Conceit

"Buy the book. Find a free weekend and a quiet place. . . .
Recall what it means to know a world through the surface
of a page, created in the words of a gifted stranger, made
uniquely yours by your own storehouse of experience and
the mystery of your subconscious."

—*The Globe and Mail*

"How to write a review in 350 words that does justice to
Mary Novik's extraordinary debut novel *Conceit*? . . . As
delightful as Virginia Woolf's *Orlando* and as erudite and
readable as A.S. Byatt's *Possession*."

—*Quill & Quire* (starred review)

"Few novels truly deserve the description 'rollicking' in the
way Mary Novik's *Conceit* does. A hearty, boiling stew of a
novel, served up in rich old-fashioned story-telling. Novik
lures her readers into the streets of a bawdy seventeenth-
century London with a nudge and a wink and keeps them
there with her infectious love of detail and character. A
raunchy, hugely entertaining read that will leave you at
once satiated and hungry for more."

—Gail Anderson-Dargatz,
author of *The Cure for Death by Lightning*

"In this gorgeous, startling, deeply moving novel about the family of the poet John Donne, the mind is shown to be one of the body's most erogenous zones. A feast, a pageant, a seduction of words."

—Thomas Wharton, author of *Icefields*

"A vivid and sensuous tale set in the world where passion and death are never far apart."

—Eva Stachniak, author of *Garden of Venus*

"Read *Conceit* not for its foods and flowers and silks and seductions—though these are here in all their lusty Elizabethan richness—but for its prose. . . . Novik's writing couples the sacred and the sexy as neatly as Donne's own."

—Annabel Lyon, author of *Oxygen*

"I loved *Conceit*, the fully formed characters, the wonderfully evoked historical setting, but above all the passion that informs the narrative throughout. The writing is graceful and fluid and the rhythms remain with you long after you have put the book down. It would do the novel little justice to speak of it as merely a work of historical fiction. It is better described as a glorious exploration of the human heart."

—Béa Gonzalez, author of *The Mapmaker's Opera*

MARY NOVIK

Conceit

– a Novel –

ANCHOR CANADA

LIBRARY AND ARCHIVES CANADA CATALOGUING IN PUBLICATION

Novik, Mary, 1945–
Conceit / Mary Novik.—Anchor Canada ed.

ISBN 978-0-385-66206-2

1. Donne, Margaret, b. 1615—Fiction.   2. Donne, John, 1572-1631—Family—
Fiction.   I. Title.

PS8627.09245C65 2008   C813'.6   C2008-901156-2

Cover image: Erich Lessing/Art Resource, NY
Cover and text design: CS Richardson
Printed and bound in Canada

Published in Canada by
Anchor Canada, a division of
Random House of Canada Limited

Visit Random House of Canada Limited's website: www.randomhouse.ca

TRANS   10   9   8   7   6   5   4   3   2   1

FOR OREST

—

The City

—

1666

It is the second of September, a Sunday, at one o'clock in the morning.

Samuel Pepys is making his way home from the Three Cranes, where he drank too much mulled sack and sang himself hoarse. He feels an odd sensation and pushes away a mongrel sniffing at his breeches. To walk well with a sword requires a certain amount of swagger and forward thrust, but he is weaving back and forth, focusing only two steps ahead. As he passes through Pudding lane, he takes little notice of the unusual glow inside the bakery. He is concentrating on sobering up so he can go straight in to his wife if she calls out. When she cannot sleep, Elizabeth likes to read to him or play at cards, and he counts it the most pleasant hour of his day. In his pocket is a new comedy that has been banging against his thigh all night. He will produce the book to divert her, if she is willing.

The baker, Thomas Farrinor, set out his dough to rise and dampened the coals in his oven before going to bed, but forgot to latch the window. When the wind came up early from the northeast, it stirred the embers and carried a spark into the Star Inn in Fishstreete. Fuelled by the straw in the stable-yard, the fire has now doubled back and is menacing Farrinor's own bedchamber. At two o'clock, he is awakened by the smell of baking dough and is greeted by an unusually red dawn and an unseasonable heat. Farrinor scrambles out onto the rooftop for safety. The houses are pitched so close together at the top that he can leap over the narrow street onto his neighbour's roof.

And so he does, for the fire is right behind him.

Told that his wife is unwell, Pepys is sleeping in his great chamber below-stairs. At three o'clock, his maid shakes him, urging him to come to her bedchamber. She leads him up the narrow staircase to her window to point out a fire burning to the west, not far from London bridge.

In the amber light, his maid's breasts appear to beckon, and he codes his thoughts in the lingua franca he has picked up from sailors. Her candle tilts towards his night-shirt, more of a threat than the fire, which the wind is driving towards the river. Musing over how pleasant it would be to tocar her mamelles so as to make himself espender, he crawls back into his solitary bed. He snuffs out his candle, lies down, sits up to check that the wick is truly out, and falls, by an erotic meandering or two, into a deep and satisfying sleep.

At seven, his maid wakes him again, telling him that three hundred houses have been destroyed in the night. He walks to the Tower and climbs up for a better look. From there Pepys sees that the fire has burnt all down Fishstreete to the bridge, and as far as the Steelyard to the west. However, the wind has now turned and is driving the blaze straight into the City. Even the stones of St Magnus's church—or so it seems in this red light—are burning after the long summer drought.

Pepys takes a boat along the river to view the extent of the fire, getting out at Whitehall and up into the King's closet as quickly as he can. Attracting a crowd, he is called to the King to give his account first hand. He warns the King and the Duke of York that unless houses are pulled down in its path, the fire will stop at nothing. Asked by the King to find the mayor and give him this advice, Pepys takes a coach as far as Ludgate, then is forced to get out and continue on foot.

On Ludgate hill, he finds St Paul's cathedral being turned into a storehouse. The mercers are piling up their yard-goods in the nave, and the booksellers are carting their books down the twenty-six steps into their parish church in St Paul's crypt, where they will be doubly safe beneath the marble flagstones. Whole bookstores are being stacked in St-Faith's-under-Paul's and small boys have been put to work stopping up the crevices in the walls with rags. A bookseller bumps his cart through the churchyard past Pepys, who picks up an octavo that has landed face-down in the grime. In this turmoil, no one cares about a single book, so he pockets it and walks east along Watling street.

Overtaking Mayor Bludworth in Canning street at noon, Pepys advises him to knock down the buildings ahead of the fire. If this is done, Pepys says, there is still hope of stopping the destruction at the Three Cranes above and at Botolph's below the bridge. However,

Bludworth has been up all night and is now spent. He rejects the Duke of York's offer of soldiers to pull down houses, for the owners are militantly against it.

The mayor does not think the fire will spread. "A chambermaid could piss it out," he says, retiring to a tavern for refreshment.

Pepys calculates the amount of fluid in a chambermaid's bladder. A pint, he guesses, perhaps a little more, hardly enough to douse a spark. He has been able to hold little urine himself since a kidney-stone was cut out of him eight years before. At the memory, his bladder tightens. He unbuttons and relieves himself against a wall.

Hearing fluttering, he looks up, and sees that the pigeons above his head are like people, reluctant to leave their roosts until it cannot be put off. The goods that people carried from Thames street up to Canning street that morning are now being removed to Lombard street, where they will most likely need to be shifted again. A cripple fights with an able-bodied man for a cart, and a slight woman bears one child on her front and another on her back. Pepys sees a sick man carried from his house, still in his bed, and the lanes stopped up by handcarts, the citizens more eager to save their goods than quench the fire. There is an exuberance to it all, a clutching of valuables, a crying out against arsonists and foreigners, a kindly touching of sleeves, and a cutting of purse strings when the uproar presents an opportunity.

Pepys walks on, as near to the fire as he can get for smoke, assessing the damage to the City.

—

Mrs William Bowles is making her way down from her house in Clerkenwell on foot, skirting the Fleet river on its journey south and staying well clear of the fire that is burning along the Thames.

In spite of its name, this river is far from fleet. It is more of a ditch, at best a backwater, although it has its source in the clear springs and wells of Hampstead. She crosses the Fleet on Cow-bridge, stopping to peer into water so clogged with refuse that even the single oarsman can make little progress upstream. His scull is loaded with his possessions, topped by a wooden lute that is listing towards the river, weeping a few plaintive notes. As the scull passes, Pegge spots a long silvery object flashing just downstream of the straining oar.

She hurries down the river-stairs and grasps a boatman's pole lying on the bank. Kneeling down, she steers and coaxes the fish towards her. Clutching it like a hawk, she lifts it free of the floating waste and teeters above the brackish water, fish aloft, heels sinking, until she regains her balance. Something is amiss, for the fish does not struggle to free itself. When she inspects it, she finds that her nails have perforated the skin like serving forks. The pike has been scotched with a knife and grilled on wood-coal, perhaps in a cookshop in Fishstreete where the fire began two days before. She lets it slip back into the lukewarm Fleet and watches it being churned towards the Thames.

Fish make her think of love. She cannot help herself, though she is aware that other women favour the honey fragrance of the heliotrope or eating sugar by the spoonful. Often she seeks out fishermen along the River Lea just to watch their sleeves shoot up and their muscles tense as they cast out their lines.

Feeling the heat rising off the water, she tries to judge the height of the sun through the smoky air. *Saffron*, her husband William would call this light, or *ochre*, never a simple pea-green or bilious yellow. There is somewhere she is meant to be. Her tongue feels for the spot where a baby tooth has been nestling in her gums for fifty years. The mud on her petticoat has already dried to a treacly brown. She shakes it off and ties up the ribbons on her stockings. Twisting her skirts into a knot, she walks quickly towards the Strand.

—

In a house overlooking St Clement Danes, the dancing-master is nodding out the beats.

"You are distante, Madame Bowles." Monsieur de la Valière elongates each syllable with a puff of vinegary breath. "Yet the fire is bien loin. No one suggests it will come here, not even the most dire prognosticateur of your Royal Society. You must reverse like the mirror, my right, your left."

"The air is too close for dancing, Monsieur."

"London has always this brown fog. It stops up the nose and the sensories." He pinches his nostrils to show her. "Even the perspirations are brown."

Why has she come here on such a day? The damp silk feels cold against her skin, unlike good English wool. The sleeves bind her arms and the fabric bunches against her thighs, as if something is trapped inside the folds. In this garment, she might as well be naked to the eye. Her father once said that draping a woman's bones with silk was like smearing birdlime on twigs to catch unwary songbirds.

"Step, dip, turn, repeat, fa fa fa," he sings out. "En cadence s'il vous plaît."

She cannot seem to please this morning. Even her shoes are unhappy with her feet. She goes to the window, leaving the dancing-master skimming about the floor in lonely minuets. Throwing open the casement, she leans out and lets the wind dishevel her hair.

There is no cool air to be had, for the easterlies are blowing scarlet heat towards them from the fire, now less than a mile away. At her last lesson, London was spread out along the curving Thames like a game of basset on a dealer's table, but today she can scarcely make out the City's steeples. The fire has burnt all along Thames street, and is now engulfing Paul's Deanery, her childhood home, in threatening grey clouds.

St Paul's cathedral stands like a cornered beast on Ludgate hill, taking deep breaths above the smoke. The fire has made terrifying progress in the night and is closing in on the ancient monument from three directions. Built of massive stones, the cathedral is held to be invincible, but suddenly Pegge sees what the flames covet: the two hundred and fifty feet of scaffolding erected around the broken tower. Once the flames have a foothold on the wooden scaffolds, they can jump to the lead roof, and once the timbers burn and the vaulting cracks, the cathedral will be toppled by its own mass, a royal bear brought down by common dogs.

"I must leave, Monsieur. I was wrong to come today." Wrong even to think of taking lessons, though she does not say that to him. She has done it only to please William, who is learning the new dances at court.

The dancing-master does something clever with his ankles and arrives at her side, dark calves flashing, his hands outstretched. "La jambe gauche, fa fa fa, la jambe droite."

Waving him away, Pegge surveys the panorama. The smoke has now cleared at Ludgate, affording a glimpse of refugees jostling to get through the narrow opening with their handcarts.

"Why should you run with the tail between the legs? Your house is well north of the dévastation and, as you see, everything goes on like habit in Westminster."

"Not everyone sleeps easily here." Pegge gestures to St Clement's below, with its parched brown garden. "My mother lies buried in that church, but I do not think her spirit has ever rested."

"Ah, that is why I felt two women in my arms just now, the light-footed one and the one who crushes on men's toes. She dances in her grave, to be sure, but you have lead weights on your hem, pulling you down when you should fly up, up"—he rises on his toes, illustrating with fluttering palms—"into a lover's arms." Then he slumps down and stares at her. "Are you the fowl or the fish? You have a feather in the hairs, but the complexion—"

He presses close, reeking of soured wine. She would much rather breathe the rank heat of a riverbank. "I must go at once, Monsieur." Brushing off his hands, Pegge flees, her shoes clattering into the winding stairwell and down the three steep flights of stairs.

"Go if you must, run, trip, fall down," he calls out after her, "be like the rustic if you will, but if you dare to come back to de la Valière after such grossièreté, wear the little slippers not those ... shoes of the farmer!"

Emerging into the churchyard, she looks up at Monsieur bobbing at the high window, still performing his foreign movements. Then his head, with its tight curls, ducks out of sight.

Soon he is back, leaning over the sill, his arm spiralling. "You have left a thing, Madame. I do not care for the English love-token."

Her old shawl flies out the window, hovers like gossamer, then shrinks into a heavy ball of wool and drops at her feet, molasses brown. Everything in the churchyard is the same burnt-sugar colour from the hot summer. The old honeysuckle has been uprooted and the bower turned into a tavern by apprentices. It stinks of piss and ale and rotting flesh. She kneels to touch a small corpse beside a broken ale-cask. On her last visit, this crow with the one white feather knocked down a wasp's nest, then stood on it while rooting out grubs with its beak. When she approached, it tried to chase her off by mimicking the sexton's irate voice. Now she feels the last few beats of its heart. Its feathers come out without pulling, staining her palms with greasy soot. Apparently it has been on a misguided foray to the east. Suffocated by the burning air, it has flown back to her mother's church to die.

The easterly has sharpened. "Monsieur," she calls up. The dancing-master's wig pokes through the window again. "You must leave London at once. On my way here, I heard this called a Catholic wind and saw a Dutchman being accused of hiding powder and grenades. He was dragged out of his house by a mob. It is only a breath from the Dutch to the French."

A face scowls at her from three storeys up. Ignoring the barrage of wounded English, she gathers up her skirts and runs towards the fire, pushing against the sludge of refugees.

Even those of good fortune have been forced to flee like beggars. A man in a wig like William's is hugging a loaf of bread. A lady's hat flies off, but she does not bother to chase after. The hot wind teases and tosses the hat, spinning it down the alley towards Pegge. She jumps and catches it, her skirts rustling, and twirls it in the air, admiring the glossy blue-black feathers anchored with stitches of the brightest blue.

—

By nightfall all of Cheapside is alight. It has taken Pegge all day to find a horse-cart for hire and willing men. It has cost her £5, enough to buy a horse outright.

When she arrives at St Paul's, the Duke of York is riding his stallion back and forth through the uproar, directing his soldiers to pull down the shops inside the churchyard. However, no man can save her father's church. It is true that the building-stones are no use to the flames, but the wooden fittings and the drygoods are burning. In their hurry to save their stock, the booksellers have left a trail of books to feed the blaze. Flaming scaffolds are now battering the roof, melting the roofing-lead and setting fire to the Yorkshire timbers. The wooden struts have already surrendered, releasing the great bells to their fate two hundred feet below, and the buttresses are beginning to separate from the tower. If the central piers collapse, five thousand tons of tower will plunge into the transepts underneath.

In Paul's choir, the two men Pegge has hired are wedging an iron bar behind her father's effigy to pry it from its niche. They loop a rope around the statue to lower it, but the rope slips and it crashes onto the cart, striking off chunks of marble and terrifying the horse. The men barely have time to curse, for the church is swirling with hot ash whipped up by the scorching wind. They throw canvas over the statue to protect it from the dripping lead, and coax the horse towards the south transept, anxious to get out before the roof caves in.

In the harrowing light, Pegge is trying to see where the fragments of the effigy have landed. She must map her route carefully, for her shawl offers little protection from the predatory heat. The wooden choir stalls are already smoking. Set free by the softening lead, wedges of glass begin to sail out of the windows and embed themselves in solid objects or shatter on the pavingstones.

All at once, the roof splits open with a monumental crack and Pegge hurtles to safety, tasting a spurt of blood as the baby tooth punctures her tongue. Six acres of roofing-lead begin to pour into the cathedral like sauce from a demented ladle. Then the roof itself comes down, breaking through the floor that separates St Paul's from St Faith's in the crypt beneath. She can now see into the bone-hole where the corpses, her father's among them, are buried in earth so dry it sparks and smoulders into flame. With another thunderous crack, the vaulting deep below gives way and the coffins begin to tilt and slide into St-Faith's-under-Paul's. Within minutes, the books stacked up in Faith's for safety are burning lustily.

Creeping along the perimeter of the choir, Pegge locates the largest fragment, but can only carry it a few feet at a time. She half-carries, half-drags it through the rubble in her shawl, picking her way over the slabs of Purbeck marble which cannot, she reasons, be attacked by fire. She knows the walls are nine feet thick in places, but nothing is certain anymore, for she has seen the earth itself catch fire this day. As she looks back into the choir, the rose window buckles, the walls bulge, the façade splinters and collapses, and the massive building-stones fly out like cannon shot.

—

At Paul's wharf, Sir William Bowles, the King's tailor, is waiting in his hired barge for Pegge. His wig askew, he is as agitated as Noah when the tide is turning and his wife is nowhere to be found.

William has never enjoyed such mystery plays. He would much rather know where people are and what things mean. He has been waiting long enough to have gone through all shades of anger and emerged in livid fear for his wife's safety. Pressing a kerchief to his nose to ward off the stench of burning tar, he holds his pocket-clock in his other palm like a silver heart. If they do not leave soon, the barge will be caught in tidal waters between Hammersmith and Kingston. Hideous sounds are echoing inside Paul's, as if the walls themselves are tumbling, and flames are shooting up the tower. Why has Pegge sent a note to meet her here? She knows their baskets were to be loaded upriver, outside the City walls. Docking at Paul's wharf is folly.

A loaded cart appears out of the strange red light, jolting down the steep grade towards him, restrained by ropes and blocks. The cart tips, and the men stop to steady the horse and balance the load. Even draped in canvas, the shape on the cart is maddeningly familiar. Of all the valuables being swallowed by the flames, why has Pegge chosen to rescue her father's effigy?

William spots her now behind the cart, a petticoat of Italian silk billowing shamelessly around bare legs. He starts to climb out of the barge to help, then thinks better of it. In truth, he is relieved to see Pegge at all. It would have been like her to disappear into the smoke, for she often wanders at odd hours in the maze of streets around St Paul's. He has seen her visiting her father's tomb dressed like a ragged child, yet she has put on her new gown to flee the burning city. Surely she did not go to her dancing lesson on such a day?

And is that Izaak Walton at her side, where it is William's place to be? They are swinging a large object between them in her shawl, putting it down every few yards to rest their wrists. Although Pegge's stockings are down around her ankles, William will ask no questions, but hasten her into the barge. He will say nothing about her father's statue, nor her old friend Mr Walton, whose hair is stuck to his scalp in the most ungentlemanly clumps. Where did she find him in this holocaust? A wretched cat is jumping at his leg, probably because he stinks of fish. It is just like Pegge to collect all the stray animals in her path.

Crates and baskets and rounds of cheese are piled helter-skelter on the quay since there are no boats left to ferry goods across the river. The desperate have set their possessions adrift, hoping to recover them with boat-hooks when they float below the bridge. William's hand flutters near his sword, ready to defend his ship and wife, but Pegge is at home in the milling crowd, squatting next to the burnt cat to calm it while the men ease the horse-cart through the mass of people and goods on the wharf. She must have paid the wharfinger in advance, for he attaches his hook to the bundled statue at once, lowering it with jerking motions into the barge. As the effigy settles into the stern, William feels the full weight of his father-in-law, John Donne, who has been dead for more than thirty years.

Pegge climbs into the barge, stepping ankle-deep in bilge. Walton swings the heavy bundle over the gunwale, then climbs in next to her. *Another pair of shoes in ruins,* William thinks. He cannot bear to contemplate the damage to Pegge's gown. Grease has beaded on his doublet and his wig is shedding flakes of ash. It has been a most untidy day.

The air is sulphurous as they set off upriver to Clewer, the shrouded sun lurking on the horizon, or perhaps it is the rising moon—he cannot read the hands on his pocket-clock even when he holds it to his eyes. Downriver, he sees an angry theatre of sky, morbid reds and blacks which bleed into the rushing water, and a colour between red and yellow he does not have a name for, a discovery he would normally find intriguing. *Like some sort of fruit. Not a peach. A ripe persimmon*, he thinks, turning his back on the spectacle to try to read Pegge's face. As she leans towards Izaak Walton, the garish light carves hollows deep into her cheeks.

When Walton came aboard, William saw the man grope dazedly for Pegge, then rest a broad palm on her knee to steady himself. He still has his hand on her leg, even though the barge is under way. The old fool is not as childlike as he feigns. There is collusion in their fire-brightened eyes and their limbs are paired like the folded arms of a drawing-compass. Have they saved the effigy or stolen it? There is no knowing what is going on in Pegge's head, if indeed anything is. As her husband, he is due an explanation, yet William cannot speak because of the power his wife holds over him, even after all these years.

The men pull slowly at the long oars, saving themselves for the rough waters ahead. William reaches for Pegge to pull her away from the men at the bow. When he loosens her petticoat from Walton's grip, their feet shift and expose the object they were carrying in her shawl—the grotesque head of her father, carved with uncanny likeness into stone, exact even to the hooded eyelids and the moustache drawn back around the teeth.

William lets Pegge go, for her nose is twitching and she appears about to cry. The barge lurches as it hits turbulent water, the grimacing head escapes Pegge's feet and rolls into the bilge, and William sits down too quickly, thumping his tailbone and startling the burnt cat under a basket.

Now both of Mr Walton's hands are free, and William sees both attach themselves to a skirt of watered silk.

YEARNINGS

—

1622–1631

I. THE DEANERY

Pegge wanted to follow Izaak Walton out to Chelsea, but was told to stay inside the Deanery. She was learning French and Latin from the tutor, and had discovered it was unwise to show her brothers up. When she recited her passage too quickly, she was sent to learn another. Now she would be lucky to catch up with Walton on his way back into London.

At last, she was able to escape. She slipped past her brother George, who was schooling his bloodied face to the razor, past her sister Constance with her head bent over her needlework, and sidestepped their old servant Bess, who was giving little Betty an enema. Pegge told her brother Jo the tutor wanted to hear his Latin, then patted Sadducee sneaking through the open door. This drooling, warmth-seeking, self-pitying stray would sprawl on the hearthstone until Bess called out her name so slowly and with such menace that the dog would slink back out-of-doors. She would hide in the flower bed until she got up courage for a new pilgrimage back to the warmth and scraps of the hearth.

Pegge could not take the dog along until she found some way of training her. Sadie did not have the knack of blending in. Just yesterday, the dog entered Paul's sanctuary when Pegge's father was performing the divine office. Misled by her nose, the dog tracked an old scent up the stairs into the choir loft and whimpered like a lost child— the sound echoing throughout the vast cathedral—eliciting smiles and bringing the Dean's performance to a jerky, embarrassed halt.

Outside the Deanery, Pegge plucked an apple from her father's tree and ate it, core and all. She cut a straight line downhill from Paul's, heel to toe, then five steps and a squared corner into Wardrobe lane, picking up speed like an Indiaman under full sail past the sign of a pie over the baked goods at Neatflyte's. She made a dog-leg through Blackfriars, up and over Bridewell bridge, enjoying the stench of the Fleet below, then broke into a run, slowing only to note a pigeon flapping its cage up and down in a market stall.

On the watch for Walton coming back from Chelsea, where he had gone to hear her father preach, she poked her stick into ditches, hoping to turn up the bones of a plague-victim to show him, or a pair of dogs locked in copulation such as her brother Jo boasted of seeing. The best she could do was a dead rat, though she had to drive off angry crows to secure it. Climbing to the top of a dovecot for a view, she brandished her rat at the mewling crows, fancying herself an Ariadne left behind by Theseus, her eyes filling with the pain of Ariadne's blind, devoted love.

Instead of Walton, she saw her father on his way back

into the City, making good speed towards the Deanery on his new horse.

Pegge ran past the King's Wardrobe back to Neatflyte's where the Bowles twins were now waiting for their father, the Groom and Yeoman of the King's Tents and Pavilions. She saw that the letters on the sign had been freshly defaced by a boyish knife, leaving the word *eatfly* hovering over the stale baked goods, and wished she had thought of this herself. One twin was moving his lips studiously as he read a folio while his brother was licking Mr Neatflyte's strawberries to make them look the sweeter. Helping herself to a small pie, Pegge took the Deanery corner crisply and found Sadie hiding behind the flowers with her tail wagging in full view. Pegge stepped in front of the tail at the precise moment that her father rode into the courtyard on his mare Parrot.

Pegge watched her father dismount. He straightened his legs, danced about to get the blood flowing, then inspected the tree he was cultivating in the small garden, which no one else was allowed to touch. Parrot nuzzled at his arm, begging for a codling. The Dean selected an apple, gave it a polish on his sleeve, then held it out on his palm. Parrot bit off half the codling and worked it to the back of her jaw with her tongue. As the horse crunched down with her back teeth, the dog surfaced from her hiding place.

"Better you than Eve," Pegge's father said to the mare, stroking her nose and feeding her the other half.

The dog began to howl, sounding remarkably like a child who had stubbed her toe. Her father did not seem to notice Pegge, although she could not be invisible for she was almost nine years old.

Without turning his head, he said to Sadie, "You don't even like apples," and then to Pegge, "Remove that animal from my prize auriculas at once."

Now that her father was Dean of Paul's, he lived from sermon to sermon, saying as soon as he had delivered himself of one that he was *with child* with another. He would shut himself up in his library, coaxing the new sermon into shape and larding it with references. Pegge would slip in to find him practising in front of the mirror, drinking in the rhetoric as if he were drinking in tobacco smoke. Every so often, he would stop and test a grimace to judge its effect on his audience.

On the Lord's Day, he would rise early and transport himself by whatever conveyance was at hand, whether a benefactor's coach or his own mare. When he was preaching at St Paul's, his children were expected to attend. The sermons were tormented by images of bodily fluids and faeces, of bones liquefying, of rotting flesh gummed down by predators and masticated into particles. He would latch on to a word and torture it. One clod of *sin* was bad enough, but what of concatenated *sins*, *sin* enwrapped and complicated in *sin*, *sin* entrenched and barricadoed, screwed up and riveted with *sin*, *sin* wrastling with the mercies of God? The word bloated up and burst from the pressure, like a bladder kicked about by her father's pointed boots.

On the hard benches in Paul's choir, the children mastered the art of daydreaming, of aping the role of listeners. They lounged about in their minds while their bodies knelt, skewered by their father's roving gaze. The boys looked up into the crumbling vault and took aim at pigeons with imaginary crossbows. The girls dreamt of amassing dowries to free themselves from their father's sway.

But Pegge listened. She could hear the bodies decomposing under her feet in the privacy of tombs. Her hearing was acute, able to pick out threads of silence, like the subhuman sounds of worms extruding casts or like the silent descenders in a printer's font.

When the sermon was finished and the children free to leave, Pegge often visited her mother's church. Now that she could read the Latin on the gravestones, she knew there was a plague of dead Donnes inside St Clement's. Mary and Francis, who were spirits. Nicholas, who had wasted away. The nameless baby who had killed her mother by dying inside her. And Ann—most beloved, most dear, most mourned of mothers and of wives.

ANN DONNE

1617 AUGUST 15

THIS STONE IS COMMANDED TO SPEAK THE GRIEF

OF HER HUSBAND JOHN DONNE

(BY GRIEF MADE SPEECHLESS LIKE AN INFANT)

WHO HEREBY PLEDGES HIS ASHES TO HER ASHES

IN A NEW MARRIAGE WEDDED

2. JEZEBEL DID PAINT

He was the Word that spake it,
He took the bread and brake it.
And what that Word did make it,
I do believe and take it.

So the Dean began the meal, the diamond ring flashing on his piously joined hands.

The sisters were sitting on the bench from youngest to eldest—Betty, Pegge, Bridget, Lucy, and Constance, who sat beside their father to help him carve and serve. Across from Pegge, who had been told to mind her tongue, was Uncle Grymes. He had brought a Mr Alleyn, a man well past his youth who had recently lost his wife. An actor in his day, he was now the Master of the King's Bears and Bulls. Pegge had been hoping he would recite something from Christopher Marlowe, some lines that would move him to a widower's tears, but though he wore black, he seemed determined to enjoy himself.

Pegge had just heard Uncle Grymes stutter out the

terms whereupon Edward Alleyn would marry her sister Constance. It was spoiling the taste of a well-seasoned soup. She bit down on a bone that had no business being there. Con, tipping her bowl politely, which she never bothered to do when the family ate alone, did not seem surprised by Uncle Grymes's proposal. Nor did Bridget, who was patting her lips neatly with a little cloth.

Con and Bridget had been so fidgety before the meal that Bess had declared them coming down with green-sickness and offered to worm them. Flat on her belly, eye to the crack of the door, Pegge had seen her sisters taking the curling rags out of their hair and painting one another's faces. Now, in the warm lamplight, Con's cheeks and bosom glowed. Pegge could detect the scent of honey-suckle though it was late October.

Her father was now holding forth about the pain of los-ing a wife and raising seven motherless children, digging up black words, sleek with memory, that the children had heard many times before. The sack bottle had become marooned at his end of the table. When the air had been rendered completely dank and humourless, Con sent the bottle on its rounds again and asked Mr Alleyn a gay ques-tion about the bearbaiting.

Mr Alleyn began talking with bread in his mouth, like an actor of the common stage. Pegge put down her spoon and stared. His coarseness had a beauty that made her catch her breath, but she could see the veins bulging at her father's temple.

When Mr Alleyn laughed and swallowed the wrong way, her father leapt. "God can choke you with a crumb, with a drop, at a voluptuous feast. He can sink down the stage and the player, the bed of wantonness and the wanton actor, into the jaws of the earth, into the mouth of hell. He can surprise you even in the act of sin!"

This was too much for Mr Alleyn, who looked uneasily from side to side.

As their father carved the goose, he sailed briskly into the story of how, two years before, he had been called to attend the King and found him heartily devouring a meal of roast meats. Though their father had ridden his mount hard, he was not offered so much as a chair.

Instead, King James said, "Dr Donne, I have invited you to dinner, and though you sit not down with me, yet I will carve you a dish which I know you love well. Knowing you love London, I do therefore make you Dean of Paul's. When I have dined, then do you take your beloved dish home to your study, say grace there to yourself, and much good may it do you."

Their father chose this moment to sever the goose leg with a savage blow, sending a tremor along the bench to Pegge, who splashed her ale. As he was about to resume his anecdote, Con dropped something on the floor. When she bent to retrieve it, their father let out a yelp and jumped to his feet, dancing back and forth. Drawing down his hose, he clapped a greasy hand to his ankle, complaining that he had been viciously attacked.

"It was only a flea, Father," Con said, a note of warning in her voice.

He sat down, wondering aloud whether a man might get rabies from insect bites or even, if left untreated, gangrene.

His priest's stockings were still down around his ankles in a frightening display of slovenliness.

Mr Alleyn's stomach rumbled and he took up his knife as a hint to his host. "A good dish of meat will settle your anxieties, sir."

His blunt words fell upon quiet, for Pegge's father was now staring morosely at the dismembered goose. The sauce had congealed and the turnip had assumed a vulgar shape. Pegge began to think her father might call off the meal and send his guests away. Con must have been thinking the same thing, for she began to serve the meat herself and pass the dishes quickly down the table.

"A flea is not as innocent as you might suppose," their father said. "It has unsavoury habits."

At the word *flea*, Mr Alleyn made a sputtering noise. "Ah, to be a flea traversing a woman's body!" he soliloquized. Having stepped upon the stage, he did not wish to exit until he had given pleasure to the ladies. "Many lewd poems have been written on the subject. I believe your father wrote one himself as a young man."

"Lewd poems?" echoed the Dean.

Mr Alleyn sniggered. "Fleas have a reputation, sir."

"So I am aware," the Dean said coolly, "just as I am aware that *certain poems* have been maliciously laid at my door."

Mr Alleyn, Pegge guessed from his smirking, had read the miscellany in which a slew of authors had imitated her father's most famous poem. So had Pegge, for her brother George had brought it home from his college to educate his sisters.

Her father supposed them ignorant of the poem which, George explained, was in a kind of code. When the flea bit the woman, then sank its jaws into her betrothed, there was an exchange of blood that compromised her honour. Why then, the poet Jack Donne argued, should his mistress withhold the balance of her favours?

The mistress? Without doubt, George informed them, their adolescent mother. Mr Alleyn appeared to be on the point of explaining the same thing, but was cut off by their father, the diamond blazing on his fist.

"The appetite of fleas is not a fit subject for my daughters. Why have you brought this old cormorant to my table, Grymes?"

Uncle Grymes did not hear the question, for at each new volley he had tilted his chair back further and swilled down more of his brother-in-law's good sack, until he was sliding down the wall. At any rate, the question was rhetorical, for their father's attention had not left his guest.

"Is this all you have to say on the subject of love, Mr Alleyn?" As their father's lips retracted, his moustache appeared to snarl.

"Love?" Mr Alleyn asked. If the old player was acting now, Pegge saw no sign of it.

"You have been oddly silent on this account," accused the Dean. "Here is my poor Con, with all her hopes and fears laid bare upon the table, while you loiter as if betting on the bearbaiting. Will you deprive me of my servant below-stairs and my companion above for such a paltry sum?"

"I fail to take your meaning, sir," said Mr Alleyn, looking towards the row of daughters as if the Dean had an ample supply of waiting-women in reserve.

"You are a cold-hearted lover. What price can you put upon my daughter's love? She has offered you all her riches."

What riches were these? Unless Pegge had missed one of her father's thrusts, all he had offered was a lease worth a scant £500 at Michaelmas.

"I have matched your offer," Mr Alleyn said, shifting his buttocks.

He was a big man, and prolonged sitting had stiffened him, filling up his legs with blood. As he worked the pain out of his large hams, Con sprang up and grasped the bottle of sack. Pegge watched her sister lean over to pour him a measure and let her hand glide down his arm, until his neck reddened and his eyes met hers.

"She is young enough to be your daughter," their father persisted, doing the calculation on his bony fingers, "in fact, your granddaughter."

There was a skill to this that Pegge admired. Mr Alleyn was made to feel ashamed of claiming a woman forty years his junior when, at twenty-one, the bride was past the flower of marrying. Con had been losing currency for five years and even Lucy and Bridget were being discounted daily. Lucy would be bartered off next, then Bridget, then Pegge. Her father was playing the hypocrite by arranging marriages for his daughters, though he had made a famous love-match for himself.

The Dean's lesson in arithmetic seemed to have frightened Mr Alleyn. "I shall be most generous upon my death," he blurted out. "My widow shall receive another £500 when I die."

"Much can be said in favour of an older husband," acknowledged their father, his tone more cordial now. "I am sure that you can be persuaded to find even more love where you have found this much already. What say you to £1,300?" Without allowing time for a rebuttal, he clapped his thigh and stood, his priest's stockings still cowering around his ankles. "Come into my library, Grymes. Let us draw up an agreement for these young lovers. Enjoy your glass at leisure, Mr Alleyn! Constance, the sack, do not begrudge the sack, our guest is thirsty."

Uncle Grymes cast a regretful glance back at the bottle, and Con slipped into his chair to dish out Mr Alleyn's pudding. She helped him to some syrup, as if he could not tip the jug himself. Pegge let the syrup run off her own knife and drizzle onto the table, until Con kicked her in the leg. Was this the man who had played Tamburlaine the Great, declaiming the immortal lines of Marlowe? Mr Alleyn had proved a disappointment, content to have the spittle wiped from his lips, a bitten and sorry bear.

And what of that flea bite upon her father's ankle? He was fond of pointing out the dangers of such minuscule things. Pins and combs and pulled hairs could gangrene and kill, he told his children, and men could laugh themselves to death. That flea bite had looked remarkably like the points of Con's scissors to Pegge. She had often received a bite from them herself when she had provoked her sister. Her arm was pinked with Con's anger, a row of chicken feet blooming from wrist to elbow.

A pink was a small thing, a pale-red flower or a squinting eye. Even the small finger on which her father wore his diamond ring. But it was also, Pegge knew, a small and deadly warship.

—

Pegge wanted to be the first to tell Izaak Walton about Con's betrothal. Down on her knees in St Paul's the next morning, Pegge ran her thumb over the initials *Iz. Wa.* scratched into Duke Humphrey's tomb where, later in the day, the loiterers would play cards and drink, barely turning their backs to relieve themselves. Their wide boots made their hips thrust out like ships rolling at anchor, but Walton had an easy sway, a confidence of bone and sinew. Unlike the other youths, he smelt pleasantly of river, not tobacco. An ironmonger by trade, he now seemed to do little more than make tackle for his fellow anglers.

The cathedral was a city unto itself. All of London took exercise in Paul's walk and posted notices at the Si Quis door, where Walton posted his signs for tackle. Taking a shortcut from Cheapside, butchers wheeled sides of beef through the transepts and down the hill to Paul's wharf, bickering with fishmongers pushing their loaded carts back up. When the clatter broke into his sermons, Pegge's father strode out from the choir to reprimand the tradesmen, stretching out his arms like Christ to block the raucous thoroughfare.

But the young idlers in the nave were worse. Only a few, like Izaak Walton, would straggle into the choir to hear her father preach. Afterwards, Walton would follow

Constance into Paul's walk, trying to discuss the sermon while she admired the Blackfriars actors walking up and down, learning their lines in their tight hose. But Constance liked toying with Walton well enough. Tormented him, in fact. He had been hanging about her for months, desiring more than laughter from her lips.

Now, from behind Duke Humphrey's tomb, where she had hoped to intercept Walton, Pegge saw the two of them coming down Paul's walk. Constance stopped near a pillar, bestowing a salty kiss on his cheek, while he blushed right into the roots of his limp golden hair. Then she whispered something into his ear. Pegge knew that Con was telling him she was betrothed by the way Walton slumped like a dead-hearted grayling, a winter fish that sank to the bottom.

Pegge watched him stagger out of Paul's, and followed his drooping fishing rod to Tottenham. When he disappeared over the hill, she tied up her skirt and ran after the sad pole, her boots sticking out beneath her petticoat.

As she fell in step, he lengthened his stride. After a while, he gave up trying to outpace her and said, "You had better go back. I am not coming home this night or two."

"Then I must go as well, to stop you doing yourself some injury. Unrequited love," she explained, blowing out a plume of air.

"This is between me and Constance and Edward Alleyn, who does not deserve her. Turn back at once, Pegge Donne."

Pegge fell behind, imitating his gait from a safe distance. He threw a few rocks at her to chase her off, but when one of them grazed her, he put down his pole to adjust it until he saw she was unhurt.

"You cannot come with me. I would have your father to answer to and I have had enough pain on your sister's account."

"I will marry you instead of Con," she offered. She held out her finger to show him the iron band he had made himself. "From Con's sewing basket. I saw her hide it after you gave it to her."

She walked beside him for a while, but he looked so downhearted that she returned the ring. It was too big for her anyway.

"You are only eleven, a child who knows nothing of these things." He dropped it into his pouch, then said more kindly, "At any rate, your father would never agree. He has set his mind against ironmongers since his father began as one."

"By the time he has shifted Lucy and Bridget, he will be more eager. If you don't marry me, he will barter me off to an old mackerel like Mr Alleyn. There was a nasty stink about it, though Mr Alleyn got the worst, Con being Con."

"You hardly know what a wife must do. There are things that pass between husband and wife that—" He turned his eyes away.

"I know more than you think, for I have read my father's poem about his mistress coming to bed." She saw his grip slacken on the fishing rod. "You needn't be so indifferent, Izzy. I must take off everything in order. First girdle, then spangled breastplate and happy busk, then gown and coronet and shoes. It is not so hard and I shall manage quite well without Bess, for I don't wear all those things that other women wear."

He tripped over his feet and struggled to get them back underneath his body. When he was properly upright he said, "I do not want you for a wife, Pegge Donne. You have spoken plainly and so must I." He added quickly, "But with your ingenious small fingers, you will make a good angler. You may help me twist hairs into lines and catch live bait, for each fish is partial to one kind."

To learn to fish would be something. Perhaps he would make her a rod as long as his. It must have been all of four-teen feet. She crouched to inspect some mud pulsing along-side the path and flushed out a wintering frog, blue with fright. When she picked it up in her muddy fist, it jumped back into the ditch.

"Why does everyone think me such a child? My father went up to Oxford at my age and I am learning French and Latin as he did."

"Then do not marry, for it will all be wasted. That is the fate of women, Pegge. Constance is marrying Mr Alleyn to please your father. You know the power the Dean holds over her."

This was too irksome. "My father is not to blame. You have never understood Con. She wants the Master of the King's Bears and Bulls, not a simple angler." She pointed to his head, which was well protected from the heavy mist. "What is that hat? It is hardly a lover's. Where is your powdered hair? Your perfumed gloves? What love sonnets did you write my sister?" She could not stop herself now.

"She calls you Pissy-Issy because you have a fishy smell as if you leaked all over your hose!"

She was about to tell him she could not abide tobacco and perfume herself, but he had gone as soft and grey as the lead in St Paul's roof. She was glad she had taken his gutting knife for safekeeping. Clutching his stomach, he broke off towards the river, weaving blindly through the muddy field, running then stumbling towards a grove of trees stripped of their summer greenery. Crowned by empty crows' nests, the ebony limbs stretched up into the darkening sky.

All at once, there was a dreadful thump and Walton fell to the ground, nursing his head. She ran towards him, mucking her petticoat with so much filth there would be no sneaking it past Bess. He had taken a jagged gash to his temple and she wiped the blood off with her hem. As the stink of manure drifted over from a cottager's field, the rain began to pelt in earnest. A hedgehog darted out of a bush and scurried off. The sky would soon be bereft of light. Just before the clouds blacked it out, the dying sun shot out a squib of gold and the wind parted Izaak Walton's hair like barley sheaves laid up for winter.

"Come, I'll help you to the nearest tavern," she said, resting his pole on her own shoulder. "It was only a low branch, not a fatal blow from Aphrodite."

The red spot on her father's ankle did not go away, but seemed to swell and shrink according to his moods, and he was as morose as Izaak Walton, who had become an open, festering sore.

Perhaps it was the fault of the book that Mr Alleyn gave her father, Robert Burton's *Anatomy of Melancholy*. The bulging quarto would depress anyone's spirits, Pegge reasoned, carrying it to her own chamber and opening it cheerfully. Choler, she read by candlelight, made a man furious, short-tempered, and subject to apparitions. Melancholy sank him in low spirits, making him think himself bewitched or even dead.

Melancholy could reside in the liver, heart, womb, or hemrods. It could come from overexciting the fancy, agitating the passions, or eating red meats. Most likely her father had scholarly melancholy, or perhaps only a windy hypochondria that would require evacuation with one of Bess's enemas.

Of all the types Burton listed, most curious was love melancholy. The philosophers had once cut up a man who had died for love. His heart was found to be combust, his liver smoky, his lungs dried up, and his soul roasted from the vehemency of love's fire. Beauty was a cause of love, and beauty, Burton said, could be made vehement by artifice. Certainly Con had employed a wealth of Bess's ointments in the service of love. Or was it lust? *Of woman's unnatural, insatiable lust,* Burton wrote, *what country, what village does not complain?* This curious fact went a long way towards explaining Con's hold over Mr Alleyn and Walton, who was acting as if he had been disembowelled.

Burton's cures for lovesickness included stuffing camphor down the suitor's breeches to stifle his urges and hiding his beloved's excrement under his pillow. Neither remedy was within Pegge's grasp. Camphor was as costly as saffron, and though Con was as regular as their father's striking clock, she was fastidious about disposing of her movements.

More promising was the idea that the suitor could be made gluttonous with two mistresses, the second spoiling his appetite for the first. Perhaps, Pegge hoped, Walton could be made to fall in love with her. She scraped his dried blood off her petticoat, then poised his knife above her thigh to draw her own blood for a love-potion. But what, she brooded, if she carved too deep and bled to death, or if the wound gangrened and killed her? What good was a love that moved the sun and stars if she was underground with maggots?

Pegge turned her attention back to her father, unwilling to let him succumb to his ill-humour. Soon it was Martinmas, the time for slaughtering animals, and a dozen chickens arrived from a parishioner. Carving up a capon for Pegge and her sisters, their father announced that he had put Con's wedding forward, so that if he died—such was his frame of mind at losing his eldest daughter—Mr Alleyn could not renegotiate the terms. Even Con looked dispirited, since she would have little time to sew her wedding garments. Pegge was the only sanguine one, welcoming the day she would slide closer to her father along the bench of daughters. She had already talked him into giving her Con's bedchamber, a roomy one which butted up against his own.

Pegge inspected her new chamber on the eve of her sister's wedding. Sitting on the window-sill in the dark, Con was hugging a pot of heart's ease that had withered from cold blasts near the pane. Pegge squeezed beside Con and surveyed the room, twice as large as the one she shared with Betty. Con was warm and drowsy and her robe swung loosely in the moonlight, the colour of ripe summer plums, revealing the roundness of her breasts and belly.

Con's face was flattened against the glass. "I wanted to marry on St Lucy's eve, when father himself married, for it is the longest night of the year, a night for lovers."

"What are you looking at, Con?"

Con pointed to the shadowy lane below the window. "Jane Shore's meeting place."

Jane had been one of King Edward's mistresses, Con said, the one Thomas More had called the merriest harlot in the realm. As far as Pegge could see, this was the only information Con had ever retained from a book. According to More, Jane coupled with William Shore before she was well ripe. Soon her old husband was impotent, and Jane was in full appetite. With her pretty foot and pleasing tongue, she made the King her thrall, then bewitched his stepson and his chamberlain. Forced to do penance for her lust, she carried her taper to Paul's Cross dressed only in her kirtle, which made the gawking onlookers her slaves as well.

Pegge touched her sister's arm. "Which man did she love best, Con?"

"Thomas More did not say, but I am sure it was the King."

—

On Lucy's eve, Pegge was awakened by the sound of laughter outside the window of her new chamber and knew at once that the ghost of Jane Shore was abroad.

Sadie was hiccuping under the bed, having got herself into the Deanery and up the stairs by stealth. The dog had been sneaking in ever since Con had gone off to live with Mr Alleyn, leaving the household to stew in its moroseness. Pegge hoped Sadie would not pine away and die of grief, as melancholy dogs were known to do.

Pegge pulled on her boots and the old purple gown, soft with washings, that Con had left behind along with her wilted plant. Pegge was sure that Jane Shore would not pass up such a night as this. Peering out the glass, she tried to spot Jane's flickering taper in the lane. Pegge was ready to follow, to see where Jane took her lover and what she did to keep him so in thrall. Pegge was dozing against the window when she heard Jane's merry, cajoling spirit coaxing her lover through the December fog and cold with her laughter.

The King responded, "Sweet mistress, where are you?" A noble lovesick call, though his voice was hoarse from a century spent in his damp grave at Windsor.

Jane's spirit was hovering a little above the earth, provoking and enticing. "Come hither, love," she called.

And then Pegge heard the noble response, drifting hoarsely through the night: "As the grave is your house, we two shall make our beds together in the dark."

Pegge leaned out the window, but something was not quite right, for the King's aggrieved and muffled voice had not come from the lane, but through the wall—in fact, from the adjoining chamber.

It was the father of night, *her* father. He was calling out in a melancholy dream, but surely not for Jane Shore? Pegge entered his bedchamber, staying away from the glowing coals. There was no need to hide, however, for he could have had thorns in his eyelids and thistles in his hose for all he knew. He was fully dressed on top of the bed, in some sort of trance, his tongue working uselessly, as if half-formed words were struggling to escape in poems. What sweet, tormenting thoughts were still inside him, what black-butter dreams?

Her mouth against his ear, she whispered, "Come hither, love," to entice his lips to form the words.

At this, he jerked himself up and off the bed, snatched his hat from the hook, and stumbled down the stairs. Collecting the lamp kept near the door, he trimmed the wick. This seemed particularly clever for a man who was walking in his sleep. She waited for his hat to merge with the shadows in the lane, then followed.

Pegge had never been out-of-doors in such a loose garment. As she rounded the Dean's corner, where the wind
always blew, a cool finger of breath lifted the neck of the
purple robe and slid into her clavicle, breath marrying
bone, then traversed her breastbone, and burrowed into her
navel like a flea trying to get warm. Then the flea danced
back out, took a bite and kissed her flesh, its hollows and
mounds, assessing how much she had grown, how her hip
bones jutted in the loose gown, how her nipples bristled in
the cold, and how her womanhood was held like an unripe
peach between her legs, the pale hairs ready to burst into a
dark, vigorous clump like Con's.

Was this how a poem felt when it came whistling over
naked parchment? Her pale hairs only awaited a poet's call to
break through the skin like new teeth in a baby's tender gums.

But where was that poet, her father? He had almost got
away, dreaming on his feet. It was a fool's pursuit, for by
now Jane would be entertaining her royal lover with more
than laughing words. Perhaps Pegge's father was headed
towards one of the taverns along Fleet street where such
liaisons were rumoured to take place. But now Pegge saw
where he was going. Not on some noble lovesick mission,
but sailing at a good clip, like a merchantman with the
wind at its back, on a voyage of his own undertaking.

—

On St Lucy's day, Pegge was awakened by her father talking loudly in the hall below. Her head aching, she leaned
into the stairwell to listen.

It seemed that Lucy's eve was not only a night for lovers' trysts but also a night for vandals, for the vicar of St Clement's had come round to report that the tomb of Mrs Donne had been broken open in the night. Still bone-cold from chasing after her father, Pegge stumbled back to her chamber.

At noon, she rose to find that the sacrilege had driven her father to bed with an angry pustulous fever. Bess was tying a bread poultice over the spots erupting on his feet. When he shouted at Bess, she tied the poultice even tighter. Then, stirring up the coals, she left him sweating in his misery. Pegge sat down beside him, feeling the warmth seep back into her flesh at last.

By mid-afternoon, the spots had begun to march up her father's calves. Doctor Foxe ordered that all books and tobacco be removed from the sickroom, for the patient's humours were too volatile. At this, it took all the doctor's powers to calm her father, who shouted that his wife's ghost had escaped from her grave, taken up residence in a flea, and bitten his ankle in a fury. Nothing could rattle Doctor Foxe, however. He took Pegge aside and told her that the Dean was allowed one page a day, and one page only, on which to void his manifold anxieties.

Pegge bought a stack of folio sheets from a bookseller in Paul's churchyard, giving her father the first huge page at once. He covered it in a furious crabbed hand, then lay back in exhaustion. Touching his brow, she found it both shivery and scalding. She applied a cold flannel, but he flung it at the wall, where it left an ominous wet stain for hours. When the doctor returned the next morning, he read the page with dismay and conceded that the patient might be allowed a little tobacco, after all, to cool his heated mind.

Day after day, Pegge hovered near her father's sickbed, fearful of his blackening mood. A cold morbidity wrapped around a hot fever, a riddling distemper—how much further could he sink? The whiskers thickened on his jaw, for he refused to call the boy to shave him. Each morning, she carried in one printer's sheet, his box of pipes, and a soothing ounce of tobacco. Each evening, she added the new page to the feverish stack and carried out the box of pipes. There was never even a fleck of tobacco to return to the tin.

On the thirteenth day, the spots broke through the barrier of smelly poultices around his waist and erupted above the mustard plaster on his chest. As night fell, the Dean blew his battered trumpet to call his children to him. The suffocating heat dampened their noise as they entered. Propped up against his Turkish pillow, he commanded them to their knees to pray for their mother's soul. Then he recited the evening prayer and required them to give the answers.

After the last faltering response and peevish correction, he announced, "You have lost a second mother in Constance and now you are about to lose a father. I am ready, I may say I am eager, to be taken by God."

Lucy threw her face into her dirty petticoat and wept, exposing an undarned rent in her stocking the size of a goose egg.

"Do not sniff, Lucy," George said, trying to make light of it. "You are a good girl, though none too clever. I am sure some foreign nunnery will have you."

"Oh my God, my God," their father called out, his hands raised towards the ceiling, "you have made this sickbed your altar. Will you accept a spotted sacrifice, or do you seek only unspottedness here?"

Bridget plucked at a loose thread in her needlework. Since Con's marriage, Pegge had never seen Bridget without this half-embroidered bridal under-garment.

"Father," Bridget said, "this is a very poor time for you to be dying. Can you not put it off? I am to marry soon. You said you would arrange it."

"When I am dead, you will go to Constance with your sisters. Jo and George will not return to Oxford, but must take up their careers at once. I am well content to send one son to the church and another to the wars."

This announcement was as unwelcome to her brothers as it was to Pegge, who had no particular wish to live with Con.

"You are not so ill that you cannot recover, Father," Bridget complained.

"The sickness has broken out into malignant boils!" their father shouted. "Many die of its virulence within three days."

"Then you have passed the worst," Jo said, pushing his hair back from his forehead. "You have lasted thirteen."

"I have been fifty years in this putridness. I have no appetite for life, I cannot sleep, and I can barely sit up."

He looked as agile to Pegge as he had ever done, though a red spot had just erupted on his nose.

"You are weak because you are fasting, sir," said George, perching on the bed and filching a lump of food from the uneaten supper. "And you would feel better if you shaved."

"We die every day and we die all the day long." Each word was dropping like distilled liquor from a boiling retort. "The skin over these bones is but a winding-sheet. Each bell that tolls for another hastes my own funeral. My body will soon be with your mother's in her grave."

"And what will you do there?" asked little Betty in spite of Pegge's jabbing elbow.

"Await our joint resurrection," her father boomed, as if to the deaf.

Even Betty knew of the resurrection, though she was hazy on the mechanics of getting there. Pegge saw her scratch her bottom quizzically through several layers of wool. After their mother died, their father had declared himself *crucified for love*, a phrase passed down in awe from the eldest to the youngest. Even now, Pegge could not drive it from her mind.

"Since your mother's soul was ravished into heaven, my mind has been wholly set on heavenly things."

"But it didn't, did it?" said Pegge.

"Didn't what?"

"Didn't go to heaven," she said stubbornly. "On Lucy's eve, you seemed to think that my mother's soul was buried with her body underground. You brought this spottedness upon yourself by roaming through the streets that night."

Pegge met her father's stare, remembering the cold that had driven deep into her marrow, then rooted her feet deep into the boots that had been Bridget's, that had been Lucy's and, long before that, Con's.

—

On Lucy's eve, a fortnight before, Pegge had followed her father along Fleet street past the Cock and Key and the Boar's Head. By the time he was abreast of the Star and Ram, she was sorry she was wearing the loose purple gown. Once he passed the Queen's Head, she knew where he was going.

He entered St Clement's just ahead of her, then disappeared. She was huddling behind a screen when she heard the sexton's crowbar scraping all along the nave. Wielding the iron clumsily, her father finally got it wedged deep enough to shift a pavingstone to one side. Then he knelt on the cold floor, speaking lover's gibberish to the underworld while she wished herself back under her old blanket. One of his poems had hinted at an unsavoury graveside reunion, amusing when read by candlelight in her warm bed but lacking in all humour in the draughty church in which her father's cries now echoed.

"I have come to keep my promise, Ann." He threw the crowbar into the gaping chasm with a horrid ringing. "We two shall make our beds together in the dark." Dropping nimbly over the edge, he landed in the bone-hole.

What about us? Pegge thought. *My scattered flock of wretched children*, as he liked to call them when chatting to the bishop. How much more scattered and wretched they would be if he pulled the flagstone down on top of his head for good.

Just then Sadie hurtled in, her coat as frizzled as if she had been running for an hour after the wrong scent. Going straight to the Dean's discarded hat, she worried it with her teeth. Then, paying no attention to Pegge, who guessed she was too cold by then to have a scent, the dog sniffed around the gaping hole—which was filled now with the thud of iron against lead, now a cracking like a rib cage being fractured, and now a terrifying stream of cryptic poetry. Her ears outraged but her loyalty unswerving, Sadie sat on her hindquarters and howled to call her Orpheus back from the underworld. In this she was at once successful, for Pegge's father broke off his unwholesome tryst and scrambled out of the bone-hole, dragging the crowbar with him. He took out his striking clock and shook it, unable to believe until it chimed that it was really midnight. He looked about the church, then at the dog wagging her tail at his feet. Flinging the crowbar across the aisle in anger, he chased the yelping animal into the night.

As the yelps and curses faded down the Strand, Pegge squatted next to the chipped flagstone and felt a rush of foetid air escape her mother's tomb. It was certainly the darkest night of the year, though so far she had seen little to do with love. The fallen lamp cast dreadful shadows and the mustiness crept down her throat and into her lungs like pleurisy.

Was her father trying to bed her mother right there in Clement's, or was he digging out poems he had rashly buried with her corpse? The horrid thudding had told Pegge he had pried the coffin open. What did he feel when he stuck his hand into the clammy void—parchment verses or papery dried flesh? Perhaps the corpse hadn't yet turned to mummy, dry and brittle with age, but was like the slimy pigs' jelly that Bess sometimes made Pegge eat. Her mother's corpse might still be in the liquefaction, the colliquation, the melting of the bowels that her father said took place in the dead. It was impossible to tell from this angle, and Pegge was beginning to think she would rather not see. The fallen lamp had begun to flicker like Jane Shore's ghostly taper, and a thin reedy sound was coming from the bone-hole. Was that Jane's penitential sigh or Ann's trapped soul she heard?

Pegge did not wait to hear it a second time. She picked up her father's hat and bolted from the church, counting off the taverns as she ran down Fleet street—the Queen's Head, the Devil, the Hand, the Falcon, the Star and Ram, the Bolt-in-Tun, the Boar's Head, the Cock and Key—running up Ludgate hill and darting south through the narrow passage to the Deanery, holding her breath past Jane Shore's trysting spot in fear of lingering spirits, and—quietly, quietly now, her heart jumping like a captive frog—creeping up the stairs to her new bedchamber. She had just crawled under the blanket with her boots on, counting her breaths to slow them down, when Sadie shot into the room, too witless to bark, and slid underneath the bed with such momentum that she smacked against the wall. Pegge's father banged in next, lathered and shaking in a fury. The bed rattled as he tried to pry out the dog, but she would not come, gripping, Pegge had no doubt, the bed frame with her paws. When her father thumped down on the bed, coughing in violent spasms, Pegge heard Sadie skitter out and slide bonelessly down the stairs.

Now, in the sickroom, tobacco fumes obscured the image of Mary Magdalen on the wall. Their father sat cross-legged on the bed, impaling Pegge like a traitor on his steely gaze. She removed her eyes from the boil that had burst out mutinously on his nose and looked down at her tightly laced boots. Her father knew that Sadie followed those boots everywhere. Had he deduced how his old black hat, now chewed around the edges, had found its way back to its hook?

"Have it your way," he said at last, weighing each word against the jutting of Pegge's chin. "Your mother's soul is *with her body in her grave*. Be that as it may. Since she enjoys her long night's festival, let me prepare towards her now."

"But Father," Bridget blurted out, "I thought you wanted your soul to see the Blessed Face of God, not go with your corpse to Mother's tomb."

"And surely," added George cheerfully, "you cannot be buried in St Clement's when you are Dean of Paul's. You must take your place with the other Deans beneath the choir floor."

They had all seen his latest porphyry-and-marble testament to fame. He had barely been Dean a month when he had pinned the first design for his sepulchre on the library wall, to be followed by another, and another, each more grandiose than the last. Pegge had seen him studying the sketches as he took his pipe of tobacco. Then, blowing smoke through his nostrils, he would admire his image in the gilt mirror in which he appeared to hang between the two paintings—the Blessed Virgin and the Crucifixion— nailed upon the wall.

"You must fight this disease, for aiding your death is self-murder," Jo said.

"It seems you must recover, Father," George said slyly, handing his cold supper to him.

"Ah," said their father, waving back the meal, "but surely self-homicide is justified if used to fly evil and seek good?"

"The taking of a life is always a sin," said Jo, pushing the hair out of his eyes doubtfully.

"Who are a little wise the best fools be." The Dean picked a fleck of tobacco off his tongue and scrutinized it, as if counting the idiots perched on the head of a pin. "Then are the martyrs sinners? What of Christ's volition at his crucifixion? Sharpen your arguments. You might be in a pulpit soon, God help us."

"Self-homicide is not so naturally sin that it may never be otherwise," Jo offered.

"Source?"

"*Biathanatos*."

"A book written by Jack Donne. I suppressed it so it would not fall into the hands of lazy thinkers, but it has done so all the same. What of Samson? If you must affect his disorderly hair, then try to fathom his triumph."

"Samson pulled the temple down on his head for the glory of God," said George, coming to his brother's aid. "But martyrs who seek personal glory commit a sin."

"That is better. Now put pen to paper each of you and write me a case against self-slaughter. If you cannot convince me, I shall fast to speed my death." He selected one of his long clay pipes, pressed in a fingerful of tobacco, and lit it with a taper. "I have no wish to live amongst philistines a day longer than Samson had to."

Nothing was expected of Lucy, who was now so distraught she was rocking back and forth, nor of little Betty, who was spoiling a sheet with gigantic sloppy letters. The others set to work, leaning against the wall or sitting on the floor. Pegge filled her page with cyphers and twining foliage that branched into the leaves of night-blooming tobacco. She hated these exercises he set them when her brothers were home from school.

One by one, Jo, George, and Bridget rose to stammer out their cases while the judge sat with his legs crossed rigidly, unwilling to exert even a facial muscle to defend his life. After each had presented a lacklustre case, their father became apoplectic with spots, dismantled their arguments with brutal logic, and pronounced himself a step closer to his grave through the ignorance of his own children.

Pegge was almost choking from the pipe-fumes. The tobacco that Doctor Foxe had prescribed seemed to be luring her father into a fatal oriental languor. Even now, his head was stiffening into sculptor's marble under the embroidered nightcap that was Con's parting gift. If he could not be talked out of this bout of hypochondria, Pegge would be forced to live with Con and be subject to her tyranny.

Feeding her page to the fire, Pegge collected his things as she usually did at this hour. She seized the pipe from his hand and pushed it back into the box.

"There is some tobacco left," he protested, gripping the air a moment too late.

"You must stop smoking, Father, for tobacco is a cure and you say you wish to die. Of course," she offered, turning back towards him with the box of pipes, "if you prefer to be cured and serve your King and God as Dean of Paul's—"

His hand was still feeling the air, hoping for the pipe to reappear. "Your argument has surpassing merit," he conceded. "Ergo, I shall continue to smoke tobacco as a cure. I will not fast. I will cheerfully await God's leisure till he calls, but not," he pointed his finger at George, who was smiling openly now, "so overcheerfully as to be loath to go when he commands me."

Wooden clogs pounded up the stairs towards the bedchamber and Bess entered, carrying a cloth in a large basin.

The Dean quickly uncrossed his legs as Bess thrust the steaming basin at him. "My sickbed is a rack and my spots malignant and pestilential." His voice was muffled by the hot wet cloth, which Bess was swathing around his face.

"I'll sweat this nonsense out of him. Throw some coals on that fire, one of you," Bess called to the children, who were fleeing from the room. Plucking the ornate nightcap from his head, she fished a knife out of her pocket that looked like the one she used for paring turnips. "You haven't been shaved since Constance left. I'm here to scrape every blessed hair off you myself. Pegge, take away that box of pipes and fetch my boiling kettle from the kitchen."

4. ANGLING

Pegge's father produced twenty-three devotions—one sheet a day for twenty-three days. Then he rose from his mattress as slickly as Lazarus, cleanly shaved and brimming with new sermons. Out of his illness came a poem written in a code to God. To celebrate the Dean's recovery, the choristers of Paul's set the new hymn to music and sang it with gusto. Pegge knelt on aching legs, enduring the puns on her parents' names and wishing her father back in his sickbed. Why did his love for her mother—the love he had *wallowed in a score*—require such public penance?

From Mr Margrave, who kept an angling shop in Paul's churchyard, Pegge learned that Walton had not been acting rashly because of Constance after all. Instead, Mr Margrave suspected Walton was after a new fish that had come into England at the same time as the turkey. The monks had kept these carp to eat during Lent, but when the monasteries were destroyed, they escaped from the fishponds and bred wild.

Pegge began to follow Walton again, singing Mr Margrave's tune.

Hops and turkeys, carps and beer,
Came into England all in one year.

Walton did no useful work that she could see and was happiest setting one foot ahead of the other, preferably along a river path. On the bank of the River Lea, Pegge watched him lose himself in conversation with other anglers, casting his line and recasting. When he was alone, he let Pegge help him with his bait and tackle, finding more and more uses for her clever fingers.

He showed her how to put moss into a bottle, then tend bait for him in this little garden. Once she found a bright caterpillar beside the river. They knelt down to take stock of his excellent features: yellow lips, purple forehead, grassy underparts, red spots in an X across his shoulders, and fourteen handsome feet. She gave him a twig of privet to gnaw at like a bone, and took him out to show Walton every hour.

Walton's rod kept growing, for the longer the rod, the further he could get across the river. It grew to fifteen, sixteen, seventeen feet, then broke into two for easier carrying. Pegge plucked strands from horses' tails along the path and twisted them into supple lines while Walton fished, skeins of love-language taking shape within her head. Soon her own hair would be as long as a horsetail, and he would beg to use it for his rods.

Before long, Pegge calculated, she would be old enough

to marry, for at fourteen women sprouted hairs and yearned for a male. Perhaps her father could be made to change his mind about having an ironmonger for a son-in-law. Though of a watery slow humour, Walton had an inquiring mind and gentle character. Pegge hinted to her father that Walton might do for one of his other daughters.

For three years Pegge waited for Izaak Walton, for three years Walton waited for Constance Alleyn, and for three years Edward Alleyn's heart beat on. Lucy died while visiting Con in some mysterious way that Con could not bear to relate, King James died and King Charles took the throne, the City was brought low by plague and recovered health again. Then, just as Pegge became fourteen, the news arrived that Mr Alleyn's heart had given out, freeing Constance to seek the embrace of a younger, more virile suitor.

Con was once more at the Deanery, sleeping in her old bedchamber. She served their father his meat at table, and Pegge was shuffled back along the row. Pegge perched on the wooden bench like a nun in a brothel, listening to her sisters' idle talk of marriage. At night, in the narrow bed Pegge shared with her, Betty was expressing an annoying curiosity about the subject.

—

Pegge was waiting at the Frog & Pike when she saw Izaak Walton coming towards her, his newest rod balanced on his shoulder and his lips sweetly curved in welcome. Pegge had sent a letter asking him to meet her near her father's parish of Sevenoaks. This summer her father had taken her to assist him with his writing for the week because he had strained his wrist.

Walton must have started out at daybreak to walk the twenty-five miles south from London, unable to resist the new stream she had described flowing into the River Darent. As they walked along the path clinging to the river, he told her how the inn came by its name. A tremendous pike had been floating sleepily when a frog leapt from the riverbank onto its head. The frog held fast in malice, biting and tormenting the fish until it sank to the bottom. And that was why, Walton said, there were so few pike left in the Darent.

It was an artless tale, and Pegge did not bother to correct it. When he had told her the same story along the River Lea, the frog had stuck fast to the head of a salmon and so killed that noble fish and all its unborn progeny.

The August heat had sucked the Darent dangerously low. Walton pointed out dry patches of riverbed and the obstructions, built by ignorant men, that slowed the trout on their journey upstream.

"The river rises in the pure springs of the Greensand," he said, "but the mills have broken its back—" A bird's cry interrupted him.

"A bittern, over there in the snipe bog."

"By the grace of God there are some marshes left. Where is our stream?"

Pegge gestured to the row of trees, just visible in the summer haze, which grew along the healthy tributary she had found.

Walton made a good figure in a new mossy-green doublet and breeches the colour of the woodcock scrambling past. Although he had cast off his old leather jerkin, he had still taken care to blend in with the undergrowth. She could not say that of herself, for she was wearing Con's scarlet bodice. On the morning Pegge left for Sevenoaks, she found her sister sprawled asleep in bed, wantonly uncovered, and took the bodice without asking. In any case, Con was supposed to be in mourning. Now Pegge tugged the bodice lower in the front and let her dark rope of hair swing back and forth across her breastbone as she walked.

Walton took a sideways look. "How old are you, Pegge?"

"Almost fifteen." She lifted her bare throat to the sun's heat.

"I am twice your age." He turned his head back. "Are you sure there are no gates and mill-dams on your stream?"

"Not twice. You are ten years older, the same as Constance."

His eyes were fixed on the row of trees ahead. "How she has suffered at the death of Mr Alleyn."

Pegge wished she had not mentioned Con. Soon he would be pressing her for details with a preposterous eagerness on his face. Why did men always pity Con? Pegge pitied Mr Alleyn, sure that Con had hastened his death with sweet syllabubs and jugs of sack. What else had been done to the poor man in the privacy of his marriage-bed?

Pegge stopped to examine a lump the size of a pudding-stone that was buzzing on the path, then broke off a corner of the cow-turd and gave it to Walton.

"A dung-beetle," he said, merry once more, "and one that sings in better tune than you."

As they walked, they ate radishes from her pocket, enjoying the coolness in their mouths. Pegge left the biggest one to last. Taking a bite, she gave the other half to Walton. A fine, philosophical look came over his face as he contemplated the half-eaten radish.

"What do you most wish for, Izzy?"

"Herbs and salads, and fish straight from the river. A man needs no more than such pleasures."

Nothing else? Not love? she wanted to ask.

"Did you know that whales once swam up the Thames as far as Richmond?"

This was a story she had not heard. "Have you seen one?"

His head shook slowly. "The great river is now so troubled with silt and weirs that a haddock can barely squeeze through." He quickened his steps towards the row of trees ahead. "This new stretch of river, you say that it is warm?"

"Reedy and turbid, and even more sluggish through the grassy shallows."

His sigh was appreciative. "You did not say which bait to bring. What are our chances of a bream?"

"A fearsome pike patrolled the shallows when I was last here."

"You say there are weeds? Pikes are bred by pickerel weeds. The pike is a gentleman, continent and chaste, that breeds but once a year, and always with his mate."

"Izzy, if he has a mate what need has he of weeds? You forget how you used to show me the males beating upstream with their hooked jaws and gaudy jackets. If generation required melt and spawn when I was ten, how can it now require only weeds? I hope you do not think me simple-minded at fifteen. And as for fish being continent, why every she-loach and minnow we have ever caught has been big-bellied with roe."

He seemed confused. "Why I do not know, for it must be when the pickerel-weed is ripe. And some eels are bred this way as well," he added, his neck colouring.

Why this new delicacy towards her? The rivers had not changed, nor had the fish. She fell a little behind, playing with the drawstring on her scarlet bodice and feeling her nipples rubbing underneath. That must be the reason. It was she who had changed, and Walton who had noticed. He now considered the spawning of fish unsuited to her ears. At this new thought, she hummed a tuneless song.

"Now Pegge, do not argue," he said, misunderstanding her cheerfulness, "for here is the river before us, with the shallows as slow-moving and grassy as promised in your letter."

Walton laid his pouch on the bank and walked into the river with his shoes on. Before Pegge had draped her skirt over a mulberry branch and pulled off her boots and stockings, he was up to his hips in the reeds. He was crossing well downstream, heading towards the still water past the swift on the far side.

An eel shot out of the riverbank as she waded in. Although her father was fond of eels, she could not take him one, for he would guess at once where she had got it.

She was still in the shallows when she saw Walton climbing the other bank with his rod on his shoulder.

The swirling current was twisting her under-skirt, pulling her off balance. She dug in her feet, determined to spot the marauding pike before he did. Tipping her head, Pegge listened for the fish as he had taught her. A clump of green-life floated past with a damselfly laying her eggs in the glinting sun, and something was stirring up the mud on the bottom, sucking in the ooze and spitting it back out.

Then a scatter of maple leaves fell on the water. Looking up, she saw Walton bending a sapling and letting it fly to get her attention. Behind her, under an overhanging rock, there was a great splashing and roiling as if several eels were fighting to get into the same hole. Walton waved her back and was soon lurching up the bank beside her with water surging out of his breeches. Unbuttoning his new doublet, he dropped it, then thought better and folded it neatly on top of a rock. Now even his shoes and hose came off, something she had never seen him do. He was rolling his sleeves up above the elbow. Above his walnut-brown hands, his arms were startling white, and as muscular as a water-carrier's from hoisting his rod and throwing his line.

He pointed under the spreading mulberry branches. "Slide out as far as you can on that rock and tell me what is beneath it."

Pegge got down on her hands and knees, first crawling, then sliding, leaving a glistening trail from her wet clothing. Walton was snapping open the bait-boxes and the warblers were quarrelling over the ripe fruit in the tree above her. When she reached the narrow outcropping, her hands were as purple as the fallen mulberries. She lay on her stomach and wriggled the last few feet to peer over the edge. Beneath the rock, dark ovals swayed gently in the weeds.

Soon Walton was standing at the foot of the rock, almost hopping from one leg to the other, his face daubed with clay to blend in with the riverbank. "Can you see below?"

"Just shapes."

"Is it a trout? Lean out further, I must know what bait to use." He was back rummaging through his boxes, inspecting the cow-turd and tossing it away. "The beetle has escaped. Why did I not bring red worms or paste? But I do not think it will be a trout," he consoled himself, "for the water is not swift enough."

"You hardly need bait," she said. "I have one in my hand."

Now he was in a fever, creeping along the wet rock towards her. He crouched over her ankles at the neck of the rock, for there was no room beside Pegge on the narrow overhang. "What fish is it?"

"I cannot tell." It was hard to concentrate when water was dripping all over her legs from his heavy breeches. "But it is not long enough to be the pike."

"And its bigness? Is it only a gudgeon?" He tugged at her petticoat to make her answer.

"As big as a bream, but not so round."

He let out his breath and pushed up closer. "Then it is too big for a roach, which is well, for it is a foolish, simple fish. What sort of fins does it have? The tench has large fins and smooth scales," he prompted.

She ran her fingers along the spine of the fish, which seemed drugged by the warm sleepy water. "Only one fin on top."

"Then it cannot be a perch, for it has bristles like a hog."

"Here is another brushing past," she said, as it rubbed against her palm.

All morning the rock had been gathering heat, and now she melted into it, a new and not-unpleasant feeling, her breasts tender against the hardness. The rock was talking to her body, and her body to the rock, but what they were saying could never be written down, not in the King's English as taught to gentlewomen. Steam was rising from her petticoat, causing an uncommon moistness all about her.

"I hope it is not a pair of ruff-fish." He sounded deflated.

"There are more than two, Izzy, there must be half a dozen, and they are not ruffs. They are slipping in and out of my hand as if they are tame. Come, lie next to me and touch them. I cannot tell you how it makes me feel—you must stroke them for yourself."

"We must call this only *the river*, Pegge, never by name. We will take them straight to the Frog & Pike. How shall we have them cooked, on the coal-fire or in a pan with oysters?"

"First help me catch them," she said, laughing. "Then you must eat them howsoever you choose while I run back to Sevenoaks before my father discovers I am missing."

Above her, the warblers were fighting again, dropping as many mulberries on top of her as they were eating. Without warning, a red fin rose out of the rippling water. As a huge, protruding mouth scooped up the floating berries, Pegge saw her face reflected in a single row of giant scales. The belly was fat and quivering, the best eating. A female, bursting-full of spawn. Now Pegge knew what they were, a shoal of them, scarcely a foot beneath the overhang. She turned to Walton and mouthed the word *mirrors*. Then she mimed the belly of the female.

"The queen of the river," he whispered. "The big she-carp. Some call her the water-fox, for her cunning. I once tried for a week to catch one using cherries. She also comes for a sweet bread paste, or for a ringing bell. Oh, say you have brought a bell, Pegge Donne, and I will love you better than your sister Con, for I have no white bread and honey!"

"If you help me, I'll get you something better." She slid towards him, her petticoat riding up above her knees, then sat on her heels, shifting her heavy rope of hair out of his way. "Loosen the ties that fasten my bodice up the back." His fingers fumbled—the same large fingers that were quick and deft when working tackle. "Lower, there is a loop at the bottom."

Taking his hands, she placed them on her waist. His knees straddled her hips as he tugged and eased the bodice up and over her head. Now only a lawn chemise clung damply to her skin. She let him feed his eyes, to see how the sun had kissed and swollen her young nipples.

He was holding up the bright cloth like soiled laundry. "But how are we to catch them?"

She pulled the drawstrings tight around the neck and arms. "Do you see?" she said. "It is a bag. And scarlet—for look how they come to mulberries! It will be as easy as snigling for eels."

She rolled onto her stomach and slid back along the narrow overhang, then tipped on her side to make room for him. As he inched forward, first her leg, then her arm, crossed over him to hold him steady. His hair brushed her face, and his lips curved an inch away from hers, as if to ask *what next?* Then he turned away, dropping his beautiful white arm over the edge towards the moving shapes beneath.

"The fish are throbbing! Do you feel that, Pegge?"

The raw heat of the sun and rock, the blows of her heart, the prickling of her skin, which did he mean? She could feel everything, and nothing would ever be the same. Her belly was trembling, as it had done when she was little and her father blew on it to tease her. She wondered whether a brace of carp would buy a night's lodging at the Frog & Pike. While she was waiting outside the inn, a young couple had passed by boldly. Calling for the landlord, they took a room for the night. They would not wait for nightfall to taste their first embraces. Even now, at the noon of day— with the warblers carolling, with the mulberries raining from above, with Izaak Walton's buckle pressing hard against Pegge's belly—the young couple would be consummating their love in the Frog & Pike.

"Are you ready, Pegge?"

Several carp were splashing on the surface, mirroring the sun so brightly that it blinded her. It was clear now what was happening. There was only one female, and she had attracted six or seven large mirrors to her spawn. They were in the very act of spawning, the melters bearing up the spawner who was rubbing herself against Pegge's hand.

It seemed a shame to take her, but Walton had never balked at catching spawning fish. It was too late to dull his appetite. If she argued for the mirrors' progeny, he was likely to contend that the sun and fertile weeds had generated them and treat her like an ignorant child again.

Walton lowered the scarlet trap downstream, careful not to splash or cast a shadow. "I must lean out as far as I can. Hold me fast so I do not fall in." His head swivelled around towards her. "You have the look of a trout fresh from the river. Are you ill, or sickening for something? Open your eyes. This is no time to fail me, Pegge."

"It is just the mulberries staining my face." She gripped his breeches with her free hand. With the blood pooling in her head from hanging over the edge, the last thing she was thinking about was sliding the fat-bellied carp into a hot pan with oysters.

Now Walton was urgent, and in command. "Just tease them into the bag," he ordered. "Do not squeeze or push, just tickle them towards it—tickle them sweetly, and let them go."

5. MIRRORS

Pegge was in the Deanery frying bread in dripping when Constance swept past with a plate full of lather and whiskers. She threw the soapy water into the courtyard, splashing Sadie, who had dug herself out of the flower bed to see what Con was bringing her.

Pegge had returned from Sevenoaks with her father the previous night, for he had grown tired of cucumbers and rural conversation before the week was over. As soon as he had woken, he had blown his trumpet for his eldest daughter and asked her to untangle his hair and shave around his beard.

When Con came back in, smoothing her dark gown, Pegge speared the hot crust and blew on it. "Will you teach me how to shave him, Con?"

Con wiped the inside of the shaving plate and laid the razor across it. "There's no need now that I am home." She took a looking-glass out of her pocket and propped it on the shelf.

"But you might marry again," Pegge said, eating her fried bread.

Con licked her finger and curled a strand of hair around it. The black curl stayed obediently in place as she stood back to consider the effect. Pegge had her father's hair—thick reckless handfuls of auburn down to her waist. Up to now, she had thought it childish, twisting it into ropes to tame it, but this morning it held the fragrance of mulberries and Izaak Walton's fingers. By the end of the day, it would reek of kitchen fat and coal-smoke once again.

"Will *you* teach me, Bess?" Pegge squinted at her reflection in the grimy window, judging her hair too long to fasten up like Con's.

"Now the kitchenmaid has run off, I need you here." Bess was ferrying goods from the larder to the kitchen table. "A load of cucumbers came from Sevenoaks this morning. This was on top of it, for the Dean's daughter." She pushed the bulky object towards Con.

Con pressed another curl in place, then unwrapped the bright cloth around the parcel. Underneath was a thick layer of leaves. As she peeled them off, a clump of moss appeared with a puddle forming around it. When the moss expanded then contracted, Con took a quick step back.

At the end of the moss, Pegge could see a large golden mouth opening and closing with a quiet sucking noise. She pulled out some green tufts to reveal a pair of eyes that bulged like a monk's awakened from a long sleep. Then she stripped off the rest of the moss and saw a row of tiny long-haired Pegges reflected in the giant scales.

Bess came around to look. "It's a good enough fish," she admitted, probing under the gills with a finger. "And it could not be fresher."

Pegge filled a deep pot, then slipped her hands under the fish and plunged it into the water. When the fish came up to the surface, she fed it a cube of bread soaked in milk.

"Why does Mr Walton do such things?" Con asked, perplexed. "I have done nothing to merit this . . . this . . . *flounder!*" She wiped her hands on the cloth, realized it was wet, and threw it back onto the table.

"A mirror carp," Pegge corrected, "a love-poem from an angler." She was already weighing and discarding inferior phrases, rehearsing her thank you to the fisherman, for she was sure the gift was meant for her, not Con.

Con was taking a closer look at the scarlet cloth it had arrived in. "How did he get my bodice?"

"You can't wear that colour," Bess said. "You're in mourning."

Pegge crossed to the bucket, lifting the dipper to hide her face. It was good water from the conduit, not the muddy Thames. She took a long sip, then let the rest fountain off the dipper onto the carp. *The mirror*, she thought, feeding it another morsel.

"So you took it, Pegge, and gave it to him," Con said. "Is that why your face is red?"

Bess slapped a bunch of leeks on the table and pushed a knife towards Con. Ignoring the chore, Con went back to the looking-glass, stretching the neck of her bodice this way and that to judge which would expose the most pale flesh.

Pegge bent her ear to the carp. For a minute there was nothing, then a soft *puk puk puk* came out of the golden lips. The mirror had been sent to Dr Donne's daughter, but Dr Donne had four daughters, not just Con, who seemed to think she ran the household. It was Pegge who had shown Walton the secret river. The fish had gone quiet again, and was listing to one side. Pegge held it under the water. When the carp surfaced, it made a quiet *puk*.

"That'd be better off dead." Bess heaved a foot onto the stool, then a second foot, and reached up to the ceiling to untie a string of garlic. Con was showered with dust as the bulbs fell onto the table. The stool wobbled and Bess stepped down, cursing the absent kitchenmaid. "Peel those," she said to Con. "I've got a fish to cook on top of everything."

"Not everyone cares for garlic with fish," Con said. "You can't taste, Bess, because you can't smell." She kept on talking, though Bess was banging about the pantry. "There is plenty for you to do in the house without doing the cooking too. The bishop has offered us his second cook and I don't see why—" A stack of pots fell over in the pantry and Con left the kitchen swiftly.

Bess carried a joint of beef to the table. "I'll need that dripping-pan," she told Pegge crossly.

Before Pegge could stop her, Bess was pulling the pan off the fire with her bare hand. She dropped it on the hearth, and smoke from the burning grease began to swirl out of the fireplace.

Pegge sat her down and examined the red welt. "You should be more careful, Bess." Pegge put some butter on the burn, then wound a strip of linen across and around the smarting hand, tying the ends snugly at the wrist.

"That'll need cleaning. Bring over some of your father's malmsey."

Pegge splashed the bandage, then handed the jug to Bess who took a long pull and planted it at her elbow, not bothering to replace the stopper. Lately, there had been more of these accidents—burns and lesions, cuts in her large, roughened hands. Alarming nicks and bruises were appearing all over Bess's arms and legs. She was now chopping the roots off the leeks and scoring the ends deeply, the knife flying dangerously high and fast.

When had Bess got so old and stiff? Perhaps she would be safer out of the kitchen, though Pegge knew there was no point saying so. She stood the scored leeks in a pot of water to clean themselves. It was curious how the vegetable captured the grains of earth inside it as it grew. Pegge extracted a leek and scrutinized it. "What is it like to be in love?"

Bess roused herself, looking in an exaggerated way from left to right, and Pegge dropped the leek back into the pot. As she suspected, Bess knew less than she did. Picking up the razor, Pegge scraped it across her arm, watching the hairs fly off one by one.

Bess took the straight-blade from Pegge's hand, then reached for a slab of fat. "Why don't you ask your father? He was the one who addled your mother's brain with poetry." She shaved off thin slices of fat, shifting her fingers a fraction with each stroke, then butted them over the joint, so that none of the meat showed. When the joint was larded, Bess took another gulp of malmsey and splashed a thimbleful on the bandage. "I hope this is nothing to do with giving your bodice to that fisherman. What were you doing all that time at Sevenoaks?"

Pegge reached up to the mantel where Bess kept her ball of bits and pieces of string. Unravelling a long piece, Pegge looped it crossways around the meat. Bess pressed her finger on it while Pegge turned the string and knotted, turning and knotting until the fat was secured against the flesh. Then Pegge lifted down the spit and drove it through the beef. She fitted the spit into the grooves above the fire, sliding the dripping-pan underneath.

This was the time that Pegge liked best, when the smells began to fill the kitchen. For the next half-hour, Bess would sit in her old chair and put up her feet, listening to the meat brown and sizzle. Often Pegge's father would be drawn in from the library to inspect the joint. If things were behindhand, he would bluster about, saying he had half a mind to hire a proper cook, but one scowl from Bess would silence him and he would go off with a slice in his hand to tide him over until the meal was ready.

Pegge knelt beside Bess and snugged up the damp bandage for her. "What was my mother like when she was my age?"

"More womanly than you." Bess snorted. "More like Constance and just as useless in the kitchen. At least peel that garlic while you're talking. Not with that," she said, as Pegge reached for the straight-blade. "Just crack it with your hands or it'll take all day. Put some muscle behind it."

Sadie came to the doorway, settling down on her paws to watch the joint turning on the spit.

"You're an outside dog," Bess warned, as Sadie crept forward. "You'll get no food from this kitchen." Bess snapped her apron to drive the dog back over the threshold, then heaved her feet off the stool. Lifting the carp by its tail, she looked it up and down. "Your mother once saw the Queen in a gown sewn all with mirrors. But she wasn't full of eggs like this, for she never had a man." The carp dripped all the way to the table.

The row of mirrors was now flying off the fish towards Pegge. It was too late to explain how well the scales would have looked on a platter in front of her father. Bess cut off one red fin, then flipped the fish and cut off another, flipping and cutting from belly to back, back to belly until, pinning the head and cutting towards her injured hand in one final, brutal *whack*, she took off the last fin and the head together, barely missing her thumb. With a chop, the tail flew off, the trimmings fell onto the floor, and the carp lay mirrored in a pool of its own blood.

The next Pegge knew, Bess was spooning out the roe and the head was trotting out the door in Sadie's jaws. Sensing something amiss, the dog dropped it in the courtyard and backed away, trying to stare down the bulging eyes. The mouth made a plaintive *puk*, then the head tipped over and Sadie ran whining to the flower bed.

Bess stabbed her knife into the table. "I was just a servant, and before I knew a thing, your mother had thrown away her dowry and was no better than a servant herself. That's love for you, better left to dogs." She wiped her forehead with a rag. "Stay away from it, Pegge. Let your father find you a husband, like he did for Constance. But first you have to get your monthlies. If you don't hop to it, little Betty will get them before you."

"I wish you wouldn't talk about it, Bess." The kitchen was far too hot. The rope of hair was heavy on Pegge's neck and the smell of the joint was turning her stomach. She shoved the heap of peeled garlic towards Bess and stood up.

"That'll never do," Bess said, pushing her back down. "I'll need four times that."

Pegge went over to the shaving mirror to remove the fish scales that had landed on her face, but one of them began to bleed. "The scales won't come off."

"Come into the light." Bess pulled Pegge over to the door and tugged her hair to tilt her head back.

"What is it, Bess?"

"As if I didn't have enough trouble. Now you've come all over with a blistering rash." Bess rubbed at Pegge's cheek with her finger. "It's your skin itself that's scaling. Bless you, Pegge Donne, you've got the pox. I hope you didn't catch this from that fisherman of yours."

———

Pegge smelt the carp all through the house, but tasted none of it, for Doctor Foxe forbade strong foods and salt foods and sugary foods and solid foods, confining Pegge to her room so her sisters would not risk disfigurement. Allowed only bread soaked in milk, she concluded that his treatment for every illness was to deprive his patients of all comforts.

On his way back from a sermon, her father was intercepted by a letter from Con warning him about the small-pox. He wrote to Pegge, saying, *I am in fear for your life*. In the next sentence, he announced that he would detour to

Uncle Grymes's house at Peckham rather than risk contagion at the Deanery.

In the daytime, Pegge dreamt of lying with Izaak Walton
beside the curves of a sinewy green river, but at night, when
she could not control her thoughts, she dreamt of eating.
In a small book, Pegge made a list of fishes she would
devour when Doctor Foxe allowed it. She drew a river that
rambled across the pages from a cold, clear winterbourne,
through slow middle reaches, and finally into the broad
flat-marshes of an estuary. Adding pictures of fish to be
found along the way, she wrote meticulous notes on their
bait and habitat to show to Walton. But though she waited
day after day, he did not come.

By now, Walton would have hunted down the monstrous pike and tamed it to feed from bread-paste in his
hand. Even now, he might be carrying the prize towards the
Deanery to share with her. *First, open your pike at the gills*, she
wrote in the sextodecimo,

and if need be, cut also a little slit towards the belly. Out of
these, take his guts; and keep his liver, which you are to
shred very small with thyme, sweet marjoram, and a little
winter-savoury; to these put some pickled oysters, and
some anchovies, two or three; both these last whole, for the
anchovies will melt, and the oysters should not; to these,
you must add also a pound of sweet butter, which you are
to mix with the herbs that are shred, and let them all be
well salted. If the pike be more than a yard long, then you
may put into these herbs more than a pound, or if he be
less, then less butter will suffice.

If fat slathered around beef heightened its flavour, surely butter would sweeten a bony pike? But if it melted straight out of the pike's belly, more would be needed in the sauce. She filled yet another page in the tiny book.

> Let him be roasted very leisurely; and often basted with claret wine, and anchovies, and butter, mixed together; and also with what moisture falls from him into the pan. When you have roasted him sufficiently, to the sauce you are to add a fit quantity of the best butter, and to squeeze the juice of three or four oranges. Lastly, you may either put it into the pike, with the oysters, two cloves of garlic, and take it whole out, when the pike is cut off the spit; or, to give the sauce a haut goût, let the dish into which you let the pike fall be rubbed with it: The using or not using of this garlic is left to your discretion.

Pegge was certain this dish would be most tasty, for she had put everything she fancied into it. On the cover, she drew a handsome pike lying in the pickerel weeds with his loyal mate beside him. Then she wrapped up the sexto-decimo and addressed it to Mr Izaak Walton of Fleet street, near Chancery lane.

Not even a minnow arrived from Fleet street in response. She began to think that something had befallen him. Perhaps he too was laid up with the pox. It seemed to attack the furthest points of flesh—the hands, the feet, and the complexion. She thought of his sweet bruised ankles and his smile, and wondered who would care for him.

—

Each night, Bess stripped Pegge to the waist and rubbed her with cream to stop the itching. Pegge's eyes were bathed with a cotton ball dipped in saltwort-water, the relief immediate and exquisite. Each morning, Pegge woke to the scent of almonds clinging to her skin, her breasts like tender, aching buds.

Giving her a sponge bath after a week, Bess pointed out the straight sparse hairs between Pegge's legs. Only so much as a brown mallard, thought Pegge, blushing, or a speckled fowl. But at least they were not falling out like the hairs on her head, which were coming out by handfuls. Nothing could slow the ravage of the pox, not even the gentian violet painted on her scalp. First the scales on her cheeks turned into pustules, then they plumped up like mulberries and burst with a running pus. Even Con was moved to compassion, begging Pegge through the door not to scratch the sores and blight her hopes of marriage.

Fearless of contagion, Bess lay beside Pegge through the hot nights, telling her stories to drive off the persecuting dreams of food. Ill with hunger, Pegge cried out for radishes, but the doctor still insisted that the disease be starved, else it would get a foothold in her stomach. When Pegge could not eat another spoonful of bread-in-milk, Bess brought up an apron-load of the Dean's cucumbers, cold and smelling of the country. She pared the largest, dropping the narrow green peels right on the bed, as Pegge's eyes hungered after each long, rivering pull of the knife.

"Nothing in it but water, in case that doctor asks," Bess

said, handing the white fruit to Pegge, and reaching for another one to peel.

—

At last the pox retreated, taking Pegge's hair with it. Her head felt lightly bulbous, an angelica flower bobbing on a reedy stalk. The boils scabbed over, tightening the skin across her cheekbones. When Doctor Foxe declared the danger past, her father brought in some codlings from his tree and knelt at her bedside, thanking God that *it had not much disfigured her who had it.* Little Betty was more honest. *You look like a six-spotted moth,* she said, counting the scabs on Pegge's cheek.

Now Con sat beside Pegge's bed with her needlework. "I am making you something to wear until your hair grows back. How does it look?" She balanced the cap on her own head.

Like a splash of flowers on a field of jet, but on Pegge's naked skull? At least Con had not carried in the looking-glass. Eyesight blurring, Pegge pressed her face into the mattress.

"But this would look so well on you." Puzzled, Con turned the cap in her hands.

"I will take your hood, Con, if you have no more use for it, for I see that you have put off black."

"You cannot know how tiresome it was. Even my sealing wax had to be black! Why should father insist upon full mourning?" Con spun out her hair, more glossy than the flowers she was stitching. "When you mend a dark garment, Pegge, you cannot even see to thread the needle.

I am so glad you did not die, for it would have meant another year of black—" She broke off, reddening.

Pegge swung her legs over the edge of the bed, waiting for the dizziness to subside. "Did Izaak Walton get the pox?"

"Why should he?" Con looked up in surprise. "He came once or twice to ask after me and looked quite well."

Ask after Con, when it was *Pegge* who had almost died? Pegge watched Con's needle feathering strokes across a sun-drenched flower. "Remember the minnow of green silk I asked you to sew for him, Con? It meant nothing to you, but he still carries it everywhere."

"Well, he is an angler, and they are not the brightest of men." Biting off the thread close to the cloth, Con checked her stitches in the window-light.

"He is devoted to you, yet you spurn him. Let him marry someone else if you will not have him!"

"You have missed more than your dinners by being in bed. He *has* married someone else."

Walton married—had Pegge heard right? The air scented with apples, the first solid food settling into her belly, cores and all, her sister sewing comfortably beside her—it was too much to keep the tears from spilling down her face.

Mr Walton was betrothed long before Pegge got the pox, a good twelvemonth ago, Con reported, just before Mr Alleyn took sick and died. Even Con admitted this was galling for Walton, though his betrothal saved her from telling him to his face that she would not marry him.

"He will be doing no more angling." Con licked her finger, then knotted the end of her thread. "His new wife will not let him wander about the countryside all day, for she is Rachel Floud, the linen-draper's daughter."

This explained the new mossy-green doublet with its starched collar. No wonder he had folded his clothing so neatly on the rock beside the river. Pegge curled into a shivering ball, keeping her wet face turned from Con.

Married while the carp were spawning, perhaps even the same day he sent the fish in its bed of moss to Con. For it had been sent to her sister, there was no doubt of that now. After Pegge had bruised her ankles in swift cold streams for him, listened to his deep voice carolling the angler's song, agreed to call their new discovery *the river*, to keep it secret to themselves.

Con raised her eyes from a particularly garish flower. "At least you will be spared hearing it from his lips."

The sympathy was Pegge's undoing. She uncurled and leapt out of bed, bending over at the waist and vomiting. Perhaps the doctor had been right to limit her intake of solids, for they were now staring at her from the floor-boards, a horrid curdled puddle, and Con was running down the stairs for Bess.

After they had lain like man and wife, his face daubed with clay, their hands entangled in the weedy shallows, teasing and tricking the spawning carp. She had swum as blithely into his trap as the mirror had swum into the scarlet bodice.

Betrothed to Rachel Floud and still adoring Con. Pegge hoped he smelt of fish when he climbed into his wedding-bed. He was as oafish as Con thought him. And worse—a coward, not daring to risk contagion to tell Pegge to her ravaged face how cruelly he had deceived her.

—

The scabs fell off gradually, leaving deep scores in Pegge's cheeks, but she no longer cared. What matter that the disease had plundered her long swing of hair? No man would finger it now, and what man would she want, Izaak Walton being taken. Each night, she scrutinized the new growth angrily and trimmed the tufts close to her scalp with scissors.

Soon she heard Walton debating the text of a sermon with her father, for Walton had no better occupation now. Before long, he made some pious connection between fishing along the Itchen and casting a net in the sea of Galilee that won her father over. Finding Walton underfoot, her father discovered uses for him, small literary chores that he would no longer entrust to Pegge. One day Pegge saw Walton in the library, admiring the latest design for her father's effigy. She was about to confront him when he took out the sextodecimo with the pike drawn on the cover. As he jotted down a scrap of information, she passed by without a sound.

For what could she have said? Told him that other fishermen called him *that crazy ankler* for walking into rivers with his shoes on, and for preferring live bait to artificial lures? Accused him of marrying Rachel Floud to get her father's shop in Fleet street? Perhaps Pegge could have listed off his wife's lumpish features, her quivering goose-flesh and hairy forearms, for Pegge had been inspecting Mrs Walton from close and far.

Still Pegge followed him, the slope of his back, the sweet curls of hair over his new starched collar, though he went nowhere near a river now. Perhaps, she told herself, that was punishment itself.

On St Clement's day, Pegge was copying out her father's sermon from the notes she had taken down in Paul's. He was supposed to be resting in his chair because he had an ulcerous sore throat from too much preaching, but he was pacing restlessly behind her.

He reached out to rub her hair against the grain. "As short as a caterpillar's fur," he said, "and the colour of lapis lazuli." His eyes lifted to the Virgin's robe in the painting on the library wall.

Pegge did not need a mirror to tell her that he saw blue hairs sticking up in tufts like mould on cheese. Bess's attempt to lighten the gentian stains by rubbing them with chicken fat had only made Pegge's head so greasy that her hood had taken an embarrassing tumble in the cathedral that morning.

Now her father pulled at a tuft to see whether it was securely rooted. "It does not seem to be growing, yet even a dead man's hair gets longer in the grave."

She wished he would sit down. His beard was so close that she could see the little comb-marks in it. Con had shaved him cleanly around the edges, and raked his moustache with a miniature rake.

He turned the paper sideways to see what she had written. "I do not recall using that turn of phrase. Look up the text if you do not know it, Pegge." The bible thudded near her elbow. "Someone with less gift for writing would do a better job. It is time to put you to other work. While Con is with us, she will teach you household skills."

She jerked the paper back. "I do not need to learn husbandry, for I mean to be your Margaret More." Dipping her quill, she tapped off the excess ink and stroked out the offending phrase.

"A man is King and men must be the scholars. I cannot change the world to suit my children. Even the daughter of Sir Thomas More did needlework."

He had often been of two minds about her, but since the pox he seemed to have settled upon one. "Bess will teach me what I need to know."

"You must spend less time with the servants and more with Con."

"It will do me no good until I have Con's looks."

He studied her face for a moment. "I shall offer as big a dowry as is needful, but you shall be married." He ran his finger along her scarred cheek, then plucked the paper out of her hands. "Is this your old argument that dogs have souls? You are like an elephant with your opinions."

"You once wrote that *women* did not have souls."

"Long before I met your mother." This brought its own hush with it, for he seldom spoke of Ann.

"How did my mother—"

"*How* and *why* are dangerous and infectious monosyllables!" Then his face softened. "I will grant," he conceded, "that I was as opinionated in my juvenilia as you are in yours. But it is more becoming in a man."

Dogmatic, she thought, but did not risk the pun. Aloud she said, "You could be equally wrong about dogs. It is not fair that Sadie is put out in the cold in winter."

"Enough quibbling. My text was Revelations 22, they

are dogs that are without. That does not mean outside the kitchen door, but *outside the Church*, meaning we should not give alms to drunkards or unchristian beggars." His voice was reaching pulpit volume. "They are dogs that are without, and the children's bread must not be given to dogs. Matthew 15. This is not about dogs, Pegge, this is about men."

She wondered whether he had seen her feeding Sadie from her plate, against his orders. "Then let us talk of men, Father. Izaak Walton is idle, but you do not mind his idleness. He licks your heels like Sadie, but you do not begrudge him crumbs from your table."

Walton's idleness had got up her nose, down her arm, and out onto the paper, but her father's wrath was closer and more dangerous. His knuckles were drumming out a dreadful rhythm. Although he had never struck her, she shifted the ink-pot between them just in case. She knew that he had a fear of spilling ink, having been punished by his tutor for staining a white shirt when he was a boy.

"Mr Walton is a cautious, careful man," he said.

"His fingers are so thick they can scarcely hold a pen."

The ink-pot was vibrating. "He had Greek and Latin at grammar school."

"So did my brothers and little good it did them." Then, more obediently, "I admit I have no Greek, but I will gladly learn it, Father."

"So you can translate my Greek as poorly as you do my Latin? And what of my English? Mr Walton writes what he is told to. This"—he was waving the paper, though it hardly seemed to cool him— "bears little resemblance to what I preached."

She moved a safe distance away to inspect the Blessed Virgin hanging from a nail. "Perhaps I will be a virgin. And a martyr. For am I not descended from the Catholic Mores, and named after Margaret More herself? Chastity will suit me admirably."

He smiled, an event so unusual as to strike a spark of fear in Pegge. "Margaret More was no virgin," he said. "She married the man her father chose and had five children by him. You have too much curiosity for a virgin. I know you have been reading my love-poems, for you left my cabinet unlocked." When she tried to speak, the diamond flashed on his hand, forbidding her. "You will marry, Pegge, so quell your opposition. I may not be here to care for you much longer. Today the canons announced my burial-place, near Dean Colet in the choir."

Colet's sepulchre was noted for its grisliness. Crowned by skulls, and featuring a full reclining skeleton without even a string of flesh or shred of muscle to clothe it, the effigy had been Pegge's favourite place to read the *Anatomy of Melancholy* when she was younger. Why had her father requested a burial-place so soon? She would not venture the question, unwilling to unleash complaints of swollen glands or fallen arches. With his grave-site beckoning in Paul's, he was likely to become mired in the pit of hypochondria, where he already spent too many of his waking hours.

"As for Mr Walton," he said, "his brotherhood of anglers has already proved its worth, since he has found a patron for my effigy, a true supporter of the funerary arts. My monument will overshadow Colet's, for I shall have the best Italian marble and Nicholas Stone to carve it."

6. A JET RING SENT

Pegge was standing in Fleet street with a cold head, hoping for a glimpse of Izaak Walton under the sign marked *R. Floud, Linen-draper*. She had stopped clipping her hair, but it had lost the knack of growing on its own. Each morning she brushed the hairs until they stood like bristles, then brushed them back the other way. One way they looked flatter, and the other way they had more shine, but brushing had not made them one whit longer.

After a while, Pegge gave up on Walton and went along to St Clement's to visit her mother's tomb. Through the window she noticed Con in the churchyard, dressed in black, although she had put off mourning a year before. Then a man came through the gate, a widower Pegge had often seen tending his wife's grave. From inside the apse, teetering on the sexton's chair, Pegge saw the widower pause as Con approached him. Coming from a grave herself, or so it appeared, Con dragged her feet in grief, a piece of stage-craft worthy of her dead husband. Pegge was sure that her sister had paced out every step beforehand.

Greetings were exchanged at the crossing of the paths and Con faltered, clutching at the widower's sleeve. Steadying her elbow, he led her to the honeysuckle bower, where she withdrew the lace from her bodice to dab her eyes, exposing robust curves. Sorrow, Pegge saw through the window, had cast a sheen of pearl all down her sister's throat. Now the widower was fingering the lace, exclaiming at its dampness. Pegge imagined the foolish words that were then shared about the mingling of their tears.

Pegge tugged her hood over her eyes just before the lovers passed beneath the window. Had they glanced up, they would have seen the sexton rubbing the dirty pane briskly with his fist, but they were intent on going through the gate, their arms linked, to share their grief along the Strand. Pegge traced their footsteps backwards to the garden, marvelling at the resilience of the human heart. The fragrance was overpowering, a thicket of wayward vines and sweet-briar. Why did midday bring out the worst in flowers? Pegge poked angrily at the foliage with a stick, poked and prodded until she determined that it was the low heliotrope, not the climbing honeysuckle, that gave off the cloying scent of honey.

Within a few months, Mr Harvey appeared at the Deanery, his clothes damp with excitement, asking Pegge for an audience with her father. While he waited, she brought him red wine to calm him and sat to keep him company. Soon his lips were purpled from the drink, and he was staring at Pegge's skull. She knew what he was seeing, hair as short and brown as Sadie's.

"The scars will fade in time," he said. Then, in a spurt of words, "I believe hair can be brushed to health again."

"It has not lengthened an inch, although I brush it vigorously."

A kind-hearted man, too kind for Con. Pegge was sorry for his fate at her sister's hands. However, Samuel Harvey had no one to blame but himself for, as it now spilled out, he claimed some knowledge of the heart, prime mover of the body, being kin to William Harvey, physician extraordinary to the King and author of the newly published *Exercitatio Anatomica de Motu Cordis et Sanguinis in Animalibus 1628*. In the art of greeting fathers he had been well coached by Con, for this was the little book he had brought wrapped up in stationer's paper for the Dean.

"Look," he said, tearing off the wrapper and thumbing to a diagram. "The blood is propelled through the body by the action of the heart. If you stand on your head, hairs will gush like water from a pump."

At Mr Harvey's urging, Pegge struggled through the Latin. First the title, *On the Motion of the Heart and Blood in Animals*, then the passage in which the heart was compared to the machine inside a firearm which, when the trigger was pulled, dropped the flint, struck the steel, elicited the spark, and ignited the gunpowder, thus forcing the flame into the barrel and propelling the ball to hit the mark.

If the heart was a firearm, Pegge wondered, what was love? The lethal ball that ripped open the chest and quickened the demise? And what was lust—the flint, the trigger, or the spark?

Samuel Harvey might have been in love, but he was far from melancholy. He was mildly discomfited after the Dean interrogated him in the library, but still sanguine, merry and red in the face and short of breath. If not for meeting Con, he might have been spared love's pain and met a slower, kinder fate.

But hungry dogs would eat dirty puddings and soon Con was swooping down the passage towards him, wearing her cap of yellow flowers. There was a flash of jet upon her finger, a gift from Mr Harvey which their father must have just approved. She had done something to her hair, dressed it with oil so that it swished as darkly as a raven's wing. As her sister passed, Pegge caught a whiff of something feral, like a drag left by a fox. Perhaps Con had milked the scent ducts of otter or stoat.

Soon Bridget and little Betty came down to delight in Mr Harvey's charms. Pegge could hear Con praising her betrothed as a learned man, the cousin of the King's physician. Then Sadie arrived to sniff him and declare herself quite willing to be petted.

Their father emerged from the library, waving the agreement to dry the ink and calling out to Bess, who was hovering nearby. "Fetch two bottles of my best sack from below-stairs and the large round of cheese, the one sent down from Hertfordshire. Come, Mr Harvey," their father put his arm around that poor man's shoulders, "let us drink a cup to seal the bargain."

—

As midsummer's day approached, the household grew in agitation. The impending marriage set them all adrift, Bridget and Betty quarrelling over who had better ankles and Con talking endlessly about her wedding garments. Pegge could not bear five minutes with any of her sisters. Even the servants had splintered into factions. The Deanery was either too hot or too cold. Someone opened windows and someone closed them. Caught by the Dean unlatching a casement on the landing, Bess was thrown off balance and tumbled down the stairs. When Pegge reached her, she found a human pincushion. Blood was dripping out of tiny perforations from Bess's elbow to her shoulder. All the pins Bess had collected on her sleeve throughout the day had stabbed her in the arm.

Night in the Deanery was full of noises. As her wedding loomed, Con's dreams became more vocal and their father was assailed by bouts of night-sickness. Awakened by his sounds, Pegge would stand inside his bedchamber, wondering whether going closer would comfort him or put him in a deeper fright, for his appeals to God to ravish him sounded more like agonized love-cries than holy prayers.

If his corpse was turned over to the philosophers when he died, what would they find when they cut him up? His lungs, she guessed, would be tobacco-black and his heart combust, but what of his spirit—would it be a pious white or vehemently roasted by love's fire? From what she had heard from him in his bedchamber at night, riddled with doubt about the state of his soul, he did not seem to know himself.

—

Pegge was not as interested in the soul as in another organ. For some time now, she had made the human heart her study. She would open William Harvey's treatise to the diagram of the labourer's arm with its large veins, labelled B, C, D, etcetera in a scholarly pen. A lady's hand with a lace cuff pressed on valves H and O, demonstrating the curious fact that the blood did not flow outward from the heart, but along the veins back to that centre.

William Harvey likened these valves to the floodgates of a river, and it was only a leap from this to the River Darent, with its springs near Sevenoaks, its tributaries and distributaries, its weirs, pumps, and sluices, and from thence to the secret river teeming with spawning carp. In a single bound, Pegge found herself staring at the strong white forearm of Izaak Walton and it was *her* fingers that were stepping across the flesh, pressing on the valves and bidding the arm to do her pleasure.

For days she could not go anywhere without The Arm, plainly labelled, and plainly a labourer's arm. It accompanied her to bed at night, as close as butter to cheese, so that when little Betty curled up next to Pegge, then threw her arm across her sister, the arm that touched Pegge was plainly Walton's arm. In the daytime, The Arm lay around Pegge's waist, clearly marked in scholarly ink, should anyone debate its purpose, and her hand danced, yea danced, in the labourer's hand as she ran the twenty-five miles to the Darent valley.

But one night when Betty's arm thudded across her, Pegge sat up with a start, struck by the plain fact that The Arm might at that very moment be fondling Rachel

Floud. Several dark nights were spent upon this problem, before a knock from Betty's elbow woke Pegge to the new fact that another arm might give her equal pleasure, for there were more men in her great City than the oafish Izaak Walton. And this was such a diverting thought that she fell into another dream, her fingers on the valves marked H and O, marvelling that she could command a man's blood to rise and fall and do her bidding.

—

On midsummer's day, Constance Donne married Samuel Harvey and went off to live with him at Abury Hatch, near Barking. Pegge was glad to see the back of Con and to be spared her needlework and household arts. Ill at the thought of losing his eldest daughter, their father followed her to Barking, but returned in worsened spirits.

Back in the Deanery, their father wrote out his Will laboriously. He was attacked by tooth-ache, deafness, sore-throat, vapours from the spleen, and such damps and flash-ings that made him too feverish to go forth, a round of ailments as frequent as the feast-days of the Roman church.

He could not summon up the strength to preach all winter, complaining of the ticklishness of the London pulpits. Paul's was the worst, for he saw disobedience everywhere in the cathedral, dogs at one another's throats, sheriffs refusing to kneel in divine service, and children laughing as they played at bowls. Candlemas passed by without his customary sermon. Perhaps it was just as well, for Pegge, who inspected his notes, saw in them an excruciating lecture on the hour-by-hour putrefaction of the corpse.

But there was one pulpit he could scarcely avoid, and that was the King's. Her father sickened as Lent approached, and starved himself for days before his sermon. He was carried to Whitehall stretched out in a coach, and carried home six hours later in the same position. If his face showed some relief, it was because he had rid himself of the tormenting anxiety of preaching before King Charles. From the notes he was clutching as she helped him down from the coach, Pegge surmised that he had also rid himself of his bloated, over-ripe harangue.

7. THE EFFIGY

On the day after the sermon at court, Pegge was creeping back into the Deanery at dawn when Bess caught her. Pegge made things worse by standing up for herself. *Talking back,* Bess called it. She had some notion that Pegge had stayed out all night with a man. *What man?* Pegge asked herself, refusing to admit to Bess that she had only climbed Paul's tower to gaze out over the City because she could not sleep.

Bess had finally worked herself up to telling the Dean and was digging her calloused fingers into Pegge's ear, yanking her forward into the library. Pegge knew her father would be in no state to listen, for his shroud had arrived that morning in the arms of Rachel Walton. Then Walton himself appeared with a train of bearers behind him—a man with an urn under his arm, another two struggling with coal-braziers, and an artist with a coffin-lid and a box of drawing instruments.

Pegge felt Bess's grip on her ear slacken as they entered the library, for directly ahead of them was the Dean, standing on top of the funeral urn with his eyes closed. Dressed in the new shroud and facing smugly towards the east, he was swaying back and forth while the artist sketched him on the coffin-lid. The air was thick with coal-smoke from the rented braziers, which flamed up mightily on either side in a scene worthy of the Blackfriars theatre.

Walton was perched awkwardly on the stool that Pegge had used as a child. As the artist's eyes flicked between his drawing and the Dean, Walton was reading the tale of the seven brothers from the gospels. When the eldest brother died, he left his wife to the next brother, who also died, and so on, until she became the wife of the seventh brother. Pegge knew this was a trick the Sadducees were playing on Jesus, but Bess was not interested in hearing the conclusion. She tugged Pegge closer and got a footing on the Turkey carpet in front of the swaying Dean.

"Never mind those dead brothers. What's to be done with this daughter of yours? She's seventeen and still going about the City like a boy. Those are breasts she's getting under there."

Walton planted a finger on the verse to hold his place and looked directly at Pegge's bodice. Pegge crossed her arms and stared right past him at the artist, who lifted his eyes from his work in amusement.

"In the end she'll make her peace with God like the rest of us," her father said. "The body is but a handful of sand, so much dust, and but a peck of rubbish, so much bone."

"Dust and rubbish," Bess agreed. "And what's to be done with Bridget and Betty? They can't all three of them go to Constance." Her voice rose a notch. "We'll be put out of the Deanery when you're gone."

Pegge thought she saw his eyelids throb. The artist's nib made a *scritch-scritch* on the wooden plank and Walton pretended to be making out a difficult word, his thick finger almost obliterating the line.

"Speak to my executors."

"You can't give your children away in your Will."

"They will go to Constance and to their Uncle Grymes at Peckham."

Bess sniffed. "A drunkard if ever I saw one."

"A gentleman."

Another sniff. "The worst kind, because they never run short of drink."

"He will marry them off as quick as he can, so as to have as little expense as possible," said the Dean. "The very thing you have been urging me to do yourself." There was a momentary tremor as he veered too far to one side and righted himself. "I have a mind to Thomas Gardiner for Bridget. He is pompous enough to suit her. Betty will be easy to please when she is older."

"And this one? Tell your father where I caught you." Pegge was pushed closer, but her father's eyelids stayed gummed together. "Sneaking back into the kitchen at daybreak, it was." A loud snort this time. "Who knows where she's been."

Her father went as still as a plumb-bob, then began to undulate once more. "What do you say to one of the Bowles twins, Pegge?"

A man she barely knew, when her father had married for love? Pegge kept her arms crossed over her chest, though it was the artist's eyes that were straying now, not Walton's.

"They say that one of them will make a man of science," her father said. "He is reckoned quite clever. You might prove useful to him." One eye opened to gauge her reaction.

Surely he did not expect her to believe this? He had told her that no woman was wanted for her learning, except perhaps to teach her sons.

"As my mother proved useful to you—by dying in childbirth?" Pegge's legs were trembling. "I shall stay as I am."

Now both his eyes were open. "You will go to Constance, who will see that you are married," he ordered.

To put Con in charge of Pegge's fate was unthinkable, cause for the worst sort of sisterly mutiny. They both knew that.

He turned to Bess, who had gone rather pale. "And you will go to Peckham with Bridget and Betty. After they are wed, Sir Thomas Grymes will see that you are taken care of."

"I have always tried, sir," Bess said, mollified. "I'm sure that even Pegge—" She was about to blurt out something else, but the hands gestured dismissively inside the shroud.

"See that you do something about those pock-marks on her face."

Pegge tested the sharpness of her baby tooth against her tongue.

"I will use ceruse, sir. It will make her look more of a gentlewoman."

"That will be well." There was an agonizing pause. "And the nose?"

"She will grow into it."

Pegge bit down and tasted a spurt of blood.

"Thank God for that," her father said, closing his eyes. "Now, let me get on with this last work of mine."

Bess grasped the bellows and pumped furiously at the coals. Pegge doubted that her father would die any time soon, even if he had drawn up his Will and preached his own funeral sermon, even if the flesh was falling off his bones, not while he had a single breath left in him. After all, he had survived the French pox and the spotted fever. Even a violent falling of the uvula.

The artist's eyes were now flicking between Pegge and his drawing, and she went swiftly behind him to see what he was doing. On a page tacked to the coffin-lid, she saw a girl wearing little but a solid, dependable nose. Her hands were crossed over plump young breasts and her nipples protruded shamelessly between her fingers.

Pegge pressed her boot down on his heel, and he reapplied his nib to the Dean, sharpening the point on the beard and twirling up the sanctimonious moustache. The man had stripped the piety from her father's face as cleverly as he had stripped and embellished Pegge's figure. When her father died, this folly would be carved in stone and enshrined in its niche in Paul's for a parade of Londoners to ogle.

Walton was watching the Dean sway back and forth, swaying a little himself as he waited for direction.

"Read," Pegge whispered fiercely.

Walton resumed the tale of the seven brothers. *"And last of all the woman died also. Therefore in the resurrection whose wife shall she be of the seven? For they had all had her."* As Walton paused to let this remarkable fact sink in, the artist caught Pegge's eye and smirked. "*Jesus answered and said unto them, ye do err, not knowing the scriptures, nor the power of God. For in the resurrection, they neither marry, nor are given in marriage, but are as the angels of God in heaven.*"

Walton stopped, feeling some need to comment. "A husband," he ventured hesitantly, "will be glad to be rid of his wife when he enters the gates of paradise."

It was an odd sentiment, Pegge thought, for a man so recently married. Her father seemed to think so also, for the idea that there would be no marriages in heaven struck a sour note. The Dean snapped open his eyes and stepped off his funeral urn more nimbly than a dying man had any right to. He hobbled in his shroud towards Walton, declaring that Christ had only meant that there would be no new marriages in heaven, and that the old ones would go on exactly as before.

But Walton was determined to rid himself of his spouse at the resurrection. He rose from his stool too abruptly, knocking the bible to the floor. Pegge had never seen him so impassioned. Even as her father neared, Walton stood his ground.

"I have never heard the verse interpreted in such a light, even in one of your own sermons," Walton protested. "What of your daughter Constance, who has already had two husbands and is young enough to have a third?"

At this, her father's arm burst out of the shroud and beat the air, causing the fabric to gape immodestly. Released from his grip, the drapery now tumbled in a heap about his ankles, exposing the full mortality of his white, cadaverous frame.

Pegge stared at her father, his wondrous dangling folds, his drapery of skin. Two arms, two legs, and all the matter of a man between. He had once been a shapely fleshed-out man, but now was sadly wasted. The artist tacked up another sheet of paper, making quick studies of his model's torso. Walton tried to gather up the shroud and fasten it around the Dean, but was waved back to his infant-stool.

"Do not look to death to break your marriage bond," her father shouted. "I shall rejoin my wife in the resurrection as surely as I stand here in this mortified flesh. And so shall you. Resurrected love is not fornication. The only fornicator is the soul that turns its back on God!"

Bess was resurrecting the fires with her poker, trying to wake Pegge's father to his senses. Even over the rattling coals, the Dean's voice was loud enough to outshout all the church fathers down the bleak expanse of Christian time. He was still sputtering out his wrath when the nauseating thought hit Pegge that her father must have been the priest who had married Rachel Floud and Izaak Walton.

Bess signalled with the poker to hurry Pegge from the room, but Pegge had a word or two to say to Walton before she left. He was tilting his little stool, trying to reach the bible on the floor without drawing the Dean's eye again. Walton did not seem to know what he had done to provoke the outburst. But then, he still did not understand that he had teased and tricked Pegge into giving him her love, then run off with a woman twice her age and size to get her thriving draper's shop. And Walton had not yet weaned himself of Constance, for it was clear that he now hoped to have her in the resurrection.

Pegge's father was trying to free his ankles and pull the winding-sheet back up. No doubt he had forgotten that she was in the library. She often came in while he was at work, gliding silently about on errands of her own, though she had long outgrown the silly infant-stool. Pegge trailed her hand over the haphazard shelves of books, grazed Sir Thomas More's yellowed skull, straightened her father's portrait on the wall and sounded out its Latin inscription. *Illumina teneb. nostras Domina.* Lighten our darkness, mistress. Who was this Domina? Was it her mother, or one of the women in his erotica, the poems he kept locked inside his cabinet? Only a youth at the time, he had posed in the style of a brooding lover, with pale, delicate fingers, black hat, and a soft dark eye.

Even the blazing sea-coal could not heat her father, who was shuddering from an inner coldness, his teeth chattering in his slack old jaw. The artist was now helping him to pull up the shroud and knot it at his head and heels. Leaning on the man's shoulder, her father climbed stiffly onto the urn, straightened his spine against the wall, and closed his eyes.

"Build up the fires, Bess," he ordered, a grisly smugness curtaining his features.

Pegge could see Walton's thumb in the gospels, riffling the pages to find his place. As Bess lugged the loaded coal-scuttle across the room, Pegge manoeuvred herself into Walton's line of vision. She waited until the artist's head was lowered over his drawing and the coals were clattering into the grate, then made her lips as soft and round as the she-carp that Walton had tricked so mercilessly.

"How dare you marry Rachel Floud?" she mouthed. "You know you were meant for me."

The coals stopped tumbling and Bess turned around to glare at Pegge, a black cloud rising from the empty scuttle. Had Walton even noticed Pegge's lips moving? If he had, he certainly did not show it.

He ran his thick finger down the Sadducees and began again. "*For they had all had her,*" he read, leaning over the verses and savouring, caressing the words.

—

Pegge heard a bleat on the trumpet and found her father slumped in his chair in the library, his legs tucked up beneath him, his shroud collapsed around his shrunken body. Walton and the artist had gone, leaving the braziers behind to cool. The library walls were sweating and everything was filmed with coal-dust, as if a great wind from the wilderness had crushed her father's feast-house. He might as well have been sitting in the coals like Job. Or was it ashes? Pegge had never cared much for the Book of Job.

Propped up beside him was his new mortification—the coffin-lid with his death portrait. Pegge stood back to look at it: the shroud tied into roses at his head and feet, the sharpened beard, the stiff unpleasant grin.

She put her hand on his arm. "You must get dressed now, Father."

"I have never had good temper, nor good pulse, nor good appetite, nor good sleep. I am not alive, but God will not kill me."

He could no longer even summon up a grimace. No man could be more eager to do God's bidding and sixty, as he often said, was a good age for a man. After all, dogs and horses did not live nearly so long.

Pegge suddenly remembered Con's fondness for his mare. "May I have Parrot if you die, Father?"

"Why ask," he said morosely, "when you have already wooed her from me with schemes and sweetmeats?"

"Father, this cannot go on all night. Shall I help you up to bed?"

"Not yet, stay by me a little longer." He grasped her hand. "I am not as I was, for when I kneel to pray, my prayers are troubled by the noise of a fly, the rattling of a coach, the creaking of a stair, a straw in my eye, a chimera in my brain. Worst of all, they are troubled by yesterday's pleasures."

What about me? she wanted to cry out. *I have not yet had pleasures to put behind me.*

Walton's indifference had been scorching, twice greater than the heat from the rented braziers, thrice, even four times. He had leaned over the bible as eagerly as he once leaned over Pegge when she found caterpillars and dung-beetles for live bait. Today, his long, lovely hair was spread more thinly across his collar, but when he bent his elbow to turn the page, Pegge saw a flash of wrist that hinted at the same strong arm above it. She remembered the first time he wore that mossy-green doublet. In her imaginings, it still carried the scent of that day they lay together on the heated rock along the tributary of the Darent.

In this room, only an hour ago, she had crossed her arms and told her father she did not wish to marry because Izaak Walton was listening. In truth, she had no desire to be a virgin. That was a sham. A lot of good chastity had done her—she had got nothing from it but little Betty's knees and elbows digging into her at night. And Pegge no longer even had that comfort, for she was sleeping in Con's bedchamber alone. She was about to take back her words when the door was flung open and Betty herself came tumbling in.

Betty fell on her knees before their father, a position bound to stir up his compassion. "I must be married before Pegge, Father, for I am a woman now and she is not."

Pegge tried to calm her sister and lead her from the room, but Betty pummelled Pegge with her fists, spilling over with rage from some mysterious source. It was then that Pegge saw that her sister's hem was wet with blood. Betty was as good as a clock, bleeding at fourteen like Bridget and Con, though at seventeen Pegge seemed no closer to having her own monthlies.

Each month when Pegge's blood did not come, Bess forced tansy tea down her. She asked Pegge why meat made her queasy, whether she had left off her undergarments while running around the City, whether she had known a man, or whether she had stuffed something up herself to stop the bleeding, as if Pegge was a child who put raisins up her nose.

And now Bess was there, comforting Betty and smoothing down her tousled hair, saying, as she had often said to Pegge, "Enough fuss and nonsense, you'll come along with me."

Then Bess was turning out the flannel-room to find a soft absorbent cloth, showing Betty how to loop the ends and string this bulky padding between her legs, all in the open passage. Bridget arrived to hush Betty's cries, though it was too late to keep the household ignorant of an event of such magnitude. Only their father was oblivious, for he walked past them towards his chamber, dragging his long winding-sheet behind him.

Now the women were wrapping a blanket around Betty and helping her into the kitchen. Pegge slouched in the door frame, watching Bess at the fire stirring coddled milk. Bridget was boasting that their father was after Thomas Gardiner for her and Betty was wondering, between large bites of custard, whether Thomas had any younger brothers. Bridget brought out Con's letter, full of details of the Gardiners, and sat in Pegge's chair to read it to the others. Con was coming to nurse her father herself, Con had a new embroidery stitch to show them, Con had a new gown, Con—

Pegge turned her back and fled.

Why had her blood not come? Con and Bridget never tired of telling of the day and month it had caught them unawares. How had it been unawares? With Bess bustling about, whispering that they would soon be women, even Betty had started looking between her legs when she was only ten.

A half-hour after Con arrived, she would be in the kitchen. An hour scratching Sadie behind the ears and praising Bess's pudding, and Con would get it out of Bess: the state of all her sisters' wombs, and who would next be married. *How odd,* Con would exclaim, the spoon half in, half out of her painted mouth, *that Betty should so speed ahead! Perhaps Doctor Foxe should have a look at Pegge.* Before long the servants would get wind of Pegge's impairment and visitors like Izaak Walton would hear the tale, told and retold inventively by Con—or perhaps by the Dean himself—of Pegge's childish, tardy womb.

Blighted, like the first buds nipped by frost. If the bud did not flower, how could there be defloration? Even the stunted holly in the garden had managed to produce a crop of berries. Pegge wanted to have her fleurs like other women, to curdle milk and sour wine when her monthlies were upon her. It would be nice to have breasts like her elder sisters but, most of all, she wanted to make a man bead up with sweat, to stop his mouth with fumbling words, to dance her fingers across the floodgates of his arm, then turn his veins into a free and easy conduit of blood.

Before Mr Harvey had left for Barking with his new wife, he had knelt in front of Pegge so she could feel how sleeping on a slanted board had reinvigorated his hair. Running her fingers across his crown, she detected a clump of baby-hairs shooting up at angles. His scalp rose into her finger-pads, delighting in her stroking. It seemed a man might be fed by such fondlings, might grow in stature by the combings, brushings, and groomings of a warm, good-tempered woman.

But what man would let Pegge groom him? Right now she was as solitary as a monk, and her own hair was still no longer than a dog's. The men she wanted could never be hers. All the lovely Waltons were wasted upon the daughters of the night, the Cons and Bridgets, the Bettys and the Rachel Flouds. Even gentle Samuel Harvey was tied by a stout cord to the bed he shared with Constance Donne.

—

Pegge put on her father's heavy cloak, smelling him as she dried her eyes on its sleeve. No one would notice she was gone. She drifted along the back streets towards the west, past the rag-and-bone man who was already out collecting, past the old water-carrier hefting his vessel up from the Thames, past the neat, tidy shop of R. Floud, Linen-draper, until, her nose pinched with cold, she reached the churchyard of St Clement's. Inside the crumbling church, her feet counted the flagstones tilted up by frost until they recognized her mother's grave. Lungs aching, she threw herself face down upon the tomb, feeling the cold rise, layer by layer, through her thick woollen skirts. Even the kind-hearted Mr Harvey could not pity her here, nor see her tears spilling through the porous cracks and running deep into the earth below. Looking straight into eyes of stone, she begged Ann's melancholy damp to creep into her childish, reluctant womb.

Death's Duel

—

1631

8. LIGHTEN MY DARKNESS

Someone is treading on my grave. Now the footsteps stop and a body throws itself onto the cold pavingstones above me. Which of my children has come to mourn a mother so long dead?

Tears drip through the cracks between the stones. Pegge is the only one who weeps like this. Perhaps she has heard me speak aloud, for anyone who presses an ear to my tomb may hear me talking and, even as an infant, Pegge had unnaturally keen hearing.

People have been coming and going in the church above me, gossiping about John Donne's sickness and pointing out his wife's plain epitaph. They are saying that you preached your own funeral sermon before King Charles at Whitehall. When you were half-way through, you sank down on your knees. However, your flesh was not as weak as the onlookers supposed. Your soul had simply tired of all your hair-splitting, your gloriously pungent diction. Catching a whiff of my spirit lurking in the vault, yours shot out of your body. Getting its first taste of freedom, it spun about in the air, uncertain of the rules of navigation. I was clinging to a beam, unable to get closer for all the tobacco smoke, when your body called back your soul, and my spirit lost its chance to embrace yours.

Two of the King's men helped you rise, urging you to stop. However, you saw this as a God-sent illustration of your text, the duel between the body and the spirit. Gripping the pulpit, you coughed out every word, your face shining convincingly with perspiration. That was when I realized you were not dissembling, as you have done so many times before. When a man is dying, his soul begins to make forays outside his body, scouting the way ahead, and you have a most ambitious soul. It was not heading towards my grave here in St Clement's, but upwards into the ether.

Do you truly think I will wait out the millennium in a miserable coffin, while you enjoy the Beatific Vision? Your ambition has become a rock under my back, growing sharper year by year. You vowed to join me in the grave upon your death. So you pledged when I first joined my flesh with yours, pelvis to pelvis-bone. And so I once believed—for surely there were faster ways to bed a woman than with poetry. Our love was such a miracle, you said, that we would be made saints for our devotion if dug up in a Catholic time.

In this Protestant land, that is little comfort. I have had seven years to contemplate the meaning of your words— and seven years again—though it is not easy to keep track of time while underground. My thoughts ring clear now, unclouded by pain. I know I did not die a natural death. I was slain by love, at far too young an age.

I was thirty-three, and our fortunes were just beginning to improve. I wanted to feel taffeta between my fingers again, a maid buffing my nails to a fine polish, rose-water on my skin and pins digging into my scalp. I wanted to glide across a wooden floor in Queen Anne heels and tease the appetites of men. I wished to live the life my sisters did—after all, I was equally the daughter of Sir George More.

But instead, you begat another child on me, my twelfth, and I died from it.

After I died, you kept a vigil beside me. When the children came to fetch you, their faces streaked with tears, you fought them off. Kneeling on the hard stones, you cried, *My joys and my tears are buried here with my beloved wife.* You swore you would never remarry. How light the burden of a stepmother would have been compared to that dread oath. When our children were gone, you whispered to me, *As the grave is your house, we two shall make our beds together in the dark.*

Soon you discovered that the church floor did not block the smell of human decay beneath. That autumn, my stench drove the parishioners to unbend their knees and move to more fragrant aisles. I wintered here in St Clement's, learning that wet rot and dry rot are much the same, though wet smells worse.

Your visits grew less frequent over time. Sometimes when you spoke aloud, your ear scraped the ground, seeking an echo from these stones. In your holy writings, you painted me as your mortal enemy, but in your dreams you craved my hips and breasts, as they were when your hands first lingered on them. Once you pried up the pavingstone above me, making a dreadful clanging with an iron bar. You were about to climb into my tomb and pull the stone down over your head, dying with me as a bondsman with his queen, but that dog came whipping in and barked to warn you of the danger.

In the grave, there is time to think. Snatches of conversation in the church above tell me of the world of men. Months and years mean nothing here, but it is false to think there is no busyness in graves. There is cold to ward off, memories to refresh, children's names to recite for fear of forgetting even one—and there is passion, so fierce and sharp that it can never be locked up in cabinets of sense. When limbs uncoil in memory, the lust echoes on cold bone. My hair now reaches a tangled glory around my knees, and my soul has grown exceedingly amorous from all this waiting. Even a spirit craves a bit of flesh to burrow into now and then.

You promised to lie beside me in this tomb, hip bone to hip bone and mouth to mouth, for love dwells in the lips of the beloved. And other parts should kiss in graves as well, so that the blood commingles in a rush. You told me that this was how the joint soul was conceived, in little deaths of ecstasy. To *die*, you taught me, was a pun. When such memories possess me, my cries rise sharply into the church, like a courtesan's gasp at the moment of her lover's plunge, and the old man in the pew above me recalls with sudden clarity his first attempt upon his young wife's body.

Now you have taken to your deathbed. When I sneaked past the vigilant dog, which has appointed itself a sentinel against me, I heard you muttering that death is a divorce and that *two graves must hide thine and my corpse.* This effigy of yours is not intended for St Clement's—I do not need men gossiping overhead to tell me that. Only you could have thought up something so flamboyant as a grinning fool standing upright in a shroud. Such a monument would be out of temper with the modest tributes above me. No, this colossus is intended for the cathedral of St Paul's. You have decided that my soul must await your pleasure—that you will come to collect me when you choose, or not at all—that death will obey you as lust did—that I, who beggared myself for love, will be content to rot in a solitary tomb.

To spend a thousand years apart is too long even for ordinary lovers, and we are far from ordinary. I do not plan to spend the millennium alone. No, I shall not rest so peacefully, my love. I shall use such mirrors and such spies that you shall never be rid of me.

You will find my anger has not eased with time, but has bloated and heated like manured straw that feeds and mulches roots. When I burst out, you will see a vision less than beatific. I will flower brilliantly into the light, my mouth a violent blue, my petals feathered and flamed with ire, and our embrace will be far from the quiet reunion you have dreamt of. Out of my putrefaction, I shall produce a carrion-flower so foetid that it will out-carrion decaying offal. The most delicate of flowers, the lady's slipper, stinks of rotting fruit to draw flies to it. And so I shall set a sugar trap for you. Drawn by my perfume, you will slide into my labyrinth like a bee into an orchid. Even the most ambitious bee can be trapped at the right time of day by the right scent and colour of flower.

—

I first met you in York House, where I had been sent by my father to be schooled for marriage by his sister, who had just taken a second husband, Sir Thomas Egerton, the Lord Keeper.

I arrived in time to see my cousin Francis wed. Too young to consummate the match, he was sent back to Oxford while my aunt taught his wife, Mary, the useful arts. I was to keep Mary company, but my visit only made her regret the freedom she had lost by marrying.

Instead of dancing the courante at court, as I had hoped, I found myself breathing the stale air of the withdrawing-room with my aunt and her daughter-in-law. It was worse than the matronly pavane, a step I could do just as well in the country. According to Aunt Beth, I had much to learn before she could present me to the Queen. Most of it my aunt was teaching me herself, but Sir Thomas's secretary, John Donne, had agreed to teach me Spanish.

I was embroidering a jasmine bush on a green background, a sad imitation of the garden I had left behind at Loseley park, when I observed Mr Donne striding along the passage in a fashionable hat and doublet. I punched my needle through the backing-cloth and stabbed my finger. After a few more painful stitches, I saw my aunt's eyelids close. Mary stopped tugging on her silk and leaned towards me.

"Francis says he is a great visitor of ladies, a great frequenter of plays, and a great writer of conceited verses, but you know that already, Ann, for I heard you asking Francis about him."

As my cousin was leaving for Oxford, he had given me some verses by a Jack Donne, telling me that the bishops were burning obscene poems and begging me to hide them for him. They were in my chest, under a stack of folded garments, and I had spent several hours trying to make out what the poet meant by them.

"Francis is a little boy with his erotica," Mary whispered. "I do not think my husband knows a thing about love."

At this, Aunt Beth propped herself upright and retrieved her stitching-hoop. "Only people of the meaner sort marry for love, Mary. You must not sour Ann on matrimony. I have found it an agreeable state myself."

At this Mary made a low, unpleasant noise. When my aunt frowned, Mary said, "I have just seen the most foolish hat go down the passage. I am not sure such brash feathers are lawful for commoners. And velvet certainly is not." Mary winked at me, for we both knew my aunt would be drawn in.

"A man's station in life may be read from his clothing," Aunt Beth said. "Beware of a comely man. His breeding, not his looks, should recommend him." A twist, a pull, and a new thread was knotted in her needle. Then she looked up. "What sort of feather, Mary?"

"Ostrich, I believe, most likely Andalusian."

If Mary kept this up, my aunt would soon guess who had walked past. While Aunt Beth checked her pattern,

Mary rubbed the nap of her sleeve suggestively, then flapped her hands, our signal for a jumped-up tradesman. I would not be able to get a closer look at John Donne's doublet until our needlework was finished. If it was really velvet, the man had truly lost his wits.

"Do you think it wise for Ann to learn Spanish, Lady Egerton? I am not sure it will endear her to the Queen, for it is the language of the Jesuits. Was it Mr Donne's idea to teach her, or your own?"

I bent my head so close to my work that I could see just how poor my last hour's stitches were. And why were there so few of them? I decided I had better count them to keep my eyes away from Mary's.

I began practising my aunt's teaching on Mr Donne in our first lesson. His pose had something of the lawyer in it, and something of the brooding lover. His doublet was not exactly velvet, I learned when I got near enough to inspect it, but had a dangerous resemblance to that fabric. His sword was too long, but its insolent hang told me its purpose was not wholly ornamental.

He began by reciting the numbers in Spanish, holding up his fingers as if I were a child. Soon we moved on to the days of the week, and outdoors into the garden alongside the Thames, where he could make a better show when he strode up and down.

Before long, I suspected that my tutor was leaving me secret gifts. I walked past the first one several times without noticing it. And then, studying my reflection in the passage windows, with some idea of contriving my hair differently now that I was in London, I saw that something had been scrawled in the grime. I twisted my head and brought it against the pane: *temptatious*.

It was a made-up word, a play on *temptation*, no doubt an unflattering reference to Eve. I knew where it had come from, for who else cared about words in that house? And it would have taken a Jack Donne to get into the east wing, where the women of the household lay. He seemed to go everywhere, even to court with Sir Thomas, although when I asked him to describe the dancing he shrugged as if it meant nothing to him. Instead, he used it as an excuse to teach me body parts, pointing to his ankles and mouthing the Spanish word in a mocking fashion.

Lips, legs, and arms, he taught me. And then the word for blushing.

Fair good his plumage would do him at court. I knew enough about gamebirds from my father's covey to know that it was the females, in spite of their dull livery, who did the choosing, not the males in their stiff ruffs, and certainly not lawyers of doubtful breeding. Mr Donne was indeed an upstart crow, beautifying himself with our feathers.

One day when we were walking outdoors, Mr Donne's usual interrogation in Spanish strayed off course into the familiar—how old I was, and how long my father proposed to let me stay at York House.

"These are not a tutor's questions," I said, "but I am not surprised, since your collar is not a tutor's either."

"That is slight evidence on which to condemn a man."

Why were there sumptuary laws when every man of the meaner sort was allowed to flout them? "Gilt spurs are not allowed under the rank of knight," I said. "Those breeches have more than two yards of wool, and that sword is six inches longer than the Queen permits."

"It is true I am no idle gentleman," he said, dismissing the whole of idle Westminster with a jerk of his thumb upriver. "But since my sword did the Queen good service under Essex in Cadiz, I doubt she will cavil at its length. You would be better listing off your verbs, Mistress More."

It was clear he earned his living by his cleverness, whereas I had not yet mastered the regular verbs of Spanish. I had no doubt he was the author of the poems in Francis's collection, for I had heard his wit in every manicured line. But why lewd poems had to be so full of difficulties, I did not know—I was still trying to work them out.

He made a low, deliberate bow. "I thought I had the right to more than common intimacy," he said, "for I have also descended from Sir Thomas More. Would you care for one of the martyr's blackened teeth? My mother gave me the skull to encourage me in the old religion."

"I am not of the Catholic Mores," I said quickly.

He nodded, catching my meaning. "Though I came from a people hungry for martyrdom, I have not such a sickly inclination myself. It is unwise in this Queen's reign. You are a girl of some sense. Why have you left the safety of the country?"

Some sense, indeed—did he suppose me ignorant of the threat the Catholics presented to the realm? "To find a worthy husband," I replied. There was a small buzzing noise, from an insect in the dog-rose or from the man beside me. Perhaps it was a Spanish expletive. "It is time for me to return to the house."

"I'm sure you cannot tell," he protested, "for I have observed you do not wear a clock."

"I need only look about me. The pimpernel has closed, but the dandelion is still open, so it is between two and three o'clock. Mr Donne, I believe you have walked here all summer, but have never seen the garden at your feet. It tells perfect time."

"I have been looking at you, Mistress More."

He had been coming closer by bits as he spoke and was now near enough for me to smell a kind of perfume about him. "You would do better to reflect upon the garden," I said. "Now I shall teach *you* something. Each of these flowers opens and closes at the same time each day. This pink opened at nine and closed at one o'clock."

There was a glimmer of interest in his eyes. "Are all flowers so unbearably dull in their habits? Do none stay open at night to keep lovers company?"

His scent, mingling with the river behind us, was not unwelcome to one who had been confined inside York House with women. "The evening primrose," I offered tentatively, "and the Nottingham catchfly."

"That is not a name to inspire love. But I could grow to like the tardy primrose. I admit I have been inattentive to gardens, but if you care for them, I shall as well. Why, there are more shades of green than of any other colour. You see, I am interested already. Here is a whole alphabet of flowers that might with mute secrecy deliver messages between a man and a woman."

"You must not say such things."

"Why mustn't I?" he said loudly.

This was too public, and certainly far from mute. As I looked away, feigning a sudden curiosity in roses, a bee landed and embraced a bloom so like a lover that the bloom began to quiver, spraying the bee in yellow dust. I snatched my hand away and felt the graze of flesh. It seemed we had both left off our gloves this day, and perhaps for the same reason.

At the touch of our fingers, something stirred, so fragrant and full of colour that to live henceforth without it would be an impoverishment I could not endure. His mouth was bearing down towards me with excruciating slowness. And for once it was not speaking. With a little movement, as darting as a frog's tongue collecting a fly, his tongue would collect mine and I would taste him, sweet and salty, inside my mouth.

But all at once he withdrew, looking over his shoulder as if hearing the busy world behind him. I had removed myself from it like an expiration from a lung, but now my breath came surging painfully back.

His eyes alive with warning, he gestured at the reflecting panes of York House. Anybody could be watching. Even my maid Bess could not be trusted, for it would be like her to report to my father in exchange for a goose pie or a roast pigeon. We resumed walking a distance apart, neither of us speaking.

"The four o'clocks are opening," I said at last.

This made him angry. "You cannot go on telling time by buttercups and water lilies," he exclaimed. "The world of men goes by the clock, not in these infant ways. You have spoken no Spanish this half-hour, as you well know, unless you count this Spanish torpor. You must realize that as soon as your aunt presents you at court these lessons will be over. Perhaps sooner, if the Spanish do not improve their manners to the English."

Why had I not thought of that? I had spent more time thinking of my hair than of the continent of Europe.

"These hurried snatches of time cannot satisfy," he said. "Time passes too swiftly in this garden. Even kings and queens are but flowers, some gathered at six, some at seven, some at eight. *Carpe florem.* Surely you have learnt a little Horace? Look—" His palm cupped an extravagant white bloom. "Even the petals on this rose are damned. By the end of summer, each one will be withered and brown. Can you not see?—the very hairs on your sweet head are numbered."

Suddenly I did see. The spectre of my father rose up before me. Soon I would be betrothed and have no need of tutors.

"Oh, do not say such things. Teach me, Mr Donne, teach me everything you know! I cannot be married until I have learnt"—I cast about for something he and my aunt might equally approve—"philosophy."

My fingers slid unthinkingly over the bare skin at his wrist. He snapped his hand over mine and twisted me around. It seemed there was a power in my fingertips that had nothing to do with stitching jasmine bushes on inept tapestries.

"You are so ethereal, Ann More—it is as if you belong out of time, or in some long-past perfection of our history. I wish that all my body could be turned into tongues so that I could declare your praises to posterity."

My fingers were trembling inside his, in fact my whole arm was begging to be included in the embrace, but he had raised our two hands towards the sun to stare at them, explaining something about hours and shadows and the sun's height at noon. Then he broke from me and strode rapidly ahead, leaving me to walk through gravel to catch up.

I found him stopped in the middle of the path, rooting around in his doublet under a deep compulsion. Producing an inkhorn and pen at last, he demanded, "Where is that list of Spanish verbs I gave you?"

I admitted that I had left it in my chamber.

"Then excuse me, sweet mistress, for I am in most desperate need of paper."

As he ran towards York House, I noted the common knit of his hose and the Thames mud clinging to the gilt of his departing spurs. Wit, I reminded myself, trying to slow my breathing, was no substitute for lands and titles.

—

This time it was a very faint word, so faint I could barely see it scrawled on the pane: *conjugation*.

It had nothing to do with learning foreign tongues, for our lessons had long since turned to metaphysics. He taught me what Plato had to say, and then he corrected Plato, for he had no modesty. He talked so much that my head ached, but when he was near me his meaning was not hard to grasp. Ecstasy, Plato said, was to be found in the conjugation of souls, but John Donne said that ecstasy found pretty entertainment in the body before it rose up to the mind. This was where he differed from Plato, who kept the flesh well out of it.

I was discovering that there were many ways of alluding to this entertainment. My aunt used the word *consummation* when speaking of what was yet to come between Francis and Mary, whose skin had broken out in pustules since his departure. Bess said there was nothing wrong with Mary that a bit of *husbandry* wouldn't clear up. The way Bess said the word left me in no doubt as to what she meant. In her own way she was a connoisseur of words, vulgarities flowing out of her like mother's milk. She had been using such turns of speech since I was very young, but they had recently acquired new meaning. Even perfectly innocent words like *placket* and *sleeve* began to present troublesome images. They would pop into my mind at unexpected moments, ripe with significance. It was as if another hemisphere had sprung up which mirrored mine. I no longer trusted my eyes, for even household objects were assuming odd shapes that suggested sinister, intimate uses.

John Donne's *conjugation* rang on my ear like a beaten chalice, brazen and new. It was a word that veered from sharp to sweet, like the petals falling from an overripe poppy. That morning, while walking with him, I had stopped to stare at a flower exposing herself to raiding insects—the whole garden was bristling with indelicate activity—and then, ashamed to be seen looking at such a thing, for his lips were curving in humour, I bolted, leaving him to enjoy the garden's lewd performance on his own.

I erased his word from the pane with my fist. The next day I noticed that the maids were applying a white paste to the passage windows and rubbing it off with paper. Was this an ordinary household chore or had someone noticed the writing? I heard Bess grumbling at the work, and quickened my steps so I would not get an earful.

Now that our slate was gone, John Donne had taken to whispering the words, drawing out the syllables as he bestowed them, gifts warm from his tongue. *Labial.* A labial wooing. *Labyrinth.* The inner shell, a ravishment of the ear. Why did I not stop up my ears with wax against him? Oh, I was *labile*—docile and willing.

In corridors, in solitary rooms, whenever we met fleetingly in that great house, words spilled from his lips into the bedchamber of my ear. I fell in love with John Donne's words, darting like swallows in and out of the frippery of this world, no more belonging to it than birds belonged inside a house. Yet they did belong. I was mistaken.

—

Now John Donne had no time to seek me out, though he was quite able, I discovered to my annoyance, to go to the edge of England to carry the funeral sword for Sir Thomas's son, who had been killed under the Earl of Essex in Ireland. I was sorry for Sir Thomas, but I thought he might more easily have spared someone other than his secretary. Then Essex returned in disgrace and was held captive by Sir Thomas right under our noses in York House while the Queen decided what was to be done with him.

Everyone was in a grey mood. I would not be dancing that season, though new dances were rumoured at court, for my Aunt Beth kept to her room. All that winter, the closest I got to John Donne was in my aunt's chamber at Christmas, when he consoled her by calling Essex a fallen angel and reproached the Queen for her gaiety at Greenwich. How could she be gay, my aunt cried out to Mr Donne, when Her Favourite was so fallen from grace? I could hear the capital letters when my aunt talked of Essex. Sweet England's Pride, she called him, gripping her visitor's hand as he knelt beside her bed to comfort her.

John Donne did not seem to care that I might need some gaiety myself, or that I also craved the comfort of his long slender fingers. He hardly touched me as he took me aside, just counselled that I should guard my speech about Essex, as he guarded his, for the axe could turn either way.

As if I would waste my words on the Earl of Essex when I had John Donne nearby. How was it that men were so narrow in their affairs, so poor-sighted in their view of the world? It was household rumour that Mr Donne had taken lodgings near the Savoy and now kept a simpering French servant. Matters of state seemed to have driven me out of his head. Unless it was true, as Bess reported, that he had taken the lodgings to meet a married woman and had found pretty entertainment there.

I was incapable of chiding Bess for gossiping. Worse still, I sent her to the scullery, to the buttery, even to the stable, as often as I could, to throw her in the path of the other servants, who were as fond of gossip as she was. It had become a disease, the need to hear every syllable I could about John Donne.

And so it was that Mary found us at the hour of midnight on St Agnes's eve—the candle almost burnt out and my buttons still done up, my hair uncombed about my shoulders, the pins only taken out, nothing more done, Bess's arms at work in the air describing John Donne's latest costume—the stiffness of the ruff about his barbered chin, the scarlet hose tight across his calves, the rich lace, the excessive ambition in every stitch and dart—and my face eager with delight as I absorbed the telling, as I had absorbed her reckless tales since childhood, since the loss of a mother I had never known. It was then that Mary burst in on us, sobbing that my aunt had suffered a blockage of the heart and even now was slipping away. I was to come at once if I wanted to take my leave of her in this world.

I went, with Bess supporting me, with Mary lighting our way, down the long, dark corridor to death, realizing too late how dear my aunt had been to me. And now I lie in death's black underworld myself, weighted down by hundredweights of stone, telling endlessly such tales of life to any who might wish to stand above and listen.

Pegge was sitting on her father's great-bed, helping him sort the manuscripts from his cabinet. She picked up some papers and flattened out the creases.

"Verse letters," she said. "Should they go with letters or with poems? They are clearly dated." He did not reply, so she put them with letters, where their chances of surviving would be best.

Stacks of paper covered the horsehair blanket. Sitting cross-legged, he was inking dates and titles onto sheets, then handing them to Pegge to put in bundles. Her eyes kept shifting to his toenails, curled and yellow, unpared for months. Surely Con had not done *that* for him? He had already written to Con to tell her he was dying, but perhaps he was only counterfeiting to force her to visit, for he looked less ill than when the artist had sketched him on the previous day. Death appeared to be a tonic, putting him into a strange jubilant ecstasy.

Some of the papers were to be burnt, some published, and some fell into limbo. Every so often, debating its fate, he would read some turgid prose, enunciating so pointedly that his lips got stuck at the corners before they sprang back into shape.

"Letter to the bishop," he would announce, or "Sermon preached on Candlemas Day," writing the particulars at the top.

"This would be easier to do in your library, Father."

"When God comes to claim me, he will look for me between these old bedposts. Push that stack closer, Pegge."

"How long have you had this bed?"

"It came from Loseley thirty years ago."

Then it *was* his marriage-bed, as she had suspected. Twelve children had been conceived where Pegge and her father sat together now. His mind must have wandered in the same direction, for he was taking too long over the expenses for the chapter-house, squaring up the corners far too neatly.

"Was it all my mother received for her dowry?"

His silence did not surprise her. She knew he could not admit he had taken Ann without her father's blessing, for fear that his own daughters might do the same, though Pegge could not imagine her sisters marrying in the heat of love.

If he was really dying, his death would orphan all her own hopes. There was still time to admit that she would rather marry than be incarcerated in a foreign nunnery, or in Con's house at Barking, but she could not force this dry confession from her mouth, not with his passion for Ann hanging in the air between them. Even Bridget and Betty would soon be consorting with perfect strangers in marriage-beds, enjoying gamesome rites that Pegge could only guess at.

"When you met my mother, she was only Betty's age," she said, thumbing through some quarter-sheets. "How did you know you were in love?" It came out too bluntly, like a child's question. She knew she must sound as foolish as her sisters.

"How do you know there is a God?" he thundered back. "Whom do I tremble at, and sweat under at midnight, and whom do I curse by next morning if there be no God?" He tapped a large pile. "These are the sermons not yet transcribed. We will need Mr Walton's help with them. Send him a note to come at once."

"I can manage on my own, Father." They would not be able to sit so companionably on his bed if Walton were there, interfering.

"You will be needed to make fair copies of these holy poems." He pushed some papers towards her. "Be sure to ask about any questionable lines before I die."

"I will copy out the secular poems as well." So far she had found only five, but she could see several likely-looking sheets closer to her father. "How shall I order them? I think by date, so they will make a kind of story. You will need to tell me when they were written."

"Give them to me." He clamped the five under his left knee, a stack Pegge knew was destined for the fire.

Pegge was struggling to get a heavy table out of the library, when the table lightened and Izaak Walton's hands were on it. He had a habit of appearing and disappearing as if river-walking in his quiet shoes.

"It will go better this way," he said, tipping the table onto its side and guiding the front legs through the jamb.

Pegge followed with the back legs. They carried the table up the stairs and placed it where her father wanted it, against his bed. Walton had been there since noon, sitting in Pegge's chair beside her father to help him with his sermons. Now Walton moved his writing materials onto the table and dipped his pen into her father's ink.

"Here is the next passage," her father said. "We have a winding-sheet in our mother's womb which grows with us from conception, and we come into the world to seek a grave."

"A shroud on an infant?" Walton looked back and forth, his pen in the air.

Her father ripped open the front of his bedshirt in irritation, exposing a chest as puckered on the surface as Pegge's sleeves.

"He means a man's skin," Pegge hissed at Walton. "Let me do the writing, Father. You should not have to explain everything."

"Mr Walton need not understand it," her father shouted, "only write it down."

"I will ask no more questions, sir," Walton said hastily. "It will go faster now, to be sure."

It was dusk when Walton finally cleared his throat, resting his quill in the groove of his book. "Nicholas Stone has asked for your epitaph, Dr Donne."

Her father rummaged through some sheets and held one out. "Remind Mr Stone I must have the Italian marble, even if he has to go to Carrara to choose the block himself.

Also, tell the canons that any cathedral business must be brought to me by Saturday next, for after that day I will not mix my thoughts with any that concern the world."

Night was falling, and they had used up enough ink and paper for most men's lifetimes. The bedposts at north, south, east, and west had become the four corners of her father's world. He had not gone past these posts all day, and Bess's mutton pie remained untouched. Perhaps men could elevate literary things above solid food. Pegge had gulped her own pie quickly, though her stomach still felt raw inside. Was this the green-sickness that Bess talked about—a gnawing appetite that could not be satisfied by food?

"It is time for my father to rest," Pegge said, stopping up the ink-pot and placing it on the high shelf.

Walton's pen scratched to the end of the line, then gave up. He looked regretfully towards the shelf, then gathered his writing materials. "I will come back in the morning, Dr Donne."

"Not before noon," Pegge corrected. The room was hot and smelt disturbingly of man. She knew it was not Walton, for he smelt as fresh as he had always done. "A man need not stink until he dies, Father. If you intend to live in your bed, you will need grooming."

There was a long silence, long enough, she thought, for Con to come down from Barking to do the job herself.

After Walton eased himself out the door, Pegge found the tortoise comb that King James had given to her father. She pulled it gently through his beard and, after a time, his head relaxed upon the pillow and his lips retracted to help her shape his moustache. That was enough for now. In the morning, she would shave him.

"I have moved your close-stool beside the fire. If you are ready, Father, I will help you stand."

He looked at the apparatus suspiciously, trying, Pegge supposed, to contrive some way to keep the body's wastes inside. Yet there it was, the red velvet seat, offering relief in the warm firelight. He lurched into an upright position and stared at the thing. At last, his yellowed toenails descended, then recoiled from the cold planking. Pegge found some stockings to put on him and his legs descended cautiously once more.

While he shuffled to the close-stool, she collected the condemned poems from the bed and stacked them on the table, satisfying herself that she had seen them all before. Once on the seat, he swivelled to face the blaze, calling out, "Bring me the bundle to be destroyed!"

Soon his greatest poems were nothing but charred fragments on the grate. There was something absurd about this act of renunciation, since the poems had made the rounds of all his friends. The most complete collection was right above his head, in the chamber that her brothers shared when they were home. She was now more familiar with the verses than they were, having copied out all his love-poems for herself.

After her father had warmed himself sufficiently beside the embers, he hobbled back and she helped him climb into the bed. As she settled him, the sleeve of his nightshirt slid up, exposing his forearm. She gripped his arm and stared at it, wondering which valves to press to stop the blood from flowing back into his heart. The dark veins stood out in milky flesh that might have belonged to a saint in Catholic times. Yet this arm had performed the most erotic acts, then written about them in poems passed heatedly from friend to friend.

When a man lay with a woman, did his hands support the weight of his body? Did his knees act as a fulcrum—for surely a man did not balance upon his toes? That was the woman's part, she knew, for she had heard that a woman danced on her feet when lying underneath a man.

Even as her father was sacrificing them on the fire, the poems were being copied and recopied, read aloud to lovers and silently in beds, for no one who had read such verses would willingly destroy them. Even now, women all over England were rising in passion, having read, under cover of night, erotic poems written by her father. Yet he had betrayed his promises to Ann, and betrayed them anew that very day, burning the records of the love they had shared on this marriage-bed. Had Ann danced on her feet where he now lay? Had *this arm* curled round to give her pleasure?

What if, that day along the secret river, when Izaak Walton had crawled out on the narrow rock beside her, Pegge had twisted his legs in hers and refused to release him, twisted and tormented, danced on her feet, until she took his love from him by force, as the carp had drawn the melters to her and forced them to deliver all their melt?

Her father had fallen asleep with his arm held straight up in the air, being subjected to a prolonged and close inspection.

"Tomorrow," she said sternly to The Arm, "I will give you a good scrubbing."

10. SIX THOUSAND YEARS

On the second night after I took to my deathbed, I woke to find Pegge standing on her head, her skirts tied above her knees and her eyes bulging from the pressure. I thought my soul had risen out of my body and Pegge was left clinging to the earth below. Then she began to sway, fell backwards, and saved herself only by curling and rolling across the floor, stopping at the brink of the fire and staring at it in that peculiar way she has.

It seems that Mr Harvey told Pegge that he grew hair on his scalp by lying on a slanted board at night, a practice that Constance has no doubt put a stop to since their marriage. Pegge's hair is as short and matted as sheep's wool. Though I told her it looks shorter when flattened on the top, she will not be dissuaded from standing on her head to make it grow.

Pegge's headstands have improved, but I am no closer to rising above earth. Now she tends to me in the daytime and, at night, Bess plants herself beside me like a side of beef to prevent me squeezing any joy out of dying. She insists on a sign of life every so often—a belch, a fart, any sound will do—to show that my insides are still functioning. If I do not produce it voluntarily, she will ream it out of me, knowing I fear her enemas worse than I fear hell.

In this wooden bed, consorting with these few thoughts, I lie in prison and am coffined until I die. It is not the first time I have been imprisoned for your love, Ann. Thirty years ago, I tumbled into a cell in the Fleet. When my eyes adjusted to the meagre light, I gave the man a sixpence to bring me ink and paper. I hoped I might get poems from it, but none came. Now I cannot stop the thoughts of you, though they are old and tainted by memory. Your voice is a knell from an unquiet tomb, your beckoning finger an accusation. You must wait for my ashes, love—as ashes I will join you. But first I must die. Sometimes I wonder if you have conspired to keep me here, pinned to this bed of vain desire.

Now and then, my soul takes to the air to try the way, but before it can get an arm's length overhead, some hiccup or rumble calls it back into this prison. This is the subtle knot that makes us man, this yoking of the spirit and the flesh. When a man dies, where does his soul go? Who sees it come in or sees it go out? Nobody. Yet everybody is sure he had one, and now has none.

Pegge is shaving around my beard. As the straight-blade hovers over my throat, I hold my breath, hoping she will do me a mercy and send me straight to heaven. Then she tilts my head expertly, and scrapes at a stubborn patch beneath my chin. She only nicked me once, on the first day. She collected the drop of blood on her fingertip and sucked it off as I watched through narrowed eyes.

Now she is kneading some life back into my hands, which have been cold for days. Licking a flannel, she scrubs at the ink on my fingers, but it refuses to come off. What cleansing ritual will she devise next? She is much more inventive than Con, who dealt with me swiftly and went on her way.

When I was a boy, I angered my mother by becoming stiff while the nurse was bathing me. That was when my mother gave me the skull of her great uncle, Sir Thomas More, and sat on my bed reading from the *Book of Martyrs*. She told me that angels watched from the hammerbeams when More was sentenced. After his head rotted for a fortnight on London bridge, it fell from its pike into the lap of Margaret, his favourite daughter. That is the sort of tale that Catholic mothers like to tell their sons, and fathers their daughters. When she was little, Pegge delighted in it, for I had named her after Margaret More.

When Pegge was older, I told her how William Roper wanted to marry one of More's daughters for her education and bloodline, and came to the scholar to propose the match. Agreeing readily, the great man took Roper to his chamber where his daughters were sleeping on a trucklebed and whipped off the sheet, exposing the girls. They woke, saw the stranger, and rolled over to hide their naked bellies. *I have seen both sides now,* quipped Roper, then slapped Margaret on her bottom, saying, *Thou art mine.* Such wit was all that passed for wooing between them. If Pegge agrees to have one of the Bowles twins, she will no doubt do the slapping.

I must stifle my laughter, for it is unbecoming in a dying man. George was the only one who understood my jokes. He would grin slyly, and tell one of his own. Perhaps, God, you stay me in this place until I get my fill of punning. Death, here is thy sting: I am condemned to quibbling with a humourless God. A ten-fingered torturing, a masturbation of the skull—shall I never stop wallowing in my cleverness? Sooner a horse might climb a tower than John Donne's wit be stopped by death.

Pegge finishes cleaning my fingernails and stares at my mouth. I suppose I have been talking aloud again. Sometimes when my lips move, no sense at all comes out. Perhaps I should try to move my other end. Bess blames all my sins on that orifice. If only I could let fly a constipated fart to please her. If I cannot move my bowels by tonight, Bess will evacuate them for me with her roving tube and bladder.

The bed has begun to creak the way it used to do when we were in it, Ann. It yaws, a great ship straining at anchor. Pegge is trying to move it into the morning sun to warm me—dragging it by herself rather than calling Mr Walton from the library—and that small gesture cramps my heart. This is what comes of breeding a headstrong daughter. She squats on the floor, panting, her skin glowing with a mad feverish light. Then she puts her shoulder against the bedpost and shifts it the last few feet.

But no one can be dragged back into life.

Just before you died, Ann, you stroked my hair as if I were a child. All at once, there was a crack and your head fell sharply against your heart. Why did God give you a stillborn child you could not bear? Was it a test of your faith, or of mine?

I have done my best, Ann, with your scattered brood of motherless children. You left me with two sons to educate and five daughters to marry. I have used such stratagems and such devices as the most desperate of fathers. How else will my girls be taken care of, unless by husbands? I must make Pegge agree to a betrothal. I cannot postpone my death until a man arrives who will suit her as well as William Roper suited Margaret More.

—

A familiar bell calls me back from my wanderings. Lincoln's Inn. I must send Pegge to find out who has died.

Lucy is dead, but better a cold grave than a spinster's bed, for Lucy was not made for marriage. Perhaps George will die before me also. Of all my children, he is the least likely to seek martyrdom, but it may find him all the same. When we give our children to the grave, they do not disappoint. They are there when we come to look for them at the last.

My own brother died of gaol-fever in Newgate where he had been sent for harbouring a Catholic priest. My mother told me that when the priest was cut down from Tyburn gibbet, he sprang back to life, forcing the hangman to disembowel and quarter him. It was one of my mother's bedtime tales. Meditating on such lessons made for hard sleeping when I no longer had my brother at my side.

That bell was our prize from Cadiz, where George is a hostage now. When last I passed Lincoln's Inn, I met a face in the street that looked like George. He would put on that face whenever he wanted something. Once he challenged me to a game for a handful of tobacco, then dealt falsely, playing with more cards than are known to the deck. When I found him out, he erupted in laughter and stuffed his pipe with my tobacco anyway.

Pegge will miss George if he dies, but Jo will miss his brother even more. He could never get the best of George. They would fight over a meat pie until I ordered one of them to cut it into halves and the other to choose. George would measure the line so precisely that Jo could not profit by his choice. Never has a boy been so unfit for a holy calling as Jo, and yet he will be John Donne hereafter.

George would be safer in his grave than in Catholic hands. Thirty-five years ago I sailed into Cadiz with Essex at the helm of the *Repulse*. Ever rash, Essex entered the outer harbour ahead of the fleet. When the cathedral bell rang out at two in the morning to warn the city, we had no choice but to attack. We went in at dawn and the running sea defeated us. It is not easy to walk on water wearing armour, especially in the Protestant cause. The Spaniards planted our dead upright at the tidemark. When the tide turned, the flotilla of bodies sailed out past our ships, shining in the moonlight like the Catholic heads I had seen as a boy on London bridge. In several hours, the flowing tide would carry the corpses past us in the opposite direction. We could hear the dogs fighting for position on the beach.

We did not stay to see the feast, but stormed the inner harbour, driving their galleons aground. The Spaniards swarmed like rats, leaping into the sea to extinguish their flaming clothes. Smelling a second meal, this time of Spanish meat, the dogs began to bark.

I was with the band of English volunteers in gold lace and plumes who took the plaza that day with Essex. Why was I, a crypto-Catholic, breaching a holy city in Spain? I had no wish to become a martyr like so many of my family. I had renounced my faith for a Protestant Queen, and hoped by such bravery to find employment in her service.

Although our flesh boiled in our armour, the city and its bell were ours by dawn. Today, that bell tolls in the chapel at Lincoln's Inn, telling me I shall be next to die.

—

We are all Time's slaves. The Earl of Essex's head was taken off cleanly with Toledo steel in England, not in Spain. He had come back from Cadiz a hero, his glamour running before him like the incoming tide. On the return voyage, we trained our beards to grow like his. When he left for Ireland, the people walked for miles to set him on his way.

I stayed behind as secretary for Sir Thomas Egerton, the Queen's Lord Keeper, in York House. It was there that I met you, Ann, and there that Essex told me his story. In Ireland, he lost twelve thousand of the Queen's men. Desperate to tell the Queen before she heard it from her messenger, he disembarked at Chester, then rode for four days across England. Saddle-mad, his spurs befouled with mud, he arrived at Nonesuch unpardonably early and took the stairs two at a time. He strode through the presence chamber, the privy chamber, the withdrawing-room, and burst unannounced into the royal bedchamber. The Queen waved her women behind her and faced the intruder head-on.

What comfort it was, Essex told me, to find her in her old bed-gown with some tokens of his affection laid tenderly upon her table. He fell on his knees and called her *My Prince*, throwing himself upon her mercy and thanking God that though he had suffered trouble and storms abroad, he had found a sweet calm at home. When he finished pleading, she asked him to withdraw so that her ladies could dress her.

Only then, he told me, did he notice that she had no brows. Her skin was unpainted and her teeth black. One of her ladies was combing something on a stand. It was the Queen's wig, impaled like a traitor on a pike. For the first time since entering the room, he focused upon Elizabeth's head—pale, blue-veined, and utterly devoid of hair—and saw his fate reflected in her eyes.

Essex was quartered in the Lord Keeper's own chamber. You hardly knew he was there, Ann. You were no more aware of influence and rank than the air you breathed, but they were as natural and as necessary to you. Essex meant nothing to you, but I was his channel to the outer world. Even in his close prison, infected equally with despair and pox, he never sullied the Queen's honour. She had refused to see him, but it was not in her power, he told me, to make him love her less.

I wrote his letters in my best hand for him. The most pitiful he wrote for himself. Each night, back in my chamber, I copied out his words from memory for the Lord Keeper. Soon Essex was in court, planted upright in the stand, about to be torn apart by dogs. I can remember the exact moment—I was handing Sir Thomas a deposition in the case against the Earl—that Essex's eyes turned towards me, dark with accusation.

I can recall the exact number of steps through the unlit halls from Essex's prison in York House back to my own room as if they were steps to Golgotha, but I cannot recall, Ann, where your sweet bedchamber lay.

II. THE SUN RISING

My father took me back to Loseley park the morning after
my aunt's funeral. Sir Thomas Egerton was inconsolable
at his wife's death, so much so, he wrote my father, that
the Queen had reprimanded him for preferring his private
grief to his duty to the state.

I sat out the spring and summer listening to my father
talk about his livestock while wondering whether time
was passing as slowly for the inhabitants of York House.
Then, just before Michaelmas, I received an invitation
from Sir Thomas, who had always been fond of me, to
come to town to meet his new wife and her three daughters. It seemed he had proved all too consolable when he
had met the Countess of Derby.

The fourteen miles and three furlongs in the old carriage from Loseley to Cobham were made unbearable by
my father giving instructions to Bess on how to care for me
in London. She was holding my unfinished tapestry,
though I had told her I would have no need of it. By the
time we reached Cobham bridge, I was so shaken by the

disagreeable roads that I pushed the tapestry behind my back to cushion the hard bench. My father was sprawling across from me, his boots muddying my gown, and Bess was taking up two-thirds of the seat we shared. At Kingston-upon-Thames, I decided it was time for me to have a lady's maid, not a servant bred in the country, and began to plot how I might get my father to take Bess back with him when he returned to Loseley. I was never so glad to see the windmill turning in St George's fields and the gates of London bridge rising up before us.

I progressed cautiously into the salon, for I had discovered that my new farthingale went its own way without my legs if I moved quickly. Mary was at the virginals, with my cousin Francis at her side, playing much more expressively than when I had last heard her. By the improvement in Mary's complexion, I guessed they had consummated their marriage when my aunt's death brought him home from Oxford.

The chamber was filled with the liveliest conversation, the sort men and women engage in when determined to be publicly charming. Wall sconces and flickering candles lent a warmth to the room which had eluded it in my aunt's time, and a row of men in livery stood looking servile and idle. My aunt, with her lessons and needlework, might never have existed. I hoped that this new Lady Egerton would let me learn the latest dances.

The salon was knitted so tight with voices I did not know which strand to pick up for fear of dropping one or all of them. I wanted to absorb everything—every syllable of London talk, every jot of London news.

"I wish Mother would not say such things. Sir Thomas cannot wish his wife to be so indiscreet."

"On the contrary, he is so besotted he will let her say anything."

"Our guest will do very well, I think, for she has no sense of fashion."

"And he will do even more nicely. I cannot say how pleased I am with poets. They are far more charming than I was led to believe."

"What news of York House's infamous guest?"

"He is now at liberty at Essex House."

"I hear necklines will be lower this season—"

"But toes will be more pointed and heels rounder."

"How can he put up with her? It has been less than a twelvemonth."

"A man does not use his head in such matters, my dear."

Breathless with anticipation, I could hardly take it in. I had been away too long from society. My eyes strayed enviously to the row of pastel feet across from me. Had the three daughters shortened their hems to show off their shoes? I tried to glimpse the heels so that I could describe them to a City shoemaker.

"Come, Ann, and meet Lady Egerton," Sir Thomas said, drawing me towards his wife, who seemed delighted to find me less well shod and dressed than she was, and soon returned her attention to her daughters. "And there is my son Edward and my secretary, Mr Donne. I am surprised he is not talking to the ladies as is his custom."

Sir Thomas left me at the table where servants were setting out quelque-choses and wines. As John Donne took a sweetmeat, I overheard him say to Edward, who was washing a mouthful down with sack, "Today the Queen cancelled Essex's licence for sweet wines."

Edward said, equally low. "There's an end of him, poor man. It was folly to set him free then humiliate him. Since he cannot recover her favour, he will strike out against her. He has been heard saying that the Queen's conditions are as crooked as her carcass. God knows what he will do next, but we must stay clear of it."

"And let the birds of prey peck out his liver?"

"The pox has eaten it, more likely," Edward said. "It would be better for us all if he died. We must take the Queen's side if we wish to rise in these times. Do not forget you have further to fall than most."

John Donne's answer was too quiet to hear.

"Now, Mr Donne, stop whispering to Edward," Lady Egerton called out gaily. "I hear you have written a new elegy. You must show me all your poems as soon as they are written."

"Why, madam, I keep no copies." His bow had a trace of mockery in it. "They are mere evaporations."

"No gentleman publishes his verses," she agreed, "but since your manuscripts circulate amongst men, what harm if they are seen by women?"

Just as I was straining to catch the reply, my ears were assaulted with the dimensions of a particularly fine animal. I was horrified to hear my father praising his sow. After describing the birth of her large litter, he moved on to her slovenly habits and the incontinence of her diet, delighted to have gained the attention of the entire company.

"Sophie is a fine creature indeed," I said, gripping his arm, "and has the most amiable temperament. But, Father, since we are in town at last, should you not ask Sir Thomas what has gone on at court?"

"He refuses to speak of public affairs and keeps me talking of the country. How am I to be in Parliament," he said loudly, "if no one will tell me anything? Young man," he turned to John Donne, "what news of Essex? How does the Earl?"

Lady Egerton intervened, pulling John Donne quickly to her side. "I will suffer no secrecy where love-poems are concerned. You must disclose all your amorous goings-on."

Must the whole room hear of his *goings-on* during my exile to Surrey? We might as well hear the pedigree of Sophie's boar as John Donne's latest conquests. Edward was beside me at once with a clever remark. I laughed up at him, though I had scarcely heard. I felt a good deal more poised than when I had last been at York House.

"Ann looks well tonight," Edward said to Lady Egerton. "Her hair suits her remarkably, don't you think?"

He was a most obliging man, and it gave me great comfort to know that others were listening.

"She is but sixteen and apes a fashion she falls short of mastering," John Donne said. "Why do women delight in artifice when men admire nothing so much as simplicity?"

My hand pushed in a stray pin. Over the hairpiece, which Bess had scornfully called a rat, Lady Egerton's maid had combed my hair into a shining beehive. The effect was flattering in the mirror in my chamber, but perhaps the light of the salon was harsher.

"Men do not admire simplicity." Lady Egerton smiled. "They admire contrivance in everything."

"It is a subject for one of your risqué poems," said Edward, leaning on his friend's shoulder, "for you never flatter women. According to Jack Donne, they are all unfaithful and lack souls."

I disliked this game of talking as if I were not there. Lady Egerton was now exuding pleasure like a musk-rose, ripe and melony and a good deal past its prime. "It may surprise you, Mr Donne," I said, "that even country girls know the Bishop of London has banned your poems. I have read enough to know they deserved the flames. They are lewd and"—it took only a moment to cast about for the exact word—"*swinish.*"

The hurt on his face was cutting. "A man may write about anything, but it does not mean he has done it," he said tersely. "I am sure Lady Egerton understands the difference."

She agreed with satisfaction, and took the poet off to supper. Her hair, I noticed, had not been pinned into a tower like mine, but was coiled loosely at the nape of her neck. Her bodice clung to mature curves, exactly as intended, and her skirts followed her legs, unrestrained by a stiff farthingale. Was she the married woman rumoured to have visited John Donne's lodgings near the Savoy? Her daughters were just as jaded and forward, and the cut of their clothes was equally suggestive. I did not know whether Mr Donne most admired the mother or her worldly daughters, but it was certain his admiration was no longer mine.

As the chamber emptied and bottles clanked by in the

arms of stewards, I considered how little inducement it took for a man to betray a woman he had once spent pleasant hours with. Spurned, derided, and discarded, I might as well have been back with my father and his pigs at Loseley. The ornate stomacher pressed against my belly like a plate of iron and my great boned under-skirt swung out so far that I was twice as broad as Sophie. I cursed my country dressmaker whose idea of London fashion had proved so false. When next I had my father's ear, I must persuade him that if I was to marry well, my dowry must show in the ornaments upon my body.

Just as my eyes were filling with tears, Edward flung open the door and walked back in. He looked about as if he had lost something, noticed me standing alone, and kindly offered me his arm.

—

A few hours later, a flicker of light under my door told me that something had been pushed beneath it. I leapt out of bed, then Bess rolled off her pallet to see what the rustling signified. Her nose twitched, testing the air for perfume. Somehow she had got it into her head that this was how a chaperone behaved.

"Go back to bed, Bess. I only wish to use the close-stool."

"Can't your bladder tell proper time? I must empty that each time you fill it."

"Remember your place. You are a servant."

This was haughtily said, but my feet were bare and my chemise draughty. She stood there stolidly, like an ancient oak. I had seen this pose before. Unless I begged her forgiveness, she would never move again.

"I did not mean it," I conceded. "You are not a servant, you are— Oh, I do not know what you are!" What did I call someone who shared my bed when I was ill, but whose hands were rough and stained with bluing? "Go back to sleep, Bess, and leave me be."

"Not until you lift your foot."

I stooped to retrieve the folded page. It seemed that midnight was the best time for gliding through the women's wing, accompanied by a smoky lantern or, better, by darkness alone. I recognized the masculine script just as she took the letter from me.

"It is from Master Edward," I volunteered.

She lit a candle and held the paper to the light, turning it this way and that. I supposed that one gallant's handwriting looked like another's when you could not read. The lie appeared to satisfy her—Edward being above reproach—and she returned to her pallet. I wasted no time breaking the seal.

To Mistress Ann More,
A man may yearn and what he yearns for he may hope to have,
though that does not say he has done such things.
Come, madam, come, all rest my powers defy.
Until I labour, I in labour lie.
The foe oft-times, having the foe in sight,
Is tired with standing, though they never fight.

I presume this meant he could not sleep, though a woman

would have phrased it differently. This was followed by an elaborate description of how a woman's garments were removed before retiring—first girdle, then breastplate, busk, and gown—as if he had done it more than once himself. At last, he came to the point.

> *Off with that wiry coronet and show*
> *The hairy diadem which on you doth grow.*
> *Now off with those shoes, and then safely tread*
> *In this love's hallowed temple, this soft bed.*

At this, I sat down quickly on a chair.

> *Licence my roving hands, and let them go*
> *Before, behind, between, above, below.*
> *O, my America, my new found land,*
> *My kingdom, safeliest when with one man manned,*
> *My mine of precious stones, my empery,*
> *How blessed am I in this discovering thee!*
> *To enter in these bonds is to be free.*
> *Then where my hand is set my seal shall be.*
> *Full nakedness, all joys are due to thee.*
> *As souls unbodied, bodies unclothed must be,*
> *To taste whole joys.*

The gifts of words had blossomed into gifts of poems—a glorious rebuke for my folly in saying that his verses were lewd and swinish. I felt the upbraiding in the way he had designed, for I was flushed and willing, without a man to perform the acts so lyrically described.

After much tugging and adjusting of blankets, I fell into a troubled sleep, the page clutched in my fist. Near dawn, I woke within a dream of violation, unable to break out of cumbrous folds of green. Verdant stalks, emerald blades, the hard new green of unripe fruit, the greenish-gold of pistils and stamens bursting with unspent pollen. The deep blue-green drone of insects raiding plants. My legs hinged open like heavily scented petals, then closed upon themselves again.

Sated, I woke late, and swiftly threw the casement open.

John Donne's indifference had been a masque for the benefit of York House. In the days that followed, I discovered that he had been collecting bits of me all along—a hair, a tear, a scrap of torn lace. There was something intriguingly Catholic about all this, though he was not very tender with the relics. He collected the tear on a handkerchief which he then stuffed into his sleeve. The hair he put into his glove, where it was no doubt crushed and forgotten. Even so, I felt cherished after being banished to Surrey for so long.

Soon afterwards, while I was walking with Lady Egerton in the garden, John Donne greeted her, then slipped a folded paper into my hand. After an agony of waiting, I fell behind to remove a pebble from my shoe. It was only a verse this time, enshrining my tear in words. As usual, he suffered more than I did and said so at greater length. His tears were pregnant of me, emblems of *more*. But how could I trust poetic tears? Such crying might only be cunning, for he had begun to hint in these verses that he wished to die in my arms.

Bold and furtive, these poems invaded my peace. They made a misery of my daily tasks, lengthening the interminable hours between our hurried meetings. That autumn, I drove John Donne into a rage of writing— sweaty misbegotten verses, the metres rough and jolting, somersaulting logic I could not hope to follow. I began to suspect that these poems were aimed at someone reading over my shoulder, Edward and Francis perhaps, or students at Lincoln's Inn, where he had studied law. I struggled to catch John Donne's meaning until, forced to be satisfied that he was still a lover, I would tuck the verses into my bodice and dream of country pleasures.

Before long, the November rains were upon us, and we sought out the corners of the house. One night in the salon, when I came up behind him and touched his sleeve, he spun around as if I had raked a fingernail across his skin. I locked my gaze with his and would not let him go, would not release him until he acknowledged my triumph with a bow. Even Edward was not immune that night, for when I brushed against him, he turned away, confused and bashful at my touch.

As soon as Edward was gone, John Donne was back, accusing me of lavishing tokens of affection upon other men. He pushed me ahead of him into the unlit gallery. But once there, I was escorted up and down as if taking exercise with Lady Egerton, while he lectured me on metaphysics. Must poets always speak in code? It was a waste of time for him to state his case by innuendo when we were alone. I wished he would speak his wishes frankly with his hands, as another man would do.

I drew him boldly to the window, where the moonlight fell across my shoulder. "I too have feelings of great poetry," I confided, "for a woman longs to *die* in her lover's arms as eagerly as does a man." At this I blushed, giving away my meaning.

He pulled me against him, hip bone to hip bone, and made me swear that I could not feel our souls pulsing from our bellies to the crowns of our heads. How could I swear, for I was shivering like a goose plucked of its covering of feathers.

"Love's mysteries in souls do grow, but yet the body is his book." His lips touched mine—lightly, but with a promise of force to come. "This is our oath of love. Now we are joined, even when apart. You must marry me, Ann More. Or else I am two fools—for loving, and for saying so in whining poetry."

I had misunderstood John Donne again, for he scorned simply to bed me. It seemed he had a different idea all along. He demanded all or nothing. He would not take my body without my heart, my heart without my hand, anything without anything.

This was unfair, for this honey was not mine to give. My father owned the hive. John Donne knew as well as I did that I could not wed a tradesman's son. I must marry estates and rank, as my sisters had before me. To demand I marry wit and poetry was arrogance and passion. My aunt had taught me that a squire could be got for a dowry of £1,000, a minor lord for £3,000, an earl for £5,000. When I was ready, I would tell my father I would accept nothing lower than a minor peer. I would not give up John Donne and all his poetry for less.

And since he valued truth above all else, I did not deceive, but told him that although I loved him, I could not marry him. I do not believe he saw, in that dark gallery, the tears spilling from my eyes, and I was not about to offer them up as a subject for his verses.

—

Just because a man writes that he will die if he cannot have you does not mean he will die if he cannot have you.

A poem is only black inkstrokes on white paper, like a list of trimmings for a new gown that you might tire of before it is even sewn. A poem is only a sheet of paper pushed underneath a chamber door when a great house is sleeping.

But this poem was different.

When I felt me die,
I bid me send my heart, when I was gone,
But I alas could there find none,
When I had ripped me, and searched where hearts did lie.

This was a shard of glass plunged into a vein—sharp, cutting, clean, and bloody. This poem could not be ignored. In it, John Donne sent me his petitioning heart, fresh-beating from his chest, and would accept nothing less in return to fill the gaping hollow left behind.

Lovers might indeed die when driven apart, since I could hardly keep my meals down. I was plagued with sleeplessness, for the spectre of my father loomed the moment I snuffed out the candle. The only part of John Donne I had held for days was that paper shoved beneath the door. After eight days and eight nights of raw longing, I learned from Bess that he had offered himself to Sir Thomas as an envoy on some urgent business. *By ship to Venice*, Bess said, as she stirred up a warm drink, crumbling in heart's-ease to help me sleep.

He might as well have been going overland to China. If I was to taste love, it would not be by means of my maid's possets. No earl in England could make me feel as he had done. When Bess fell asleep, I wrote a letter in halting Spanish to Mr John Donne, offering myself as a page to accompany him as far as the antipodes, willing to die at his side. I had no fear of discovery if my message was intercepted. My penning of that language was so execrable that only a former tutor could decipher it.

—

A fortnight later, I was dancing with Edward in the great hall when a little girl swirled between the dancers, then skidded across the floor until she bumped against the lute-player's leg, causing him to drop a measure. Whose child she was I did not know. I cared only for adults this night, which ones had arrived and which had not.

As I mirrored the steps Edward was teaching me, I felt his cheek graze mine. I had seen nothing of John Donne for three weeks, but my appetite had improved when I learned that he had been sitting in Parliament for Brackley and not travelling on a ship bound to the Orient.

Now I felt the rush of silk against buffed nails, the new shoes tight across my toes. I had barely mastered the first part of the dance when the member for Brackley strode in, his breeches clinging like the taint of Papism. He stood apart from the knot of men, his eyes scouring the room. His gaze passed over Lady Egerton and lingered on her daughter Agnes, who smiled too agreeably at him.

All at once, Edward broke away and I found myself with another partner, one less inclined to pleasure. His palm rested on me heavily, his sleeve giving off a blue-black sheen. Sir Thomas's secretary had bought himself a cloak of surliness since I had last been with him.

"Have you come only to be displeasing?" I asked.

"I am not a dancer."

Edward was indeed the better partner, but John Donne knew exactly where to place his hands and there was an anger in them that I did not care for. "Agnes would gladly teach you," I suggested.

"I would rather dance poorly with you than well with any woman."

He kept to the shadows, like the stink of privet behind roses, his feet tangling wilfully with mine. When it was our turn to circle, displaying our paired steps to the room, he pulled me against his chest, so that anyone could see how unsuitably I was partnered. He had put off his courtier's ruff for a collar that exposed his throat, Italian lace that must have cost £5. I was near enough to see the threads. Less showy now than when he had arrived at York House, his clothes were better made.

"Sir Thomas must pay you well."

"A coarse man may wear fine clothes."

"I did not mean—" His phrasing had been too careful, meant to injure. "You came too close in the pairs," I said. "Next time you must hold me at arm's length."

"That I shall never do." He pulled me out of the dancers. "We will stand and watch instead."

Even his standing had a swagger to it, like a cock pheasant among hens. Edward was spinning Agnes, whose feathered mask flew out from her waist, commanding John Donne's eyes. I saw no sign that he was languishing from being apart from me. What had become of my offer to go to the antipodes as his page? A woman could make no bigger sacrifice. Surely it deserved an answer.

"You did not go away," I pointed out.

"You might yet drive me off."

Again, that stabbing wit. Would I always lag behind, his jest and slave? "I hear you sit in Parliament." Only the music and the couples' laughter. Would this tedious dance not end? "How does the Queen look?"

"Just as she should. An old woman sickening for affection. She has pined for Essex these nine months, and well she might. It took three strokes of the axe to sever his head from his body."

His eyes fell heavily upon my neck, as if weighing the chain of Loseley gold that ringed it. Perhaps he thought I was displaying my dowry to other men. I was stricken, and wished I had sent the gold back with my father.

"I have not seen you for three weeks," I hinted.

"Time is not a friend to lovers." Then, brushing irritably at his sleeve, "I found five grey hairs this morning."

I hoped he would now press Horace's argument that we should make much of time, but he did not seize the chance. He had not even acknowledged the letter I had written him in rudimentary Spanish. "Aging has made you less mannerly," I said. "Your correspondence has fallen behind of late."

Five long steps and we were in the passage, where he pinned me against the wall like a country girl. My gilt bodice strained across my chest, making it difficult to breathe.

He dug around in his doublet and thrust a much-tortured sheet of paper at me. "This has cost me a fortnight of my life. Read it if you wish to know my mind."

I scanned the poem that quivered in my hand.

By our first strange and fatal interview,
By all desires which thereof did ensue,
By our long starving hopes, by that remorse
Which my words' masculine persuasive force
Begot in thee, and by the memory
Of hurts, which spies and rivals threatened me,
I calmly beg: but by thy father's wrath,
By all pains, which want and divorcement hath,
I conjure thee, and all the oaths which I
And thou have sworn to seal joint constancy,
Here I unswear, and overswear them thus,
Thou shalt not love by ways so dangerous.
Temper, O fair love, love's impetuous rage,
Be my true mistress still, not my feigned page.

"What spies were these?" I asked. "You cannot mean my maid, who is too simple to discover any of my secrets. And my father has no dislike of you, at least none that he has spoken of. If we starved for love, it was your fault for not replying to my letter. As for rivals—"

"It is not fact, madam," he said in exasperation. "Why is poetry so foreign to a woman's thinking?"

Before I could read more, it was snatched from me and pushed back inside his doublet. Perhaps he did not care for me at all, but only wanted to get poems from me. "By this rudeness," I said, "I see it is your only copy."

"Do not mock me, Ann." He captured my wrist and twisted it sideways. "You prick my patience. As if you could pass as a man's servant! It is heartless to offer yourself to a man to tease him."

This was said like a schoolmaster, but it was not a schoolmaster's leg between mine, making four layers of skirts feel papery thin. He was as near as my own flesh, and hotter than my blood. My wrist was cruelly tethered and the panelling was jabbing into my spine. I was mortified that he had so easily seen through me. I had only hoped to convince him that, though we could not marry, we might still be lovers here in England.

"Your fingers are hard," I complained.

"From the pen." He flipped back his lace cuff to show his ink-stained hands. "Words coarsen a man."

It was true that when he touched me I sometimes imagined a tradesman's coarseness, although his fingers were long and delicate. "You wanted a poem and now you have one," I said bitterly. I counted three measures from a muffled lute before he reached for me more gently.

"A wandering rage of passion is not love, Ann. Do you

want me or do you not? For there is only one way to have me."

When I did not answer, he pulled me down some steps. Even there it was not wholly dark, for I saw a vein pulse at his neck. Was this a man's skin, then? The hairs curled moistly in the hollow of his throat, a place most gentlemen kept covered. There was a heaviness in the air, the heat of noon, although it was December. A shuffling came from further along the passage—a couple, their faces hidden, their arms a tracery of wanton light.

"We must go back another way," I said.

"We must *act*, Ann. Those two take their pleasure while they can. When your father left for Surrey, I heard him tell Sir Thomas that he is determined to see his daughter married."

"That is not a crime in fathers."

"But yours means not to wait. I believe he thinks of Edward. You know it, Ann. Do not counterfeit."

My breath came faster. "What did my father say?"

"He spoke admiringly of Edward, then vowed you should have a generous dowry."

"My father's conversation often takes strange turns."

"He spoke in metaphor, to be sure—"

"My father does not talk obliquely. What were his *words*?"

"Something about refurbishing a coach with plush," he admitted.

"There." I was greatly relieved. "My father is no poet. He was talking of his carriage."

"Do you deny that he seeks a husband for you and carries your miniature to show to men?" At my silence, he threw up his hands. "Do you want Edward? If you say nothing, I will believe it of you."

Any answer now would be a step into a snare. "And if I said I did?"

"You prick at a man's heart with a pin, and mine has bled enough. Give way to my love or deny me to my face. How much longer will you tease? *Do you want Edward?*"

The next breath went straight into my heart. "No," I said fiercely.

"Now"—he was triumphant—"do not pretend I am nothing to you." His fingers hooked beneath my busk and pulled me close, but still his lips only tempted, did not kiss. "Unless we act at once, you will find your head on a pillow with a man your father loves."

The spectre of my father rose again. "The difference between us is too great. My father—"

"Is gone." He spoke deliberately. "The only difference between a man and a woman is difference of sex, and that," he pressed his groin against me, "cries out for union."

His lips took mine, forestalling any protest, and I tasted him, as sweet as cinnamon, inside my mouth. His hands were bolder now than any tradesman's. My breath sped up and down my ribs, feeding and nurturing a most dishonest urge. When he released me, I hid my face against his shoulder, ashamed of my immodest thoughts. Where did such ripe imaginings come from—such rousing, aching feelings that more became a man?

"Will you take me as your servant after all?" My blushes betrayed my poorly hidden meaning.

"You shall never play so lowly a role as page, nor travel as far as Venice." He lifted up my chin to join my eyes to his. "But since you are eager to play a part with me, I will find you a far, far better one."

———

On St Lucy's eve, John Donne opened my door, then pushed it closed behind him, holding me hard against his chest for a full minute. Everything had been prepared against this night. Only a quarter-hour before, I had sent Bess on a fool's errand too tempting to refuse because it offered large portions of French foodstuffs.

"We must go at once," he said, pinning my cloak around my shoulders.

We went down narrow stairs I had never seen before. I wondered, then, how often he was forced to use that route. In that house, even poets were a kind of servant. When we emerged, he tied a mask snugly behind my head. We went quietly through the courtyard, then crossed the garden, stepping quickly by the light of a wind-blown candle. A boat was waiting by the river-stairs. Dark, oily waters swirled round the bow and a dead animal floated past, legs trailing in the murk. After it came the stench.

I drew back from the river's edge. "Where is my cousin Francis?"

"He has gone ahead to make things ready." He gripped my arm somewhat too firmly. "No harm shall come to you while I am near."

"And Mary?" I had not expected to be so alone.

"She will stay with Lady Egerton this night to allay suspicion, but wishes us good sport. Why these hesitations, Ann—has your heart changed since we last spoke?"

It was rumoured that when Essex was held captive in York House, the Queen landed at these steps one night. She visited him in the Lord Keeper's bedchamber—perhaps John Donne escorted her up the servants' stairs?—and what was said between them no man knew, for Essex had since gone to the block. If the Queen had the courage to meet her lover thus, then so did I.

I shook my head and John Donne's hands circled my waist, lifting me over the gunwale. As I stepped in, the bilge washed up and soaked my hem. Then his gilt spurs were in the bilgewater too, and his arms steadied me as I sat on the muddy bench.

When we landed at Temple stairs, we were met by a mob of noisy students. A donkey cart banged round a corner and hurtled down Temple lane towards us, almost pitching straight into the river. Seated unsteadily on the excited donkey, Francis hardly seemed to know me. He led the minstrels in a bawdy song, nearly falling off the poor beast as he thrashed his arms to keep his choristers in time. As soon as John Donne was out of the boat, a jug was thrust into his hands. When he did not drink at once, but looked towards me in embarrassment, the jug was tipped up for him and the ale spurted down his shirt.

Shame and love pulled me in two directions, backwards by river to York House or forward to my waiting lover. I was shrinking back into the miserable boat when John Donne, being led uphill by merrymakers, blew me a kiss.

Taking the boatman's filthy hand, for no cleaner one was offered, I stepped onto the wharf. The law students converged, decking me in rosemary and bay, mistletoe and ribbons, then boosted me into the hay-filled cart. Smacking the donkey's rump, they drove it braying up the hill, with Francis clinging drunkenly to its back. I gripped the sides of the cart and stared at my cousin's head to calm my heaving stomach as we jolted through Temple gate and up Chancery lane.

At Lincoln's Inn we were met by John Donne's party, as full of ale as my own muscular band. I was heaved aloft by two stout men and carried into the chapel. Decorated with torches and winter boughs, it thronged with masquers and stonefaced youths dressed up as barristers in robes and horsehair wigs. For a moment, in the flickering light, they took on the grisly shape of judges and my courage faltered. What was I doing in such a place and with such drunken men?

Wearing a long bedshirt and laurel wreath, Francis raised his hands to start the gaudy night, proclaiming it the longest night of the year, an ideal time for nuptials. This year, our Poet told us, John Donne had begged the coveted role of groom and Francis would take Donne's usual place as Master of the Revels, reading the wedding-poem that Donne had written for the annual rites.

Francis began the *Epithalamion* with gusto. As he read out the first lewd stanza, I was carried down the crowded nave into the chancel, where I was put down and given a shove towards the vulgarly dressed groom. When I stumbled at the sight of his comic phallus, the mob surged forward, but John Donne reached me first and raised me to my feet. Although my clothing was wet and streaked with tidal mud, John Donne was wetter and smelt like a granary of fermenting wheat.

When Francis reached the stanza's end, the students shouted the refrain—"Today put on perfection, and a woman's name"—then thrust their fists into the air, splashing more ale upon themselves. Francis could scarcely make his next stanza heard and I retreated, betraying my faltering resolution.

"Will you turn back now," John Donne asked softly, "and deny our love before God and this company of men?"

The mob was pressing closer. "Are you sure God is here?" I asked.

"God is always in a chapel, even when he is being mocked."

I hesitated on the altar steps. The mock-chaplain looked no more than a boy in his mummery of a hat, his robes too large, as if he had picked them off a peg on his way through the vestry. The drunken students were crowding in, calling out ribald encouragements to the groom. No doubt this was the audience for which Jack Donne had written his licentious poems, and I was sure it had relished every one.

"Close your ears," my bridegroom said, "and look into my eyes. Will you go up into our night of love or down to safety? A man is waiting with the cart to take you back to York House if you choose. The kitchenmaid can play the part of wench as she did last year. She has braided her hair with flowers in a most becoming way." He smiled, knowing how to touch me. "If you swear you do not love me, I will let you go."

As his thigh jostled mine, my courage rekindled. Here was no threat, only a promise, a promise no kitchenmaid was going to enjoy in my stead. I stepped towards the altar as the Poet recited the next verse. The students knew it better than he, contributing rude sounds and gestures to accompany each line.

After we had exchanged our solemn vows as bride and groom, the great bell from Cadiz was struck and hoots and jeers rang out. More jugs of ale appeared and baskets of pies soon offered nothing more than crumbs. Dancers filled the nave, and minstrels attacked a battery of pots and pans. When we had been so toasted and so made merry that we were damp with ale, both inside and out, my two stout scholars heaved me up and followed Francis, who was reciting another stanza of the wedding song. A noisy band came after, illustrating by uplifted fists—as if the groom needed repeated instruction—the vulgar act he would soon be called upon to perform.

The wedding bower was decked out with vanities from all the chambers of the Inns of Court. Every student had contributed some frippery, from tattered garters to farthin-gales of yellowed bone. John Donne carried me the last few yards, like plunder from a captive merchant ship. My dowry gold shone round my neck, a bridal ransom, too showy to be thought real by anyone except my lover. Looking a little wistful, the kitchenmaid with her love-plaits turned down the bed in readiness. We were showered with grain and made to kiss, the first time since we had been declared mock man and wife. Surely, I hoped, the worst would soon be over and they would leave us quietly to ourselves.

The scholars loosened the groom's doublet, pulling out his ale-soaked shirt and unbuckling the oversized phallus he had worn throughout the ceremony. Chipped and battered, it had evidently done good service in past revels. Tipping it over, they stirred up a posset in the crude cup, sack to inflame the groom and honey to make him gentle. Sickly sweet, its real purpose, I suspected, was to make the bride easy. I could not bring myself to touch the cup, but when John Donne raised the drink to my lips, I swallowed deeply, having more need of it than he did to keep the tears and shame inside me.

The students shoved me forward, but my hands were too unsteady to perform the next part of the annual rites. Without a blush, the kitchenmaid stepped in and unlaced the bridegroom's hose and scarlet codpiece, ribbon by ribbon, bell by bell, until he stood as proud and naked as the risen sun. Stripped of his comic art, he was again John Donne, though I had never seen John Donne attired in so little. In the passage of York House, when I had welcomed the leg thrust between my thighs, and felt the answering rush inside, I had not thought this far ahead. A naked man is a brave sight, but not the first time a young girl sees it.

Francis was straining to make his verses heard, and at last reached the climax of his song, "Thy virgin's girdle now untie, and in thy nuptial bed, love's altar, lie."

This was the moment I had most feared, but I had been well instructed how to act.

"This bed is only to virginity a grave," Francis sang out, "but to a better state, a cradle."

After my greenery and outer garments were removed, and many coarse jests and innuendos suffered, I was laid like a sacrifice upon the gaudy bed, certainly the most authentic maiden who had ever played the part. After the youths had shouted the last refrain, Francis held up his hands for quiet, declaring the bacchanalia over.

"Now," he announced, "the bride and bridegroom must soberly perform their duties." Pushing the students out the door, he allowed himself a wink before he left us.

Now we were truly alone, and only God could see how well we played our roles. I struggled to untie the ribbons that held my shift together. Unable to discover how Bess did it, I made impenetrable knots. In spite of the sparking fire, I was shivering, loathing the river damp and stink upon my skin.

John Donne pinched out the candle and untied my mask, then worked loose the knots all up and down my shift. Tugging off my wet stockings, he warmed my toes in his palms. Then he removed my under-garments one by one, tenderly and with a wise affection. If he knew how to undo a lady's garments better than she did herself, I did not accuse and he did not trouble to deny it. Each time his fingers trailed over me, in search of some lace or string that needed untangling, my body rose a little more towards him. Before long, I was warm through and through. Even my feet had happily forgotten the cold bilge in the river boat.

Now, we were so close that there was neither shred of cloth nor grain of wheat nor breath of air between us. Our hip bones met and I was no longer afraid of what might lie ahead. I had chosen this role, and play it well I would.

"Tonight," my lover whispered, "put on perfection and a woman's name."

12. THEY APPLY PIGEONS

Arriving with a kettle of hot water at dawn, Pegge found Bess asleep in the chair beside her father's bed.

He had been speaking in mangled and mutilated tongues when Pegge came in, but now he was wide awake and shouting. "This ecstasy doth unperplex! We see by this it was not sex!"

Bess woke with a jump and scowled at the Dean, who fell back against the old Turkish pillow. Then she stumbled past Pegge and out the door.

The fumes of burnt poems still lingered after a week, casting an oddly tactile scent about the chamber. Pegge broke off a piece of bread and dipped it in some milk, but her father's lips closed tight against it. His skin was taut over the cheekbones, as if God was tugging him both east and west. Perhaps he did have the wasting disease, though he would not drink the milk that Doctor Foxe had said would cure it. He would not admit to starving his body, for that would be considered self-murder, protesting instead that he was feeding his soul. More frightening to Pegge, he had given up tobacco.

Pegge poured the water into a basin, then pulled off the bedcovers. Her father looked as flat and numb as a sole in a cold buttered pan, but when she rolled his nightshirt up to his armpits and stripped it off, he flinched.

"Where does it pain you, Father?"

"I am but a volume of diseases bound up together, a dry cinder, and yet a sponge, a bottle of overflowing rheums, an aged child, a greyheaded infant, and but the ghost of mine own youth."

When he talked like that, she had no idea if his pain was real or philosophical. She began to lather his skin, starting with his face and soaping gently down his bony arms. As she dried each limb, she covered it with a heated blanket. Rolling him onto his belly, she scrubbed his back with a soft bristle-brush, working the soap into a foam then wiping it off with a flannel. When he was washed, she propped him up to face the window and brought another blanket from the fire to warm him.

She took out the straight-blade and began to pare his long curled toenails, now blackened by corruption. When her blade slipped into the rotten flesh, his knees jumped up to his chest and he uttered a cry like Saint Sebastian being tortured. She calmed his legs and straightened them, the tears in his eyes telling her the pain was real and her father a long way from dead.

"I'm sorry, Father. I will not cut your nails again."

"Those will take away the sting," he said, gesturing to a basket sitting on the floor. "They came last night from Izaak Walton."

Pegge opened the latch. Pigeons—to lay on his feet to

draw the vapours down from his head, a remedy suggested by her father himself in his *Devotions*.

His feet were now nestled in the cavities of the pigeons, their necks intertwined like cooing doves.

"I shall read your holy sonnets to you, so you can check the wording before they go to the printer."

She had found twelve of them, but could make no sense of their order. In one, he spoke of the soul's black sin, in the next of it being crimsoned by Christ's blood. But what if the first had been written after the second? As she read, his breathing grew hoarser until he fell asleep.

She was having as much trouble ordering his love-poems in her room at night. They bespoke a fury of love, a worship so rarefied that, like angels, the lovers were no longer male and female. And yet, this love was so carnal it drove them mad, sweeping them up into a whirlwind of lust. If the poems spoke true, her parents had spent days inside a single room, hardly caring whether they ate or cleaned themselves. Their bed—*this bed*, Pegge reminded herself—had been the navel of the known world, their little room an *everywhere*, but now he wanted to cleanse himself of the taint of having loved.

He began to mumble from deep inside, opening a vein clotted with rich, red words. She sat on the bed and stroked his hand, hoping to bleed some wisdom from him.

"You promised that your body would lie next to my mother's in her grave," she prompted.

"So I did, so I did." A ghost of a smile elongated his lips.

"It is not too late to cancel your great tomb in Paul's."

"Do not vex a dying man with trifles."

This was said quite firmly for a man in sleep. *Trifles!*—he had sucked his fill of sin, but she had yet to taste even a drop. Love was folly and beggary, love was— But Pegge did not *know* what love was, in truth was no closer to knowing love at seventeen than she had ever been.

How many fathers invented words like *sex?* Her brothers had found it in a poem and sped off with it to school, earning the admiration of other boys, but what good was a word like *sex* to a girl who was forced to stay at home, then betrothed to a man she barely knew?

In one poem, her father had canonized the two lovers, saying that he and Ann had died and risen in the mystery of love. When Pegge explained this to her brothers, Jo cast rude doubts on this conceit, pointing out that every oaf in Paul's alley knew what it meant to *die* in a woman's sweaty arms. The boys delighted in finding the tricks in their father's poems, reading the besmirched lines aloud to their sisters.

"What starts with P and rises out of its own ashes?" Jo asked, wriggling his ears. "What palsies the body and greys the hair? What gives a man gout?"

"Playing with his phoenix," George responded, illustrating how it was done with quick strokes of his wrist.

There was no good telling them that the phoenix in the poem was the two resurrected lovers, for even the rising sun had been reduced by her brothers to a male member standing to attention at break of day. Their favourite conceit was the drawing-compass—an object Jo imbued with lewdness by driving the legs apart with his thumb and then snapping them back together. They found the compass in a poem written to convince Ann that, even when separated, their two souls were joined like stiff twin compass legs. Ann was the fixed foot left with child in England while John travelled to France, growing *erect* and longing to *end* where he began.

Now Pegge knew the puns better than her brothers. In their imaginations, all the poems blended into one. But so they did in hers, though Ann and John's story, as she knew it, was no longer shared by another living being, for her father had driven it into some phantom limb, then cauterized it.

As her parents sank in poverty, his poems spoke of desperate thoughts and deeds, the man's heart ripped beating from his chest, the woman feverish and dying. Then he turned to writing holy poems, and before long Ann was truly dead. However, Pegge had learned from his deep mumblings that her father's weak-kneed God could be chased off by one pungent memory of Ann, one putrid whiff of decomposing female flesh.

And now these holy poems were the only ones he wanted saved. Reading such betrayals, Pegge became her mother's subterranean ally, their voices knitting into one. Night after night, Pegge lay with Ann in the damp cottages described by Bess, bearing a child with her every year. But Bess needed a quart of sack to be primed for storytelling, and her tales were never the ones Pegge craved. Though Bess could recall every remedy she had dispensed in the

Donne household for thirty years, she could not recall the story behind a single poem that John had given Ann.

It had fallen quiet in her father's chamber, a heavy-lidded silence like dusk along a country lane, and Pegge was watching her father slumber, trying to decipher his twitches and contortions.

She felt a draught and saw a shadow in the doorway. Izaak Walton in his old riverwalking shoes that did not even squelch in warning, admiring the pigeons roosting on her father's toes. How long had he been standing there listening to Pegge and her father?

She stopped him at the door. "Why have you come while he is sleeping?"

Walton dismissed her anger with a cheerful wave. He was just looking in. "Now the Dean is so happy as to have nothing to do but die," he said, leaving dull footprints behind him.

She watched Walton's back and legs going down the stairs. He had not lost any of his shapeliness while running errands for her father. In the absence of the Dean's sons, Walton had set himself up in the library as a secretary. Men had been coming and going for days, talking with Walton about her father's Will and the disposition of his manuscripts.

However, Jo had arrived that morning and his voice was now drifting up the stairs. He had come, she heard him tell Walton, to take charge of his father's papers, but Walton seemed reluctant to turn the library over to him. The printer John Marriot was with them and Pegge stepped into the stairwell to listen.

Offering hard coin, the soft-spoken Marriot had come to pry as many manuscripts from the Dean's stewards as he could. He knew that Pegge was ordering the holy poems, and Walton the sermons, but he was concerned about the fate of the Dean's early poems. Marriot became distressed—his voice rising so sharply Pegge need not have bothered descending to the landing—when Walton announced that the Dean had destroyed some of his old papers.

Walton was in high spirits. "His poems were loosely, God knows too loosely, scattered in his youth," he was saying. "It is fit and right that such impieties be burned, for he wished to witness their funerals before his own."

Pegge heard Marriot's indrawn breath. He wanted to print, he said, from copies written in the Dean's own hand. Pegge knew that Marriot would have better luck with Jo, for her brother was already hemming and manoeuvring, leaving the door ajar to take the printer's money as soon as they were out of Walton's hearing.

In this Pegge could be of some assistance. "Mr Walton," she called down, "my father is waking. I believe I hear him calling out your name. Soon he will be propped up on his pillow and have some little task for you."

13. LOVE'S DIET

I once said, Ann, that I would rather owner be of you one hour than all else ever.

Chills, palsy, grey hairs—I have them all. Only my ruined fortune has repaired. My thoughts rattle in this pomegranate-skull and the dogs gather at my deathbed, smelling a cadaver as they smell sex upon a cleric's hose. What do they know of love? What is its quality to such as them? I pay my debts with my bones, paying for the wastefulness of my youth with the beggary of my age.

Voices squabbling over my manuscripts. Mr Walton ushering great men in and out. Our eldest son arriving. Pigeons bound to my feet to draw the vapours away from my head. The hands of our daughter preparing my skin for death. Every so often, she hesitates, frowning at Mary Magdalen swinging on a loose nail above my head.

For fourteen years, you have pursued me from your grave. Let me go now, to face my God alone. I must die in the first person and rise omniscient. I will collect you when the time is right, for Time cannot weary you where you lie now. When you are six thousand years old, you will have not one wrinkle of age or one sob of weariness in your lungs.

—

The body of a woman but the reasoning of a girl—what a drug was there! You were barely fifteen when I met you in York House.

Each day I studied the perfection of your limbs, ripening into womanhood. In my chamber at night I wrote poem after poem. Not all my verses were pure of heart. I thirsted after you, claiming you with my words. I warned you to take heed of loving me, for I was insatiable. My love expanded to such cumbersome unwieldiness and burdenous corpulence that it had to be dieted, fed with only one sigh and one tear.

Years later, I became a priest and this youthful play at dieting became sour truth. When did you begin to collect your sweet salt tears—when I began to thirst for God, not you? Before I took orders, I found you crying in our chamber, your hand supporting your back, for your womb was full of Pegge. You reached to tidy the wisps of hair at your neck, a gesture I had not seen in years, but now your hair was grey. So was mine, but I did not tug it out by the handful. I took you by the arm and led you to Bess, who found some way to calm you. I had no choice but to become a royal chaplain. King James refused to prefer me to any other post, and eleven years in the country eating salads and onions was enough.

Pegge fought her way out of you with such ferocity that you did not have the strength to name her. Called *the baby*, she slept in a box beside your bed for months, a stout, robust infant. As a priest, I could not come to your bed on fast days and feast days, I could not come when you were bleeding, or suckling, or with child, or even when you had given birth but not yet been churched. Such dieting sat ill with both of us, making your belly ripe with another hastily sown child.

When you were churched after Betty was born, I could not wait for night. I unlaced your gown and all your undergarments for you. In the afternoon sun, your flesh breathed in and out like a live sponge. I laid you on the bed and was quickly finished. My fingers left holes that would not close, for the blood had oozed out and gone elsewhere. You were a map of veins, a spongy hydroptic cushion. The image tempted, but I could not get a poem from it, no matter how many pages I blotted in my library.

You announced you were with child for the twelfth time while Bess was carrying a spotted-dog to the table. She raised the pudding high enough to throw it at me, then slammed it down and cut it with a knife. The children quarrelled over the squares, arguing over who should get the biggest. They poked their fingers into the pieces and poured cream into the holes. Then they sucked out the cream as rudely as they could. Bess refilled the jug to keep them quiet, but Pegge would not hush. She had just learnt a new word, *maggot*. Hearing it, the older children stopped their sucking and looked at you. Another birth, they knew, might mean another death. The cream from your pudding dripped over your chin and spotted an already unclean bodice.

Bedridden for weeks, you let the children make a play-house of your bed. I told Bess to chase them out, but she said they did you less harm than Dr Donne, who had made your belly a house of death. Afraid of night, the children slept with one another, leaving beds empty elsewhere in the cottage. Sometimes I woke to find that Pegge had crawled under my blanket and curled into a ball behind my knees.

As the birth neared, the doctor eased your bloating by making pinpricks up and down your legs. The children stared at the morbid fluid weeping from you until Bess finally took them out. After a day and night of labour, the doctor warned me you were too weak to deliver. A small foot emerged and I baptised the infant while it still had a soul to save. Your eyes opened as my lips closed. I will never forget that look. You brought forth that twisted child more in anger than in pain. Your reason escaped in a single tear, though your body wept three days longer.

Your father handed me a list of sculptors, wiping his eyes with the back of his wrist. I took it without a word. Dumb, blind, crucified—what metaphors did not apply?—I chose one for his name, and composed an epi-taph for Nicholas Stone to carve. *This stone is commanded to speak the grief of her husband John Donne (by grief made speech-less like an infant) who hereby pledges his ashes to her ashes in a new marriage wedded.*

This was no idle conceit, for my grief was unutterable. What tears were left to shed? I had become that very stone, that infant without a mother. I buried you next to your five dead children in St Clement's. I still have the accounting.

for the burial of a stillborn
child of Dockter Dunes
    for the grave in the church...... iiii s
    for the knell................... viii d
for the burial of Mrs Dun
    for the knell..................... v s
    for the passing bell........... iiii d

Should I have withdrawn my seed like Onan and spilt it on the floor? You might have lived another thirty years, but God counts onanism a crime. Since your death, I have paid a price that would make Onan blush, for your fingers call me forth each night to share remembered pleasures. I sometimes wonder, my gentle wife, if you are taking your revenge.

Four years after your death, when I became Dean of Paul's and moved the children into this house, I found Bridget's tinder-box with nail parings. She confessed that she had clipped your nails as you lay dying to entice your soul back to collect them. I rooted out all the children's relics—the hair that Constance had combed out of your brush, the flannel in which Jo had caught one of your tears. I threw them on the fire as the children watched, and condemned such Catholic idolatry. In truth, I had no wish to encounter your soul gliding about the Deanery at midnight, seeking lost nails or hairs or tears, and rousing allies to avenge imagined slights.

The children have outgrown their memories of you, except for Pegge, who refuses to be weaned from the few she has. Once in a while, when Sadie barks for no reason, Pegge looks about as if a spirit might be present in my chamber, then lays a hand on the dog to quiet her. For months the dog has shadowed me, even into the chancel of St Paul's, tracking the rank odour of human flesh. I do believe the animal has some gift, for she knew before my own doctor that I was dying.

My marriage-bed is now a deathbed. You must leave me, Ann, to the corruption of my body. I can smell it beginning. Let me putrefy and vermiculate, incinerate, dissolve, desiccate, and be dispersed until I am motes of dust. When God is ready, he will call back each mote from wheresoever it has flown, in whatsoever filth, and from these particles he will reintegrate and recompact my body, and revivify it in the blinking of an eye. At the last busy day, when the numberless infinities of souls arise and go to their scattered bodies, my ashes will wed your ashes and we will be young again in one another's arms.

14. ENGLISH LAW

At first light, I was jolted out of John Donne's embrace by the pipes and clanging pans outside our window at Lincoln's Inn.

"Good-morrow to our waking souls," my lover said, tying my shift for me.

My clothes were only just back on when the law students burst through the door to toast our health from the leather phallus once again. The hoots and jests were so loud I thought the window-glass would shatter. According to Francis, rubbing his cold hands, they had spent the long midwinter night on Lincoln's fields where a tavern called the Blue Balls kept late hours.

John Donne's face was flushed, but not half so flushed as mine beneath my hastily tied mask. He looked well pleased with our night's revelry, for there had been nothing mock about this part of the ceremony. This had been a mingling of blood, a bargain entered into willingly.

But now we had to leave separately. Francis had to get me back inside the east wing of York House, while John

Donne resumed his duties for Sir Thomas. It would be some time before we could manage such a night again. We had known this, and had to be content to feed ourselves on memories of love.

On the following day, I was walking restlessly about York House at midnight when I heard hooves striking and ran into the courtyard, hoping to see my lover. A man dismounted and lost his footing on the frosty pavingstones. I recognized Anabel, my father's mare, and heard his familiar curses. He had come, he said with an ill-mannered oath, to take me back to Loseley.

Though it was dark and foul, he insisted that we start out at once. What had he heard that brought him back from Surrey in such haste? His face purple, he pushed me ahead of him down the passage, shouting for Sir Thomas. When that poor man stumbled out in his nightclothes, my father demanded his dead sister's carriage. I gathered that my father was annoyed with something Edward had done, or not done, and that Sir Thomas had betrayed a trust and now owed my father a sum of money. But how these things were connected in his mind, I was too terrified to ask.

When the lawyer in Sir Thomas came awake, voicing objections and stating facts, my father began to blow in another direction, saying that Sophie was expecting another litter and that he would have me home for company. Finally, when he had sputtered out like a spent candle, we got ourselves quietly into my aunt's carriage and onto the Strand. No one was there to see me off—not even the gallant Master Edward.

A long, dead night, it was the worst possible for a thirty-four-mile journey on bad roads, though this time I was well cushioned by my late aunt's plush. I endured the ride in fearful speculation about what was going through my father's mind. Had Bess somehow got word to him that I was receiving letters from Edward? But that could not be, for my father was never silent when angry with his children.

One thing I was sure of—my father could know nothing of my night of love, for even Bess was ignorant. She had not been in my room when I returned, but had staggered in, reeking of garlic and strong drink, some time after I got myself to bed. It had not been difficult to undress myself, for I had not been properly fastened. John Donne's skill lay in undoing women, not in lacing them back up.

My father slept all the way to Shalford. When the carriage knocked along the village lane, he began to talk himself awake, cursing Sir Thomas for shadowy crimes. Dawn broke, an ominous yellow, as we entered the grounds of Loseley park. Bess finally quit snoring and my father felt for the velvet bag that contained my dowry gold. For my part, I had thought John Donne's poems more worth saving, and for hours they had been comforting me next to my skin.

—

The days passed slowly, like the mist swirling around the apple tree below my window. Bunches of mistletoe perched on the bleak limbs like oversized crows' nests, and the lowest branch almost dragged upon the earth, weathered and glistening. It had seemed high off the ground when I was three and Bess lifted me on top of it. Ten years older than me, Bess had climbed up to reach the pippins, polishing the best ones for me on her apron.

My father had taken offense at all of London, preferring wet, inhospitable Surrey to any warmth the town might offer. I could not discover why we must wait out the winter at Loseley and was too afraid to ask directly. The only cause I could see was Sophie, who had indeed been bred and now was swelling. Her boar had been chosen with the care lavished on daughters of high rank. Sometimes I went out to feed her acorns. It was too cold outside to wallow but, inside her private sty, Sophie was building a nest out of straw and my father's old, discarded shirts.

In the evening, I sat with my father in front of the chalk fireplace in hopes of getting some news from him. As the January weather worsened, so did his temper. His sentences consisted of few words, and most of those were directed towards his chaplain and his steward. The gout stiffened his knees and ankles, depressing his spirits further.

Late one afternoon he came in from outside complaining of the muck and rain. He stirred up the coals and threw himself into the depths of his chair, making piteous sounds. I kept him company on a little chair that had been my aunt's, making a show of embroidering a silk handkerchief for him.

"You should not sit so close to the fire, Father. It heats up your legs too quickly and gives you pain." He shifted his chair an inch closer and shut his eyes against me. "Do your eyes trouble you?" I persisted. "You should dictate your letters to me to spare your sight."

He had always found writing tiresome, and I longed to be privy to his correspondence. If any letters had arrived from my cousin Francis, or any occupant of York House, they had been locked up at once in my father's study, and I was desperate to know what John Donne had been doing in the month since I had seen him.

I tried again. "My aunt said my penmanship was equal to her own, and she was one of the Queen's maids of honour." My aunt was dead now and could not dispute this fabricated claim.

This time I was rewarded with a grunt. "My writing is good enough for other men to read."

Then he *was* writing to men, but to which ones? "You would be more companionable in London, Father. You would have no need to correspond with your friends then, for they would all be near you."

"I shall return when Parliament is called, not sooner."

He had set his heart against London and nothing I could say would revive his civic duty. Perhaps I would do better with a domestic theme. "Is it true that my aunt worked one side of this chair and the Queen the other?" A grunt, possibly a licence to continue. "Aunt Beth said Her Majesty was always glad to see you. You have not forgotten I am to be presented at court, Father?"

A churlish oath. "If the Queen wishes to see you in this unspeakable weather, she may travel on the filthy roads herself to Loseley."

Perhaps sullenness was preferable to activity. When the weather improved, his attention would turn all too quickly towards me. Soon he would be riding his prize mare about the countryside, assessing neighbouring estates, tallying livestock and weighing crops still ripening in the field. Any day now he would begin to scrutinize the bloodlines of country squires for his fifth son-in-law.

—

The jasmine had begun to crowd the winter house the gardener had built for it. On warm days, he opened the panes so it would not overheat. One morning I heard him beneath my window with a saw, pruning the apple tree to make way for new shoots. Before long, he would be netting the tree against marauding birds.

It had been two months since I had seen John Donne, two months of guessing what my father was plotting, when I was called to sit at table with his visitor, Henry Percy, the ninth Earl of Northumberland. As I entered, my father was complaining about his lazy swineherd. The Earl stopped feigning an interest in rural economy and gave me a sharp measuring look.

Could it be that my father, a rabid anti-papist, had decided to match me to a Catholic peer three times my age? I hung upon every word, hoping to find the Earl already settled in life. I was relieved to hear of a daughter, and soon hoped to hear of a mother for her. If he was widowed, surely he would have mentioned his loss when my father said that our sow Sophie had been named after my dead mother, but no—the Earl's eyes were dry and watchful. I was heartened. His wife must be alive. But if so, why did he stare so pointedly at me?

In the dynastic portrait behind my father, I leaned on the knee of my dead mother, who was petting a small fancy-dog. Either she had been copied from an earlier picture, or my face had been painted over a dead child's, for I had never known her. Everything I knew about my mother was on that wall, and none of it, perhaps, was true. Even the dog's name had been forgotten. Perhaps it had died of sorrow at her death, or been killed by my father in a fit of grief.

When the first hot dish was carried in, the Earl stood up so abruptly that the bench teetered. "I have brought a letter for you, sir." He reached inside his doublet.

"Read it," said my father, cutting himself a liberal slab of pork.

After a moment of doubt, the Earl began.

> To the Right Worshipful Sir George More, Knight
> SIR,
> If a very respective fear of your displeasure did not so
> much increase my sickness as that I cannot stir, I had
> taken the boldness to have done the office of this letter by
> waiting upon you myself to have given you truth and
> clearness of this matter between your daughter and me.

As a fish rode past on Nellie's platter, the Earl paused to steady his breathing. I had recognized the Jesuitical style of the opening and was now in fear of just how wrongly the writer would judge my father's temper.

> So long since as her being at York House this had
> foundation, and so much then of promise and contract

built upon it as, without violence to conscience, might
not be shaken. At her lying in town this last parliament
I found means to see her twice or thrice. We both knew
the obligations that lay upon us, and we adventured
equally; and two weeks before Christmas we married.

Here the Earl stumbled over some sentences, and I did not
blame him. The argument seemed to turn upon the fact
that had my father known of our *adventure*, he would have
impossibilitated it but, now that the act was done, he should
pardon us at once. This was like putting a whip into a
man's hand—a man who had never, to my knowledge,
spared his horse's flanks—and forbidding him to use it.
There was more.

I know this letter shall find you full of passion, but I
know no passion can alter your reason and wisdom, to
which I adventure to commend these particulars—that it
is irremediably done; that if you incense my lord Egerton,
you destroy her and me; that it is easy to give us happiness,
and that my endeavours and industry, if it please you to
prosper them, may soon make me somewhat worthier
of her.
Yours in all duty and humbleness,
J. Donne
From my lodging by the Savoy
2nd February 1602

My husband had chosen as his viceroy one of the most
important men in England, a man I had heard called the

Wizard Earl. Perhaps making his acquaintance was what had taken John Donne two long months. I studied the stripes on my skirt trying to will the parallel lines back into focus.

The Earl placed the letter in front of my father and judged it best to remain standing. "I have been sent to collect Mrs Donne and take her to her husband."

"There is no such person here," my father replied, digging out a fish eye with his knife and holding this delicacy out to me.

The Earl looked at the eyeball on my father's knife, then looked at me.

"I am Mrs Donne." I was shaking so horribly that the words came out in spurts. "I shall not eat the eye today, Father. My stomach—"

My father placed the eyeball in his mouth and crunched it. The Earl's face whitened, as if he had only just grasped the danger of his commission. He moved towards my end of the table to inspect the tarnished family armour hanging on the wall. "Gather your servants and your things," he said in a low voice. "The more quickly this is done, the better."

"Tell him this is nonsense, Ann," my father ordered. "I believe I recognize the name J. Donne. I am not one to forget a thing so easily. It is that foppish man of Sir Thomas Egerton's, is it not, the one who is always making jokes about his own name? I gave him a coin once for writing me a letter as garrulous as this."

"He is not foppish," I said quietly, "and this is no jest."

"Speak up, speak up, Mistress More! I cannot hear you. My ears fail me. Answer your father, girl. Tell me you have not wed that fool of a secretary!"

"The ceremony took place at Lincoln's Inn," the Earl said, "as part of the Christmas revels."

"Ah, then it was all a mock. This is some Inns of Court foolery. It was a student, not a chaplain." My father's jaw clamped shut with satisfaction.

"It is true he was newly installed in orders," the Earl acknowledged. "Only the principals knew he was a lawful priest."

"Ann More was no lawful bride, since she did not have her father's blessing."

"I am now Ann Donne." Perhaps I would convince myself, if not others in the room, by repeating it.

My father's knife was now back in the air. "You are a minor and have defied both civil and canon law. What is worse, you have deceived your own father. I shall have this marriage stopped—mark me, I shall—by trial of nullity."

"Not if it has been consummated," the Earl said sensibly.

"And that it has not!" My father was certain on this point. "She has not been breached. This is no country bitch in heat. My youngest daughter is a true, most perfect virgin."

The Earl had no ready answer. His eyes met mine, then fell to his boots.

"We have five witnesses to the consummation," I said, rather too loudly, "all students of law at Lincoln's Inn who are prepared to testify in court." I had been coached on this point by a man who was no stranger to the law himself—the Lord Keeper's own secretary. In my mind's eye, I could see the bed we had lain on that night. "If proof is needed, they will produce the bloody sheet."

Even the Earl was disconcerted by this homely detail and seemed to be searching for his gloves.

"I shall see all five of them in leg-irons," sputtered my father. "If I find out that it was my nephew Francis who led you like a mare to stud—"

"No one at York House was party to it," said the Earl. "The bridegroom told me so himself."

This was true so far as it went, for Francis would by now have come of age and inherited my aunt's estate at Pyrford.

"And you believe the stallion, a known womanizer, a Jesuit who wants a Protestant wife to raise himself at court." My father's fist was rattling the pewter on the table. "He would sleep with his stepdame sooner than take the Queen's oath."

"You can hardly expect me to think ill of Catholics," the Earl said, "being bred one myself. However we have both foresworn the old faith out of loyalty to the crown."

"It will be the end of my daughter's chances with the Queen."

"You said yourself he is eager to rise at court."

"He is an arrogant, insufferable—an idler seeking her rank and lands."

"His blood is better than you might suppose. His mother is descended from Sir Thomas More, as you are yourself. She fell in love with a City ironmonger who gave his son the best education that could be bought."

This was too much. I wished the Earl had stopped short of documenting my husband's blood lineage.

"Oh, Annie, Annie, to throw yourself away on an iron-monger." My father fell down on all fours and squeezed my knees, his eyes filling with tears. "You are beautiful enough to have any man in England. And for this I kept your mother's wedding lace—for this she died giving birth to you—for this—"

He had not called me Annie since I was little, but I knew I must not give in to his distress. I had seen him like this before, his gout making him swing from fulsome rants to crying. I must hold myself together until he was done.

"He is a poet, Father, not an ironmonger."

"A poet who cannot afford his own horse. What kind of poet is that?"

"Oh, Father, you know nothing of poetry. He has little need of money."

"It is you, Ann, who knows nothing. Do you realize how much it costs to feed and dress you for a year? More than that fop will earn in a lifetime." He yanked at my gown, smearing it with pork grease. "This petticoat alone cost £10. And that bodice—" To my relief, he could not remember the amount. "He can give you no jointure, and I shall give you no dowry. For £800 I could have got you a wholesome country squire. I'll not pay a penny for this tradesman."

I thought it wisest to remain silent. Nellie was making more than enough noise, banging the trenchers as she stacked them in a lopsided tower. She was taking far too long and earned my father's glare.

"And servants—I suppose you have no need of *them*? There are fifty servants on this estate, whose names you hardly know. You cannot even get out of bed without two girls to help. Bess herself has three women to command,

and then there is your dressmaker, your silkwoman, your laundry-woman—" He had his fingers out to count them.

I thought of John Donne's slender fingers caressing my skin as they unlaced my shift. We would manage quite well by ourselves. I had long been suffocating under Bess's care. "My husband will help me in and out of bed," I said softly.

At that, he erupted into choler. "He shall not touch a single hair upon your head. I'll make him a widower before nightfall. I shall cry all the hounds of heaven upon you, you foul disobedient bitch!"

He was on his feet like a champion in the tiltyard, casting about for a weapon. Nellie stood by the stack of trenchers, making tatters of her apron. Then the door was swinging and she was gone, taking my father's meat knife with her.

"Your daughter is no longer yours to hit." The Earl was pulling on his gloves. "Only her husband may discipline her now."

The Earl's satin breeches flashed once, then twice as they passed through the door. Perhaps this was why he was called the Wizard Earl, but I knew better than to run. I stationed myself in front of Queen Elizabeth's coat of arms, newly carved on the chalk fireplace.

Nellie was back now with Bess behind her. They stood on either side of me, like iron firedogs around a blaze. When my father made a sally towards me, Bess planted her solid frame between us.

"You, at least, are mine to do with as I please," he said to Bess, pulling the ladle from the soup bowl. "You are no better than a bawd. Where were you when this whoring took place?"

"Just you try me, Sir George," Bess taunted, raising her fists into the downward path of the ladle. "Be you never so fearsome I shall fight you, I shall."

When the blow struck, Bess landed hard on her nose, spitting curses in the midst of broken crockery. After a few more half-hearted swipes, my father collapsed on his back, his hand whipping the air and his breath coming in short bursts.

I knelt to unfasten his jerkin so he could breathe more freely. "Do not thrash so, Father. Let me unbutton you."

"Sophie, my darling Sophie, do not die."

"He has lost his wits, mistress," said Nellie. "Be off at once and leave him to me."

Bess struggled to her feet. "The boy is saddling two horses for us. His Majesty the Earl waits for us by the gate."

I raised my eyes to Bess's bloody face. I had not realized how tall and valiant she was. She blotted her nose with her starched cap, then blew it for good measure, starting the bleeding again. Stripping off her livery jacket, she threw it to the floor.

"You cannot come, Bess. It would be worth your life."

"What life is here? Sir George'll whip me when he comes to his right senses. If I must die, I will die at your side."

It had almost a poetic sound, but there was no time to thank her. Hurrying down the stairs, we got through the buttery and into the kitchen as quickly as we could, barring the door behind us. Once outside, we looked about for the saddled horses. Instead, we heard a bolt driven home in the iron gate ahead.

The Earl had gone, and in his place stood my father's steward with a face of granite and a loaded gun.

—

Cloistered on the upper floor of the house, I was now even more ignorant of my fate. Since my father had forbidden me to step foot on the great staircase, Bess carried my meals upstairs, complaining at the extra work.

Cradled in wool, I sat by the fire and drank warm ale. I told time by Bess's broken nose, watching it go through every shade of plum on Loseley's trees—from purple-black, to green, to murky yellow. She sat on a stool nearby, mending my clothes or helping me make scarlet tassels for new bed curtains, her large fingers making delicate stitches. Sometimes I looked at those hands to pass the hours, wondering if they would ever touch a man as mine had done.

Picking at my dinner on the ninth day, I accused Bess of letting my food go cold and demanded something hotter. For a big person, she was swift on her feet, disappearing into the tapestry on the wall. In a few minutes she reappeared the same way.

"This should put you in better temper." She threw some letters into my lap.

"How did you get these? My father keeps his study locked."

"But not the servants' door between it and the hall. Be quick about it, for he will be back at dusk."

The first letter was from York House. Apparently, my

father had written to Sir Thomas at once, saying that he had applied to the High Commission to annul the marriage and demanding John Donne's blood. But the Lord Keeper was in no mood to oblige, for he had just discovered that his son Edward had married his stepdaughter Agnes.

Lady Egerton had arranged it all behind his back—such was the tale that came out in his letter. More than one mischief had been done. She had tricked us all, putting Agnes up to smiling at John Donne. Edward's attention to me was another blind. By such deception, the three of them drove John Donne mad with fear of losing me. He carried me off in a passion, dwarfing the evil of their own crime.

It seemed that York House had been full of spies and matchmakers. I had been thrown in Edward's path by our two fathers from the moment I arrived. Even the dowry and jointure were agreed upon, the down-payment of the carriage made, hands all but shaken, but when time dragged on and Edward did not speak for me, my father returned to claim me and my aunt's plush coach. As my father had been most blind—tricked by all and trusted by none—he was most angry.

If Sir George More was to suffer, others would suffer with him. Sir Thomas's second letter revealed that the young chaplain had been imprisoned in the Marshalsea and John Donne tossed into the Fleet.

The last letter was from John Donne, pleading his case to my father, for he swore he was falling headlong to his destruction. Was he fearful of dying from gaol-fever like his brother? I read hastily, my ear attuned equally to melancholy in my husband's letter and my father's boots thumping back into the house. *All my endeavours and the whole course of my life*, John Donne promised, *shall be bent to make myself worthy of your favour and her love.*

At those most welcome, most moving words, my tears spilled dangerously upon his letter.

Two more days of agony passed until, looking out my window, I saw our boy guiding a strange horse towards the stable. Someone had come for a visit with my father, expecting to stay for several hours. I sent Bess down to listen.

Before long, she was back. "Another earl or bishop of some kind," she reported. "His gentryship was a time coming out with it, but at last he pulled out some letters and your father chased him off."

The stableboy was now leading the horse past my window, stopping to tighten the hastily buckled saddle. The gelding had barely got a mouthful of Loseley oats.

"Go and look for the letters, Bess. My father will be taking dinner in the hall. If he is angry, we do not have much time, for he might burn them."

"And risk my life for you again?" She dumped a cold pie in front of me. "I'll wait until your father rides out to inspect his grounds."

The tapestry on the inner wall appeared seamless, but when I ran my hand across the pastoral scene I felt the narrow door, barely wide enough for a milkmaid to squeeze through. There was no knob or latch, just a finger-hole. My father had not needed to forbid me to use these hideously dark stairs, for he knew I had been badly frightened in them as a child. However, if John Donne could use the servants' passageways, then so could I.

I held up my candle and pulled, stepping into the marrow of the house. Every so often, I saw a spear of light and felt for a finger-hole. Testing to see where each door led, I finally emerged through the wooden panelling of the study and reached for the letters stacked on top of my father's table. They were all from John Donne.

My husband was back in his rooms under close arrest. He wrote to my father that enemies had been blackening his name for deceiving some gentlewomen and for loving a corrupt religion, and he feared this poison had reached my ears. *Some uncharitable malice*, he added, *hath presented my debts double at least.*

What rumour was here that I had not heard before? That he had written poems to other women? That I knew. That he was Catholic? That I cherished, for what other faith made saints of its women? That he had debts? We should remedy that state together, for poets and their wives lived frugally, if not entirely upon fresh air.

From his next despairing letter I learned to my anguish that Sir Thomas had let his secretary go, crushing his hopes of rising, for no one at court would employ a man dismissed by the Lord Keeper of England. My husband could not strike off such fetters with his own hammer blows. A torrent of self-pity was unleashed on page after page—wild, feverish writings that would have melted a fiercer man than my father. On the last page was scrawled a desperate pun: *John Donne. Ann Donne. Undone.*

Though I went down the perilous, dark stairs each night, I found no more letters, and the cold ashes in the grate did not reveal what verbal thrusts and parries now took place.

It had been four months since I had lain with John Donne, and four months since Sophie had been bred. In spite of Bess's eavesdropping, I could not discover whether the High Commission had annulled my marriage. Perhaps I no longer had a husband. I knew now what it meant to swear *I will die if I cannot have you*, what it meant to cry tears *pregnant of thee*.

In the daytime, I worked on the tapestry I had begun at York House. Now I could survey the garden I was stitching. Over the months, I had added small figures—the steward with his loaded harquebus, Nellie feeding her pullets, and the bent form of my father shuffling to the pig house to feed acorns to Sophie, who was almost ready to farrow. Sometimes he looked up and saw me at my needlework. Perhaps good manners would one day inspire him to touch his hat, as King Henry had done to his imprisoned daughter Elizabeth.

For a week, four birds sat calling on the garden wall. I stitched them into my work, along with the cat lurking below them. I wanted to tell it that an archbishop was allowed six blackbirds to a pie, a bishop four, but commoners and tomcats none. This was no shroud for past love that I was making. I wanted my commoner in my bed. Each morning, I put a cross-stitch for a night we spent apart. It was now past Lady Day and I had one hundred and fifteen.

I was stitching a rose-bush when Bess entered, dangling a raw chicken by its feet. By its stench, I guessed the innards had been rotting for a fortnight. Apparently my father's blow had bruised her sense of smell.

"Take it back to the kitchen, Bess." Selecting a pale red skein, I made a French knot for a rose.

"That I will do, madam, when you have had a closer look."

"There are flies on it," I said, annoyed that she had begun to call me madam. "Is that close enough? I hope it is not intended for my supper."

Nellie arrived next, looking for Bess. "Give me back my poultry. I know what you are up to and it's no kindness to Mistress Ann."

"What do you mean, Nellie?" I asked.

"My sister thought she was stuffed by that pample-mousse who got between her legs, but now that she's not, she's trying to find out if you've got a bellyful."

This took a moment to work out, but John Donne's conceits had given me good training. Nellie had likely got this idea from stuffed carriage seats or cooking hens.

"What happens to a woman with child when she sees a chicken, Nellie?"

"It's more the smell, mistress. It's a vomit, anybody knows that."

I would have to take better notice of such things in future. I had not known that Bess and Nellie were sisters either, though I could see the resemblance now that it had been pointed out. Certainly they shared the same coarse speech.

"Look at Bess, her neck is like beetroot," said Nellie, pleased.

"Would you care to tell me about this . . . this *Frenchman*, Bess?"

"You know Jakes well enough, that fast-fingered weasel. You set him to pluck me, with his sweet wines and his foreign talk."

"What sort of name is that?" Nellie hooted. "Did you plant your buttocks on this jakes, Bessie?"

Jacques, of course—John Donne's servant. On the night of our wedding in Lincoln's Inn, Jacques had been told to take Bess to a tavern, feed her copiously, and keep her plied with strong drink. That he had done, for she had come home reeking. But it seemed he had gone further on his own initiative. I waved Nellie out of the chamber.

"Have you heard from him, Bess? Did he ask if you might be carrying?"

She wiped the back of her hand across her nose and sniffed. "What difference would that make?"

"You might have married him," I said gently.

"A Frenchman?" she snorted. "A polecat that greases his fingers to put them who-knows-where? And then weasels off to France in his master's best suit? As if I'd be tricked by such a one. I'd never have gone," she said righteously. "I promised your mother on her deathbed to care for you."

There was that upward thrust of the jaw, that bluster. With Bess, it was hard to know how much was true, but this sworn bond was not good news. She would never budge from my side now.

Despite the rotting chicken, I was managing to keep my meat and drink down. I picked up my needle in relief. I had not known how to tell whether I was carrying and had refused to beg Bess for the information. It was a mercy that the only female who would produce a litter at Loseley park was Sophie.

"We should both be thankful we are not with child," I said, hoping to make an end of it.

"Not exactly, madam." She jiggled the chicken back and forth a little.

I stabbed the needle into the tapestry. "Why are you so exasperating, Bess?"

"Sir George wouldn't be asking half of London to stop the marriage if you were great-bellied, would he? Then any blockhead could see you'd been rightly bedded." She swung the chicken a little more freely now. "Surprised you didn't think of that yourself, madam, you being so close with poets and all."

A little upholstery pillow, stuffed under my bodice like dressing in a roasting hen, bought my release from my father's cloister. He was easy to gull because he had refused to look at me for weeks. I approached the pig sty from the upwind side while he was showing a suckling pig to his chaplain, my hands clasped discreetly over my well-upholstered belly, my eyes downcast, docile.

The Right Worshipful Sir George More, Knight, of Loseley Park, Surrey, wasted no time writing to *J. Donne, Esq., in his lodging by the Savoy*, to come to collect *Mrs Donne* at once. After showing me the page, my father held out the quill so I could add an encouraging postscript.

Within a day of receiving the letter, my husband rode up on a rented horse in his second-best suit of clothes. No French servant danced attendance, but in his hand he clasped a permit that had taken him four months and £20 to procure. It had the seal of the Archbishop of Canterbury and declared the marriage of *Ann Donne alias More* and *John Donne* legitimate and sound in English law.

15. FLAT MAPS

When she could no longer bear the stink of the rotting pigeons, Pegge made Izaak Walton carry them out by their slimy legs. He returned with a jar in which white grubs were feeding on a woodmouse, a treasure collected on a stroll. Scooping out a handful, he arranged the maggots on top of her father's blackened toes, then cocooned the feet in moss and secured the moss with gauze.

Each morning, Pegge picked off the maggots glutted with dead flesh and put on hungry ones. There was an endless supply, Walton assured her, delighting in his role of purveyor of services to the dying.

Now Walton sat in Pegge's chair beside her father, their hair mingling in an irritating way. She was standing at the window watching the bedsheet dry on the bare limbs of the apple tree when she noticed a papery growth under the eaves. The first three cells of a wasp's nest, though there was little sign of spring.

Inside the room the talk was of the sorts, species, and genders of worms, a subject dear to both men, worms of the dunghill, basilisks or blind worms, scarabs or silk worms, squirrel-tails and brandlings—found in cow-dung or hog's-dung rather than horse-dung, for the last was too hot and dry, Walton was adamant on that point—and of the abundance of flies which adorned and beautified the riverbanks and meadows and whose breeding was so various and wonderful that Walton was swallowed up in the excitement of the telling, until her father steered him on to flies hastening the decay of a carcass, and whether maggots were bred in dead flesh or were drawn there after birth to feed, and whether buried flesh could bring forth grass.

Pegge was pulling the frozen bedsheet off the tree when she heard the clatter of wheels on the pavingstones. Soon Mr Harvey was helping his wife out of their carriage, which righted itself with a jolt as she stepped down. Con had gained weight, and all of it protruded out the front. As Con approached, Pegge shook out the sheet so that the ice flew sharply across the courtyard. Pegge carried the sheet in a lump into the kitchen and hung it near the fire, where it began to give off a fragrant steam.

In the passage, Con was playing with Sadie, who rolled over to be scratched on her belly, forgiving Con's desertion in an instant after pining the whole winter. Walton was coming down the stairs, his eyes fixed on Con, as if he had never laid eyes on a woman with child before. Con stood up slowly, her hands coyly supporting her back, and Walton began to stammer, unable to say two good words in a row. Although she was almost thirty, Con's hair was still a glossy black.

"Like a raven's wing," Walton whispered, possibly to Pegge, who was too annoyed with both of them to answer.

As if he could tell a raven from a rook or crow. Egg white and some secret powder—gunpowder, black bile?—had given Con's hair that avian sheen. Even in March, the scent of honeysuckle drifted from her, though no man had ever questioned its unseasonable source.

Con should have stayed in Barking to tend to her own husband, who appeared to have lost weight under her regime. Mr Harvey's scalp was sallow and unloved, and his whiskers were ragged around the edges as if she had little time to lavish on them.

"Why have you come?" Pegge asked her sister.

Con's eyes rounded. "To care for Father, of course. You know how eager he is to die. He has written of nothing else in his letters."

"Nothing else," echoed the gentle Mr Harvey, shifting his eyes away from Pegge's. "A most pious man, most pious indeed . . ." His voice trailed out the door.

Would no one talk sense except herself? "If Father dies, it will be because he has taken it into his head to let his soul feed off his body."

"Then why so downhearted, Pegge?" Con asked. "I am sure his soul is merry. We must arrange everything most becomingly, as befits his stature."

"He wishes to be buried in a private manner."

"But in that place assigned to him in Paul's," Walton added, looking uneasily from sister to sister.

"Englishmen are usually buried with their wives," Pegge said.

Con tilted her head, a bird alerted to an insect stirring underground. "Surely you did not think he would be buried with our mother?"

"He made a promise to her."

"Years ago—and in a poem! Can you not let go of that poor fable? There will be no mention of that marriage in the funeral in the cathedral. I will speak to Jo about arrangements tomorrow. And to you, of course, Mr Walton, for your letters have told me how useful you have been. He is past speaking for himself, so we must speak for him."

The boy came in at one end of Con's box, with Mr Harvey labouring at the other. As Mr Harvey rested beneath the picture called *The Skeleton*, working up courage for the flight of stairs ahead, the kitchenmaid stuck her head into the passage and asked what was to be done with the Dean's cold dish of soup. Should she heat it up or throw it out?

"I'll take it in to him," Con offered.

Walton held her jacket as she slipped out of it. "I'll come with you," he said.

Mr Harvey looked at his wife as if he had only just noticed how full and soft her lips were. Con swept her palm across her neck, preening in the heat of Walton's gaze. There was an unseemly incandescence about her skin, like a pale worm flushed out into the street by rain.

"No," Pegge said to Con, "he will want me, not you. He likes me to hold the bowl while he sips. As for other visitors," she said to Walton, "you know he has no use for you at this hour."

"I meant," Walton stammered, "only that I would read to Dr Donne while Mrs Harvey fed him. I have transcribed another of his sermons."

Pegge gripped the bowl. "If you want him to hold this down, you'll both stay out. He needs help using the close-stool now. I doubt you would care to do that, Con." Then, assessing her sister's face, "You may see him in the morning when he is rested. You must be tired yourself after the long coach ride."

Luxuriously big-bellied, bathed in male attention as pungent as musk, Con had never looked less weary to her younger sister.

"I will come in early to shave him," Con said.

"His skin is more tender now. No, I think you had better leave such things to me." Pegge hoped Mr Harvey would take his wife straight up to bed and out of Walton's addled sight. "I am sure Mrs Walton is expecting you home for fried eels," Pegge said as she pushed past him with the lukewarm soup.

—

When Pegge saw her father lying flat on his back, she knew he would not take even a sip of broth. A drop of Christ's blood would have been more to his liking. She put the bowl down on the hearth for Sadie.

The dog was baking her fleas next to the glowing coals, her sleep full of yelps and apprehensions, as if ghosts were paying irksome visitations. As old for a dog as the Dean was for a man, Sadie no longer harrowed Hounds-ditch or even ventured outside the City walls. Now it was as much as Sadie could do to sneak into the death-room to keep vigil with Pegge beside her father.

Pegge unwound the gauze on one of her father's feet and peeled back the moss. The morning's worms were feeding sweetly on his toes. He seemed to be enjoying the maggots, as if he were already in his grave, being worked into a slime by grubs. Was conspiring with maggots a form of suicide? Pegge ripped off the poultices and threw them on the fire. When the maggots began to pop and hiss, Sadie ran out of the room in fear.

Her father's nostrils twitched from the smoke. "Write this down," he ordered, his eyes closed.

She snatched the quill from the ink and lowered it to the first sheet she could find.

"Since I am coming to that holy room, where, with thy choir of saints for evermore, I shall be made thy music."

"Those are iambics, Father, shall I break it into lines?"

He nodded and recited the rest, tripping over the words in his eagerness to get them out. He must have composed it in his head and waited, a cow with a painfully stretched udder, for someone to come in to milk him.

"Did you get six stanzas?"

"Yes, six, with five lines each."

"Now check the rhymes."

She did as he asked. "I have them all."

"That is my last poem, Pegge. See that it gets to Marriot for printing with the others. I am glad it was you who came into the room just now. Of all my children, you have the most poetry in you, though God knows how you will use it."

She turned away to fold the paper so he would not see her tears. Which had he meant most—that she had some poetry in her, or that he doubted she had the talent to make use of it? A smugness was spreading over his face, because he had gotten the poem out or more likely because he needed to use the close-stool. She would have to bring the pan to him, but he disliked her asking him directly.

"Do you want anything, Father?" It came out hesitant and bleating.

His eyes opened, with a glint of triumph in them. "I want you to marry, like your sisters."

She had not expected that, said nothing, let the anger dry her tears. She decided to make him wait until morning to learn that Con had arrived, big with child. A son, Con had been most definite. How did a woman know such things?

Pegge straightened the papers on the table. "Do you wish to speak to Mr Marriot yourself?"

"I am done conversing with the living. I am as flat and foul upon the earth as a rotting horse or dog."

There was no arguing with a dying man, even one who still had strength for punning, and she knew now that he had not been counterfeiting, for gathering on his skin, in all the creases of his flesh, clinging to his hair and nails, was the odour of mortality.

—

Con had been there a day, organizing the household, but each time she entered their father's room, his eyes were closed. Now he was spread out stiffly on top of the blanket, his arms extended like the top beam of a cross. Pegge sat beside him, touching his cheek now and then to soothe him. When he spoke, it was a porridge of half-digested phrases. At least he was not asking for Con, for the name he most often called out was *Ann*.

Walton was readying the chamber for her father's death. He carried in the shroud and the coffin-lid with the death portrait, then strode back in with Thomas More's skull. "A memento mori." He held it up joyfully. "A death's head to meditate on. Has your father finished his last poem?"

His last poem—it was not much of a secret if Izaak Walton knew about it. She took the poem from her pocket and held it out. He handed her the skull and walked about the room, savaging the rhythm. Soon he would be downstairs, quoting it to anyone who would listen. But no, he would not leave her in peace, his little book was coming out, the pages turning.

"I have been writing a poem too," he said, "for the Dean's funeral, but I have yet to find all the words. Perhaps you could assist me."

"Why don't you show it to Con? I am sure she will be glad to advise you." She held the death's head at arm's length while Walton, pleased with her suggestion, made a little note. "Why do you encourage my father in thoughts of martyrdom?"

"You seem destined for that fate yourself," he said, "for if you die a virgin you will go to heaven with an arrow's speed."

She whirled around, almost dropping the saint's head she was lifting up to the high shelf. "Did my father ask you to say that?"

"He cannot see it there. Let it sit here in plain view." Walton took the skull and placed it on the table.

As their hands touched, the scent of green almond teased Pegge's nose. There was only one plant that smelt like that in England—bracken. After gutting a fish, Walton cleaned his hands on bracken, then cut fistfuls to cushion the catch on its ride home in his pouch.

"What fish are biting that make it worth braving the cold, Izzy? It is not yet the end of March."

He held a finger to his lips, nodding towards the bed. Of course. He would not want the Dean to learn where he went in the mornings. It was no wonder he was as brown and vigorous as he had ever been. He must keep his tackle near the river, since she had never seen him leaving London with it.

"Does Mrs Walton know?"

"She leaves me to my own pursuits. I am no good at linen-drapery, Pegge," he confessed, a little too happily, "no good at all. I cannot tell linen from wool." He stooped to waylay a good-sized beetle that was heading to a dark corner. "This will catch a fine trout, but where shall I keep it?"

Pegge held out a flask. As round as an alchemist's retort, it made a perfect bait jar.

"That is for his sacred wine," he said, stepping back.

"As you see, it is empty." She tipped it upside down. "The bishop came yesterday to give him his last communion."

"If he sins now, he will die without absolution." He peeked in his fist to see how the specimen was faring. "But I suppose there is little chance of that, for he can hardly last another day."

He dropped the beetle into the flask and placed it on the window-sill to admire it. "Your father's death will be exemplary. Even his effigy will start a fashion. Every churchman in England will want to be carved standing upright in his shroud." His hand fell earnestly upon her sleeve. "Will you agree to be betrothed, Pegge? It would relieve your father's mind." He looked at her closely. "Your hair will soon be long enough."

So they *had* been discussing her. Walton and her father. Con and Walton. And next, unless she kept them separate, her father and his fertile eldest daughter. What of Pegge's barren womb—had they spoken of that too? By week's end, all the servants, even the Dean's new errand boy, would know that Pegge was still without her fleurs.

—

The scent of almonds hung over the Deanery that night. Perhaps Bess had been blanching dried almonds and slipping off the wet skins to make a funeral cake, or perhaps, Pegge feared, her sense of smell had finally run amok. The coldness of her womb, the arousing dreams that poisoned sleep, her father's dying, all were mixed up with fish guts nestled in crushed bracken on some forbidden riverbank.

When Mr and Mrs Harvey had arrived with their servants, Pegge had been shunted into Bess's chamber. Now the shutters cast long shadows, fraught with dread, across the narrow ceiling. Towards dawn, the door slammed and the bed pitched sideways. Bess was jerking her swollen foot, trying to get it out of the toe of a knitted stocking. Soon the other foot was being violently extracted. At least the garlic was chasing off the troubling scent of almonds.

"Will you be groaning much longer?" Bess asked.

Pegge clutched her pelvis. "It is a melancholy womb, such as my mother had." What did it matter if she even had a womb, since it would never be wived or mothered?

"More likely it's Aphrodite's curse," Bess grumbled. "And long overdue at that. Your mother's womb was fallen, not melancholy. It wasn't made to bear a dozen of you children."

Heaving herself up, Bess opened a small cupboard, uncorking something brown and still fermenting that Pegge could hardly swallow. Bess's nighttime remedies had always been foul, to discourage the children from waking her at night.

Pegge shuddered as the last spoonful went down. "I doubt you know who Aphrodite is, Bess."

"I know this much. Something is making you sour and green, as if the pox on your face wasn't enough."

Pegge knew who Aphrodite was and why she had scarred Pegge's face. She had asked for love but Aphrodite had denied her. Try as Pegge might, she could not break Con's hold over Walton. Even Con's two husbands, even Walton's own wife with her thriving shop, could not cure him of his lovesickness. Con had stopped up his arteries of sense with some love-potion.

"There are too many sick dogs moaning in this house," Bess said. "You're in that old man's room too much. A wife wouldn't do the things you do."

"How would you know? You've never been a wife." Pegge was too pigheaded to stop now. "Do you think Con would give him better care?"

Bess considered this, then let it go. "Maybe you want to rub up against that fisherman. A sorry mess this household's in. He's a lickspittle to your father and you're a lickspittle to him."

"That was years ago, Bess, before I had the pox."

"I saw you on the landing yesterday, eavesdropping on him and Constance." Bess poked around in the cupboard again. "Tomorrow, I'll show you how to fill in those pockmarks with paste." She yawned and produced a pessary from somewhere. "Have a look down there. We can't wait forever."

Pegge held up the blanket to screen her thighs. The hairs had grown a little darker, but still the blood refused to flow. She shook her head, ashamed. Bess showed her how to use the pessary, whipping the padding between her own legs, catching the loop and tying it around her waist. The whole thing came off just as swiftly and landed, as Pegge crimsoned, in her hand.

"I don't need them anymore," Bess said. "You can have the lot of them." Then a bristle-brush came out, Bess's remedy for a red, itchy scalp caused by anything from fleas to ringworm. "Let me brush some life into that hair for you."

"Oh, please, do not!" Pegge cried, burrowing underneath the blanket. Even her hair was sore this night.

The mattress sank to the floorboards as Bess heaved up her legs. Pegge had no choice but to lie with her back to Bess, shivering from the ache inside.

"We must get you married off as soon as your father is finished this last business of his," Bess said. Something was catching in her throat. "If you go to live with Constance, I'll see no more of you."

Pegge was afraid to speak, in case her own throat was afflicted. She had not thought of going somewhere without Bess. This damp, dreary night would never end, Pegge hardly able to breathe for lack of space, in danger of flying off the bed if Bess's weight shifted by so much as an inch.

"If you married, that would be different," Bess encouraged. "I could come to live with you."

"I would like a man," Pegge admitted in a whisper, "but if I tell my father, I fear he will get me the wrong one."

"What's wrong or right about them? I had a man once. Little good it did me."

Pegge had not heard this story. "Who was he, Bess?"

Bess snorted. "A Frenchman with slippery hands."

"Is he the one who broke your nose?"

Another snort, and then a snuffle. The heat from Bess was like a blast furnace, making sleep seem finally possible. In an hour, the ceiling would be stitched with light and Pegge would be needed at her father's bedside.

16. NECROPSY OF LOVE

When I left Loseley park with you as Ann Donne, my sweet husband, I took only the mare I was riding and Bess on a black nag behind me. Later, my father sent my oak bed to us on a wagon, but whether he was being kind or could not bear it in his house, I never did discover.

One or another of our children was always ill. In letters to your friends, you called our cottage at Mitcham *my poor hospital* and said your wife had fallen into a discomposure. You complained of being circumcised for bread, forced to eat cucumbers and onions in the country when you might have fed on melons and sweetmeats at court. You could find no employment equal to your talents. *Patronage*—how your lips caressed the word. To be ambassador to Venice, secretary of Virginia or even Ireland! The best you could do in all those years was Sir Robert Drury.

While I was carrying my eighth child, you travelled to France as Sir Robert's secretary, although I begged you to stay with me. You told me that we would be yoked together like a drawing-compass even when the legs were spread apart. Was a clever poem worth a dead child? Labouring to give birth, I sent my spirit to find you, but you did not spring back to my side like the promised compass leg.

It was a year before you returned and moved us to Sir Robert's estate. After eleven years of languishing in the dullness of the country, you were in London at last, where more patrons might be wooed with John Donne's flattery. However, illness followed us to Drury cottage. When Francis and Mary sickened, you bargained with God, offering to bury your poems if he spared your children, but Francis and Mary died. After they were lowered into the cold earth, you locked your poems into the safety of your cabinet.

Then, the post of Clerk of the Council became vacant. You borrowed a horse and rode it hard to Theobalds to beg for the seat. King James refused, saying, *I know Mr Donne has the abilities of a learned divine and will prove a powerful preacher, and my desire is to prefer him that way, and in that way and no other.*

No man was less suited to being a priest, but you set about making ready. You called in your scattered verses hastily from friends, thinking to publish them while you still could. While you were out, I lit a candle in your library under the portrait of Jack Donne as a brooding lover. Rank satires and elegies were spread across your table—verses your friends had thought worth saving that I had never seen. The female body was anatomized with its ripe menstruous boils and sweaty breasts, its warts, weals, and hanging skin, its limbs strung up like sun-parched quarters on the City gates. A man's member was likened to the mouth of a fired gun pouring hot liquid metals into a woman's body. Who would have thought poetry to have such malice in it?

Your puns on my name were odious. Was this all that I had meant to you, this vulgar act? Worst of all was the poem that mocked our wedding night in Lincoln's Inn. I was only seventeen, and my pretense to womanliness was but a girl's bravado. The stain on the white linen terrified me, but you called it our bargain of blood, the baptism of our joint soul.

"Now none can do treason to us," you assured me, "except one of us two."

That morning, as you sweetened my pain with your fingers, I thought I heard the moving spheres, only to discover it was the law students making a din outside our window. You did not mock me then, but gave me your wedding gift—a very small word, *sex*. So prolonged and seductive in my ear, so fresh with new meaning, I swear you had invented it that moment.

Twelve years after that long midwinter night, you took a priest's vows and split our soul apart. You sold yourself to God on the very day and at the very hour that Pegge fought her way out of my exhausted womb. Staggering down Drury lane like a drunken man, giddy with doctrine, you did not even look into the birthing room until morning.

After my churching in St Clement's, you pulled me into our bedchamber, your hands damp from the font. Pushing upwards to an aching sweetness I could not hold to, I conceived another child, but when my monthlies stopped, so did your visits to my bed. Coupling while I was great-bellied was no better than adultery according to the church fathers. Once an *everywhere*, our bedchamber was now too cramped for your ambition. You moved to a more spacious room, furnished with a feather bed from Lady Drury.

Overnight, you transformed your past into an apprentice-ship fitting for a royal chaplain. Deciding not to publish your poems after all, you thanked God for delivering you from the Egypt of lust and from the Egypt of domestic cares, by which you meant your numerous children and a wife who could no longer meet you in conversation. That child died in my womb, too young even to count, and soon I had con-ceived another. Your children had become an annual crop to you, like acorns collected in the woods each autumn.

What sort of God boarded priests like whores, drove them faint with longing, made them pregnant with hopes of resurrection? What sort of jealous God called conjugal love a sin? By then, I had found my own god with her own commandments, and Aphrodite had no mercy for men who scorned her. Her favourite punishment was petrifica-tion. You were easy to discipline, for you had already begun to turn yourself to stone.

—

I was snapping off tulip heads in the garden behind Drury cottage when you rode past me in your priest's robe to preach at Sevenoaks.

Aunt Beth had embroidered tulips on silk for the Queen, who read symbols in the flowers. The country was full of girls named in her honour—Beth, Betty, Betsy, Eliza, Lizzy, Elsbet, Isabel, Lisa, Libby, Bess. I had named the new child Betty, but for my dead aunt, not the dead Queen.

England changed for girls after the Queen's death, for the King did not wish to have educated women about him. King James liked to say that to make women learned was to make them cunning, but you, my husband, fancied yourself a Thomas More who educated his daughters.

Born the year the King was crowned, Constance had no use for such lessons. Fourteen now, she was impatient to be married. I could smell her outside the door before she came bursting into rooms, a smell to bloody mirrors and drive men mad. Sour milk and stratagems—even you rushed to obey her. Bess took her aside, whispering of *these* and *those* as if I no longer cared about such things.

Nicholas's wooden car was going down the lane. He would not have the strength to ride it back, though Pegge, a year younger, could do it. She would push Nicholas off and propel it up the hill, leaving him to suck his fist. She had learned to walk the same month that he did. Crawling backwards one day, and passing Nicholas walking forwards, she stood up and began to run, overtaking him in seconds.

Why were the tall nodding angelica permitted in this London garden? They were indiscriminate, attracting flesh-flies and greenbottles. My thumbnail hesitated at the neck of a yellow-and-blue parrot that was infested with greenfly. Some alchemy made the tulips break into these exotic patterns. If I let the tulip go to seed, the seeds would not be true to the parent, but if I broke off the blossom, the bulb would draw the complexion of the flower deep inside it. Only then would the daughter bulbs, which grew like off-shoots from the mother's body, inherit the same colours.

Before I deadheaded each tulip, I studied the pattern flaming up from the pale base. The best were unique, like a baby's footprint. Only eight of my children had lived— Constance, Jo, George, Lucy, Bridget, Nicholas, Pegge, and Betty—and Nicholas seemed to be shrinking. And now I was weighted down by a new child in my belly, my twelfth in fifteen years.

—

On the day that Nicholas died, the sparrows gathered as they did every year. The pinks opened as they did each morning, just after the pimpernels. Once the bees moved on to the celandines, the sparrows began to circle the garden. First one, then a pair, then the whole flock attacked the dark centres of the pinks, stabbing them with their beaks. Hundreds of sparrows swooped in front of me, blotting out the solid form of Pegge who was squatting in the flower bed eating the bee-mint. Her hands flew up to protect her eyes. Even a child of three has that much sense.

You found me in the garden with the blinded pinks. The sparrows had fled and Pegge was talking to herself in a hollow of muddy earth. First the tulips had been beheaded and now the pinks destroyed. I would have to be watched all the time, in the garden and in the cottage. I might behead small boys next, or peck out the eyes of little girls.

"Mad," you muttered, rescuing Pegge. "He is stark mad who ever says that he has been in love an hour."

Perhaps you thought I could no longer hear. You stood opposite me, my sweet priest, your eyes telling me how much you suffered. We had lost four children in three years. Was it any wonder I sorrowed for them?

You stayed away from my bed until desire ulcerated you and made you raw. When the new child had so swollen my belly that I could not see my legs, you came slinking into my room like a Catholic martyr on knees of pain. But what I got was not the love I had so missed in your arms, the quickening of our joint spirit through our mingling blood, but a soulless act—the payment of the marital debt. You knelt beside my bed, twisting the church fathers' words to excuse conjugation with a great-bellied wife when it would prevent a more heinous crime, the spilling of semen by the man himself.

A woman's body does not have the resilience of a man's mind. When I saw that you would do the act without a spark of love, I locked my spine and protected my belly with my hands. When you withdrew, I felt a deathchill echo deep within me.

Blinded by pinks and tulips, by feathered petals and parrot hues, I began to rot from the inside out. Pegge was the only one still climbing in and out of my great-bed. She was such a sturdy, practical creature, already capable of telling one flower from another, the only one of my daughters to breed true. Extracting her, Bess stood her on the floor and sent her scuttling, but within minutes she was back with another armful of flowers, roots and all, feeding me petals to make me well.

At summer's end, you were called out of a sermon to witness the birth of your twelfth child, as cold and hard as stone.

—

There is some comfort in the grave, for there is freedom to do as one wishes without regard for husband or for children. There are no pregnancies and painful birthings. Yet there is excruciating loneliness and far too much time to think. At first you would come to tell me about your grief and my poor motherless children, but once you became Dean of Paul's I seldom heard your footsteps on the pavingstones above my head.

Why did you stop visiting me? A conversation between lovers should never end. My amorous soul lives for its outings, my visitations upon your body. What once was pleasure has become addiction.

Memory, my accomplice, prickles your skin when you least expect it. Your body rouses and claims your attention at the most unfitting times. An erotic memory assails you as you choose a text for a new diatribe from the pulpit. First your pupils darken, your penfingers twitching, dipping, and stroking across the paper in a drowsing rhythm as you lose track of thought. A rude pun slips into your sermon, a labial knot in a knot-garden of prose. You strike it out with a swift line of ink, but it is never quite erased. It is always there, half blotted in your mind.

As you are preaching, you stumble over the word *sin* and your mouth becomes dry. The notes blur on the sheet before you. Your voice gets louder, your arms gesticulate, and your parishioners think this sudden passion meant for them. You extemporize, trying to drive the word *sin* further from your mind, but it insinuates itself into every sentence, concatenating and proliferating, enwrapping and complicating, animating the sermon into a paean to lust. In the audience, attention creeps out on its belly serpent-like, seeking lush gardens with illicit fruit. Ears redden, and blushes climb pruriently up cheeks. Later that night, husbands greet wives with unexpected joy, wives respond ardently in kind, and another of Donne's sermons becomes legendary.

But now I remember—you are on your deathbed, and I must keep by you at all times, ready to claim your soul before God fires it straight to heaven. When you pledged yourself to God, you defied your solemn vow in Lincoln's Inn. You were wrong, my husband, labile. It was treason to give away something that belonged to me.

On our wedding night, you wanted nothing more than to die in the act of sex and share a single grave with me. You told me we would die and rise the same, and prove mysterious by this love. I have not forgotten, though it seems to have slipped the busy mind of the high priest of St Paul's. Did you really think that I who had given up the whole vast world for love would be content to lie alone in this narrow tomb while you went to a far more splendid grave?

True marriages are not divorced by death, nor are lovers' vows so easily unknotted. God has not the power to curb my love, whatever violence he has done to yours. Now you sicken in the great oak bed I loved and died in. At times, your soul rises and scouts around, checking the way ahead. Whether you are taken by flood, by fire, by fever, by plague—or more likely, I see now, by decrepitude and age—I will lay claim to what is mine. At the exact moment that your soul springs from your body, I will be there to trap it with a long, devouring kiss.

17. SALT

An unfinished conversation echoes in my skull. But where did we leave off, Ann? I mourned as much as any husband, but I was no Orpheus plunging into the underworld to save my beloved at the risk of my own soul. You had found a kind of peace, while I was forced to stumble among men and raise your children. Having betrayed Essex, it was not hard to turn my back on you.

Visitors push into the room, but I keep my eyes closed. I am marooned on an island with a festering wound, but these spectators are not driven off. Spit in my face, ye Jews, and pierce my side. Why not scoff, scourge, and crucify me too?

Someone says impatiently, "Foulness signals a quick end."

It is our son Jo, still not wearing a cassock. Does he think me deaf as well as dumb? He has been here a week going through my papers, hoping to find some manuscript to make his fortune. Constance comes in on the arm of Samuel Harvey. They hover, proud of their fecundity, hinting that they will call their first-born John. Perhaps they will begin to appraise the plate or remove the pictures from the wall. She leans over me, her eye slipping the diamond from my finger. But Constance has been away too long, and it is Pegge I want now, at the last— Pegge and Walton, whose little notebook has finally become an asset.

They leave, not a moment too soon, for I cannot be far from death now. When Walton arrives, I will send him to the sculptor to ask whether he has purchased the marble for my effigy. Even now in the quarry, the agent might be running his knife along a block to check for suppleness and colour. It will be brought by ship and carted up the hill into Paul's yard, where Nicholas Stone will contemplate his line into the marble. Fourteen years ago he carved your epitaph. More sought-after now, he will carve only my face and leave the shroud to his assistants. But first he will wait for my Will to be proved and the deposit to be paid.

And for that to happen, I must die. Oh, Ann, break off this last futile lament and let me speed out of the prison of my body. Your finger beckons impatiently, though you know I cannot come. It is not wrongdoing to decompose in separate tombs. Death *is* divorce. Why should husband and wife be manacled in the grave like prisoners in Fleet gaol? When I die, my soul must go ahead to chart the way, while yours lags behind to burn off its amorousness. As ashes I will come, according to my pledge, but first I must go to a far more worthy place.

—

Bess cares for me at night as she cared for my children, regulating the function of my organs as she regulated theirs. Now she peers into my chamber pot with thin lips, displeased with my stingy offerings. Her basins hold the ministrations of the devil. Mustard poultices for hoarseness in my chest, and purgatives to loosen my bowels. If that does not work, a greased finger will shoot up my anus, digging out a plug of stool to start the process going. Why has God seized my bowels and put this steward at them?

Bess leaves me naked as long as she can, then covers me with the itchy horsehair blanket and throws a bucket of coals on the fire. I might as well be locked in a jakes with a lusty whore. Must I share my last cell with female infidels? The most cowardly is this mongrel who sulks and wheezes beside my bed, observing every humiliating rite I am put through with wry philosophy.

"The dog has fleas." Did I say that? No doubt I did. I have thought it more than once in these past weeks.

"No more than you." Bess swats at the old blanket, then secures it so tightly I can scarcely breathe.

Balaam could not have been more surprised when his ass spoke than I am at hearing Bess say this. And yet Balaam's animal was full of wisdom. Can it be possible that God has sent such gatekeepers to catechize John Donne and test his worthiness for paradise?

What has Pegge done with Thomas More's skull? I am sure it was here, for I heard her arguing with Mr Walton when he carried it in. There it is—on the high shelf. I can just see it if I tilt my head. Much more comforting than the sight of

Bess settling herself in the chair beside me and unwrapping a hog's pudding.

When Pegge was little, she would curl up in my lap with the skull while I worked on a sermon. I feared she would block the passages, knot and slow the tumbling phrases, but instead I wrote faster, outpacing time, fleuve and effluvium, tumescence and detumescence. When I finally wearied, her fingers were white from clutching the bony eye sockets. Once she asked me what Margaret More did with her father's bloody head after she caught it in her lap. I said that she buried it under her tulips so that when his soul returned to collect it, he would be forced to collect his daughter too.

"Then, Father, how did the skull get *here*?" Pegge's eyes were wide with the injustice of it.

I had only been trying to console her, for no man can hunt down the bones of all his children, especially when he has fathered twelve, as I have done. In truth, it was my old fear of burial in a shallow grave, dressed up by More's skull and a few tulips to make a tale for Pegge. In my nightmare, a dog would dig me up, chewing off my face and dragging my skull as far as Bedlam gate.

Pegge liked to play in my library, fingers eager for my nib, her small body squirming as she watched me write. Once I found miniature words wedged into the white spaces of a sermon. The paper was ruined, so I gave it to her. Soon it was covered with minuscules and majuscules, the spurts and blottings she called stories. As she grew older, her penwork became more vain, the letters petulant, the words indelible and rude. Wedged in the fair copies she made of my sermons, I would find digressions I had never preached.

Sometimes they had a kind of brilliance to them.

Now here is Pegge, bumping and rustling, pushing Bess out the door. She snuffs out the candle and opens the draperies, quoting my own poetry at me. "Busy old fool, unruly sun, why dost thou thus, through windows and through curtains call on us?"

I do not return her smile, for the warmth coming through the glass might now be fatal. Last night, Bess's snorting ensured my wakefulness but now sleep, death's vanguard, launches his attack.

I want to die awake, not die asleep, for I will risk falling into Death's yawning pit before my soul is able to escape. If I relax now, I will slump down past reverie, past sleep, into the boiling vat which melts the flesh off bones, swilling with pigs' feet and cat-skins until the fat has cooled and coagulated and the bones are extracted and laid in the tomb, where centuries will mulch them into earth. That death might do for a commoner, but not for the Dean of Paul's, whose soul must speed at once to heaven.

"Quick, Pegge, a lemon."

She looks startled. This is the price I pay for speaking in metaphor all my life, talking what Bess calls *stuff and nonsense*. I cannot possibly mean what I say. Or perhaps Pegge is surprised I can still talk.

"Salt," I cry.

This time she understands and clatters out the door, the mongrel at her heels so bursting-full of morning piss that she can barely waddle. This morning the dog's reeking breath is a foretaste of hellmouth. Yet this bitter hound has mastered metaphysics, saving my soul more than once by coughing and wheezing just as I was about to fall into a mortal sleep.

Pegge is back with a straight-blade, a lemon, and a bowl of salt. She halves the lemon, almost slicing off her finger, and squeezes it into the salt. Then she rubs the coarse mixture on my feet, just sparing my toes, grinding the cold salt under my arches, over my heels, past my ankles, twisting out hairs mercilessly as she scours up my calves, like a kitchenmaid attacking a soot-blackened pot.

The citrus stings my nostrils and makes my eyes smart, and I am as happy as a martyr in a hairshirt. Then my Magdalen dries my bleached, hairless legs and props me up on my pillow facing east. Cleaned and trussed, confessed and ready, I am a joint of meat salted and put down for winter. And so we begin another day of waiting for my God.

—

Visitors have come and gone, and the curtains are open to the night sky. Bess is sprawling across the chair with her eyes closed. *Keeping watch*, she calls it.

When will you speak in your loud voice, God, bidding me to take up my bed and walk? I must not drift off now. A man must be alert, not lax, at the moment of death. How many have evacuated their bowels? Become, against their will, aroused?

Batter my heart three person'd God, for I—except you enthrall me—never shall be free, nor ever chaste, except you ravish me. My body will fall down without pushing, but my soul will not go up without your pulling. I hold my breath as it rises a little and hovers above my head.

Bess rasps through her broken nose and I return to my body with a thud. How can my soul rise with such braying down below? It might as well be the arch-fiend snorting at my side. Can a man not die without a woman's body taking centre stage? I feel like a supernumerary at my own funeral, a wad of excrescence travelling down an intestinal pipe guarded by Beelzebub herself.

It is nearly dawn and I am in despair that God has been chased off once more. Pegge must think me comatose, for she is an inch away, scrutinizing me like an upturned bug and prodding me with a finger.

Now she plunges her hands into some salve and rubs it briskly on my skin. The scent is provoking—I hope it is not myrrh. My lips move to tell her I am in no danger of sleep now, but no sounds come out. Instead, the lines of a poem jump neatly into my head.

> When I am dead, and doctors know not why,
>   And my friends' curiosity
>   Will have me cut up to survey each part,
>   Then they shall find your picture in my heart.

Made thus to think of you, Ann, I am transported to your bed of sin, the root and fuel of all my sickness. I am laid on a pile of fagots. Desire becomes the bellows, and memory the embers and hot coals.

My fingers itch with remembered pleasure, and that which God would have me remember with shame I remember with delight, imperiling my divine spirit. I am charged with lust, my buttocks flattened against the mattress, hairs rising on my scrotum like grasses fanned by an exotic breeze, my member like a compass leg, leaning and hearkening and growing erect as it draws closer to its mate.

All at once, the sun whips round the courtyard, blazes over the Deanery wall, and spears me through the window. I exult as God begins to split my body and soul apart—two married hemispheres divorcing, a two-sided coin, two hands cemented with a fast balm, two prisoners manacled face to face about to be rent splendidly asunder. Just as I am working out the exact metaphor, for my God is a metaphorical God, and I am an exultant poet composing my own death-song, I apprehend it is not the face of God I see crowned by this blinding aura, but the triumphant face of you, my vengeful wife. God has not *done*, and there is *more*—

Your hair brushes my cheek and your tongue plunges between my lips, pulling me into the hot mouth of death, the labyrinthine end. My fornicating soul is sucked down with my body into a subterranean grave, your toothed and fatal vaginal embrace.

But a priest is stronger than a woman's kiss. I hold out long enough for death to unjoint my soul from my skeleton. My face is anointed with Adam's sweat and Christ's blood, and my death becomes my resurrection. My soul takes flight and my earth-born body plummets to its fate.

18. A NOCTURNAL

Pegge was sitting beside her father's bed, trying to get him to sip water from a cup. Con was eager to return to Barking, but still he lingered, his shroud hung ready on the bedpost. It had been a month since he had worn it for the artist, but he was past admiring his likeness on the coffin-lid.

When he finally died, the lament would sound at Paul's, eclipsing all the other City bells. Women would wash his body, then wrap him in the shroud. The canons would nail him inside a wooden coffin and encase it in a larger one of lead, lowering him into the cold earth between the floor of St Paul's and the ceiling of St Faith's beneath. Even as the pavingstones were levelled, his legend would begin its sanctimonious ascent.

Con was welcome to wash his corpse for burial. It was his live body Pegge wished to care for. She was no longer shocked by its white boniness, nor by the mortal nooks and crannies that fell open to her eyes. No more aware of his incontinence than an infant, he sometimes called Pegge by her mother's name. This evening, although she held his head for him, the water was dribbling out of the cup and down his chin.

Walton came in, saying cheerfully, "He has no need for water now."

She handed him the dripping cup. "Stay with him while I find a sponge."

When she returned, Walton was leaning over her father, telling him that his immortal soul would soon be disrobed of its garment of mortality. Someone—did Walton mean himself?—would press an ear to the Dean's lips and hear a muffled expiration, an easeful *sploosh* like a dipper going into a bucket, as his body melted into earth and his soul vapoured away in glad expectation of the Beatific Vision. At least that was how Walton pictured it to her father, looking as jubilant as if he would be vapouring off himself.

And her father was just as much a fool, coming back from wherever he had been and resting his hand on Walton's wrist, muttering, "I were miserable if I might not die."

Walton scribbled it into his little book. He stopped up the ink-pot just as Bess burst in with enough meat and drink to last her through the night, chasing both Pegge and Walton out.

—

Some hours before dawn, Pegge returned to her father's chamber and shook Bess awake. "Let me sit with him now, since I cannot sleep."

"Nothing goes in the man and nothing comes out." Bess knocked the crumbs off her lap and lurched out the door, her clogs pounding up the narrow flight of stairs to bed.

The room was full of the cool mystery of spilt milk. The front of her father's nightshirt was soaked from Bess trying to get some liquid into him. Pegge felt in her pocket for the sponge. She had been so annoyed at Walton, she had forgotten to give it to Bess. Dipping it in water, she held it to her father's lips. He would not refuse, just as he would not move a finger to hasten his soul's flight, for fear it might be thought self-murder. He was beyond thinking, sucking like an infant, a mindless rhythmical suck.

A thrill was pulsing in the vein at his neck, tempting the hangman's noose or the butcher's axe. His lips invited the suffocator's palm, yet he was rock still, not moving a hair, a breath, an inch, towards the instrument God chose. His body was aligned towards the east and squared—hips even and flat, arms outstretched. His legs were splayed for the rapist's plunge, his feet bared for the carpenter's nails. He had been waiting all night, but his God had not come.

Something must be about to happen, some last words before she witnessed his soul escaping from his body. A formal leave-taking. Some wisdom passed from father to daughter. But what if he never spoke to her again?

"Father, why must you—" She blurted out all the wrongs he had done to her and how she felt and why she had hurt him back in turn. Still he held out for more, and at last she said, "I will be betrothed if you wish it, but I would rather marry for love, as you did."

His eyelids opened and he looked clear through her.

Out of his death-mumble came a sudden clarity. "You were always my favourite." Then his lips snapped back into a narrow line as if they had never moved.

Pegge did not believe what she had heard. He must have meant Con, getting bigger with child each day, or Jo who was studying for the priesthood, or Lucy who had died a virgin, or George who made him laugh, or Bridget or Betty who were more marriageable—but Pegge could not stop the sudden greedy joy that fountained up at being finally, justly, inexplicably, loved.

His body now had a mutinous stink about it and an absurd complacency was spreading across his face. His hands were joined in prayer, ready for the winding-sheet. He would not suck at the sponge Pegge held to his lips, and the thrill was pulsing ominously at his neck.

Pegge rolled up his damp nightshirt and stripped it off. His flesh was the black and white of church tiles, but he was not dead yet. When she ran her hand across the hard lump in his belly and up over his chest, his heart sprang alive, cramping and writhing. Something was dithering around in his rib cage like a boy's stick propelling an iron hoop.

She washed his hands and dried between the fingers with a flannel. At one time, these hands had been as familiar with a woman's body as hers now were with his. She squeezed water over his blackened toes, gauging the pain by the twitch of his eyelids. Holding up his legs one at a time, she washed them, before and behind, above and below. Then, pushing his knees towards his chest, she soaped right up into the crack between his buttocks with the sponge.

"Full nakedness, all joys are due to thee," she sang out. "As souls unbodied, bodies unclothed must be to taste whole joys."

She could recite what she wished, for he could no longer object to his own erotic verse. She rinsed and dried the creases, then let his legs fall slack against the mattress. A passive prone receiving female, he was stuck in a marriage-bed waiting for a God who came and went in the small hours like an adulterous husband.

Why would he not tell her what she wished to know? His smug face sucked the pity right out of her. Later, she would hold herself accountable for each lost minute, but now she warmed an aromatic salve in her palm, rubbing it over his skin from west to east. The blood was rushing out of his arms and legs, which were whitening at an alarming rate, and accumulating in his groin, reddening his skin just where her fingers rested.

She thrust her scented hand between his thighs, right up to the shrunken old plums, and asked tormentingly, "What is love?"

A force that had nothing to do with wedlock, that she knew. Only her father had the answer, for Con had certainly not married for love, nor had Walton, nor anyone else Pegge knew. Bridget and Betty would take any man who would take them. Her father and mother had married for love, caused a scandal that had cost them everything, yet even exiled to a country cottage he had written exquisite love-poems to her. Her father alone knew love, but he was about to bury that knowledge beneath the marble floor of Paul's.

His pulse was slowing to an aboriginal rhythm and from his throat came the *tick tick tick* of stillborn words. She thought she heard *open* and *window* and went to open it, then remembered the thrill at his neck and spun around. The vein had stopped pulsing. As the sun rose in the east, the hairs at his brow became erect and moist, and paleness crept in a feathery wave from his forehead down his throat and chest, chasing the blood back into his heart.

He had awaited the exact moment that it was God's pleasure to pluck him, ripe and willing.

And now he had been plucked.

She could see one eye half-open and the other gone white like a new-baby eye, and knew that the soul had gone straight out the window when her head was turned, that it had snuck past her, darted out like a rebellious schoolboy, and that there was nothing left in that old carcass now. Saw the lips gone slack and the hands freed from their noose of prayer. Saw the baby-eye bulge out as if escaping the socket. Pushed it back in with the ball of her thumb. Leaned over and closed the eyelids, this time for good.

She had turned away and missed the event, the instant his whole life had been hastening towards. She had missed discovering whether the soul was a jelly, or hot and sharp like the tip of a speeding arrow. Would it go straight to God, or into his coffin as worm-meat with his body? Perhaps it had not left through the window at all, but had hidden in the old black hat that Sadie always barked at, for Pegge knew his soul would do any mischief to get itself to heaven.

She pressed her lips against her father's but they were as cool as Sadie's nose. He might have gone to eternal bliss, or limbo, or a much worse place, but he was certainly no longer in his bed. Only a corpse lay where her father had just been.

Sadie pushed the door open a crack and slunk in, reeking of civet. She scratched herself with her back leg and looked quizzically at Pegge, as if asking what mutiny had transpired while absent from her post. Wheezing guiltily, Sadie edged forward to tongue his hand until it shone with dog-spittle. Then, tasting the rot beginning, she forsook his arm and nosed the door back open, bolting down the stairs.

The pain intensified behind Pegge's breastbone and a muscle in her leg began to spasm. She reached out a quivering thumb to touch her father's cheek. It was then that the noises started, first a murky, gulping sound, then a prolonged and awful hiss. Pegge did not care to hear what her father now had to say. She had heard too many of his sermons, and a dead man's verse would hardly scan or rhyme.

The sun filled the room and Con's shoes were tapping up the stairs. Pegge heard her stop on the landing to talk to someone down below. In a minute, the door would be flung open and Pegge would be forced to share her father's death. Wrapping his cloak around her shoulders, she stepped through the window, pushing it firmly shut behind her. She crept along the rooftop and climbed down the ladder he had kept there in case of fire. It was a short drop from the last rung into the courtyard.

Sadie was sitting underneath the apple tree, waiting. Later, Pegge remembered one thing clearly: on her way down Carter lane with Sadie, she had passed a priest in a black frock going in the opposite direction.

19. METAPHYSICS

Pegge hurried along Fleet street and up Chancery lane to ask the bell-ringer at Lincoln's Inn to ring the death knell for her father.

Delighted to outstrip Paul's cathedral, he quoted exuberantly from the dead man. "Any man's death diminishes me, because I am involved in mankind. Never send to know for whom the bell tolls," he lowered his voice for emphasis, "it tolls for Donne." He pulled the exact number of strokes, no fewer, no more, putting out his palm smartly at the end.

Pegge emptied her pocket to pay him. She could not go back to the Deanery for fear her father's spirit would return to its dwelling place. She shook out the folds of her skirts, ridding them of any grey hairs, nail parings, and scales of skin she might have carried from his deathbed so she would not tempt his soul to hunt her down. He once said that if he had lost an arm in the east, a leg in the west, some blood in the north, and some bones in the south, his soul would circumnavigate the globe and in an instant arm, leg, blood, and bones—eastern, western, northern, and southern body—would be recompacted into one. She had no intention of standing between a soul and a lost body part, not if that soul was as zealous as her father's.

Pegge drank from public conduits and stole food from market stalls, hardly knowing what she ate. That night, she curled up with Sadie in her father's cloak in the narrow passage where Jane Shore had met her noble lover. From this trysting-spot, just below her own window, Pegge could look into the brightly lit Deanery and watch the inhabitants preparing for her father's funeral.

On the following day the cathedral was so full nobody noticed Pegge standing in the choir loft for a better view. Men elbowed to the front to pay tribute with their verses, climaxed by a piece of surpassing length and folly that claimed the Dean had died a sacred martyr. She knew it was Izaak Walton's by the inept rhymes, and by the author himself, trumpeting his verses loudly, then bowing almost to the floor at the applause.

After the eulogies, a file of men entered the Deanery to collect the rings and pictures left them by her father. Through the window, Pegge watched Con fold linens into baskets to take back to Barking, her mourning cut to show her belly proud with child. When the carriage was loaded, Con led Parrot out herself and tied the reins to the back. Mr Harvey helped his wife climb up and they set off. Only Bess remained inside the Deanery, packing the last of the family's goods. She would probably spin out the task as long as she could, in case Pegge wandered back.

Pegge crisscrossed the City for hours, listening to lost rivers running far below the streets and to buried pipes bringing fresh water from the north. They ran where Izaak Walton had showed her, silent and blue, like veins beneath the skin. Not all the water was hard and sweet. Some drained out of the hot baths where people cleansed themselves of sweat and grime, then filtered down through boneyards before springing out in rivulets a quarter-mile ahead. Waste water ran down streets into drains, spilling into sewers, and from thence into buried rivers which emptied themselves into the muddy Thames.

At Clerk's Well, Pegge drank thirstily, then unlaced her boots and rinsed her feet. By now, the flagstones would be laid down over her father's grave. She set off with Sadie towards the cathedral, around the Dean's windy corner, past the blocks of marble waiting in the masons' yard, through the Dean's doorway, and down the nave into the depth of Paul's. The fresh earth pressed into the seams on the choir floor told her where her father had been buried. Crawling into the niche where his effigy would be erected, she fell asleep, wrapped in her father's cloak and holding Sadie in her arms.

—

Pegge and Sadie had been up since dawn without a crust or bone. Waiting on the west side of the Fleet, Pegge eyed the naked buttocks hanging down through the privies suspended over the eastern bank. Threads of conversation sailed across the ditch, as mundane as the oysters at the Horn Tavern and the serving-maids at the Kingshead. Was the King ill or simply in distemper? Which priest would he name as the new Dean of Paul's? Surely no new man could sermonize like Donne?

Finally, a pair of buttocks rose and a privy emptied. Pegge stepped across the footbridge and took a seat.

Back outside, she walked the outskirts of Fleet gaol, where tenements clustered cheek by jowl. All the faces were winter-white, as if the blood had burrowed deep into the flesh. The dogs were more congenial with their country ways, nipping heels and sniffing one another's hindquarters. A woman overtook Pegge with a peculiar gait, her strides too long for her skirts, a lump in her throat like Adam's undigested apple. *An androgyne*, Pegge thought, *a creature complete unto itself that has no need of marrying and no desire for children.*

Now an emaciated cheek, sharp beard, and hollow eye were bearing down upon Pegge, putting her in mind of her dead father. Some playful dust blew his words into her ear—*consider upon what ground you tread*. She walked a few more steps in iambic time, John foot, then Ann foot, and the voice spoke again, as quick as the living. *Every puff of wind may blow the father into the son's eye*, the voice insisted, *or the wife into her husband's, or his into hers, or both into their children's, or their children's into both. Every grain of dust that flies here is a piece of me.* His soul must be perambulating, whirling about her—undergoing metempsychosis or just stirring up trouble. She felt a breath on her neck and then a blast of hot tobacco on her cheek, and she knew she must keep vigilant, for his soul was as likely to take up residence in a neighbouring onion as in a travelling post-horse or spider.

Pegge had hoped to steal a loaf from Paul's canons, but she found their brewery and bakehouse shut up to honour the late Dean, so she trudged north with Sadie close behind. One of the dog's legs was beginning to drag, and a damp weighed on the air, a suffocating wool that muffled sound. No one seemed to be at large, except a rat shuttling for cover a few yards ahead.

Past Bishopsgate, a cart drew up and a man jumped off, then pried up a cellar door. Sea-coal tumbled below ground, sending up a choking cloud. Worse than the hot stink of tar around the wharves, the coal dust hit Pegge's empty stomach like a fist. All around her, chimneys were expelling smoke from roofs that jutted out so far they blocked the light. Now that dusk was falling, the vileness sucked up by the heat of day would be drawn down to blacken the nostrils and chill the brain. Each morning of her life, the City had been filmed in this airborne soot, a fuliginous mist that corroded even iron. This noxious fog had defiled even the sacred stones of Paul's and coated her father's auriculas in wintry slime.

Pegge crossed under Bedlam gate in search of water, but found the spout tied shut against interfering hands. The garden grew foodstuffs in a warmer season, but now only stinking, half-eaten cabbages were strewn about. When she was young, her brothers had brought her here to laugh at the inmates and throw a coin if their antics merited it. Now the inhabitants were being herded, coughing, snuffing, barking, spitting, back into the cottages. A keeper was cajoling a wild-man to follow him with a bun nailed to the end of a bamboo, but before long even that diversion was locked inside.

The coal-man entered the grounds looking for sport.

Seeing no entertainment to be had, he pushed near to take a look at Pegge, who was bending under the spout to collect a few drops on her tongue. How had the dark crept up so quickly? The air was brindled, a pewter fog, which no sane person should be out in. The man was so close she smelt his rotting teeth and saw the scar that joined his twisted lip directly to his ear.

He spat out a gob close to her boots. "Who are you, then? Did they forget to lock you up this night?"

"I am the daughter of the just-dead Dean of Paul's." She backed up towards one of the buildings for safety.

This seemed to whet his appetite, rather than the reverse, for a crude hand gesture conveyed what he would like to do to her. Without taking his eyes off her, he leaned one grimy arm against the wall, preventing her from escaping, and groped at the buttons on his breeches. He pissed leisurely, sending out a spray with a rank odour, then grasped her wrist abruptly and pinned her against the wall. Her brothers had once pointed out a cottage where a mad gentlewoman had been confined and used by various men against her will in gruesomely contorted postures. Perhaps it was this very cottage, cold and slippery against her back. She wished her brothers were beside her, telling their stories now.

Just then a torch appeared at Bedlam gate and out of the brindle came a fond, familiar face, the sweet long nose of Parrot, her father's mare, come to carry her to safety. But as the fog parted and the mare drew closer, Pegge saw it was only a tall man with a brown cloak wrapped round against the damp. Parrot's sweet nose dissolved into the man's, although the eyes—a welcome chestnut brown—were indisputably the mare's.

The stranger dismissed the coal-man with a curt warning that sent him running. Everything had become too loud in her head, every word a shout, like Bess's clogs pounding on the wooden floor when Pegge was still in bed. Shaking from the vulgar encounter, she tried to brush the filthy coal-marks from her clothes.

The torch-boy held out a fragrant parcel. "The Dean's old servant said to tell you there are six more waiting for you in her kitchen."

Inside the cheesecloth was a fresh mutton pastry. Turning to hide her brimming tears, Pegge gulped it down, then wiped the crumbs from her lips.

"I was at the Deanery speaking to your uncle when this boy came to tell us he had seen you," the stranger said. "Do you not remember me, Margaret Donne? I am Mr Bowles, who may be your husband hereafter. I hoped that your father had spoken to you before—" He found it too indelicate to say.

Pegge could not answer, thankful for the night fog that occluded her complexion.

"I have just learnt the terms of your father's Will. Your uncle showed me a codicil that pertains to you."

What if her value had fallen upon her father's death, like currency when the monarch was dethroned? It was too much to expect Uncle Grymes to make good marriages for all three daughters. Bridget and Betty would be easier to dispose of. By the time their uncle began to negotiate for Pegge, she would be as unmarriageable as Bess.

Had Mr Bowles just said something?—she could not tell. How many hours had passed since her father died? She did not even know what day it was, or month, only that her body was stiff from sleeping on cold stones.

"I see you will not ask me for the terms," Mr Bowles continued awkwardly, "but I must tell you just the same. *Her portion to be £750 if she weds Mr Bowles of Clewer and £20 if she of her own fantastical brain rejects him.*"

Fantastical brain. She had no doubt the words were her father's. What choice had she now—to embrace a man, or to embrace only penury and shame? If unmarried, Pegge would be forced to live with Constance after all and be nursemaid to a brood of ill-bred children.

Pegge watched Mr Bowles fumbling with the fastener on his cloak, as if he had not yet mastered all its workings. "Can it be true you are a man of science?" she asked.

"I am William Bowles," he admitted. "My brother George is the botanographist, the discoverer of milk-white lady's smock."

"I believe the Dean had in mind your brother," she said. *The clever twin,* her father had called him.

"George is too ill to return from Venice. The physic," he cast his eyes down, his words low, "quicksilver."

The Venetian pox, Pegge guessed, from a night-walker. To spare Mr Bowles, she only nodded.

"No lady should be forced to marry such a man. Your father would have despised the union."

Perhaps so, but her father's poems provided ample evidence of his own transgressions, speaking of quicksilver sweats and sick tapers which winked when lovers were too ill to couple. However, Mr Bowles was not the man to confide this to, for he had the look of an innocent in such matters.

"By law I must marry the man my father chose or be reduced to £20 all told. I would hardly attract a fishmonger for that sum."

"Your uncle believes I am the Mr Bowles intended and there is no need to tell him otherwise unless you wish." He added this sweetening to the bargain: "I am five minutes the elder. I will be Groom of the King's Wardrobe when my father dies, and all his lands at Clewer go with me."

She ducked her head and smiled to herself. Cucumbers and turnips would suit her remarkably. By this odd turn-about, her father had provided for her better than he had for Constance.

Mrs Bowles of Clewer. The name Bowles was not what she would have picked for resonance of language. Clewer, was it? That was not so bad. On the Thames somewhat past Richmond, if her geography was right, high enough for carp and gentlemanly pike. Grander, she was sure, than Constance Harvey's Abury Hatch, and Pegge would rather go anywhere than Barking. No sea-coal would foul the air, and there would be space for Sadie and for Bess, with her vast stores of useful salves and potions.

Pegge's own brother George had wanted to be a pig-farmer, for he said that pig-farming had come down in their mother's blood from her father, the squire of Loseley park. Before George boarded ship at Portsmouth, Pegge stood with him at Smithfield market, admiring the breeding stock. Yes, she would keep pigs, as her grandfather had done.

"But why should you wish to take your brother's place?"

"The woman my father has chosen for me is not to my liking. She is too"—good breeding tied his tongue in knots but a greater fear untied it—"forward in her longings."

Pegge imagined a rural Constance, exuding musk and crowned by tangled locks, a hairy springe to trap plain country birds. No doubt whole villages, whole boroughs, complained of the woman's unnatural, insatiable lust.

He looked queasy at the prospect. "The match has not yet been concluded," he said, "and with evidence of my brother's evil—for he has foolishly spelt out his agony in letters to me—I shall persuade my father to let me marry you in his stead."

Her very boyishness was now in her favour. She had grown small, high breasts and her hairs were indeed sprouting in her armpits and on her more quiet place below. Even now, she felt them rupturing the skin like new feathers in a fledgling eager to take flight. According to Bess, marriage would cure the green-sickness, which had turned Pegge's voice rich and plummy, a fearsome thing, and made her breasts throb at night, provoking startling dreams. Worse, it had made her covet Con's old under-garments, turning this way and that in front of a looking-glass, making unhappy comparisons with her sister's ample breasts and buttocks.

Mr Bowles did not look gluttonous, but time would stimulate his appetite. Soon his will would be wholly hers by power of love and they would learn to pleasure one another, for even the gentle Mr Harvey had been able to get Con with child. Kissing and embracing were the best philtre, the sight of naked parts stirring even ordinary husbands to extraordinary, burning lust. As for herself, she could tell by the turn of Mr Bowles's ankle that he had a comely leg that would well suit her. And his arm—it would curve softly round her to drive away the perverse longings that had transported her at night.

At one of her father's last sermons in Paul's, she was taking notes when his pointed boot began to tap. As she shrank into the bench, the rhythm shot up his calf, his thigh, his torso, pulsed down his arm, and emerged in a hand quavering with the gravity of the theme. Every so often, he rose up on his toes to delay the climax, the vowels resonating in his throat, his lips in the service of a deadly grin, retracting so far to the sides she thought they would snap, until suddenly they sprang back and spat out the last few potent words like black tobacco juice.

Pegge had squirmed in horror, wondering how much longer he could keep up the performance. That was when she noticed one of the Bowles twins. His eyes fastened on the Dean's peculiar lips, the young man was absentmindedly buttoning and unbuttoning his jacket in time to the Dean's oratory. A periodic sentence. An absolute. A fragment for emphasis. A rhetorical question. Another button done up and undone. Now she knew which twin it had been: William Bowles, secure in his buttoning.

Sadie's noises had drawn Mr Bowles into Bedlam garden, where the dog was devouring rotten vegetables. As he tried to coax her up, Sadie gave out a gaseous belch and sank even deeper, rivalling the cabbages in sulphurous fumes. Unmindful of the mud, Mr Bowles took off his cloak and lay it under the dog's head, pressing his hands along her bloated flank. Sadie snapped at him, but he did not flinch.

"Your dog is sick, Margaret Donne."

Margaret rolled softly off his tongue, an exquisite sound. Pegge lay her cheek against Sadie to hide her face. "She has eaten too much on an empty belly."

"I know dogs and this one is ill. See how she salivates? A dog should not burp. I will need a tube or a needle to deflate her stomach." He called to the torch-boy, who was waiting at the gate, "Find a barrow for us and you shall have another farthing!"

As Mr Bowles worked his hands along the dog again, his hair gleamed, as sleek as Parrot's tail after Pegge had groomed it, and she saw herself in the row of ornate buttons bisecting his chest. How must she seem to such a man, covered in the filth of her late wanderings? Even her face was coated in grime. And yet, the wonder was, he had not spoken of it.

"I have been much in my grief of late," she confessed.

"Such great love becomes you," he said simply. "Perhaps your dog is pining for the late Dean also."

At this, a sad, grieving belch came out of Sadie and the burps took on a more contented tone.

Mr Bowles patted the dog on the head. "The old maid-servant is waiting for you at the Deanery. I will buy you the best funeral-cloth, tinged with purple, and will cut it for you myself. When your mourning is over and you are Mrs Bowles—"

"I shall still be John Donne's daughter. My father became a priest on the very day that I was born."

Mr Bowles considered this. "A priest is melancholy by trade," he agreed, "but his dog and daughter have no need to be."

All day long, her insides had been cramping and her thighs aching deep into the bone. Now, between her legs, she felt the first drops of moisture, like water skimming off a petal in the rain. At last the promised blood began to flow, bringing the release she had long craved. Everything from crown to toe was itching and prickling. She was finally fertile, like her sisters. Now she could sour the wine and make the meat go off as well as Con, even tarnish Mr Bowles's hereditary silver.

The boy came back along the passageway, balancing a small cart and his torch adeptly. Mr Bowles laid his cloak on top of the conveyance and bent with the utmost gentleness to lift the convalescent dog.

TONGUES

—

1631–1667

20. KINGDOM

William, Pegge discovered on their wedding night on Lucy's eve, had wiry black hairs on his chest that matched the beard he was growing in imitation of his sovereign, Charles. Though he was often at the King's Wardrobe in London, he agreed that Pegge could stay at Clewer.

Arriving at the estate for the first time, she announced happily, "I shall want to keep pigs if I am to live in the country."

He replied, "You may keep *horses* if you will, and certainly there is no harm in dogs, though they are healthiest if kept in kennels."

Bess came to Clewer with Pegge, but kept herself apart from the other servants, making much of the fact that she was from the City. Spurning the livery that William gave her, she wore her threadbare skirts from the Deanery instead. She liked nothing better than to sit outside with a horsehair blanket over her knees, watching Pegge come and go. Though Bess complained about Sadie's fleas, she let the dog lie across her feet when she thought no one was watching.

On Lady Day in their second year at Clewer, Pegge was alarmed to find Bess still in bed at noon. Something had happened in the night, blinding her but restoring her sense of smell. She asked to be carried outside each day so she could smell the earth, and died in her old chair, a week later, holding Pegge's hand underneath the branches of the ancient yew.

Sadie sank at once into a dreadful gloom. Hiding under Bess's bed, she refused to come out to eat or drink and was dead within three days. Pegge buried Sadie herself, then sat in Bess's old chair beneath the yew with the soil clinging to her hands. Even with dusk falling, Pegge could not bring herself to go inside. William brought her a young dog from his kennel, wrapped in the horsehair blanket, but Pegge told him angrily to take it back. When he returned without the dog, placing the blanket across her shoulders, she threw her arms around his neck and begged him to forgive her.

—

With Bess gone, Pegge could not bear to order the servants about, so she let them run things as they chose. Before long, she had discovered the extent of their labyrinth behind the hidden doors. Estimating where they were by their footsteps, she travelled between two points unseen, annoying William by springing without warning out of walls.

Now she was lying belly-up on the bed, admiring the play of sunlight on the coffered ceiling and twisting her hair between her fingers, for it had grown down around her shoulders.

She had taken a liking to this chamber because it got the morning sun, and claimed it as her own. If they must occupy separate bedchambers, as William's parents had done, and his grandparents before them, then at least her room had a servants' door connecting it to William's.

Even at ten o'clock she felt no urge to rise. Half-dressed, she fell back in the lazy stretch of light spilling through the window. If she stayed in bed long enough, William might come to collect her, for she had heard him arriving late the night before.

She pressed her thumb into her navel, detecting a tremor well beneath the flesh. No lover had yet protested his undying love to *her* in verse, no man had called *her* bed the world's umbilicus, its very centre. She inspected her thumb—were there really twenty minuscule lines, one for each year? She longed for her womb to swell so that her navel would shrink and disappear entirely.

When they were first married, William's fingers traversed her body, bringing the nerves to the skin, the skin to his lips, but of late when he arrived at Clewer he was tired and incurious, his curiosity spent on pinking, vizards, Flanders lace, and collars.

Now voices became louder in the corridor, the door opened, bolts of cloth were stacked on top of one another, steps receded. Pegge stayed motionless while William's heels clicked across the floorboards towards her. She could feel his eyes upon her naked arms and throat.

"What are you pretending, Pegge? Are you melancholy? Your cheeks are hardly sallow. You must tell me at once if you are melancholy."

"I am not *melancholy*, William. I am warming myself in the sun."

"You must go downstairs and make something of our servants, or go out-of-doors, you have a horse to ride."

"And suck on country pleasures childishly?"

Now he was hurt, for he had recognized her father's words. "You cannot live inside a poem, Pegge. Am I too dull a husband? You knew I was no poet when you married me. If you must sleep in this old bed, you will need new bed-hangings, for these are mildewed." He pulled out some lengths of cloth. "Which do you like best? This has just come from the Indies." He smoothed out the nap, then rubbed it with his fingers. "It would be deeper if over-dyed with indigo."

Rolling onto her belly, she tugged out a muslin so thin she could scarcely feel the weight. She draped it over her body for the sun to catch and toy with.

"That will not do for bed curtains. You will want something heavier, like velvet." He unwound some yardage from a bolt, then from another. "What colour will you have? An umber or brown ochre? There are some fine reds and Turkey browns to be got from madder. This shade is almost as rich as your hair. That is only from Essex," he said as she picked up a yellow swatch. "At least choose a saffron from Arabia."

"Will you dye this muslin for me, William? I want it butter-yellow like the sun. Come and lie under it and see how light it feels."

"It is full day. The servants may come in, even the cat is here. The steward will soon be back to carry out the bolts."

"There will be time enough for caution when we are

old. Some lovers spend whole days inside their bedchambers. Push my cabinet against the door." She pulled at his laces teasingly. "This jacket is so dreary. Madder, is it, saddened with black? What colours shall we have in the nursery? All dark satins and brocades?"

He did not answer, but ran his fingers along her pale stocking as if working out how the silken thread was spun. She took shallow breaths until he drew his hand away.

"You were in the City a fortnight this time, William. How am I to conceive at such a rate? My belly cannot grow fat on such a diet."

One side of his face had gone completely red, right down the sinews of his throat. "I fear I am not well."

"Come, you are well enough for this." She took his hand and drew it higher up her leg.

He had never undressed her or begged to be undressed himself, never slipped his hands under the back of her skirt, nor sent the maid out when she assisted Pegge at night. He had never even come to her bed with his hair mussed and his breeches already off.

William removed his hand and turned his face away. "I do not know what is ailing me. I am blue and swollen with pain."

"With *love*, William. A man should swell with impatience for his wife."

William sat down to undo his breeches. He had invented a new catch for the waist, since a gentleman, he said, was only as secure as his front-fastener. To release it, he should only have to flick his thumb. But this one was not working as designed, for William's thumb was bleeding.

"Let me help," Pegge said, reaching over to squeeze the clasp. "I do not think a man's breeches need to be quite so hard to open in his wife's bedchamber."

William stepped out of his breeches and shoes, then stripped off his hose, but when he got himself upon the bed, he simply lay on his back and looked up at the ceiling.

"William, this will not do. You have been in London more often than at Clewer. I know my horse better than I do my husband. And my mare, at least, has foaled."

Mr Harvey had already given Con three sons. Pegge's sister had brought the little boys to Clewer and displayed them on an upholstered bench. It was the baby, with his long lashes and tiny clever fingers, who had won Pegge's heart. When she blew on his stomach, he trilled with laughter, making her ache with longing for a child.

She ran her toe along William's leg, from heel to thigh, but still he did not curve his arm to pull her closer. Soon he was out of bed, doubled over to inspect his pain.

"Must you worry so, William? Is it worry for the King? Are his shirts the wrong colour? Are his tapestries still on the loom, his tents behindhand in the making?"

His face was lopsided in misery at this teasing. She sat beside him and tidied his hair with her fingers, but nothing came of it and soon they were obliged to rise and dress and take their dinner.

She saw that William could not enjoy his food. It stuck in a throat made drier by Pegge's attempt to show a sympathy she did not feel. How could their love survive such dieting? All of her father's poetry had now flown from her head, and nothing but brown meats adorned her plate. William's complaints were not endearing, everything too tart to be endured, too rough to swallow. She filled his glass with sweet wine, but when he took a gulp to wash down the dry beef, he spat it out, proclaiming it too sour to drink, the worst he had ever tasted.

—

William had orchid-fever, a sickness that made a child of a man and might, if it ran its course, render him unable to sire children. The swellings at his throat and between his legs heralded the illness. Soon he lay in a dark room with a compress on his groin that did nothing, Pegge knew, but press upon his pain and weigh upon his mind.

After several weeks, the swellings subsided and William paid a visit to her chamber, fraught with hesitations and meanderings. Pegge's coaxings could not always bring him hard again, but soon that too was overcome, and William was in better appetite in bed. Pegge still had not conceived, although Bridget, who had married the same year, had just given birth to a second child by Thomas Gardiner. Even little Betty was betrothed and would no doubt soon bear triplets.

The doctor came, deliberating while taking healthy doses of Canary wine. In his opinion, the mumps could not make an Englishman sterile. He concluded that Pegge's womb was rebellious and that William took his manhood far too seriously.

"Do not enter that race frowningly," was his advice, as he held out his cup for refilling.

Finally Pegge conceived, with the help of powdered oats, sage juice, and sitting in a tub of scarlet dye and ashes, the sight of which brought William first to tears and then to healing laughter. Enamoured of his own lustfulness, he plunged his arms into the dye-bath and carried Pegge, lubricious with colour, all the way to her bed. Whether it was Pegge who was cured, or William made less serious, they did not bother to determine.

Once she was with child, William became confidently amorous, stroking her swollen belly and laying his ear against it at the slightest invitation. The midwife came to listen as well, pronouncing it a large and active infant. Designing voluminous garments for Pegge, William neglected the King's Wardrobe for weeks at a time and gave up his work on a fastener to keep men's breeches securely latched, calling it a useless trinket.

When Pegge went into labour, the midwife chased William out, told him to go outside and shoot at something instead of troubling his wife, who had enough to do. After the labour was over, and the large and active child was finally out, Pegge held and nursed her first-born, then fell asleep, exhausted.

She was awakened by a conversation outside the door— the midwife's reassuring words, then William asserting he would go in to see his wife alone. His hose and shoes were muddy and his hair dishevelled, showing the first threads of grey. He would not look Pegge in the eye, but held up a peculiar stalk of flowers.

"A satyr flower," Pegge said contentedly.

He brought it closer for her to examine. Each of the

seven flowers on the spike had three violet petals and, hanging at the groin, a fourth misshapen one. She was surprised to see an insect still nestled in a bloom. It became motionless, thinking to avoid detection as she drew the blossom closer. She cupped her hand to trap the bee, discovering to her delight that she had caught a brown-and-yellow petal in its masquerade.

"They are bee-orchids," William said in a rush, "from the fens beyond the marsh, about three miles upriver. Once when I was a child I found them at this very time of year. And today—" He looked at the empty place beside her on the bed, too embarrassed to seek further.

She rescued the quivering orchids from his fist. "Your daughter is in her cradle. Go quietly and pull back the cover and you shall see a giant infant with a ruddy face. Since I have done all the work, I have named her Margaret, after me."

—

The thud of Pegge's morocco heels was muffled by the rush mats on the floor. The peacock shoes had deepened to a saturated blue, the result not of variegated dyeing but an accidental soaking in the river years before, and her old morning-gown was badly stained from eating red fruit in her bed. These were Pegge's clothes for when she was alone, gliding like a servant through the dark.

An hour earlier, the throbbing had begun under her left ear. Then the cramps started, announcing her fleurs, and she knew she would get no sleep until the blood began.

Her holy week, she called it. This time she left her candle in her chamber. Last month a servant had found her asleep at dawn with a pool of melted wax beside her, having almost set the flannel-room on fire.

Slipping her feet out of the old shoes, she crept barefoot along the gallery to William's study. Climbing to the top rung of the ladder, she looked for the dust streaks that told her where he had hidden the new book. At dusk the previous day, the folio had arrived wrapped in the fleur-de-lis paper used by John Marriot's shop in Fetter lane. Finding it now, she pushed the other books together to hide the gap and climbed down to read it at William's table.

Lighting the candle, she opened the book and discovered that her father's face was misshapen on the frontispiece, his left eye where his right should have been. His features had been transposed by an engraver too lazy to check his work against the original. It had taken her brother Jo nine years to gather eighty sermons into one disordered, bloated volume. But there was also something else inside the folio—something that had caused William to hide the book from Pegge when it arrived—a *Life and Death of Dr Donne*.

Izaak Walton's pious fiction began with her father's birth and schooling. *The age*, according to Walton, *had brought forth another Picus Mirandola*. After a good deal of nonsense the printer should have struck out, Walton plodded to the apex, his account of her father's death, written as if he were right there at the bedside. *In the last hour of his last day, his body melted away and vapoured into spirit, his soul having, I verily believe, some revelation of the beatifical vision.*

Walton seemed to have forgotten that he was elsewhere, still in his own bed or walking north for his morning's fishing. *As his soul ascended, and his last breath departed from him,* Walton wrote, *he closed his own eyes and then disposed his hands and body into such a posture as required not the least alteration by those that came to shroud him.* As if a dead man could reach up and close his own eyelids! Much had happened between the thrill pulsing at her father's neck and his soul making good its escape that even Pegge could not recall in detail.

Walton had not been just a milksop and gossip-monger, a hanger-on at great men's deathbeds. He was much more than that: a damager of reputations, a fulsome biographer who could not tell art from truth, a parasite—her mind was sparking—a writer of gross fabrications, who took the rind of great men's lives and threw away the meat.

Pegge had read the folio in a sweat and now the moon was riding low. She wanted to smash the book against the table, the floor, the window, whatever was hard and close, but she could not risk waking the household and being accused of harbouring a dangerous melancholy.

A woman could write a fiction as well as a man. Why did men always begin their stories at the start? Closing the folio, she spun it round.

She flipped up the lid of William's ink-pot. Her fingers greeted the quill after a long absence, relearning grip and stance. She tested ascenders and descenders, loops and angulations, her ribs draped over the table, her left ear scraping, eye pursuing nib. The ink was of good quality, thicker than water, as viscous as blood, evoking the east, intoxicant. She had learnt the quality of ink from a master,

John Donne, but it was ten years since she had toiled under his strict eye. This work would be more pleasurable. She wrote the first words boldly in the white between the lines. *Lips, legs,* and *arms:* small words that fitted into the spaces left by men.

More words quickened within her and the nib skittered across the page, explosive, blurting out syllables, quarter-words, half-words, then galloping phrases that outpaced sense. By daybreak, the pages were wet and black with William's ink.

Pegge let the leaves flutter closed and the words smear. Tomorrow, she would get up before dawn to mix ink of her own. She was stretching her arms, interlocking her fingers above her head, when someone moved in the door frame. For an instant, she could not see who it was. Then she recognized William with their daughter close behind him, mouth caressing her thumb, eyes darting to her mother's naked feet. A small arm cradled Pegge's peacock shoes.

A woman might read a book, surely, if she could not sleep? And where better to find an improving book than in her husband's study? William could not tell which folio it was, nor see her naked feet from where he stood. Of all things, this would most annoy him, even more than the frayed morning-gown he tolerated up to the hour of noon. She felt the blood begin to gather and drip along the inside of her thigh, then the familiar release as the first spots hit her feet. She willed him not to come near enough to see the spots, or the book she had defaced with ink.

An accusation began to distort his lips. Perhaps he would threaten to send her to stay with Constance, as he had threatened once when she was wilful but had not the heart to do. He began angrily, a husband's privilege, waving his hands in the air, but gentled his tone when he remembered the child, who was now chewing on a peacock shoe. He told Pegge to go into the breakfast room and eat a good breakfast—she had never in her life been told to eat a bad one—and then to retire and dress and find some useful task with which to occupy herself. And if she could not find a useful task, to pretend to do so for her children's sake.

As soon as William turned his back to leave, Pegge tucked the morning-gown between her legs to soak up the blood. The little girl took the wet shoe from her mouth and held it out. This daughter seldom smiled, but sometimes she made a little out-of-tune hum that told Pegge a good deal more than words.

"Margaret, would you like to wear my shoes today?"

The child nodded solemnly.

"We will make a game of it, but first take this book to my chamber and push it underneath my old cabinet. Then come to me in the breakfast room as swiftly as you can. And do not let a single person spy you on the way."

—

Pegge was in the kitchen with the children, beating eggs in a metal bowl, for today was the day of the picnic that Margaret, who was now ten, had planned. It was to go ahead in spite of the darkening sky. William had said so himself, forced into it after discovering that Pegge had stolen eggs from the moorhens' nests. He had made such a fuss, with such a red face, accusing her of spoiling his autumn shoot—*How many birds will hatch out now?* he'd cried in rage—that he had to agree to the picnic or else the children would have pummelled him with their fists.

Now he was at the fireplace, running his finger over the mantelpiece where the royal initials had been sanded off. "It was a day like today, a wretchedly cold day, four months ago," he related. "They say that wombs miscarried and men swooned. I myself had palpitations of the heart. When the axe was poised, King Charles asked—I thought my ears misheard—he asked, *Is my hair well?*" William looked up at the ceiling as if it were a metaphysical question.

Margaret pressed a damp finger in the scraped sugar and sucked it. "Did he wish it better combed?"

"Why no," William said in surprise, "he wanted it safely inside his cap, so when the head was held up as is custom—"

"What custom?" asked Will, collecting the egg-shells Pegge had tossed on the floor.

"Streaming with blood," Margaret hissed at her brother.

Did William think this a suitable tale for children? Pegge poured the scalded milk on the eggs, stirring all the while, added a fistful of sugar, then threw the basin on the grate, attacking it with the wooden spoon. As Emma walked in, dangling her cap by its ties, Margaret's finger dove back into the sugar.

"Soldiers carried hooks and grapples," William continued, his back now comfortably to the fire, "in the event the King did not go willingly. Before dawn, they burst into the Wardrobe and plundered the black velvet, dragging it all along the street, a silk velvet from Italy, the finest I have ever seen. The blood," Margaret and Will stopped what they were doing to hear better, "fountained like a saint's, a Prussian blue. The people dipped their handkerchiefs in it. My sleeve—"

Pegge stared at the custard coating the back of the spoon.

"My boots!" Emma demanded, pointing at her stockinged feet.

"William, surely this story—" Hearing Cook's voice in the larder, Pegge pulled the basin off the grate and covered it. "Margaret, do not stand idly, help Emma find her boots."

Now they were on their way, all but William and the baby, who was sleeping in the nursery. Pegge was carrying the pudding, with Will by her side. Behind her trailed Emma and Plum, who had shamelessly deserted her puppies for the fête, her swollen nipples almost dragging on the earth. Ahead, Margaret lifted Isabel over the ditch that kept the deer from Pegge's garden.

"A pudding cannot be a spotted-dog if it has no spots," Will complained, still smarting because they had not been able to get into Cook's store of raisins.

"Then you must pick some fruit to put in it," said Pegge. "If there are berries this early in the year, Plum will find them."

Last year, she had seen the dog eating berries the way a clever horse ate thistles, drawing her lips back to avoid the thorns in a way that reminded Pegge of her father.

Pegge assessed the clouds obscuring the sun, then Margaret's determined back. Margaret's scissors were hanging proudly from an eastern girdle, which her father had brought her from the City. She was trampling a path through the wet grass so that little Isabel, who was in charge of the wooden spoon, could get through on her short legs.

"I see a raven," Will said, then more doubtfully, as he neared the bird digging a hole in the earth, "or a crow."

"A rook," Margaret corrected, pointing to the old elm, "from that rookery. A rook has a skirt like Mother's, not hose like a man."

"Cracking eggs, cracking eggs," Emma sang out, imitating a raven.

Will plodded behind Margaret, waving his stick and glaring at her worsted stockings as if he wanted to poke a hole in them. "Women wear hose, too."

Pegge saw him take a practice thrust at his sister's leg. "Would you carry the basin for a while, Will? Hold the handles carefully, it is very heavy. It came from your grandfather's church plate."

A hush followed, the same hush that fell whenever she invoked her father, as if William had cautioned his children never to be drawn into this particular web. Pegge thought she saw a kindred glance pass between Will and Margaret.

Will took the basin gravely and quickened his steps, veering towards the Lebanon cedar where the servants were setting up a table. He stumbled, then righted himself without mishap, glancing apprehensively at Pegge. Now he gripped more tightly, fixing his eyes on the ground ahead, his legs moving like springs to keep the basin steady.

—

Pegge could not remember whether her own mother had ever been annoyed with her. As she grew up, Pegge fed hungrily on her brothers' memories of Drury cottage, where they lived before the Deanery. Their father was mostly gone, and whenever he returned, he ushered in a strange quiet. *Doctor Theologo*, George liked to call him, running quickly out of range.

Once, as Jo and George told the story, there had been angry words in the cottage and their father strode outside, dangling their mother in his arms as lightly as if her bones were hollow. The boys said a torpor had poisoned her body, making her pull out her hair. The little that was left was stringy and unpinned. As their father propped her in a chair and put a stool under her swollen legs, the word *dropsy* fell out of the air, moist and ripe like a windfall from the pippin-tree.

The boys stopped running with their pointed sticks, wary of the lesson their father was setting up for them. In the garden, it was unlikely to be Greek or Latin. A lesson in deportment, possibly, or grooming? Perhaps he would call their new servant to pin up Ann's hair. They knew they were to make something of themselves now that he was Dr Donne.

"You must stop this wasting away," he said to their mother, trying to fasten her hair himself.

"You cannot pretend I am of any use to you. You do not even come to my bed anymore."

The boys knew what this meant, or so they said.

"And what man would? It is more of a sickbed than a marriage-bed."

"I am always with child, and you always came before. You are tired of me."

"We had not one another at so cheap a rate that we should ever be weary of one another."

This witticism was chiselled in her brothers' memory. Pegge heard them recite it again and again when their father was out of hearing.

"You forget I am a priest now and must come only when you can conceive. Why not admire how healthily your children grow? Surely they are as worthy of your attention as those misbegotten tulips. Here they are, bearing weapons like half-clothed Indians in the heat. Look at them, Ann— open your eyes, your mouth—speak to them—tell them to dress like citizens of Europe!"

The children stared at their mother's blancmange face. She looked much paler next to the flowers than she did inside. Only the centres of her eyes were dark, like mulberries.

"Play!" he shouted at the children. "Let her see you playing! Why are you lining up silently in a row? Can you never run about and enjoy yourselves when I tell you to?"

—

Will was now quite far ahead, resting the basin on the ground and peeling back the cloth to inspect the pudding. Little Isabel had stopped in the marsh orchids with her spoon, looking so intensely at the sky that she wobbled backwards. Telling her to hurry, Pegge caught up to the older children.

"It is still runny," Margaret declared, crouching next to Will. "You should have cooked it longer, Mother."

Pegge carried the basin into the muddy reeds, tying some of the stalks together to anchor it. "There—it will thicken in no time."

As the pudding floated in the cool water, they sat under an elm to wait. The moorhens pecked at the basin, but it was too solid for them to tip and they paddled off to poke their red beaks under the bloodwort. Dark shapes mustered in the elm, peering down at the children.

"Now *those* are crows," Pegge said to Will. "You will need to chase them away or they will have their beaks in our pudding."

When Will shouted, the crows flew to the next tree, then the next, and the next, hopping further and further along the branches until they were craning their necks out over the bobbing pudding.

Taking his stick from Emma, Will brandished it at the marauders. "Let us be barbarous savages!"

"I will be an ingenious Chinese," announced Margaret, taking her shears to a reed. "Do you want one, Emma? Do not try to come, the ground is too soft. I will find a small one for you."

The shears will never cut a straight line again, Pegge thought, but said nothing.

Seeing Will and Margaret approaching with their weapons, the crows flapped indifferently over to the other side of the marsh. Now Pegge saw why. The basin had worked itself loose from its moorings and was floating into the marsh water. Will and Margaret tried to stop it with their sticks, but they sank into the mud. When they stepped back, the water rushed in to fill their footprints with a frightful sucking noise. The basin was now too far out, heading at a goodly pace across the pond in the direction of the crows. As Pegge and the children looked on helplessly, the cawing became unbearable. Emma stuck a finger in an eye and began to whimper.

"We must make a boat out of reeds," said Will, but his voice quavered.

"Or wade in," said Margaret, taking off her shoes. She stripped down her stockings and tied up her skirts with the oriental girdle.

"You will sink into the bog," Pegge said. "Make waves quickly, both of you. Come and help, Emma. Like this."

It was no good. The waves refused to echo as far as the basin, which mocked them by spinning in a circle. More crows flew in to join the raiding party and the chorus rose and fell as scouts made forays over the prize. One landed on the rim of the basin, getting a taste before losing its balance.

"Margaret," Pegge said, "hand me your stick and stay with Emma."

Pegge circled around and approached the marsh from the east, using the stick to flush the mudhens out of their nests and into the water. As they launched themselves, the outraged cries, the splashing wings, the legs running on the surface drove the basin back to the other side where Will, observing the pudding's change of course, had prudently stationed himself. The hens sank back on the water, pumping their heads and clucking. In another moment, they were pecking stupidly under the blood-wort again.

Will landed the copper bowl with his pole. "I have it, I have it, look how thick it has become!"

As they escorted the pudding over to the Lebanon cedar, William came up the path from the house calling out *Margaret* as loudly as good manners permitted. Both Pegge and Margaret turned at once towards him.

"This is what comes of naming a child after yourself," he said tersely. "Neither of you knows which one is being called. This must stop, Pegge. Stop. Do you hear me? I found little Isabel asleep in the tall grass just before the marsh. I would not have gone that way except for Plum, who was standing on top of a tussock, wagging her tail to catch my eye. Anything might have come of it, Pegge. Anything. If not for Plum."

Having frightened Plum into trembles and Isabel into sobs, he was almost in tears himself. Pegge held out her arms to Isabel and drew her close, kissing her damp nose. The little girl finally let go of the spoon, winding her arms around Pegge's neck. Will was making his way back to them with the pudding held rigidly horizontal.

"Is that the vessel from the Deanery?" William demanded, his face as coppery as the old basin. His arm rose almost to the perpendicular and began to wave about. "It is dangerous to keep such a thing. The soldiers have already sacked my study once, looking for your father's writings sympathetic to the King."

"It is only a bowl, William," Pegge said.

"They wanted to search your chamber as well, but I told them— You have not kept any of your father's books, have you, Pegge?"

"I don't like the name Margaret. It sounds too English," Margaret said abruptly.

The girl's face was a study. Either artless or full of art, Pegge pondered which. It was not William's face, to be sure. His arm fell as he considered his eldest child.

"If you dislike it," he said peaceably, "why not go by Maggie or Meg?"

"Meg," Margaret tongued the word. "It sounds very Chinese, does it not?"

Reminded, William felt in his pocket. "I brought these for your pudding. Berries from the New World. Not so many," he cautioned, as Will sprinkled them over the top. The berries began to bleed into the pudding, turning it a festive colour.

"But what are they really, Father?" asked Meg, moistening one in her mouth. "They taste like raspberries, only sharper." She held it out on her palm for Will and Emma to peer at. "It looks like a tiny beetle."

"Well done, Meg," said William. "It is cochineal, for dyeing wool scarlet. Mordanted with aqua fortis. Remember that, Will. You must learn the mordants. Your mother once rubbed cochineal on her lips to colour them. And scarlet has other, less familiar, uses." He looked sideways at Pegge, a blushing reference to the dye-bath that had led to Meg's conception. "Scarlet was once permitted only to gentlemen. Now Cromwell's redcoats wear it, while we must make do with Puritan black."

Meg and Will crushed the insects in their palms, spat, then rubbed the paste on one another's cheeks. They put bog violets into Emma's cap and reddened her lips, bowing and saying *Lady Emma* this and *Lady Emma* that.

Pegge burrowed her nose into Isabel's neck and nibbled at her moist flaxen curls to make her laugh. Soon the little girl was wriggling out of Pegge's arms to dip a finger in the pudding. It was now the colour of bruised flesh and emitted a peculiar odour. Unable to bear the smell, Pegge bolted into the horsetails. After a while, two white hands swam through the shoulder-high grasses towards her.

Meg fidgeted, playing with her bright girdle. "I will be called Margaret if it makes you well," she said at last.

Pegge longed to erase her daughter's forehead creases, but could not yet think how to reassure her.

"Or Pegge, after you, although I hate it."

Hearing these martyred words, Pegge dove into the horsetails once again. Surely some female wisdom should have warned her? After all, it was the seventh time she had become with child. With each birth, William had shown the same delight as with the first, whether Pegge had bestowed on him a daughter or a son. Only one had slipped out dead, a tiny perfect son.

Since Will had no great love of pigs, Pegge hoped for her own sake to bear a second boy—a son who would always stay with her at Clewer. Charles would be a good name, she thought, after the beheaded King.

21. TULIPS

Pegge was watching her daughters paint the flowers
William had arranged in an ivory jar. The well-bred flowers included only a single tulip, a white with vermilion
feathering.

Meg had grown slender and elegant like a fleur-de-lis.
Today, because she was sixteen, William gave her a new pair
of shoes and took her off to discuss her dowry. Meg
returned, limping but smug, saying that Peter Scott had
spoken for her. Pegge had no liking for the man, though he
was rector of Sunning-hill and canon of Windsor, for he
was far too staid.

The five girls were sitting with straight backs, their
drawings propped rigidly on wooden frames, while their
Aunt Constance circled them, securing the sheets with
pegs. *They need to be schooled in the arts,* William had said,
writing to Con to invite her to Clewer in spite of Pegge's
objections. He meant the useful arts, the things that Pegge
disliked. When Pegge asked to keep little Franny to herself
another year, William refused. He took Franny by the hand

that very minute and began her education by showing her how to tell time by the hall clock.

Pegge brought in some tulips from the garden for her daughters to paint as well. Although the tulips were now splayed over the green baize, the girls' brushes danced by preference over the pale lilies, irises, gladioli, and narcissi. Pegge was sorry now that she had pulled up the tulip bulbs. She had wanted her daughters to draw the whole plant, even down to the rich clumps of clinging earth, but only Franny was drudging away at the vibrant tulips, one foot bare, the other dangling in a garden clog. Pegge saw Franny rub her paper so many times the brilliant paint ran, turning the sky a weepy carnation. Pegge bit her lip, waiting for Con to swoop, for William to make peace, offering to design a pair of shoes for Franny as he had done for Meg.

The girls had the fair skin and hair that was à la mode in Europe. It must have come down from Pegge's mother, for both William and Pegge had dark hair. William liked to sketch them painting or doing needlework, sharing his hopes with them for the return of the King's son to England. His nib elongated their necks and legs, clothed them in French gowns, and paired them with gallants in wide breeches. With a few swift pen-strokes, he made the alterations they asked for, teaching them how width and length were proportionally related.

Pegge was the only one who found plain English wool, even Puritan black, to her liking. When she was a child, she hid under woollens matted and softened by her elder sisters. Now she embraced the inky black of childhood, greyed by the country sun. Sometimes when she sat writing next to the window, she heard the gentle *scritching* of William's nib trying to capture her on paper.

Six years had passed since the King was beheaded and the Royal Wardrobe turned into an orphanage. Even now, taking refuge in the country, William sometimes came into Pegge's room at night, waking her to describe his dreams of merchantmen with cargoes of mysterious printed cottons from the east. In the light of day, she would see him crumple drawing after drawing, unable to decipher the secret of the indiennes.

Now Con was at the window-ledge, writing to her sons, and William sat beside his daughters, guiding their choice of colours. From time to time, he leaned forward to convey a morsel of information.

"India yellow," he said, pushing the paint towards Emma when she started on the narcissus, "from turmeric, or perhaps only fragrant Indian corn."

Meg's brush hesitated over a row of dark colours.

"Those are for shading," advised William. "Of grey, there are several: slate, bat-wing, and plumb. That is crow-black and this—tending to brown—raven. Black is never pure, Meg. The best black, used for mourning, has a purple sheen. Here are liver-drab, London smoke, and Paris mud. This tiny cake is mummy-brown," he paused to make sure that five flaxen heads were turned his way, "from mummified Egyptians."

"Which is your favourite colour, Father?" asked Meg.

But William could not answer. His eye flitted from colour to colour, unable to decide among them. Finally, he turned to the vase, fingering a plain yellow flower tucked behind the others. "This is woad, so detested by Queen Elizabeth she forbade it near her palaces. Its leaves give up a deep blue dye that heathen women once used to stain their bodies."

Pegge stared at him in astonishment, and Franny poked Cornelia, giggling. When Con walked over to the table to see what she had missed, William made some excuse and left the room, crimsoning from his own boldness.

—

Pegge did not like to sit for long in the salon, favouring the trapdoors and narrow passages that circumnavigated the house. She crept up the servants' stairs in bare feet and walked backwards into the family bedchambers so that, when her children discovered her, she could pretend she had come up by the proper staircase. When they slipped their hands over her eyes, she would guess *Meg-Will-Emma-Isabel-Cornelia-Franny-Charles*, all run together to make them laugh.

Pegge would sneak in at night to hide gifts in the children's rooms: ebony combs, snakeskins, peacock feathers, nets for catching moths, bleached jawbones, polished stones, a chambered nautilus. Their limbs encountered rose petals between sheets at night and rosemary sprigs in morning shoes. When it rained, Pegge would take over the kitchen from Cook, who reined in his temper only so long before chasing his mistress upstairs. After Cook was appeased, Pegge pulled up the sweet plunder in her sewing basket, never used for its real purpose, and shared it with the younger children. When it was sunny and the children wandered outside to the east, west, north, and south, Pegge blew her father's dented trumpet to call them home, upsetting William's equilibrium.

They disagreed about the care, the upbringing, even the number, of their children. William counted only seven, but she counted eleven: seven live and four dead. One by one, Pegge's children outgrew her pleasures and became William's heirs. Now it was little Franny who teetered back and forth between her parents.

Year after year, Pegge looked for evidence of her father in her children, but found none. Would the child now growing in her belly resemble him? That morning, William had picked the twelve flowers from Pegge's own garden—one for each day her fleurs were late—to tell her she was with child again. The bouquet might have been an apology, or only a subject for a watercolour lesson.

Another child? Even the thought was wearying. Pegge watched Meg wet the tip of her brush, then trail it through some pea-green powder. Would Meg have a hard time in labour with her first? Meg was filling in the pencilled leaf with deft strokes, her mouth pursed. Perhaps, Pegge thought, her daughter would find some artificial way to give birth.

Pegge asked her daughters whether they would like something warm to drink, but they did not reply, not even Cornelia who liked to turn the cocoa mill and Franny whose job it was to froth the chocolate with the paddle. Pegge picked up a few tulip petals and put them on her tongue. Turkish caps. The inside of her mouth tingled.

"Are my lips red?" she asked Franny.

"No, Mama, but we are not meant to talk when draw-ing. Aunt Constance does not care for it."

Franny seemed to have forgotten that her aunt had dis-gusted her only last week. When Franny was in the parterre holding up her gloved hands like blossoms to catch a hawkmoth, Con had sailed past, telling her to *stop dawdling and come into the house.* Pegge heard a hideous crunch as Con stepped on Franny's snails and saw Franny chase after her aunt, tugging on her skirts in rage.

"Mother, how can you eat flowers?" Emma scolded. "Why are you being tiresome? We cannot work if you are playing games."

"She may not be playing," said Meg, drawing a perfectly straight line.

Con opened her mouth like a foxglove, then snapped it shut. A widow again, Con often walked with William after dinner, but whether she was hoping to entangle him after Pegge's sudden death from floral toxaemia, or was contriv-ing more matches for her nieces, Pegge did not know. Canon Scott had been Con's doing, and Pegge still hoped to bring Meg to her senses. There was a *swish* as Meg stepped her bloodied stockings out of her new shoes.

"Shall I bring you a foot-bath of gentian violet, Meg?"

"Stop fretting, Mother. You must learn to call me Margaret like everyone else." Her head rotated on its stiff ivory column away from Pegge.

"And I wish to be called Frances, not Franny." The little voice was cool and prim, like her elder sister's.

Pegge wanted to whisk Franny into the garden, where she could pretend to be a four-o'clock-flower at dusk. She could stay out all night like an evening primrose—*Hawkmoths are best caught in the dark*, Pegge longed to whisper—and collect dew from the lady's nightcap at dawn. What need did Franny have of telling time by clocks? *Bees are the best timepieces*, Pegge wanted to tell her, *for they visit the same flowers at the same time each day*. But it was too late. These daughters were no longer Pegge's. They were grafted so firmly onto Bowles stock, it was as if they had no Donne blood left in them.

—

Pegge fingered the tulips strewn across the table. "Peppery," she told Franny. "The red tastes like pepper. Try it." She held out some petals on her palm.

"Your mind is a muddle," Con said sharply. "A colour is a colour and a taste is a taste. You are always *muddling*."

Con would never say such a thing in front of William. Pegge's daughters looked down, mixing pastel colours with determined brushes. Only Franny was drawn to red. Rust, scarlet, cerise, blood. Mixed with white, red became a cooler, more palatable shade—more polite, but less to Franny's liking. Pegge saw Franny lick her brush to taste the undiluted crimson. Was there anything of John Donne in that sly darting tongue?

Con's bell signalled the end of painting and the start of needlework. While the girls stitched, Con read aloud from one of the books that she had brought from Barking. It suddenly struck Pegge that Con must have been reading from Walton's *Life of Donne* for days, since she was bearing down triumphantly on the ending.

"*To the Dean of St Paul's burial-place,*" Con read, "*some mournful friends repaired, and, as Alexander the Great did to the grave of the famous Achilles, so they strewed his with an abundance of curious and costly flowers, not ceasing till the stones that were taken up in that Church to give his body admission into the cold earth—now his bed of rest—were again by the mason's art so levelled and firmed as they had been formerly.*"

Pegge coiled a thread around her hand until it was a tight noose cutting off the blood.

"*His aspect was cheerful,*" Con continued, "*and such as gave a silent testimony of a clear knowing soul, and of a conscience at peace with itself. His melting eye showed that he had a soft heart, full of noble compassion.*"

Melting eye—how could Con read such a thing without wincing?

"*That body which once was a temple of the Holy Ghost is now become a small quantity of Christian dust. But I shall see it re-animated.*"

Pegge waited until Con had wrung the last drop of pity out of Izaak Walton's words. *Slip-slip*, Meg's feet stepped back into her shoes and the daughters escaped, leaving Con to congratulate herself on her father's saintliness. A look that Pegge detested spread over her sister's face, turning it a cracked yellow like old custard.

"May I see the book?" Pegge asked.

Con hesitated, then pushed it across the table. "I thought you disliked Mr Walton's view of father."

Pegge opened the cover. *The Life of John Donne, Dr in Divinity, and Late Dean of Saint Pauls Church London. The second impression corrected and enlarged.* Hardly the trifle

Walton called it in the preface, the *Life* had swollen to twice its former bulk.

"And I thought you disliked Izaak Walton," Pegge said. "You once drove him crazy with longing, spoiling him for any other woman."

"I suppose you mean yourself." Con stood up, her breasts straining the florid cotton. "You were hardly a woman, Pegge, you were a stubborn, boastful child. That was years ago, and the man was a simpleton."

Con adjusted a loop of hair, then ran her hands over her hips. This habitual preening, this pretense of ironing out creases in her clothing—would she still be doing it in her grave?

"A simple man is different from a simpleton, although you could never see that. But I have not seen him since father died," Pegge admitted.

"Nor I, although he sends me each new book, each windier than the last." Con read out the title of an octavo. "*The Compleat Angler or the Contemplative Man's Recreation, being a discourse of fish and fishing not unworthy the perusal of most anglers.* Why is he writing tales of red cow's milk and giant pikes bred by pickerel weeds?"

Pegge flipped past the dedication to Con on the fly-leaf, past conversations with anglers and an engraving of a trout, and stopped at a recipe for dressing a yard-long pike with butter and sweet marjoram, pickled oysters and anchovies, claret and garlic that could only have come from one source.

"Why, this is delightful, Con. In this book, he writes just as he talks."

"Since you are so pleased, why don't you tell him so? It will save me the trouble of responding." Con wound the silks back on the spools and collected the needles the girls had strewn across the table.

Walton's letter was still inside the book. It had been written to Con just after Mr Harvey's death, from a cottage in Staffordshire where Walton was living with his second wife. His penmanship was just as clumsy as Pegge remembered it. She folded the letter and replaced it carefully. Even after all these years, she sometimes felt her hands reach up to cover Walton's eyes, or touch his golden hair. Pegge had written to him in London several times, but never got an answer. Perhaps he had simply been in the country, fishing.

Pegge would write to suggest some tales for a new edition. A duodecimo would fit more easily into an angler's pocket. This octavo was too big, and one of the pages appeared to be misprinted, until Pegge studied it more closely.

"Look at this, Con. It is the song we used to sing. He has put the bass part upside down and the treble right side up, so that a man and woman can sing it across an ale-house table."

On that day along their secret river, Pegge had barely felt the mulberries raining down upon her head because of Walton's buckle pressing so hard against her belly. What if she had gone with him to the Frog & Pike and bought a night's lodging with their brace of carp? They might have interlocked legs beneath a table, drinking barley wine and singing, then climbed the staircase to the bedchamber above.

"Only his book on Father has any merit," Con said, "and that is because he got his facts from others."

"Lies," said Pegge, buffing the green calfskin with her palm. "Just lies you believe in, Con. I cannot forgive Walton for making Father into such a martyr."

"And you want to destroy his reputation."

"The truth has more need of guardians than the Dean of Paul's."

"Not this old battle, Pegge! Father wanted to suppress Jack Donne, yet you persist in digging him up. He drew the veil over Mr Walton's eyes himself." Con let out a prevailed-upon wheeze. "Why are you always *against*? At least Mr Walton had the sense to bury Father's sins."

"Bury Mother, you mean." Pegge shoved the *Life of Donne* towards her sister and kept *The Compleat Angler*. "Walton says Father's love for her was only a flattering mischief. Yet it gave rise to his finest poems, to magnificently tortured sermons! Do you really believe Ann was the *remarkable error* of his life?"

"I seldom heard her speak any sense. You saw what a three-year-old sees, taking off your boots and stockings every time I turned my back. When mother was dying, I was barely fourteen, running the household with only Bess to help."

Had Con been only fourteen? To Pegge, she had seemed much older.

—

After dinner, William offered his arms to the two sisters for a walk in the gardens, an intimacy that Pegge did not like to share with Con.

"We shall go back to London in a few weeks," he announced, drawing the women closer. "Cromwell has built a warship with his statue on horseback at its prow and ninety-six brass guns. This usurper must be stopped. Plans must be made to bring the new King back to England."

"I hear that St Paul's has been turned into a barracks by Cromwell's troops," Pegge said, "and that they are baptising colts in my father's font."

"Well, Paul's is nothing to us now," William said cheerfully. "Let the Dean's effigy preside over her ruin."

"The baby is in need of country air," Pegge said. "I will stay here with him until he is grown."

"Charles is four," William said. "He is in need of school."

"Charles is but three, and I am with child again. We will be better here."

"This will be your eighth child," Con said. "You will find more to occupy your thoughts in town."

"It is my twelfth, like Mother. She died with her twelfth."

"Now, Pegge, do not be melancholy," William said. "I am sure that Constance will come to London to help you through your confinement."

Why did Con's sons never need her help in Barking? Perhaps they wished to be rid of her and encouraged her to accept William's invitations. "If it is a girl," Pegge said, "I will call her Ann."

Con smacked away a bee investigating a yellow flower embroidered on her sleeve. "Then if it is a boy, you must call him John, after our father. Do you not agree, William?"

At least William had the sense to say nothing. They were now passing beneath the yew where Bess had spent her final days.

"If I have a son, I will call him Duodecimus," Pegge said, staring up into the spreading branches. "It means twelve."

William began to sputter, but Pegge shook off his arm and fell behind. Just as she was turning to go into the walled garden, she saw Franny catching up to William with something in her hands.

"Look what I found in Mother's room," Pegge overheard Franny saying, "on top of Grandfather's old cabinet."

From the other side of the wall, Pegge heard William take a few determined steps on the gravel before he stopped. "A pipit's nest," he said, "there is nothing wrong with pipits' nests. See the brown spots on the eggs, Franny?"

"But look what is beneath them," Franny insisted.

"It is our mother's," Con ventured, after a minute. "Or perhaps it is our father's. The strands are so matted it could be anyone's. It is a puzzle why Pegge keeps such things."

"Or one of her dead children's," said William, his voice doubtful. "You must put it back at once, Franny. She might be on her way to the house. And the nest too, be quick about it."

As Franny ran back down the gravel path, Pegge extricated a rose that had been throttled by lemon balm, then yanked up the wayward balm. She must talk to the gardener about cleaning the beds and pruning the vines. The thyme had gone all woody and brown.

"This is what comes of letting her keep country ways," William said to Con. "No doubt she will want to ride her

mare even though she is with child. She has twice miscarried since Charles was born." His voice broke, as if Con had
taken his arm, pressing herself against him, encouraging
his tears. More steps on the gravel, more comforting and
consoling. "She will be safer by my side in London. You
will come with us, won't you, Constance? You are much
better than Pegge at managing the servants."

"You know she has never been fond of me. She would
sooner have me back in Barking."

"I am sure she doesn't think it. She is completely guile-
less."

"She is completely absorbed by guile!" Con exclaimed.
"Pegge is always acting a part. As a child, she was given to
mimicry. When my father preached, we would sometimes
hear an infant mewling in the choir loft, but nobody could
ever find it. The poor dog was always blamed."

"Perhaps—"

"There is no *perhaps* about it, William. She is full of
practice. One of Paul's canons heard Jane Shore laughing
night after night outside his window. He lamed his foot by
chasing after the laughter in the dark. It finally drove the
poor man mad." A deep urgent breath. "After Father died,
Pegge took to mimicking our mother's voice and giving out
the name *Ann More* to strangers."

Con was a goose. Why did she disturb William with
such tales? She was worse than lemon balm for straying
where she was not wanted.

On this side of the wall, everything was thrusting up,
demanding Pegge's attention. She uprooted a loose stake
and drove it hard into the soil, bruising her hand. She

looked into the open throat of a clary, then pinched the bloom and extracted a bee, subjecting it to a keen examination. By its looks, she suspected that it was the kind of bee that stung its victims more than once.

22. THE RIDDLE

Izaak Walton was standing under the portico of St Paul's, watching his house in Paternoster row burn to the ground. The flames were attacking the cathedral from three sides. Only the west, where he now stood, was safe, though where the sun was nobody could see, for the fire had eclipsed it. It could be night or day for all that anybody knew.

Six years before, when the Rump Parliament fell, the churches rang a jubilee and rumps of meat turned on spits on open fires. Butchers' knives flashed, cutting off penny slices, and street boys ran up and down, calling out *kiss my rump* instead of their customary *kiss my arse*. Men drank to the King's health openly for the first time, toasting the end of the bloody rebellion of nearly twenty years. Walton had climbed to the top of Paul's that night and counted hundreds of bonfires cooking rumps both inside and outside the City walls.

It was hotter now than on the day of the rumps, and it was the house he had just leased that was being roasted. The fire had burned for two days in a westerly direction along the river, then the wind had shifted, driving the flames up Paul's hill towards his house. When he ran out to hire a carter, he found the streets already blocked by people hauling goods. Returning to carry his papers to safety in his arms, he was waved back by his neighbours, who stood in Paternoster row with rags held to their noses. As he watched, the fire jumped over his doorstep and sped into the house, making a meal of all his manuscripts.

Now the roof was collapsing onto the lower storeys. He had stood there in a daze for so long that the wooden ceiling of the portico was smouldering above his head and the refugees taking shelter with him had scattered to find sanctuary elsewhere. He woke to harrowing sounds ringing in the cathedral at his back and saw someone dancing out of Paul's walk towards him, dragging a heavy bundle along the pavingstones. It looked, until Walton rubbed the smoke out of his eyes, like John Donne dressed up in a skirt. Walton grappled the apparition, netted it, laid it on the riverbank: Pegge Donne, whom he had not seen for more than thirty years.

A stray cat, smelling the fish on his hose, leapt onto his leg, digging in its claws. Before he knew it, he was cradling the wretched animal and looking for somewhere to put it, so he could grasp the end of the shawl Pegge was pushing at him. Soon they were swinging the bundle between them down to Paul's wharf, with the burnt cat following close behind.

He wondered how old Pegge was. After the Dean died, she married Mr Bowles of Clewer. Near Windsor, with good fishing up to Henley, but not good enough for him to visit. When his *Compleat Angler* came out, she wrote to praise it, diverting, at the midpoint of her letter, into a wild attack on his biography of her father. She wrote several more letters, but he was afraid of taking up with her again. An odd child, she had likely grown into an even odder woman.

Now that he recognized the huge shape on the cart in front of them, he was sure of it. The carters blocked the wheels halfway down Paul's hill to shift the effigy back to the middle. Walton doubted it would see the inside of St Paul's again, for Pegge had detested it when it was no more than an artist's sketch. In the fiery light ahead, Sir William Bowles was standing in an immense barge, his hand hovering at his sword, and Walton dropped his side of the bundle, making Pegge struggle the last few yards by herself.

The barge took a night and a day to travel upriver because of the currents, arriving at the Bowles estate at nightfall. The men lay down their long oars in exhaustion. The servants had seen them round the bend, and were on the bank to guide the barge to shore. Even before they moored, the cat leapt out and disappeared into the long grass. Sir William ordered his servants to fetch his draught horse and block and tackle to lift the effigy out of the barge.

As Walton scrambled up the bank, soaking his shoes and hose, a pony-cart lurched to a stop, almost knocking him back into the Thames. The driver introduced himself as Duodecimus Bowles. No more than eleven or twelve, Walton guessed, looking about for a safer way to travel.

"Sit here, Mother," the boy said, wrapping his arms around Pegge.

Unless Walton wanted to stand outside all night, he would have to squeeze into the seat beside Pegge and her son. When he stepped up, a caterpillar fell out of a tree onto his shoulder. The boy picked it off and inspected the stripes, then counted the number of legs on the small creature.

"A lovers' knot," said Walton. "Put that in a glass with a bit of privet and it will get you a good fish. Live bait is best, young man."

Something flew above them in the darkening sky. "Bats," the boy said, smiling.

"First the swallows come out and then the bats," Walton corrected. He was reminded, not unpleasantly, of Pegge at the same age.

Walton could smell the honeysuckle as soon as he entered the great house. All at once, he was back at Constance's feet in the Deanery, fetching the pale green silk from her embroidery basket that she needed to sew the minnow's belly. When she reached to take the spool from him, he almost fainted from the scent clinging to her body.

Now he wandered through the rooms looking for Constance until one of the maids, a small girl with a Welsh accent, took pity and told him that Mrs Harvey had indeed been visiting. She had been called home as a result of the fire, but would return to Clewer in a day or two.

At breakfast, he noticed an ugly fly perched on the slice of cold mutton in front of him. He tried to flick it away without being observed, but in his clumsiness knocked the dish to the floor and broke it. The Welsh maid brought him another slice of meat with an even greater fly perched on top. She stood by his side, waiting for him to lift his knife. He was becoming irritated at this game when a thought struck him. He pinched the wing and held the specimen up to his eye.

"The gadfly or whame," he announced, exhibiting it between thumb and finger, "commonly known as the horsefly, the females of which suck blood. It is very like." He looked towards Pegge, who was engrossed in eating, and then to the eager maid.

"Madam made it herself. She learnt how from the old groundsman. It takes almost a day to make each one."

He thought he saw a smile cross Pegge's face, though it might have been a wave of indigestion.

—

Each morning a new fly appeared on Walton's breakfast, and the maid hovered until he identified it. The miniatures became more exquisite as each day passed, but still Constance did not return from Barking. They began to infest his shoes and stockings and alight upon his nightshirt and pillow. Each morning, outdoor clothes, decorated with a dragon-fly or pond-skater or even a daddy-long-legs, were laid ready in case he might have use of them, but each day he stayed indoors waiting for Mrs Constance Harvey.

At last, holding a lame-fly to the light to tease out the source of its iridescence, it occurred to him that there might be a use for these flies. He asked Pegge if a servant could take him to the river to see whether there were any fish to be caught. She was so pleased that she took him herself, wearing a dreary brown stuff dress. From her shoulder hung a wooden box fitted with a leather strap. On the bank, it opened to reveal fifty compartments, each with a tiny, vibrant creature. He lifted one out: a tuft of badger's hair, the softest yellow hog down, and a white dove-feather, twisted together with white silk. It was then he recalled that he had once made a promise to build her a rod, but never kept it.

After that, they took the pony-cart to the river each morning to read the water and the fish. Formerly, he had put live bait into the middle or bottom of the stream, but now he devised a way to buoy a horsehair line with quills so that it would float one of her flies on the surface. He dropped the fly on a crisp stretch of water, then made it dart up and land a few inches away. Pulling in the line by dibs and daps, he jumped the fly across the river, deceiving the fish into biting. Each day, he wet his line in a new and more seductive patch of water until even the tender-mouthed graylings rose for Pegge's flies.

On a day with a good south wind, they entered into battle with a majestic pike. Walton pulled in eighteen feet of rod hand over hand until he gripped bare line, while Pegge waded in and grappled the prize into her skirt. She came out of the water halved at the waist, brown above and black below like a Derbyshire coach-fly. When they arrived back at the estate, Pegge went straight into the kitchen to stuff the fish herself, dripping Thames water across the tiles.

She appeared for supper in a dry gown ornamented with curious tufts of fur and speckled feathers and carrying the dressed pike on a bed of garlic. He ate the garlic with reluctance, mindful that it was said to elicit black vapours from the brain and breed unwholesome dreams. As he left the hall, the maid drew him aside and told him in her soft Welsh accents that Mrs Harvey had arrived but gone straight to her room. He went to his chamber with garlicky pike clinging to his soft mouth tissues and the promise of Constance luring him to an early breakfast. For the first time in thirty years, they were widow and widower at the same time. Perhaps, he mused, falling into a garlicky sleep, she now dreamt of a simple life with a country angler.

He certainly did not expect her to creep into his bedchamber, but that was what she was now doing, gliding through the door and standing at the foot of his bed, her flesh gleaming against the blinding moon, her hair falling over her shoulder like a raven's wing. Then he must have swooned, for he woke to the touch of fingers in his hair and a torturing nocturnal scent. A moral decency buttoned up his hands, but all the fibres of his being sang. This was the Constance he remembered from the Deanery, the ripe Constance of twenty-one, a scent-drunk blossom heavy with its own destruction, the Constance who, night after night, year after year, had invaded his bed, crowding out his wives—first Rachel, with her roughened fingers, and then the dear devoted Kenna who had never risen to anything that in the least resembled passion.

"Izzy," his night-visitor whispered, twisting it to sound like *Issy*. Perhaps it was *Pissy-Issy*, but he could forgive her even that tonight.

He was ashamed how readily his body responded, so free now of its kinks and aches, how quickly his blood rose and expanded to fill the space between them. A thumb traced a line from his breast-bone down to his belly, a palm slipped with practised skill along his inner thigh. These were no rough linen-draper's hands, though lurking beneath the honeysuckle was a darker, furtive scent. She began to slide her body on top of his, pinning his hands against the sheet. It could not be!—he could not believe the pressure of her limbs.

"Do not move so, Constance," he managed to choke out, "or I cannot be held responsible for what will come of it."

It was indeed an uncontrollable—yes, a very uncontrollable—urge in a man. In spite of what the church fathers said, it was not at all like wiggling the ears, for such uprisings could not be curbed by the power of the will.

"My dear, you must stop, you cannot mean to be doing as you do. Your chamber must be next door, not very far—" It was easy to lose one's way in a dark house, for all beds looked alike in the moonlight, and with such a disturbing scent as this! "My dear—oh, my dear Constance—you must not— you cannot blame me for—I cannot prevent—"

He was late going down to breakfast the next morning. He had kept his hostess waiting and was ashamed that the maids were even now making up his bed, discovering what he knew was there to be discovered, like wax that had spilt from Psyche's candle. His dream had been extraordinary—not just a senseless paraphrase of his waking thoughts, or of the business of the day past, or the result of over-engaged affections when he betook himself to rest, such as he had always thought dreams to be. No, he had been visited by riddling tongues of fire, the illumination of the soul in sleep, for he refused to believe that he had simply undergone an involuntary, and ungentlemanly, emission of nocturnal fluids.

On the breakfast table stood a great slab of country cheese topped by a spectacularly engorged and vulgar bluebottle. Half-eaten crusts and sticky honey trails littered the table, and Pegge was not inclined to conversation. The Welsh maid confided in her soft voice that Mrs Harvey had left in haste at dawn, without any explanation. She had not even had the time (*or charity! decency!* Walton screamed inwardly) to write a note excusing her departure.

He did not like the dark circling Pegge's eyes, or the cloying scent of honeysuckle on her breath, as if she had devoured a hundredweight of those delicate, nocturnal flowers. Her drab gown had taken on a gaudy, blood-red glow. She was still eating, and appeared to have been doing so for hours, for honey was spilt all down her bodice. Her lips tinged with tell-tale yellow, she was enlarging before his eyes, like an elephantine hawkmoth he had once seen glutting itself on a ridiculously small bloom. All at once, she lunged across the table and gripped his wrist with her sticky fingers. If not for the glimmer in her eyes, he might have thought her gone completely mad.

"You are looking particularly unkempt this morning, Izzy," she said. "We really must do something about the tangles in your hair."

———

Pegge washed Walton's hair clean of soot, then stained it with saffron to bring back the colour. Now he was sitting on a stool in her bedchamber listening to her skirts rustling from the cat that hid underneath, rubbing at her legs. Never far from her, it had become sleeker and more cunning in the fortnight since the fire. He leaned back against Pegge as she untangled the strands with her fingers.

"Like gold to airy thinness beat," she said.

She had not lost that disturbing knack of plucking her father's lines from memory. As she dipped her tortoise comb into the bowl, he thought of the tortoise in its natural element of water. The sun was cascading through the window, turning the liquid a shimmering turquoise. Every few minutes, Pegge would set down the comb, dip her fingers in oil, and rub at a lump of tar until the heat of her hands dissolved it. Sometimes she tugged at his scalp so hard that tears came to his eyes. The worst knots had to be cut out with scissors.

"It is better than shaving your head," she said. "I cannot forgive William for sacrificing his beautiful long hair just because the King cut his."

Now Pegge began to brush Walton's hair. She had a good casting hand, steady and quiet. His head followed the brush into her hand, moving towards her warmth with each stroke, a maternal rhythm perfected on her children. Every so often, she ran the comb through the brush, then pushed the strands into an enamelled hair-tidy. This must be where she got the hair for her flies. Dyed the colour of grass and marigolds and autumn leaves, the small bundles were displayed on her cabinet next to her ear-drops and crystal rings.

Pegge no longer had any children to groom, for her daughters were young women of fashion with their own maids to comb them. Walton had seen their portraits in the hall, observing to Pegge that women, with their patches and paint, were like trout, most fresh when first taken from the river with all their maiden spots and colours. Pegge's own hair still had the deep burnishing of its youth, and the same curious dimples spotted her cheeks, like sun dappling her skin through mulberry leaves.

He reached towards a shank of matted hair on the cabinet, but she tugged at his temple with the brush to bring him back to her. Oddly familiar, a straw-colour gone to grey, it might have been Ann More's hair, for the cabinet was unmistakably John Donne's. Some curls were being pressed in a duodecimo that was badly discoloured from blotting up dye. His heart quickened when he saw it was the second edition of his *Compleat Angler*. Had she liked it, thought it worthy? Suddenly, her opinion mattered more than anybody's.

"I added pictures of the ruff-fish and roach, so they are not so subject to confusion," he prompted, "and this edition is printed smaller, as you suggested."

"It is lovely, much lovelier than your biography of Father."

Giving with one hand and taking away with the other, as she had always done, unlike her sister, by far the sweeter of the two. Constance would never have forgiven him if he wrote ill of her father. "Constance liked the *Life of Donne*," he said, though in truth she had only written an indifferent line on the back of his own letter.

"You painted him with a white brush, you know you did," Pegge scolded. "You made a plaster saint of him. You're an old fool, Izzy. My father used you just as surely as Con used you with her kisses in Paul's walk. He might as well have kissed you on the mouth himself."

How did Pegge know such things? At any rate, Paul's was now destroyed and so was his own home in Paternoster row. The image of the flaming house swam up before him, his eyes watering as the smoke from the fire stung them anew. He saw the windows of his study burst outwards, showering the street with glass, and the flames devouring all his papers for a new edition of the *Life*. He had been collecting John Donne's words for years—begging letters to patrons, flattering epistles to great ladies, anything Walton could get out of the hands of others and into his own study. He was not after the fish itself, but the vibration of the fish in the water, a quiet pooling shape which rippled outward year by year, gradually embracing conversations, letters, hearsay, scraps of half-heard tales and verse.

Pegge's breath was teasing the thinning hair on his crown. Was she still talking? Perhaps he had been deafened by the crashing timbers of his house. Who would want a deaf old fish-tickler? He did not know where he would live, since it was unlikely he could persuade Sir William to let him stay on at Clewer. Though Sir William had behaved with impeccable courtesy, he had avoided Walton at every opportunity.

After his wife Kenna died, Walton had wandered about the countryside. One gloomy afternoon, he filled his pockets with stones and walked into the River Ouse, but while still in the shallows, not yet into deep-running waters, he caught sight of a large pike—a solitary, lachrymose, and bold fish—beating upriver like a prize bully, of a weight, he reckoned, to be exceptionally good eating. He waded swiftly to the bank, unloaded his murderous ballast, and baited his line with the first caterpillar he could find.

He could have used Pegge to run upstream that day, for he had not been fast enough to overtake the pike. Duodecimus, her youngest, was the right age to learn how to fish. If Walton stayed on at Clewer, he could make the boy a short fir-wood rod, grinding the colours into linseed oil and laying them on smoothly with a bristle brush. He could teach the boy to tickle carp in the pool Pegge wanted dug next to the spring. In him, Walton could see the faint imprint of the great Dean of St Paul's. Certainly, the boy had the same taste for tobacco, for Walton had seen him smoking inside the piggery where the smell could not be detected.

Pegge was still brushing with that deliberate, easy motion. "Your father's sermons will always be revered," Walton said.

"For their cleverness, their wit, but do not look there for the man, Izzy. Such mysteries are only found in poems."

One hundred, two hundred, three hundred strokes—when would her hand tire of the intoxicating rhythm? He knew Pegge wanted him to show Ann in a better light. But what good was it to recover the wife's reputation at the expense of the husband's—Ann More, who was nothing compared to John Donne? Walton was set hard against Ann, more adamant against such passion now that his night-visitor had so rudely bolted, leaving at such an impolite hour to go back to her house at Barking.

"Love carries men as hotly into error," he said, "as whirlwinds carry feathers."

"But that is love's power, don't you see?" She twisted his hair around the brush and tugged. "I liked you better when you were less pious, Izzy. You must stop printing that biography. I cannot bear you turning my father into such a bloodless creature. You should enlarge the *Angler* instead. That is the book that Izaak Walton will be loved for."

Perhaps she was right. As the brush untwisted, he sank into the chair, his hand toying with the minnow in his pocket, his mind drifting downstream. He had no need of notes for his book on angling. It came to him voluntarily, begging to be told, fountaining up as he walked along a river path or took refreshment in alehouses with other anglers, his earlobes pricking when he heard a tale worth telling.

When she was finished, he would ask Pegge to take him to the river. The day was cold but sunny, with a slight breeze that might fool a grayling into thinking that a thorntree fly was real. When he had rooted himself with the wind at his back, he would cast his line, the breeze carrying it out before him, and dap and dibble the bait back across the water. Pegge would sit on her cloak on the bank and open her dubbing box with its silks, wax, hooks, feathers, and little packets of dyed hair, and tie flies like those they spotted in the air about them.

If the water was too calm, he would stand rock-still facing the sun, waiting for the dark shapes to emerge from beneath the overhanging bank, for even the shadow of a pole or horsehair line would betray him to the vigilant fish. On such a day, if the fish refused to be deceived, he might lie with his head on Pegge's lap until the clouds became dizzy, bestirring himself only to hand her a speckled feather when she asked him for it. She would have the scent of violets about her, the same scent as a young grayling fresh from a chalk river.

She was brushing his hair over her fist to form damp curls as his own mother had done. He could feel short bursts of breath as she bent close to his nape, talking of Ann and John, how they had first set eyes upon one another, how they had sworn fealty, risked all, promised everything, even to share a single grave—the story veering further and further from known truth. Walton picked up odd words and mated them, breeding a more wholesome tale to tell himself.

His thoughts swirled and bred in the warm waters downstream from the rock, like pockets of spooling water. There was something about Pegge's mouth today, her hands, the swell of her breasts pushing against his back, something familiar about the curve of her thigh as it rubbed against him, about the eros gathered in her hands. It was in him to remember, almost to recall, that he had once lain with her as man and wife, but not of his own volition—no, somehow she had persuaded him—when had this been? When she had taken him to the secret tributary of the Darent? But each time Walton circled round, drumming upstream like an otter after a spawning carp, he foundered on the rock of Constance Donne. Constance who had married the Master of the King's Bears and Bulls, Edward Alleyn. Constance who had married Samuel Harvey. Constance who would probably never, even now that she was finally free of swooning, pestering admirers, marry him, Izaak Walton.

23. MAISON RUSTIQUE

Pegge was in the garden, collecting leaves one by one. A meditative act, it reminded her of picking up grains of rice in the Deanery, a penance devised by her father to make her contemplate her errors. Behind her was a trail of stones weighing down piles of leaves.

A fine red dust from the Sahara had carpeted the garden, mingling with a layer of ash from Cheapside. She had been finding scraps of books all day. Since the fire, words, phrases, paragraphs of her father's had been coming back to her at the strangest moments. When she was sitting on her close-stool that morning, a sermon had sprung to mind with the word *bladder* embedded in it. And now this haunting wind, whistling the dust into her eyes and ears as if her father's mischievous spirit were abroad again.

From where she stood, she could see William coming up through the physic garden past the blackened statue. The stonemason had reattached the head and was now bent over the effigy, scrubbing it with a coarse brush.

"Why is everyone acting so oddly?" William asked. "Constance arrived an hour ago and got straight into a quarrel with Izaak Walton. Even our new maid came in for some harsh words. Then Mr Walton took a horse from the stable and rode off towards the river with a very red face. I suppose that is the last we will see of him till evening."

Pegge hid a smile. Was it her fault that the Con who had arrived that morning was sharp-tongued and tight-lipped, far from the phantom who no doubt graced Walton's memories of the Deanery?

"Now Constance is reorganizing my closet on some new principle brought down from Barking. I wish you would go in and calm her, Pegge. After all, she is your sister."

"If you want to please me, you will send her home."

"If I do, will you send Mr Walton away?"

"I think you'll find he has already left. He will have gone north to fish before winter sets in."

"On *my* horse?" William was trying to brush the red dust from his doublet, but only succeeding in driving it further into the weave.

Walton would be on his way to the Wye in Monmouthshire to catch young salmon. He would tie crimson ribbons on their tails and slip them back into the river. Perhaps he would write to tell her of his researches, but more likely she would not hear from him for at least a score of years.

"What is to be done with that grotesque statue?" William asked.

"I will train bindweed to grow around it."

"I refuse to have Clewer garden turned into a sepulchre."
She reached down to collect a few more leaves.

"Let Angus do that." William gestured towards the dark
figure slouching off with a half-full sack of leaves. "Why
do I employ a gardener when you put him to so little use?"
He began to swat at the folds of his breeches, turning this
way and that.

"The bees will be gone in a minute," Pegge said. "It is
time for them to visit the star of Bethlehem."

He jerked his head around. "Why don't you use your
father's pocket-clock?"

"I gave it to Duodecimus."

"He will lose it, to be sure. Well, I shall get you
another—one with a minute-hand like this." He flipped
open the lid of his clock. "This is the most remarkable
invention, Pegge."

The tomcat landed at her feet with a bushtit clamped in
his mouth. She pried open the cat's jaws and the bird flew
out. The last time he had shown off such a trophy, only the
beak and a pair of feet had fallen to the earth.

"Constance brought us a *London Gazette* with a report of
the fire," William said. "After we got away, the wind turned
south and drove the flames into the Thames. Only nine
people died, but thirteen thousand houses and eighty-
seven churches were destroyed. Thirteen churches were
saved, the same as the number of taverns."

Thirteen thousand homes! The City had been folded
down from quarto to octavo size. Another scrap of book-
paper crumbled in Pegge's hands. "Were all the books in
Paul's crypt destroyed?"

"They burned for a week and the booksellers are wholly in ruin, with £150,000 of stock in cinders. Pegge, are you attending? When your sister's coach pulled up, she saw you walk off in the opposite direction with something in your hand. She said it looked like a rat."

"It was a dead mole that I found under the leaves. I wanted to show Duo what an odd nose it had, but he was gone."

"I cannot have my wife playing with dead animals. What was Constance to think?"

"I presume she told you herself." Pegge assessed the espaliered pear tree. While she was in London, it had been crucified with nails. She must find something else for Angus to do. His hands were like mangles and he had no idea how to prune. "I was not in the mood for her bullying. Why did you send Duodecimus back to school without telling me?"

"Do you think you are in a fit state to mother him? What made you go into the City when the fire was raging? Cheapside was an inferno. Had you no fear of being set alight, or crushed by falling timber? I would never have learned what became of you."

"There was something I needed to do on my own." He had not seen that, just as he had not seen that this was the cat that had been burnt in the fire.

"You took that daft old Walton with you—was that *alone?*—and stole your father's effigy right from the heart of Paul's. What earthly use is that colossus? You should have let it go up in flames." His hands fell still. "Pegge, there is a bee on my sleeve."

"It thinks you are a flower. Be quiet and it will go away."

An anxious minute passed. "I am being quiet, but it is still hovering."

"There it goes. You are all right now."

She had tied up the stalks of the white lilies and would need to lift the bulbs after the first frost. *Alabaster* or *ivory*, William called the colour, *opal* or *pearl*. He never used a plain English word like *white* when a foreign one would do. She felt the tom underneath her skirts, chafing her ankles, and tied it to a stake a little further off.

"That beast is more to you than I am. Why do you torment me? You are like a cat playing with a garter. You will say nothing, tell me nothing—and yet I see you writing morning after morning in that book of yours—"

"Let me be, William," she said softly. "You should have married one of my sisters instead. Either Bridget or Betty would have taken you gladly."

"I wanted *you*," he said. He sat stiffly on the bench observing the cat tumbling in the mint, seemingly on the verge of some discovery about the animal.

"I told you that I was John Donne's daughter, that I was Ann More's child, that I could never stop being what I was, but you took me all the same."

"You knew I wanted something beyond the ordinary—" He broke off, colouring. "Why do men have such yearnings, if they cannot be satisfied?"

When had William become such a philosopher? "There are different kinds of wanting," she said. "Some are like games." She knew she had chosen the wrong word as soon as she tasted it like a tart plum in her mouth.

"And you, Margaret, what is your sport? You must stop walking about like a madwoman, picking up feathers and scraps of fur. The stableboy tells me that you stripped most of the hairs from your mare's tail."

"For the fishing line I will make for Duo. Don't curl your lip, William. What do you expect me to do? You have sent my sons away to school and married off my daughters." She counted them on her fingers. "Mrs Scott, Mrs Spelman, Mrs Tempest, Mrs Wight, Mrs Bispham. Their husbands will never be free of their ambition. They seem so little of my body, I am ashamed to have bred them. Even my dear little Franny."

"Let us not talk sadly of Franny," William said in exasperation. "She is doing very well with Thomas Bispham."

"What does a girl of sixteen know?"

"If you must have the truth, it was all Franny's doing. I defy any father to wed his daughters to men they dislike nowadays. It cannot be done."

Poor William, his doublet was looking far too tight. "But he is such a tiresome man. I do not know where you and Con find them."

"I daresay you thought me tiresome too, though we have learnt to get along well enough. You will be lonely here with Franny and Duo gone. I wish you would be more welcoming to your sister. She was like a mother to you after your own mother died."

"Is that what Con told you?" Pegge ripped out some spreading pimpernel. "She has no business here now that our daughters are married. Since Walton is gone, you must send Con away as well."

"It is not good for you to be alone at Clewer. Come to London with me to help Franny with her baby," William said, "or ask her to come here."

"Franny doesn't want me."

"I think you'll find she does."

"I have years of neglect to put right in this garden. I must have my fish pool to breed carp in, William."

"And your goose-foot paths, your serpentine tunnel—"

"And my grassy solitude."

"Next you will want to build a folly for the Dean's effigy. To think it almost cost your life—why on earth you tried to save it in that raging fire—and that cat, yes, that very cat," he pointed to the well-groomed tom, "to pick up a filthy stray! I suppose I shall never get you back to the City again."

He would bluster himself out in a minute. "It must be past four o'clock," she said, "for the bindweed is closed. The stonemason will not finish cleaning the effigy today."

"Even if all the flowers in Christendom nod off, I will not let you put yourself in such danger again. Are you attending, Pegge?" He raised his index finger. "You know I can be fierce when I want to."

"And I must have a new gardener, William. Angus is impossible. I will begin the fish pool in the new moon when the wind is from the west. Soon we will have carp biting. You must let me have all your pheasants' tail-feathers for my flies."

"Be damned, Pegge, you can have the whole covey if you ask for it. Only let the servants bring the birds to you, don't go scrambling after them yourself. You have the bad habit of frightening my birds out of laying."

She turned towards him and unbuttoned his doublet. "Open your chest. Breathe in the air. A deep breath, William, not a flutter. There, I saw a smile. You must work harder at being a quarrelsome husband, for you have had so little practice at it. We are a poor pair of quarrellers if we cannot keep it up for more than a few minutes at a time."

—

William watched Pegge lift up her old gardening skirts to shake them out. "Have your feet been bare this whole time? Have you no sense, woman? It's almost Michaelmas."

The wind was whistling the leaves into hollows, then whirling them up and scattering them. He put a branch on Pegge's leaves to hold them down until Angus slouched back with the empty bag. Pegge untied the cat from the stake, brushing her face against its fur and settling it into her elbow. Her other arm slipped under William's, letting him lead her back towards the house.

"Will you eat a freshly caught grayling, William? It will put you in better humour. You are in the country now, and must study to enjoy it."

"Did that fool Walton catch it?"

"It is a tasty fish all the same."

"And is he truly gone? I suppose you will want some of my claret," he said grudgingly. "I do not know why I bother to employ a cook. Grayling, you say?"

"You know you like the way I dress it."

She leaned against him, a faint odour of smoke about her, as they walked past the stonemason putting away his tools.

"I want to stay in the country, William. London is no place to be after the fire. When the King calls, you must go back to the City alone. Duo will stay here with me. Angus can row him across the river to school each day. Let me have my last child a little longer."

"I do not think—" He felt her finger on his lips, calming their sputtering.

"Don't answer now, William."

They had been married more than thirty years, yet he still wondered at the unfathomable brownness of her eyes. After the fright she had given him, when he was sure she had been consumed in the blazing streets around St Paul's, he would give her anything and bear everything.

"You will have your fish pool and your conservatory and your maison rustique. You will have everything you wish, Pegge, for you know I can deny you nothing." *Only do not die before me, for I cannot live without you.*

24. A FLATTERING MISCHIEF

Why did he lack the courage to ask Pegge what had been disturbing her since the fire? Of all things, that was what William most wished to know. She had been walking about the house at night, tempting him to follow her into uninhabited corners, until he came to believe that she was playing with him.

William had just been called back to London to assess the repairs needed to the King's clothing as a result of the fire. That morning, when he went downstairs to tell Pegge, he heard her in the breakfast room, reading her book aloud to the burnt tom, telling a mad tale that only a cat would understand. As he came up behind, she shifted position so he could not see the book, her face only an inch from the page.

"Why are you still writing, Pegge? I thought this nonsense would stop when Mr Walton left."

She began to say something, hesitated, then wrote a sentence.

"This cannot go on," he said.

She closed the book on top of the quill.

"Show me what you are writing." It came out sharper than he intended.

"You must promise you will not ask me that again." She drew the book towards her with a pathetic gesture.

How dare she turn him into some sort of ogre? After all these years of forbearance, of explaining her to everyone, to the servants, even to her own children! Held against her chest, the book looked absurdly fragile. He suddenly realized that it had shrunk considerably in size. What if there was more than one?

He went upstairs and took the key from its hiding place. She had asked him never to look in her cabinet, but now, he told himself, polishing the key against his cuff, checking that it was right side up, he was fearful that she was becoming melancholy. A husband had a right to guard his wife. Had a *responsibility*, he corrected himself, turning the key, to protect her.

Her father's old cabinet had no space for the idle curiosities of women. He found it choked with books, lopsided, at all angles, so that when he extracted one, the others tumbled onto the floor, spilling open shamelessly. Over the years, without his knowing, Pegge had collected all the posthumous works of John Donne, defacing— scribbling over and ruining—each and every one. This was not simply jotted marginalia. The pages were black with smudge, the writing abandoned, deranged, indecipherable, full of animal cunning.

So *this* was where her father's books had got to. It was Pegge who had stolen them from his study, not the parliamentary soldiers in their raids on Clewer. She had probably disordered his shelves herself to make it look as if the Roundheads had done it.

The cat leapt onto Pegge's old bed to get a better look. As soon as he and Pegge were betrothed, the lacquered cabinet had arrived in a wagon from the Deanery riding on top of the monstrous bed, which William had always hated. He had slept there with Pegge only the previous night, a night of joy, their last together for some time since he was going back to London on his own. The impertinent cat had watched the whole performance, inciting William to complain about the bed's unpleasant creaking and to threaten to turn it into firewood. Afterwards, stretching out her limbs, Pegge confessed the history of the bed. Not only was it her father's marriage-bed, she said, but he had also died in it. She would never sleep in another, so William must never speak of harming it again.

How could he come to Pegge's bed knowing that it was her father's? And to tell him only now, after all these years, to confess it with such equanimity as if it were a nothing! This was a more alarming crime than stealing her father's effigy and hiding it on William's property.

William was no poet, but he knew that something was amiss. He was on the verge of telling Pegge he was tired of John Donne and his notorious passion, but the cat was staring rudely, as if it were William who was doing something wrong.

At any moment, Pegge might come upstairs. What if the books had been in some nonsensical order and she could tell they had been tampered with? He could not risk sparking an argument with her in her current state. Fitting the books into the cabinet as best he could, he replaced the wad of matted hair—surely it was not Izaak Walton's?—and returned the key to her old shoe. Then he jostled the cabinet, knocking the ornaments off the top, as if the cat had done it.

William waited in the hall, his eyes fixed on his new pocket-clock. The minute-hand was making a most satisfactory haste to the top of the hour and his baskets sat ready for the coachman. At ten o'clock, the coach pulled up to take him back to the King's service. As he walked to the door, his cloak held firmly over the book underneath, he could hear Pegge at the top of the stairs, upbraiding the cat in the gentlest possible tones.

In London, all talk was of the fire. William learned that a young French watchmaker, Monsieur Hubert, had been condemned at the Old Bailey for starting the blaze. Escaping from the drudgery of his father's clockworks at Rouen was no crime. Nor was turning his back on Catholic France. Hubert's mistake, William concluded, was to head towards Protestant England, since he was accused of hurling a Papist fireball through the window of Thomas Farrinor's bakery in Pudding lane, *devilishly, feloniously, voluntarily and of his own malice aforethought*, though it was more likely he had enjoyed the flames from a ship moored in the Thames.

Now troublemakers were thirsting for exotic blood. William heard stories of Papists, Hollanders, and Frenchmen left in the streets for dead, and strangers attacked for no greater offense than speaking butchered

English. Even the Catholic Duke of York was accused of being an incendiary for seeming too gay upon his stallion as he fought against the flames. Pegge's dancing-master, de la Valière, had been chased back to France and Monsieur Belland, the King's firework-maker, had hidden under the King's own nose in Whitehall, trusting his life to Charles's fondness for French wine, dances, clothes—and fireworks.

However, William knew that the royal taste could change, just as the royal locks had greyed and William had been forced to shave his head and don a wig of human hair. Before the fire, the King wore his breeches slung low on the hips like his cousin the French King's, but now public feeling was against it and Charles prudently declared that he was giving up all things French. Since vast sums were needed to rebuild the City, he would teach the nobility thrift by wearing only simple English vests, swearing to be in the fashion within the week.

William had to cut quickly. The King's Wardrobe had burnt to the ground, so he was working out of Hatton Garden. He found a length of velvet in a new blush colour that had been purchased for a lady's chair and draped it over his shoulder in front of the mirror. He cut freehand, shaping as he went, until he had cut and basted together a long flared cassock in the Eastern manner. Ruffling the breeches over the thighs, he trimmed the white stockings with ribbons and the high-heeled shoes with bows.

The King declared that he liked William's new fashion so much he would never be out of it. The royal mistresses admired the King's new colour, calling it *pink* after the flower of the same name. However, Lord St Albans said that the royal thighs were puffed up like pigeon's legs, and pointed out that the coat flapped when the King walked, wagering that the King would soon abandon his *skirts*.

"Look," St Albans said loudly to the ladies, "His Majesty blushes like his suit."

The King had no choice but to laugh and enter the betting at a hundred to one.

William was in court two days later when Lord St Albans strode in wearing a strikingly plain black cassock and a justaucorps with buttons in a strict row from collar to hem. The breeches were tight and clean, without a ruffle or a ribbon. The whole effect, William saw with misgiving, was frankly masculine. The King was outraged, accusing William of dressing him like a capon or, worse, a Persian eunuch. He commanded William to pay the £100 he had lost on the wager and sent at once for St Albans's tailor.

William was now back making tents. On his table was the box of drawing tools inherited from his father, who had been the Groom and Yeoman of Tents, Toiles, Hayes, and Pavilions for Queen Elizabeth, King James, and Charles I, dying just after that monarch was beheaded.

William's compass bit into the paper, inscribing a circle the diameter of a pomegranate. In front of him was the six-sided fruit that Pegge had grown in her garden at Clewer. The bumpy peel conjured up extravagant textures and fringes for the pavilion he was designing for the King's next ball. The rich colour would make it fit to hold a harem of royal mistresses. He imagined Blackamoor eunuchs crushing pomegranates with their feet to extract the dye for nine

hundred yards of Egypt cotton. From the leftover fabric
William would make a smaller tent for Clewer garden with
a poufed top and tasselled corners, into which he would
entice Pegge to take the shade with him in summer.

Why did Pegge so love red fruit?—crunchy unripe per-
simmons, mulberries, red apples and pears, gooseberry fool,
stewed winter plums. He recalled the flash of white ankle
as she placed the pomegranate on his palm the night before
he had left Clewer. She had neglected to put on her stockings again—done it to tease him, he was sure, so she would
have less clothing to take off when they lay together.

William had fallen in love with that boyish calf thirty-five
years earlier in St Paul's. He had hardly attended to the
Dean's sermon, for he had just discovered that his new doublet buttoned right over left, not left over right like a man's,
which lessened the pleasure of the garment. Afterwards, he
went into Paul's walk, stopping beside Duke Humphrey's
tomb to note the cut and stuff of the fashions that passed
by, especially the women's, for he was of an age to marry.

In the shadows a girl stood looking out at him. There
was no modesty in her eyes, just an English brown. Her
hair was beguilingly short and soft like flocking, and her
nose was bred for wisdom, not for flattery. He knew this
was Margaret Donne, one of the daughters the Dean was
seeking husbands for, since he had seen her at her father's
sermon only a quarter-hour earlier.

Taking a pomegranate from her pocket, she placed it on
the tomb, sawed through it with a straight-blade, then
popped the seeds out of the leathery skin and scooped

them up with her teeth. Above her blood-red lips, deeper than madder, deeper than any red that he had ever known, her dark eyes mocked him, forthright in their wit.

The first time William had heard the Dean preach was when he had made enemies of the ladies at court by saying that painting the skin was prostitution and wearing silk an excuse for women to go naked in clothes. No wonder this daughter hid herself in drab woollens. Yet her hips swung charmingly as she walked away, proof to William's eye that she put no store in layers of under-garments. Unveiled, she would be a slim, nude statue of the finest marble.

William had heard odd stories about the Dean and the children he had raised himself. And yet his own father thought a match with Margaret Donne desirable for William's brother, writing to George, *You could do worse. Her bloodline is itself a dowry, fetching back to Sir Thomas More.*

George was in Venice at the time, confined to a surgeon's care. *The pain of the ulcers,* he wrote to William, *is like none I have ever known. A woman's touch is excruciating—and in a city which numbers four prostitutes to every priest! In no case must you tell our father of my indiscretion.* William was to send money for the sweating cure and for silk, the only cloth George could tolerate against his skin.

Then the Dean died, and William was by his own good management betrothed to Pegge himself. After their wedding supper on Lucy's eve, they retired to the bridal chamber, he climbing expectantly into her high bed, and she dismissing the old servant who had helped her into her garments—*Leave us, Bess, I shall unclothe myself.* Dipping a sponge into a bowl of water, she washed away her alabaster face and turned towards him, her cheekbones blushing a delicate shell-rose. In a flash of anger, he saw that her skin was deeply scored with pocks. What he had thought were beauty marks were scars.

Years before, when his mother's face had been disfigured by small-pox, his father had said that a woman whose face was filthy by nature must mend it by art, like Jezebel. William's mother died and his father took a younger wife, saying privately to his sons, *You might well wonder why I put my neck into the halter a second time. Marriage is a bondage, a thraldom, a yoke, and yet a man needs such release as can only be found between a woman's legs.*

On his wedding night, William felt cheated, but only a little, and only until Pegge slipped under the bed linen to join him and her leg snaked over his calf, hooking his foot, her strong limbs locking tight with his. Her body held no disfigurement he could discern, the skin unblemished and undefiled, a pale creamy marble, though much warmer to the touch, her breasts as decorous as fledgling doves.

Afterwards, she fell asleep, her arms and legs outspread and her short chestnut hair sticking up in flocks, and he could not stop thinking of a silly rhyme about Queen Elizabeth that his mother had taught him as a child.

Her bosom, sleek as Paris plaster,
Held up two balls of alabaster.

Thank God Pegge had not died of small-pox. Over the years, the marks had faded to a dimpling on her cheeks, hollows to tempt midday shadows to bed down in.

It was dark outside William's workroom and the pomegranate was warm in his hands. This was his east, his India of need. He placed the fruit on his drawings as a paperweight, putting away his draughting tools. He took a coach as far as he could, then walked past the empty shell of Paul's towards one of the thirteen taverns that had survived the fire.

—

When William entered the Three Cranes, he saw a man sitting at the back showing something in a wooden case to a serving-maid.

"You must be Mr Pepys, for there is nobody else about. Lord Sandwich said I would find you here. I am William Bowles." He slid onto the bench and sent the girl for some hot sack. "It is bitterly cold this night. What is that object, Mr Pepys?"

"My kidney-stone."

Pepys handed it to William, who inspected it politely. A frightening specimen, it was as big as a tennis ball and a good deal heavier.

"It was cut from my groin eight years ago." Pepys told the harrowing tale in a ringing voice, then restored the relic to the padded box.

The dark alehouse suited William, though he could have wished for a more discreet companion. No doubt Pepys had heard about the King's disastrous new fashion, and William did not need his wounds rubbed with coarser salt. He knew Pepys had come up rapidly in the King's service and was now Clerk of the Navy, weathering even the recent sinking of a ship. Under a vast untidy wig which must have cost a full £4, Pepys was wearing one of the new masculine vests, but so plain and thin at the back that he seemed pinched with cold.

Pepys's talk was peppered with vulgarities no better than an ordinary seaman's, though he had a greater intimacy with foreign tongues. When the girl brought the hot sack, Pepys expressed a desire to tocar her mamelles and put her mano against his cosa, a seasick mélange that had barely crossed the Channel. *The man is as much a cheat as his waist-coat*, thought William, but at least Pepys did not seem inclined to discuss fashion, and for that William was grateful.

He unwrapped his parcel and pushed the battered folio in Pepys's direction. "I have come to ask your opinion of this book."

Pepys ran his hands over the binding and read the title, *LXXX Sermons preached by that learned and reverend Divine, John Donne, Dr in Divinity, late Dean of the Cathedral Church of St Paul's, London, with The Life and Death of Dr Donne by Iz. Wa.* Then he examined a few pages. "With so many books burnt in St-Faith's-under-Paul's, this folio would fetch a ransom, yet it is hardly worth a penny in this condition." He looked accusingly at William. "It is so defaced I can barely make out the print."

William tried to curb his impatience. "It is not the value that concerns me, it is this strange annotation. Lord Sandwich said that you know code."

"It is not in code."

"Come, man, it cannot be read!"

Pepys tipped the book upside down, then opened it from the end. "It is written in the Chinese manner, from back to front."

"Never mind the manner. What do the symbols mean?"

"It is tachygraphy, a system devised for taking down sermons, and written in a woman's script." Pepys plunged in, sounding out the words. "*I was enticed to London to dance the*—here is a foreign word, perhaps *coranto*—*at court, but found myself breathing the close air of the drawing room instead. It was worse than the*—and now she names a country dance she despises, I think the *branle*, or it may be the *pavane*, for the writing is very blotted."

William's teeth were aching from the sack and he was sure his head would pain him in the morning.

"If I am not mistaken," Pepys said, leafing through a few more pages, "this was written by the woman who became John Donne's wife. Look, their names are here—*Ann More, John Donne*—and afterwards she has written *Ann Donne* in the manner of a besotted girl." Turning the book around, he tried to make out Izaak Walton's biography beneath the handwriting. "Mrs Donne died many years before this book was printed. How could she have written in this volume? The dead cannot write."

They can speak, though, William thought, assailed by fear. He felt in great need of some strong drink, for the sack was far too sweet. "The dead think only of their own needs, they care not for the living." He extracted the book from Pepys's grasp, restored it to the wrapper and tied the string vigorously, knotting it several times for good measure.

"I would be glad to read some more," Pepys protested.

"There is no need, Mr Pepys, no need. I have the gist."

"Then later, sir. You may wish me to translate the rest."

"I should not think of troubling you. If you will tell me where to find the key, I shall perform the task myself." William shoved the parcel underneath the bench. "And now, I insist on buying you a supper."

"I would rather read ten pages of that book you have spirited away," Pepys said. "John Donne, Ann Donne, undone—do you know the story?" William must have shown his dismay, for Pepys hurried on. "Of course, everyone has heard it. But do you not think it odd that the woman is writing from her grave?"

"The lady who wrote this is not dead, although—" William stopped, wishing the words back in his mouth, and his mouth wrapped round a tankard. He took one straight out of the serving-maid's hand as she went past.

"Then why is she playing such a masquerade? The woman believes she is someone else. This is no idle game. It would have taken months to write."

"I have seen several volumes in the same condition," William admitted, "but I do not dare confront her, for she is subject to fits and distractions. You know what is said about sleeping dogs."

"Let them lie, let them lie," Pepys said peaceably, rooting around in his wig with his finger.

"If she thought she had been found out, she might do some violence to herself. Discretion, Mr Pepys, discretion is best where women are concerned."

"I understand you perfectly," Pepys said, stroking his

nose. "I shall press you no further, but if I could do you service as translator . . ."

William downed a numbing draught. "What do you say to a cask of oysters?"

"I shall not say no to oysters," Pepys replied, "for you know their reputation. Though, in truth, my wife allows me to lie with her but seldom. Of late, her spaniel has been sleeping on her bed and growls when I come near her."

The more crowded the room became, the more it was needful to yell, and the more at ease William felt. "You are fortunate to have your wife in London, Mr Pepys," he shouted. "Mine cannot tolerate it."

When the serving-maid returned to ask how they did, Pepys sang out "Come aloft" and pulled her onto his lap. While he fumbled at her, saying picturesquely in his sailor's polyglot that he wished to hazer his cosa in her eglisa, William consulted his pocket-clock.

"What an amazing instrument," he announced when Pepys's hands were back on his drink. "It will affect every aspect of our lives." He showed Pepys the new minute-hand, then pointed out the engraving on the back. *Hubert. Rouen. 1666.* "A young man of that name has just been hanged at Tyburn. We live in a paupered kingdom, my friend, if we cannot trust the French. He died because of a fire he did not set."

"So did my little shoemaker, though he never set foot out of Fleet street in his life. Today his shoes have taken me from my home in Seething lane to the King's dressing chamber in Whitehall, from thence to the Navy Office, and then here to the Three Cranes."

"I was once a Gentleman of the Bedchamber, but am now reduced to making tents as my grandfather began."

"But surely you have sons," Pepys countered. "My wife has given me none."

"Mine has given birth to three."

"So we each covet what the other has, and wish our own lot changed."

"And so doth all humanity. Let us drink to that." William thought of Duodecimus slouching along the backs at Clewer, keeping to the upwind side of the sty, his arms heaped with winter pippins for the swine. "My eldest son is a spendthrift and my youngest talks to pigs," he said gloomily. "I can scarce see myself in the boy. There can be bitterness in sons, my friend."

"Perhaps your wife came from a lesser family?" Pepys ventured.

"My wife had the education of a prince."

Pepys selected a fat oyster and slid it down his throat. "In this new reign, most think a woman learned and wise if she can distinguish her husband's bed from another man's."

"My sons could have no better pedigree. My wife's bloodline descends from one of England's Lord Chancellors. For that genius to die out is unthinkable, yet it is easier to breed good dogs. When I wish to improve a pointer, I choose a bitch and stud with good ancestry and, from the resulting litter, I pick the best bitch and breed her again with the same stud. Within a few generations, I have a superior dog. But with humans, it is impossible to breed true, for no one breeds uncle to niece, nor grandsire to granddaughter, though it might improve the race a hundredfold."

Pepys rooted in his wig again, considering this point. "Well, sir, the worst I can see is that you have sired rich tailors, and I will always be the son of a poor one. Neither of us will starve, and neither will make baronet!" He toasted William with his tankard. "May I ask the name of your wigmaker, sir?"

"A Frenchman still in Paris, but I fear that source is drying up."

"This ship came with a vicious cargo," Pepys said, squashing a louse between his fingers.

"Have your man powder it well and the nits will come out in the comb."

"You will always have a job in the Navy if you know how to get rid of lice," Pepys said. "Now here's a frigate anchoring in your port."

The girl was at William's elbow. When he held up his tankard for refilling, his arm brushed against hers— accidentally, he hoped, burying his nose back in his drink.

Pepys hit his fist against his palm. "You will never make junior officer if you seize her as tamely as that. When she docks again, you must hook your thumbs under her gunwales. Now here's how it's done."

As the girl returned with their suppers, Pepys clapped her on the breech and steered her into harbour. The two locked arms and sang a verse of "She Cannot Keep her Legs Together." William had never been so foxed with drink. He fiddled with his pocket-clock, scarcely able to read the dial until the girl sailed off.

"You seem a man of science," Pepys said. "You must join our society of virtuosos."

Over a venison pasty, Pepys reported on the experiment at the last meeting of the Royal Society, in which the blood of one dog was transferred to another. The first dog died on the table, but the second did very well, Pepys said. The success of this experiment gave rise to jests about the blood of a Quaker being let into an Archbishop, with many coarse asides, leading the members to speculate whether blood could be let into the mummified corpse which had miraculously survived the fire in St Paul's crypt.

This mummy, Pepys told William, was rumoured to be the great Dr Donne, whose marble statue had vanished mysteriously in the fire. An enterprising man had wired Donne's remains to the wreckage of the cathedral, to the amusement of passers-by, who declared it uncorrupted both by time and flame. The most daring paid a penny to climb up the man's ladder to kiss the mummy's stiffened lips.

Some said this incorruptibility was proof that Donne should be made a saint, but others jested that—given the lewdness of the man's elegies—they should bring in a whore to work a different kind of art. Pepys told this tale rather too gaily, as if he had kissed the mummy on the lips himself.

The bench was digging into William's thighs. This was certainly not the time to divulge that he was John Donne's son-in-law, a fact he had shared with few acquaintances. The effigy grinning in Paul's choir had been public show enough. Izaak Walton had stirred up the dust with his biography of Donne, and there was no need for greater fools to canonize him. William hoped he could keep the news of this uncorrupted mummy from reaching Pegge in the country.

William saw Mr Batelier approaching their table, a welcome diversion. Batelier had come to report that he could get no more French wine for Mr Pepys because of the King's ban on importing goods.

"No more French fabric either, Sir William," Batelier declared. "All garments must henceforth be made of English cloth."

Even corpses, William learned, must now be dressed in loyal wool and under-garments made of itchy homegrown stuff. The ban had angered the King of France, who was mocking King Charles's new fashion by putting his menservants into two-piece suits like the ones the English lords were wearing.

"What an ingenious affront for one King to make upon another," Pepys said admiringly.

William was well out of it. He would make the new pavilion out of plain Suffolk-cloth, for he had advanced the King £2,000 since his return to England. What need for eunuchs to crush exotic produce underfoot? English beetroot would do just as well for a King who did not pay his debts. Fixed with alum, it would dye the royal tent the same shade as would eastern pomegranates.

Made merry by Batelier's tale about the French, Pepys was whispering to the serving-maid that he would have her both devante and backwards, which she would find a bon plazer. It seemed there was no law against importing foreign words. Pepys was forward with women, but there was no denying that the King had entrusted an entire navy to the man. Since the sinking of the unsinkable *Double Bum*, that nonsensical double-bottomed ship, had not soured Pepys's reputation, all his talk of gizmos and mamelles was not likely to scuttle him.

William stood up to go, feeling unseaworthy himself from all the drink. As he struggled to get his legs over to the door, he heard Pepys call out, "Sir William, your folio!" and saw it travelling towards him on top of the wooden box which held Pepys's kidney-stone.

As they left the tavern, a lurking dog fell in behind them. Pepys swore and kicked it away halfheartedly then admitted that it was his wife's pet come to fetch him. Its behaviour was odd, Pepys said, for up to now there had been no love lost between them.

A breeding experiment gone wrong, William thought, bending to inspect the dog through the intelligence of drink. "A toy, bred as a lapdog like the King's spaniels," he announced, "but it came from working animals. Train it to the leash and it will heed you well enough. Take my advice, Mr Pepys," he yelled at his parting friend, "and train her to the leash!"

25. VIRTUOSO

Samuel Pepys stumbled home in the vertiginous shadows, following his wife's spaniel through streets bereaved by fire, unable to discern the truth of the shapes weaving around him in the dark.

Inside his house, he went straight to his library. Closing his eyes, he called up the size of the book he was looking for, then opened the correct bookcase and put his hand on it at once. Walton's *Life of Donne*, not the first edition with the sermons, but a smaller second one. He was convinced that shelving books by size was the most logical method and could not understand why no one else adopted it.

He found his wife sitting up in bed wearing the loose morning-gown he called her kingdom for the ease and content she had in the wearing of it. The spaniel was already on top of her blanket, chin down, eyeing Pepys with new respect—or was it mutiny? On their walk home together, Pepys had warned the animal that if it snarled at him again, he would throw it out the window.

Now he leaned back in a chair, his eyes closed, as Elizabeth picked out the passages in the biography that interested her, a habit that annoyed him. As she read aloud, he drifted, worrying about the ache in his cods and thinking of what he would record in his diary before climbing into his own bed. *Strange*, he might write, *with what freedom and quantity I pissed this night, which I know not what to impute to but my oysters . . .*

But soon he was listening, for Elizabeth was reading from the year 1612 when John Donne left his wife with child in England to travel to the continent. In Paris, he suffered a dreadful vision in which Ann passed before his eyes, her hair down about her shoulders, carrying her dead infant in her arms. Days later, as Walton related the story, Donne discovered that his wife had indeed given birth to a stillborn child on that very day.

"This is a relation that will beget some wonder, and it well may, for most of our world are at present possessed with an opinion that visions and miracles are ceased," Elizabeth read. *"And, though it is most certain that two lutes, being both strung and tuned to an equal pitch, and then one played upon, the other will, like an echo to a trumpet, warble a faint audible harmony in answer to the same tune, yet many will not believe there is any such thing as a sympathy of souls."*

Elizabeth's voice caught and she laid the book aside. "Is it possible for such a thing to pass between two lovers, Samuel?"

Pepys shifted, cleared his throat, made a show of picking up the book to read it for himself, although his sight was blurry.

Elizabeth took his hand and drew it over her body, sliding it beneath her kingdom. This act was so intimate, this coolness of his hand on the warmth of his wife's belly, that he was ashamed, as he had never been ashamed with all his mistresses in all his acts of unfaithfulness. He tried to withdraw his hand, but she put hers on top and pressed down, wanting him to feel the riches growing there. He did not wish to think about this child. It could not be discussed lightly, shared with drinking companions in taverns. In desperation, he recalled their former housemaid and tried to feel wronged because Elizabeth had forced him to give up the girl, but he could not summon any righteousness. Instead, his eyes began to water.

"Do you feel it?" Elizabeth asked.

He could almost feel a small heartbeat below his wife's unsteady, excited one. It was a palpitation, a small miracle. Perhaps this *was* a sympathy of souls, for Elizabeth could not be with child. He thought of the sage water and holland-drawers and all the other schemes she had tried in order to conceive. He knew that long ago she had added barrenness to her list of shortcomings, along with her tin ear and untidiness and her lack of skill at drawing, letter-writing, and household economy. He had grown to accept his fate, for even a king might wed a barren queen.

Sometimes, in the theatre, Pepys heard wind-music so sweet that it ravished him and wrapped up his soul so that he felt truly sick, just as he had when first in love with his wife and ravished by her youth and beauty. Elizabeth Le Marchant de St Michel had been but fourteen, with sideways glances and dark hair à la négligence. He had been so desperate to have her that he took her without a dowry. Forced to sell his lute for forty shillings, he had not felt the poorer. Since they could not pay a servant, she had carried in coals and carried out his chamber pot and washed his foul clothes, all with her young soft hands.

That had been ten years ago, when her beauty had tempered her wilfulness. But after the fire, Elizabeth had taken umbrage at the odious verses circulating about the Papists and at the arrest of Monsieur Hubert, who was French like herself. She took Hubert's martyrdom upon her head, and worked herself into such a rage that her hair began to fall out. Much as Pepys tried to convince her that Hubert was a known madman, and that it was foolhardy to take up his cause, Elizabeth was resolute. He feared that at any moment she might fly into a fit and cry out that she was Catholic in front of the servants, which would be as good as slipping a noose around both their necks.

In the weeks after the fire, the pain in what she called her *chose* worsened, and her eyes darkened when they lay together. Even though he told her that the wife must feel pleasure in order to conceive, she lay stiff and afraid beneath him. After supper one night, when the maid was combing his hair and he believed his wife was asleep in her bed, Elizabeth suddenly reappeared and found him with his hand under the maid's petticoat and, indeed, with his hand on her cunny. Though he endeavoured to put it off lightly, Elizabeth was not pacified. She flew into a tantrum, threatening to slit the maid's nose and squeeze his cods with the hot fire-tongs.

For twenty days Elizabeth rose in the morning to comb and dress him with her own sweet hands, so that the maid would not need to do it. The grooming would begin tenderly, but would soon shift into a witchhunt for lice. At last, he was forced to send the maid away, and on that night slept with great content with his wife, writing in his diary, *I must here remember that I have lain with my moher as a husband more times since this falling-out than in I believe twelve months before, and with more pleasure to her than I think in all the time of our marriage.* Within a week he could record that his home was in *a tolerable peace full of pretty kind words* and that he *did hazer con ella to her content* when they lay together, imploring God *to give me the grace more and more every day to fear Him, and to be true to my poor wife.*

And now, since she had felt such pleasure, Elizabeth thought herself with child and he was once again an exile from her bed. For several days she had stayed in her chamber, enjoying the luxury of maternity, although she was only a week late with her fleurs.

His hand still rested on her drowsing belly. If he withdrew it, she would wake, and he could not bear the joy he would see on her face. He knew now that the maid was only a passing fancy, and that this profound ache he felt for Elizabeth had driven it away. In all of his dalliances, he had never fathered a child, and in spite of her music, drawing, and dancing-masters, and all the other eager voluntaries who had come her way, including Lord Sandwich, Elizabeth had never been unfaithful. For if she had, Pepys knew she would have conceived. And all of this Elizabeth knew too, but some faint hope, some aberration of the female character, had caused her to believe, once more, as she had early in their marriage, that they might conceive together after all. And so she slumbered in her lavish kingdom, dreaming of carrying the son and heir to Samuel Pepys.

And this thought—that she had indeed felt the sympathy of souls, like a lute-string reverberating in her womb—must sustain him while he endured, as he knew he must endure (since her fleurs would bloom again), her tears and barren heartbreak.

26. GOING TO BED

William was at the table beside his bed in Clerkenwell, making notes by lamplight in a neat secretary hand. Working from the key that had arrived from Samuel Pepys—a tachygraphy book from Pepys's own library—he was discovering that Pegge had muddled the system by introducing symbols of her own. He rubbed his hand over his eyes, fearful of discovering foreign words such as Pepys used when three sheets in the wind.

William was making poor headway, but he could not face returning to Clewer until he knew what Pegge had written. Her angry smuts almost obliterated the print in Walton's *Life of Donne*. Surely it was not some amorous dialogue with that peculiar man?

While Walton was at Clewer, William had come upon Pegge leaning out an open window with him, their hair touching, Walton's a surprisingly youthful yellow. When William crept up behind them, they began to talk about the chances of good weather and a favourable breeze— perhaps a code of some kind that they shared? Soon afterwards, Walton had ridden off on William's horse, but a horse, William had since concluded, was a small price to pay to get Walton away from Pegge.

He closed the book and undressed for bed, aided by a manservant who stank of spirits. The man appeared to have spent the better part of the fire and its aftermath drinking his way through William's cellar.

Since returning to London, William had been having a dream as troubling as Nebuchadnezzar's. In the dream, the fire melted his gold and boiled his claret, then invaded the upper floor. It bore down upon him as he knelt in an uncombed wig in his bedchamber, surrounded by books which he was trying to sort into baskets by the system Pepys had described. Most of the servants had gone ahead to ferry his goods up the Thames. William was to take the baskets—and his wife—in the last barge, but Pegge had vanished. Not, he hoped, to a lesson with her dancing-master. The fire began to sizzle the back of his wig, and the horrid stench of scorched hair filled the chamber.

He tried to pull off the burning wig and awakened bolt upright, his hands clutching air instead. In fact, he was sitting on the edge of his bed with an itchy, unshaven scalp, staring at the wig on the bedpost, where his lazy manservant had hung it. His pocket-clock told him he had slept only an hour. He lay back down, determined not to think of Pegge.

As soon as his head was down, the dream resumed. This time, he was splayed upon his table, tied down securely by his hands and feet. His manservant was holding a bottle of brandy and a funnel. It was a puzzle gone horribly wrong, a blind-man's trompe l'oeil. A doctor

sharpened his knife on a whetstone under the eye of the
burnt cat, who was sitting on top of William's lungs,
squeezing out all the air. Could it be true that the lungs
were but a bellows, the human heart nothing more than a
mechanical pump? Pepys's tales were swilling in William's
head and he was gripped with sudden terror that should
he lose too much blood, the surgeon would try one of the
new blood exchanges, turning the insolent cat into the
King's tentmaker and William into a burnt, hairless tom
fastened to his wife's ankle with a string.

William felt the brandy funnelling down his throat as
the surgeon inserted the itinerarium into the mouth of his
penis, then fed it down by rapid twists and jerks, then
down further yet, by the same harrowing wrist-movements,
into the bladder. The surgeon tested the point of his rapier
against his thumb. He scored William from scrotum to
anus, then plunged in his thumbs and spread the halves
apart as neatly as splitting a ripe peach. A stone the size of
a tennis ball popped out of William's bladder and landed in
a wash of acrid fluid on the floor.

"Three minutes," the surgeon proclaimed, tapping
William's pocket-clock, "from the incision to the closure."

The surgeon calculated the weight of the specimen and
the amount of urine the bladder had expelled, as if present-
ing to the Royal Society, alluding to the possibility of
impotence only as an afterthought. The manservant made
a crude jest and finished off the brandy in one gulp.

William woke in his boarded-up house in Clerkenwell
and called out in distress for Pegge, who was not there. The
bed was rolling like a ship in heavy seas, and seasick doubts

were reeling in his head. He was in a sweat, yearning for his wife to comfort him, with only an indolent servant to inquire after his needs.

—

William pulled on his old cloak and walked towards a coffeehouse that had escaped the fire because it was made of brick. The landlord, who was doing a good business, took a pot off the grate, pouring William a penny-bowl. The same size had cost only a halfpenny on his last visit. Since there was no longer any competition, the landlord had not bothered to build up his fire. Even so, the coffee seared William's tongue and he pushed it aside. There was a faint whiff about his clothes which put him out of temper. What was the point of keeping a house in town when he had to live alone, except for servants who came and went like cats?

Outside, the wind was blowing away the coal-dust suspended over the City, exposing a French-blue sky with lacework clouds. In the distance, past a row of houses levelled by the fire, William could see a group of men gathering near the Si Quis door of Paul's.

Inside the coffeehouse, he smelled chocolate and looked for a woman. Instead, he noticed a small man with a roll of draughtsman's plans drinking down his bowl without taking time to sit. It was apparent that the man's three-quarter coat offered no protection from the cold, for he stood as close to the dying embers as he could. As the man wiped the chocolate from his lips, William recognized Christopher Wren, the surveyor appointed by the

King to assess the damage to the cathedral. When Dr Wren tried to button his coat, he discovered that the sides would not meet in front. Giving up, he went out the door, crossing the churchyard to join the gathering of men.

The buttons, William wanted to shout after him, *are purely ornamental!*

Soon, William thought, he would be the only gentleman in London dressed warmly, for he was determined never to wear the King's new two-piece suit. Another gust of cold came through the door and a hawker entered, peddling broadsides. Spotting a regular customer in William, he thrust the elegies under his nose. William gave the man a sixpence. As soon as he was gone, William tossed the poems on the grate, where they gave off a satisfying heat. He had only needed to read the words *Dr Donne to his Mistress to Come to Bed* to know the contents. Every lewd poem by every incompetent rhymester in the City had a similar title. William could have papered Paul's with the copies he had bought to keep them off the street.

Feeling a good deal better now that the fire was blazing up, William drank the cooled coffee, finding that it relieved the churning in his stomach. Then, hearing a commotion outside the window, he wrapped his cloak around his chest and went out to have a look. He followed the curious along Paternoster row, passing the burnt timbers of Walton's house and thinking unkind thoughts about the owner.

Along Panier alley, a farm wagon was scraping through the rubble with the sharp ring of metal against stone. The heavy load was barely clearing the foundations on either side and people were clambering on top of the ruins to watch the spectacle. The curious bodies were soon pressing so close that the horse balked at pulling the wagon further. It stopped in front of a sugarer's boy, pushing its nose against the boy's stomach until he stumbled backwards and dropped his brittle loaves. As the horse lowered its lips to scoop up the sugar, William noticed that its tail was too bedraggled to even bat a fly. It was Pegge's mare, which often liked to nudge their children backwards to make them trip at Clewer, and the woman comforting the boy was his own wife.

Now William looked more closely at the wagon. Steadying the load were his gardeners, Angus and his eldest son. On the top, scrubbed and cemented together, was the marble statue that William had last seen, languidly recumbent, in his own garden. Still connected to the soles of the Dean's feet, the marble urn was a ludicrous appendage when he was prone, like a leg-iron that weighed down a dead felon.

Why couldn't the man stay put in his grave? William could not seem to escape his father-in-law no matter where he went.

Grateful that he was wearing his new full-bottomed wig, which no one at Clewer had yet seen, he tugged it down over his eyebrows, then stepped back into the crowd.

27. THE WAY OF ALL FLESH

Pegge picked winter plums on the day that William left for London, spitting out angry words as she stripped the branches. Holding the basket, with good as well as mummified fruit hailing down upon him, Angus finally protested that she was murdering more than her plums.

She stacked the winter-sweets on William's bed, making them spell out his angular shape as if he were still there.

Just before William left that morning, Pegge noticed that her cabinet had been shifted. The tom might have jumped on it, but he certainly had not put the key into the wrong shoe or removed the folio of her father's sermons that she had written in. Anyone could have come into her room and stolen it—anyone alive, or even one of her many dead.

As winter drew closer, her monthlies became erratic, and an idea began to haunt her like a half-formed child within. She would wake at night, feeling her lost children like splinters in her fingers, but when she held her hand up to the candle, only bones shone through the translucent flesh. When she lay back down, twisted phrases echoed in her bedchamber. Sometimes Con spoke, and even little Franny uttered a word or two. Perhaps it was Ann stirring things up, choking Pegge with half-digested words. No wonder Cook complained of voices in the house.

The scrubbed effigy lay flat in the garden, waiting for William to come back to Clewer. He had told his servants that no man was to erect it until he returned. On All Souls, when William had been gone a month, Pegge ordered the gardeners to set up the block and tackle, then led Fox straight through the physic garden, which pulled the ropes smoothly through the pulleys, tipping her father smartly up, his feet still attached to his marble urn.

Before going to bed, she wrote one satisfying line in her book: *The wheel is the key to moving a great weight without men.*

Martinmas came and went, without even a letter from William. Servants were clothed for winter, beef was salted and hung. Pegge lifted her lily bulbs and carried her rare plants into the conservatory. Then she dug up the potatoes, brushing off the earth and arranging them on the children's empty beds with their eyes towards the ceiling.

That day Pegge received a letter from Franny, telling her mother that she had gone past the wreckage of St Paul's and seen a mummy fastened to some crude scaffolding. A huckster with a ladder was charging passers-by a penny to embrace the man he called John Donne. *Selling dead kisses,* Franny wrote, her penstrokes sullen and disgusted.

That night, a spicy embalming scent drew Pegge to a casement left open above the garden. Outside, the gleaming statue was illuminated by a cold coral moon. She walked out in her bare feet, the spongy earth oozing between her toes, and looked at her father's hooded eyes and vain moustache. Around the neck, where the head was cemented, there was a line like a bruise from a hangman's noose. She knew why William so disliked the effigy, for the grin was far too lifelike.

Pegge could remember little of her father's last moments. After all, she had been only seventeen, a child nursing a dying man. Sometimes, when she had visited the effigy in Paul's, she thought she saw it breathing faintly, as Walton reported in his *Life of Donne*. But in this garden, where everything was green and changing, she could see that the grin was lifeless marble. Any life in the statue was due to the sculptor's art.

Her father was never going to speak to her—how could he? He had become mute stone, calcined and pure from death.

—

A week later, Pegge left Angus with the farm wagon on the outskirts of London at dusk and rode ahead on Fox to check the route. It was the twelfth of December, St Lucy's eve, a night so long that she could return the effigy unseen.

Three months had passed since the fire had ravaged the City. As she rode up Fleet street towards Ludgate hill, the blackened skeleton of Paul's grew larger. She found Ludgate badly damaged, with rubble and new building bricks clogging the street. The pavingstones were heaved up haphazardly from the fire, worse than an attack from flood or ice. She would have to take the loaded wagon through another of the City's gates.

Five crows were skating on the air currents above the battered cathedral, a sign that a wind was building, a great troubled wind out of her father's sermons. A gust was already whistling at the Dean's corner and a newssheet flapped past, making the mare jump sideways. Fox's hooves were clattering, but there was no one to wake here with the noise. Only the burnt-out shells of houses now peopled the lanes. The City had never been so quiet, for even the church bells had been silenced when they had melted in the fire.

The wind was making the mare uneasy. Pegge dismounted and led Fox south to see whether her father's apple tree had survived the fire, but where the Deanery should have been was only a charred foundation with a few weeds taking root in the slimy black timbers. Pegge heard the old sexton dragging his lame foot as he took a shortcut through the Dean's court. When he was gone, she coaxed Fox through the broken wall. Pegge rested until the moon began to rise, then left the horse with a bucket of water from the old well.

The mummy was where Franny had told Pegge it would be, stuck up as high as a traitor outside Paul's for all to mock, on a piece of scaffolding that had survived the fire. The bellman called out the hour as he rounded the Dean's corner. It would be two hours before he came that way again.

The wind caught a bony foot and rattled it, scaring off a crow pecking on dried skin. Her father's beard had grown several inches in his coffin, and long, curved fingernails now dug into his thighs. The huckster had taken his ladder home with him, but Pegge climbed up the blocks by squeezing her fingers and shoes into the gaps the way she had done as a child. She was now face to face with her dead father. No life was on these lips either, only a greasy shine from penny kisses.

Holding onto the scaffold with one hand, she tried to free the skeleton, but it was bound with wire, impossible to loosen even with her knife. He wasn't mummified after all, for only a few threads of flesh still held the bones together. Pushing her fingers into the eye sockets, she snapped off the skull, then climbed down with it in her skirt and vomited until her stomach was dry. The crows retreated, then waddled back for a closer look, squawking like hungry infants. Pegge took a plum from her pocket and ate it slowly, throwing the stone to drive the birds away, then ate another, and another, until she had driven the crows away three times.

Climbing back up, she caught hold of a foot, twisting the shin bone until the leg broke apart at the knee. She dropped the bones on the pavement, then climbed higher, twisting the thigh bone until she had forced the hip joint asunder. She wrenched the pelvis out from under the wire and threw it down, then pulled and snapped and broke the rib cage, rib by rib, until she had taken her father apart and thrown all the pieces to the ground. Then she laid him out, from big bones right down to fingers and toes, on the pavingstones outside St Paul's.

Why was it that the bones of the dead fractured more easily than the bones of the quick? As she was straining to see the marrow in a broken bone, a dog shot out of the dark and clamped his teeth on a rib. When she tried to tug the bone out of his jaws, he let it go, snarling and baring his teeth. Two mongrels appeared out of nowhere to fight over her father's skull. One carried it in his teeth a few feet then dropped it, then they tugged it back and forth, until the skull had been grabbed and rolled and pushed across the churchyard. Soon a pack of scavengers converged on Pegge, darting in to steal the bones at her feet one by one, until she was left with only the thigh bone she was holding in her fist.

She chased some of the dogs into Paul's nave, where they burrowed under the rubble to gnaw on dried flesh cleaving to the bones. Above her head, the roof was open to the stars and the cold winter moon. When she stopped, so did the dog behind her, lowering its head, lunging and snarling when she turned her back, hungering for the thigh bone but wary of the arm that brandished it. Then a rat scurried past with some half-eaten filth clamped in its jaw, and the dog chased after it.

In the choir, the December wind blew through the blackened stonework, whirling up ash and human refuse. When she looked down into the gaping bone-hole, she thought she saw something moving, perhaps a vagrant sheltering next to a corpse or a few embers. Now ruptured and overturned, the coffin of one dean looked like another's. A great man's grave was as mute as a poor man's. Even the bone she held might have belonged to the thigh of another, lesser, man.

—

Three months before, a wind like this had caused the flames to spread, but it had been blistering hot that day in Paul's. No dogs had braved the church, only the single frightened cat that now made its home at Clewer.

On that September day, Pegge stood in the burning choir, dodging cinders and riots of sparks. The carters she had hired were easing her father's effigy out of its niche when some molten lead dripped on one of the men. He jumped, loosening his grip on the rope and letting the effigy crash onto the cart. The neck broke and the head rolled down the aisle into the fiery void.

In their hurry to swing the cart around, the men knocked the statue against one of the weight-bearing columns, shifting it a fraction. A jagged scar shot up the pier. They had chipped the urn this time, and sent one of the handles flying. Pegge helped them drape the canvas quickly over the statue, then one man pushed on a wheel while the other pulled on the horse's bridle to lead it out.

Picking her way towards the altar, she collected the marble handle, then saw her father's head grimacing just beyond the smoking choir stalls. It was too late to call back the men. Coughing from the fumes, they were already in the transept, trying to get the frightened horse through the south door. From there, it would be a torturous, slow trip using restraining ropes and blocks down the steep grade to the wharf.

Pegge could feel the cathedral tilting and settling into the ancient sand far beneath her feet. The pavingstones were moving and the blocks themselves were shifting in the walls. As she edged towards the head, she heard the Yorkshire timbers cracking high above her in the roof. All at once, there was a blast like gunpowder igniting and she ran into the aisle, crouching against the outer wall. The timbers and stone vaulting thundered down, buckling the church floor and exposing the centuries of burials in the layer of earth between Paul's and St-Faith's-under-Paul's.

Battered by the heat and violence, the lead coffins began to twist and soften, tipping and sliding towards the gaping crypt. The lids shunted sideways, revealing corpses as parched as tinder, or awash in liquid and reeking gloriously of putrefaction. As the fire attacked the insides of the coffins, a nauseating odour sickened the air, like the stench from the City's tanneries. It took Pegge a moment to grasp that the odour came from the dead—great statesmen and churchmen all—who were roasting in the vast stone oven. Some with relief, some with vengeance, the escaping souls took to the scorching air in plumes of jubilant smoke. It was then that the thousands of books laid up in Faith's burst into flames and charred bookpapers flew out of the crypt like rabid bats.

She could not recognize her father's casket in the sinister light. No longer in a cool repository for deans and bishops, he would be hotter than a minor canon relegated to a parish churchyard. In minutes, the pavingstones would be too hot for her to walk upon. John Donne would have to take his chances with the others, lurching and tossing on the selfsame sea of fiery rot.

As Pegge rolled the marble head into her shawl, a vengeful spirit shrieked behind the altar. A form leapt out and fled towards the nave—not one of her father's books come hellishly alive, but one of Paul's cats driven mad by the scalding wind. She stumbled after it, carrying the head as far as she could, then dragging it in the shawl behind her.

That was when she found Izaak Walton huddled under the smouldering portico, his hair stuck bleakly to his scalp as he watched his house burn to the ground.

—

Now, three months later, a cold wind tore through Paul's, uprooting charred timbers and sending them clattering.

By some miracle, her father's corpse had survived the inferno in its corner of the bone-hole, only to be hauled out and desecrated by the huckster. The great tower had also withstood the force of fire. Gripping the thigh bone, Pegge climbed the stairway to the top and looked down over the skeleton of Paul's. The spine of the vast roof was broken, and only a few ribs of vaulting protruded here and there. As a girl, she had surveyed all of London from this height, trying to spot blood on the pinnacle where a man had plummeted while hauling up the weathercock. Now there was no pinnacle for a man to spear himself on, nor even a scrap of lead where a girl could scratch her name.

To the west past Ludgate, Pegge could make out a swinging lantern as Angus led the farm wagon towards their meeting place at the conduit. They would need to circle the wall to the north and enter the City through Aldersgate. At Bladder corner, instead of turning towards Cheapside past St Michael's, which bulged out into the street, she would squeeze the wagon through Panier alley. From there, it would be downhill all the way and easier on the mare, but she would have to take the risk of being seen, for it would be dawn by the time she got the wagon safely to Paul's churchyard.

Far below, near the scaffolding where her father's corpse had hung, she saw a violet flash. The dogs were fighting over his bones again and the crows, still hungry and awake, were making sallies towards them, mimicking their peevish snarls. Pegge threw her father's thigh bone as far as she could into the square. It splintered as it landed, driving away the dogs and scattering the crows in a cloud of violet-black feathers. Soon they were back to collect the slivers and waddle off to shelter. At first light, they would lurch off to deposit them on rooftops, where they could pry at them at leisure, far from the scavenging dogs. Before noon, her father's remains would be dispersed and mingled with the dust of every dunghill and swallowed in every puddle and pond.

28. PASSIVE VALOUR

When the muzzle coated in white sugar had lifted, William found himself looking straight into the brazen eyes of his wife's horse. For once, he found himself agreeing with John Donne, for he was never more sure that animals lacked souls.

Pegge looked as if she had been sleeping with the wagon. She must have carted the effigy all the way from Clewer by road, not trusting it a second time to the currents of the Thames. No doubt she had worn out his servants and his draught horse, reserving the showy finish, where the streets narrowed through the City, to her highstrung mare.

Angus was scowling from exertion. He and his son were guiding the wheels while Pegge held Fox's bridle to coax her forward. In front of them, William could see two stone buildings connected by a bridge, barely taller than the reclining statue. When the horse refused to duck under the bridge, Pegge unharnessed her and took her around the longer way. The gardeners lay on top of Dr Donne, propelling him through the arch with the strength of their legs, like a barge through a tunnel. As Pegge rode up on Fox on the other side, William fell back into a lane, holding his pocket-clock like a heart in his palm. It had taken five minutes to leg the great Dean through the arch.

Now William could see why Pegge had chosen this route, for the lane sloped downwards, opening out past the burnt husks of bookstalls, then dropping like a plumb line straight to Paul's. There was no need for the horse to pull here. In fact, it was all it could do to hold the wagon back.

Ahead, Christopher Wren and the assembled dignitaries were emerging from the Si Quis door to assess the damage to the cathedral's exterior, gesturing and consulting, calling out measurements, beating off stray dogs and then, hearing an ominous clatter, turning as one body to stare at the approaching colossus, reined back by rough workmen with their legs braced and led by an outlandish woman, her face streaked with dirt, riding a prancing brown mare. Behind her was a mob, which was making a loud holiday of it, and keeping pace with them was an enterprising band of meat and drink sellers, their merchandise strapped to their bodies by every kind of box and contraption. Paul's pie-man was hailing fresh pies at two a penny though the pastries smelt, as they passed William, at least a fortnight old. William had pulled his wig almost down over his eyes so Pegge would not recognize him and call out for help—to climb atop his recumbent father-in-law and leg him through the Dean's low doorway into Paul's, or to ride him through the nave towards his appointed resting place.

All at once Christopher Wren broke from the dignitaries and strode uphill to halt the wagon. As Pegge leapt down from her mare to speak to him, William sagged against a wall. His wife was going to greet the King's surveyor, the man who was being called the new Archimedes, wearing her gardening clothes. Where her old brown skirts had ridden up, where a lady's white stocking should have been, William saw a flash of bare and bloodied ankle.

At something Pegge was saying, Dr Wren walked around the effigy, subjecting it to a closer look. Then he came forward to point out some technical feature of the route ahead and, as his hands flew in the air, William saw the difficulty. The slope of the churchyard, multiplied by the weight of the marble statue, would accelerate the wagon to such a pace that it would ram the horse, catapulting the effigy and its entire apparatus—wagon, woman, horse, and gardeners— against the cathedral like a maddened war-machine. In its weakened state, with the pillars already off the perpendicular, the blackened shell might be brought to its knees.

In spite of the cold, Dr Wren was removing his new three-quarter coat and tying it over the horse's eyes, certainly the best use William had seen for that impractical garment. Pegge took Fox's bridle and turned the wagon around, calming the animal with some nonsense chatter. The gardeners spit on their hands, looped the guy-ropes about their waists, and braced their legs. The mob became quiet as the load rolled slowly backwards, the mare's hooves skittering as she strained to keep her footing on the stones. Using the mare as a drag, as directed by Wren's lively hand signals, Pegge eased the wagon down the slope, manoeuvring it all the way into the churchyard until the wheels sank deeply into the soil inside the masons' yard.

A bottle was passed hand to hand over the gawking heads to Pegge, who tipped it back, spilling wine over her throat and clothes as the mob cheered her on. One of the pedlars shone a piece of fruit on his filthy sleeve and tossed it to her. She caught it with a laugh, spun it in her hand, then threw it in a perfect arc, past the dignitaries now examining the colossus in their full-bottomed wigs, the sun striking brightly off their shoe buckles and gilt swords, past Angus unharnessing the mare, and back into the appreciative mob. Without thinking, William stepped forward to catch it, the largest he had ever seen. *This colour should be called orange*, he decided, *red mixed into a rich primrose yellow*. The backs of his legs tingled at the discovery.

Dr Wren was running his hand along the statue's flank, admiring its curves. Then he was studying the marble face and Pegge was looking straight at William. It was too late to push the orange into his pocket and slink back to Clerkenwell unseen, for Pegge was smiling to thank William, as if he had arranged for Wren's help instead of cowering at the back of the vulgar crowd, hoping she would not see him.

Pegge called to the pie-man, but William got to her first, smelling the mare's sweat all over her—or was it her own? Angus, he told her, would take the horse and wagon back to Clewer. Her woollens soaked with perspiration, she had begun to shiver from the cold. He wrapped his cloak around her and peeled the orange, getting juice all over his sleeves as he fed the pieces to her.

This madwoman would be the talk of Westminster by nightfall. It was a mercy that William had already been dismissed as the King's tailor. At least that humiliation was past. The sky was an old green cabbage overhead and the air reeked of hot mare's urine hitting straw, but his hands smelt pleasantly of orange. William took Pegge gently by the elbow and led her past the curious dignitaries, past the Duke of York who had just ridden up on his stallion and given William a sharp, familiar glare, past Christopher Wren's knowing look—he had finally, William guessed, deduced exactly who Pegge was—past the scaffolding where the Dean's mummy had been kissed by every ragtag apprentice in London but, mercifully, had been taken down before Pegge saw it. William looked at his wife's pale smile and felt a pain behind his ribs. He dared not ask what she was thinking, for fear of the answer she would give him. He must get her warm as quickly as he could.

As William led Pegge towards the nearby coffeehouse, a playful gust stirred up the rubble, tossing up hats and feathers and periwigs, sifting and quickening, mixing the sacred ashes from Paul's with common playbills from the theatres. Pegge twisted in his arms and looked backwards at the dust whirling up from Bonehill in the north, where human remains were being carted from all the churches gutted by the fire.

"They were clearing out St Clement's as I rode past yesterday," she said.

Just at that moment, a strangled note sounded in the distance, no doubt a child practising on the recorder. However, Pegge's face told him it might as well have been

John Donne blowing his old trumpet to call the numberless infinities of souls back to their scattered bodies.

With her finger, she singled out a wisp of ash spiralling purposefully upwards. "A conjugation of souls," she said, "like a small quantity of Christian dust re-animated."

Smoke from a blast-furnace, he thought, unwilling to correct her.

He uprooted her and pulled her forward to the coffeehouse. An infusion of coffee was the best remedy. It would not matter what explanation he gave her, for she would still believe her father was circumnavigating the earth collecting pieces of his body. From souls flying around in some heretic limbo, it was only a step to Papist fireballs and his wife being thrown in the Old Bailey.

Pegge's cheeks had quickly regained their usual ruddy health. She seemed to pull colour into her as salt pulled colour, hiding it under a drab façade. As she walked beside him, her skirts swirled around her ankles, the worn nap giving off a chocolate sheen in the morning sun. If pinks and oranges could be colours, why not chocolate and coffee? Why not lemon? He would feed her lemon cakes and coffee—an intriguing milky brown—and take her back to the country, staying with her as long as the King would let him. If he was correct, King Charles would be in no hurry to have him back.

Now that he was no longer the royal tailor, William had no need to tend his body, stay the same height and weight as the young King, keep himself for show, immaculate. He could slouch and spread, indulging a discreet wrinkling in out-of-fashion suits. A tentmaker could eat a baked apple when he chose. There was much to be said for tents, for they could be designed equally well in the country as in town. A tent could have a raffish elegance. A tent could be dyed to match a China orange, or even a common English pippin.

As for Pegge's writings—he would take the key out of her old shoe and slip the book he had removed back into her cabinet. There was no need to say anything about it. Perhaps she had not even noticed that the volume was missing. He knew, without asking, by the look on Christopher Wren's face when she had jumped down from her horse, that she had introduced herself as Ann More, a woman dead for fifty years.

29. UNBUTTONING

Franny had arrived at Clewer that morning in a great hurry, putting the baby down on the floor and leaving her with Pegge. William followed Franny's heels up the stairs to her old chamber. He meant to ask whether it was wise to leave the little girl with her grandmother, but instead found himself asking why Franny had run away from her husband.

"What do you know?" Franny burst out at him. "You are a husband too."

Yet Mr Bispham had been Franny's choice, not his. Perhaps, after all, it was unwise to allow daughters to choose their husbands. When Franny's crying finally drove him out-of-doors, William wandered musing in the shade. Soon afterwards, Cook came out of the house and walked smartly past.

When William called after him, he replied sourly, "Madam is in my kitchen again."

He did not bother to end the sentence with *sir*, just slapped his jerkin on top of the hedge as he went down the path. Now William was standing in the kitchen garden trying to puzzle out what was wrong with everybody.

It is a very hot day, he decided, wondering if that had anything to do with it. The mad-apple was splayed against the bricks of the house, its fruit like purple goose eggs, indelicate in the extreme. He was not sure it was the sort of vegetable a gentleman should have on his estate. Had Pegge been rash enough to eat it? She had begun to cultivate unusual plants from the New World. Now that he was retired from public life, it was unfair she had so little time for him. For all the attention she paid him, he might as well have remained in London.

At least in the summer Pegge would not poke up the fires in a slapdash way or drop a lit candle on the stairs. All winter, his stomach had cramped with fear that she would set the house aflame. He tied a rope to an upper window so they could climb down in case of fire. Sometimes, in dreams, he heard the sound of breaking glass and saw a swinging rope of chestnut hair disappearing out the window. He would wake perplexed, wondering why Pegge had gone into the holocaust in Paul's. Had she been in the choir when the timbers gave way and the stone vaulting came crashing down? The thought was like a blowfly that laid eggs. Nothing could stop the larvae growing and taking flight.

Everybody else seemed to be going somewhere. Duodecimus was just now tramping across the grounds. He disappeared—as if he had dropped off the edge of the earth—into the ha-ha that kept the deer out of Pegge's garden. Three minutes later by William's pocket-clock,

Duo sprang up a furlong ahead, making towards the pig-gery. He must have crawled inside the ditch until he thought he was out of William's view. This was what came of letting the boy stay at home and cross the river to school each day as Pegge had wished. But then, why had his mother haunted the Fleet? Two separate streams, pure at their source, had converged into that filthy London ditch.

William went into the buttery, leaning against the damp stone wall to cool himself. When he opened his eyes, he could see Franny's naked baby on top of the great kitchen table, looking like an apricot made shiny by the heat. Her legs did not seem to have ankles, just feet pro-truding at the end. As William watched, she pushed her-self up and walked across the table until she stood with her toes curled over the edge, trying to see what was underneath. He almost leapt out of the buttery to catch her, but held back when he heard Pegge's voice.

Pegge was placing raspberries in a row across the table. The little girl sat down to watch the line grow longer, testing a berry by squashing it with her thumb. She did not appear to have wrists either, William noted, just hands coming straight out of arms. When the last berry was in place, the baby shoved the first one into her mouth, then pinched the second between finger and thumb. She held it close to her eye before swallowing it, then reached for the next berry in the row. William could not comprehend why she did not eat them all at once.

"That does not seem safe," William said, stepping out. "I thought you were looking after the child for Franny."

"I am." Pegge lifted the baby off the table and set her on the floor.

Below the table was an upside-down bowl weighted by a rock. The little girl saw it at once, crawling underneath the table to push off the rock. The bowl jumped up and out came a mouse, a little disoriented, wobbling back and forth. With a terrible *whoosh*, Pegge's cat leapt from the window-ledge straight onto the groggy mouse. *Surely*, William thought, *this is not a suitable game for a child.*

Pegge got out her quill and ink bottle, settling down at the table with her book. "What kind of death do you wish, William?"

He spun around, alarmed.

"Slow and easy, or quick and painful?"

Was this a Catholic question involving martyrdom? The kitchen was unbearably close. Through the window, he could see a summer storm blowing in, with shades of grey from smoke to gun-metal. "Where were you when the vaulting fell in Paul's?"

"In the barge heading upriver with you. Where else should I have been? You are too fretful, William. Loosen your vest."

The baby stopped playing with the bowl. "Vest?" she asked, pointing at William.

How had the child learned to speak? Was it possible that, in spite of a sobbing ninny for a mother and Pegge for a grandmother, the little girl might yet amount to something? He scrutinized her sober round face for anything of Thomas More or John Donne in it. Where was William to find her a suitable husband? It could not be left up to her foolish parents.

The gathering tempest was driving Pegge into a passion. Plucking the quill out of the ink, she began to write before it had stopped dripping.

Why did she fancy herself an author? John Donne's other children had no such ambition. William hoped she would not make a spectacle of herself like the Duchess of Newcastle, who thought herself a writer, though a woman. It was a very inconvenient business. William surveyed the kitchen and saw no signs of a meal. He had not seen a kitchenmaid all day.

"Why have the servants all run off?" he asked.

"It is a feast day in the village. Let me get this down, William, or I shall go quite mad."

Perhaps it was best to let her write. "What shall I do with Franny's child? Is she hungry? Should she not have her clothes put on?"

Pegge did not answer, so he reached for the little bodice and under-things and tried to figure out which should go on first. At the sight of the knitted drawers in his hands, the baby ran away. He caught her, laid her down flat, and pulled on the drawers, but when he tried to pull on her stockings, she stiffened her legs. Giving up on the stockings, he squeezed her head through the neck of the shift. Why were children dressed like miniature adults? He laced up the baby's stays, but after he had lowered the stiff embroidered bodice over her head, he found he could not do up the tiny buttons.

"You've put it on backwards," Pegge said, without looking up.

"Many a man is a wonder to the world whose wife sees nothing remarkable in him." He whispered to the little girl,

"Montaigne said that. These are silly garments. I shall make you a country suit with buttons you can undo yourself. You must help me draw the pattern."

The child climbed into his arms, her hands clinging damply to his neck. Why had husbands so little to do with children when they were so much better at it than wives?

"I am sure she understands every word I am saying, Pegge. I don't remember Franny being half so clever."

As he turned to look at Pegge, bent over her book, his heart knotted in fear, for her head was bathed in a Prussian blue. Then her body shifted and he saw that the light was coming from the window behind her. He had seen this once before when he was a child. An ignis fatuus—light clinging to the village spire just visible between distant thunderclouds.

He carried the little girl to the window to show her. "What do you suppose God is thinking?" he asked.

The sky was now as matte as the blackcloth worn by priests. One cloud crossed over another until there was layer upon layer of moving clouds, as if strong black arms were pressing wood blocks into dye and then onto cotton, this way and that way, cobalt and scarlet and amber, one on top of the other, pattern upon pattern, into a layered richness of shape and texture—the secret that had long escaped him, William realized, blinking back an eyeful of English monochrome, of the oriental print, the indienne.

All of a sudden, there was a crack and a blinding streak of phosphorus cut across the sky, followed by a whiff of sulphur, as if a flint had struck steel and ignited silky black grains of gunpowder, propelling a ball out of a gun's barrel and into the thunderous air.

The wind was now an angry bawd, yanking and stretching the clouds. John Donne had preached that at death God would cleave flesh from bone, blowing the dust to the four points of the compass. Then at the last busy day, God would force each Christian soul to hunt down each speck of its anatomy—every morsel of saliva left inside a lover's mouth, every seed sprayed out in heedless passion, every heartbeat lost in childbirth, every hair and nail trimmed, every tear cried—until every seed and hair and teardrop had been collected and the soul fleshed out to human form again.

And what then? William asked himself, as the rain began, for England was no longer Catholic. Would lovers still contrive for their souls to meet at one another's tombs by exchanging tokens of hair and bone? Once reunited, he supposed, they would embrace one another in the resurrected flesh, as moist and young as when they had first coupled.

But this was nonsense, for a man wanted his wife in bed right now, not after a millennium of frustration. William was full of yearning for Pegge this very minute, as they had not slept together since he had brought her back to Clewer. Even though William had returned the book he had taken, placing it inside her cabinet next to the wad of tangled hair, she still had not come to him at night. A man could not go without release for ever because his wife was too stubborn to visit his bed. And yet, and yet—sometimes he had such vivid dreams as made him almost think she had.

The birds, assuming it was dusk, were making a racket outside, and the baby was tugging at William's sleeve to be put down. Instead, he held her tightly to his chest, pushing the lazy cat off the sill and leaning out the window so the baby could smell the rain-freshened earth. He was glad Pegge had taken the effigy back to Paul's. They were all better off without the dreadful thing.

On the horizon was an odd shape. It might have been a dog, or a flapping stick-man to fend off crows. But on closer look it was a rain-soaked Duo skulking back from the piggery, carrying something draped awkwardly over his arms. When Duo had got as far as the ha-ha, William whispered, "Watch!" to the baby and turned her head with his hands. The moving shape disappeared into the ditch, then popped up a few minutes later, holding a giant pike.

"Look! What is it," William asked, "what is it?"

As Duo neared the house, his grin became wider and his grip on the long fish more nonchalant.

The baby's eyes were fixed on Duo's arms. "Bird. Fish. Cat," she said, pointing to it in excitement.

Duo carried the pike past the kitchen towards the salt house. When it was out of sight, the baby objected, squirming in William's arms. Thrusting his hand into a bin, he pulled out a turnip for her to play with.

When William brought Pegge back to Clewer, he had found the estate in disarray. On top of her cabinet, for all the household to peer and poke at, was a jar of blackened teeth, no doubt from some martyred relative's jaw. Someone had broken off the hour hand on the big clock and plums were drying on his mattress as if Pegge had expected him to stay in town all winter.

Pegge was writing flagrantly, in any room of the house, in any slatternly garment that she chose—or barely clothed at all. Once when he interrupted her, asking when all this folly was going to end, she bristled and threw her gardening clog at him. Yet sometimes she glided joyfully around him, practising her dance steps and begging for a partner. Perhaps her monthlies were at fault. They had always turned the household into pandemonium, although now she kept their ebbs and flows a secret from him.

During Lent, he found Pegge in the conservatory, feeding her plants a red liquor. When he asked what it was, she told him it was blood, sweet and mingled with water. He watched as she cut potatoes wildly with her blade, each chunk with an eye, then carried the pail outside and plunged them deep into the earth. Why did she seek novelty in vegetables? He could not bear to think what foreign uses they might be put to.

Each evening, he sent away his manservant. Though he dropped his shoes loudly and unbuttoned his breeches as slowly as he could, she did not enter through the connecting door. He lay alone, fearing that the lumps between his legs were growing as large and indelicate as the mad-apples on Pegge's vine.

He could not go through the door himself, for he had sworn not to lie with her in her old bed. Every time he slept there, he came away with flea-bites, though the fleas did not seem to bother her. But more than that. Now that he knew it was her father's, his manhood would wither in that bed, though he could not bring himself to tell her such a humiliating fact.

When the potato shoots pushed up through the soil, he could stand it no longer and entered her bedchamber. He found her sitting on the monstrous bed, which was draped all in summer muslin like a tent, cleaning her hair with oatmeal. She must have been outside in her shift, for he could smell the sun and wind burnt into the cotton. Ignoring him, she brushed her hair forward over her face, then tossed her head, spinning the hair out in a circle, flakes of oatmeal swirling, spiralling, wafting, until the room was filled with shards of floating light.

Still she did not come to him in bed. Oatmeal and citrus invaded his sleep, making him toss as restlessly as he had done as a young man. He was fragrant with a need he could not fathom. Why did God make machines of men's hearts and then, when least expected, turn them back to flesh?

The wind had died completely and the sun was back. How long had he been staring out the window wondering whether his wife had ever loved him? William glanced at the child in his arms. The hairs had dried against her scalp in stringy clumps and she was holding the turnip with both hands like a mouse, making neat teeth marks all around it.

Pegge had not even heard the storm come and go. The symbols were still flashing boldly between the printed lines, her hand smudging them as it pushed past. Why this unending, meaningless chore that carried her away from him? She had rejected the book he had returned, like a bird rejecting a nest that smelt of human hands, and was now writing upside down and back to front in a book of poems.

He leaned forward, the baby cradled against his chest, feeling the warmth of Pegge's shoulders through his loosened vest. From this angle, he could just make out some printed lines. To his horror, it was "To his Mistress Going to Bed," the Dean's most pirated elegy. The wet ciphers were swelling, undulating, obliterating whole lines of print. Pegge's words—if they *were* words—had a queer foreign look, more frightening than if they were wholly gibberish.

What if someone in a badly cut uniform rode up, confiscated the books, and delivered them to the Lord Keeper? At least there was no question of anyone untrained in tachygraphy understanding a syllable. Some act of twisted love, of homage to her parents—that was the most he had been able to make out in all his weeks of trying.

He hoped she was not writing poetry. Surely not lewd Catholic poetry such as her father had written? The appetite of men for such things was insatiable. He had a horrid vision of broadsides by a female Donne being circulated around the City's coffeehouses to fuel the dreams of vulgar men.

Pray God these were just the inchoate scribblings of a woman. He must not provoke her into any rash behaviour. If he humoured her, she would continue to lock her writings in her father's cabinet, by far the safest place for them. He must watch that nothing was sent by post and that no visitors arrived from London for her. His retirement began to take on a purposeful tint, a rich velvety conspiracy, as if his family's safety—perhaps the safety of the entire realm—was now in the capable hands of the King's tailor.

All at once Duo was there, smacking the cleaned pike on the hearth. Taking the baby, Duo tossed her high above his head, flying her out into the garden, flapping and squawking like a baby crow.

William had no idea that Duo was so familiar with the child. He wondered whether his son also had a gift for cookery. The potato, William had heard, was thought erotic, as was chocolate. What of pike? Most cooks baked it just as it came from the river. Pegge was the only one he knew who stuffed a pike with sweet butter and garlic and basted it with claret. But was it fit food for the little girl? He eyed the gutted fish, uncertain what to do, then carried the prize into the cool buttery. It would seem a pity to serve it plainly. *On the whole*, William thought, *I believe I prefer my pike with garlic.*

Pegge was now asleep on the table, her face pressed against the open book. When she turned her head, William saw ciphers imprinted on her cheek. Her thumb twitched an inch from the abandoned pen. She appeared boneless, as if she had neglected to put on her stays. One foot dangled, too short to reach the floor, and the other was tucked up beneath her, filthy from going barefoot. Ladies' shoes were much more on view now that the Queen was in short petticoats. He must send at once for some new shoes for Pegge, for it paid to be careful in such times. After all, the Duchess of Newcastle was considered mad as much because she had a beard and wore eccentric garments as because she thought herself a writer.

When Pegge woke, she would slam the jacket closed and push the book aside. If she were pleased with William, she would stand on the stool and take down an old straight-blade from the high shelf—his heart slowed at the thought of her fingers near it—and finding they were out of apples, slice potatoes with the blade instead, layering them in a pie-dish with scalded milk and raisins. She would pull butter out of the well and roll cubes in cinnamon to scatter over the top. When it was cool, she would cut the sloppy pie with such wild movements of her blade that he would choke back a fear that she would stab herself. She would laugh at his cowardly face, pick up a runny slice, and feed it to him on her palm. It would taste of apples burnt by a Persian sun.

30. FLEURS

A violet beetle crosses the moonlit floor, headed towards the shadow beneath William's bed. The scent of honeysuckle and jasmine drifts through the open window. On such midsummer nights as these, children will be conceived and old men die, souls will be engendered and emparadised.

I came in after my lover fell asleep, his wig on a stand and his turban on his head to ward off the night chill. For some months he has been making a show of undressing himself with the connecting door open to lure me into his chamber, but I do not come and go like an ordinary wife. I saw the look on William's face this morning when he found the baby naked on top of the table. He will need to watch me more closely now, since I may eat eggplants next or walk about unclothed, complaining of the heat.

Called to supper, William and I found only a pile of knives and spoons. Duo had taken over the kitchen since Cook was at the village festival. After a time, Duo carried in a huge pike with a tremendous jaw. When he put the platter down, the pike almost slid off its bed of buttery garlic onto my lap. Then Franny appeared with plates, which she skimmed across the table as if serving in a tavern, while ignoring the trilling and babbling in her old bed-chamber at the top of the stairs.

"What is wrong with the baby?" William glanced at Franny, then at me. "Perhaps I should—"

"She is just talking to herself," I said, pressing his knee to stop him rising.

"Like you, Mother," Duo said wittily, through a mouthful of fish.

William looked a little anxious at this comment. It was true that, when I picked up my pen, it was sometimes hours before I counted a minute gone. Like eating a fresh buttered pike, I could not stop until my belly cried out that it was glutted. Perhaps I did speak aloud at such times, though I saw nothing wrong in that. I was more companionable than Franny, who had barely spoken since she arrived at Clewer. At the table, she rejected all her father's overtures at conversation, even when he inquired about fabrics currently in vogue in London, a subject she enjoys as much as he does.

At last, disturbed by Franny's sulking, William produced a letter from her husband, masquerading as news about St Paul's. William read it aloud while Duo and I ate cherries and Franny pleated her bodice cruelly with her fingers. Mr Bispham said it was now so hazardous to enter Paul's that Dr Wren proposed to take it down block by massive block or, if that work proved too dangerous, to use battering-rams and gunpowder to destroy it. In its place he will erect a cathedral to rival the Catholic monuments of Europe. There will be a special niche for John Donne's effigy—the only one, Mr Bispham told his father-in-law, that had survived the fire.

"Too large for Clewer garden," William interjected, his most cheerful comment of the evening.

The real point of Mr Bispham's letter was at the end, where he demanded the return of his lawful wife and infant daughter. At this, an unladylike noise spurted from the nostrils of Mrs Bispham.

"Why did you marry him, Fran, if you hate him so?" Duo spat a cherry stone past his sister's ear and out the window.

"There is a little more," William said hurriedly.

In the postscript, Mr Bispham asked William to send Franny home with *some memento of Dr Donne (a grey hair or flake of skin or incisor from his jaw) as evidence of Mrs Bispham's kinship.* This makes me wonder whether he wants Franny for herself or for her bloodline. I know that he is eager for her to bear sons, though she is just seventeen. Yet, in spite of his demands, I suspect Mr Bispham cannot do without Franny for more than a few days at a time, a fact much to his credit.

William placed the letter near Franny's uneaten supper. As she slipped it into her bodice, I saw a softening in her chin. I do believe that Franny is with child again and has not determined how she feels about it. I will speak to her about staying with us for several weeks. That way, Mr Bispham will be forced to travel to Clewer to collect her, and she will gain the upper hand with him.

William went to sleep on a stomach so achingly full of pike that he must have been sucked at once into a black, garlicky dream. I came to him while he was dreaming and kept him so, for no visitor is so sweet as a night-walker. My touch was light and purposeful, my purpose to arouse but not awake.

It is not the first time I have come to him in the night. These fingerings are shorthand for a long affection. No victim of my nocturnal visits has ever complained. In the dark, there is only sensation, the dreamer adding scent and colour according to his whim. Tomorrow, when William wakes, he will find only a rumpled sheet and blame an amorous soul. Such spirits are thought to give off a violet glow and leave a trace of phosphor, or perhaps a jelly as does a fallen star.

But this time, instead of enjoying my lover, I have been watching him sleep. William is no longer young, and I have begun to worry about him. When his head turns, his turban shifts, exposing the grey stubble on his scalp. It must have been itchy under his wig all day, since his manservant went off with the others to the fête. William would be astonished if I offered to shave him myself, but I once was fairly good at grooming men.

Now I am jostled by another night-creature, her feet going step by step up the ladder of my leg. Not yet weaned, my grandchild nuzzles at my breast, puckering her lips like a hawkmoth searching for a bud. I tug her higher, making a buzz in her ear so she will buzz me back in mine. She pushes me away and reaches for William, but I pull her back so she will not wake him. There is no room in a love-bed for a child. When I was about her age, I also had to learn that nothing should come between two lovers but their skin.

—

I once lay next to you like this. I had been present at my own conception—why should I be absent from your further acts of love? Crawling up from the foot of the bed, I pushed myself between you and Ann, earning your confused and drowsy fumblings. Reaching past me, you cupped your hands around her breasts and lay your face into the hollow of her neck. Soon we were both exiled from her bed, for Ann was dying.

You buried my mother in St Clement's with her five dead children. We all knew what the Latin said above her tomb, but you had not been made speechless like an infant. Far from it. To avoid Betty, who had come back from the wet nurse with sharp baby teeth and scratchy toenails, I crawled into your bed and curled up at the back of your knees, fingering the dark rivering veins that led upwards to your heart. At any moment, your body might begin to jerk. You would sit upright, gesticulate as you did in the pulpit, and hold forth—poem or sermon, I was too young to tell. Then you would look about wildly for a woman and find only a shivering child. *Ann*, you would cry, and I would answer, *Yes*.

This wraith beside me now is cool to the touch but far from innocent. When she is told she must not sleep with William, she will kick and complain, as I did when Bess took me from your bed. *Too old to sleep with a man*, Bess said, putting me back into the smelly cot with Betty. Even Bess with her broken nose could see the problem. *Not again*, she scolded, taking Betty off for a cleaning and another suit of clothes.

I hear a dull reminding chime. Surely William has not brought his clock to bed? But no, it is in the baby's fist. When I pry it from her, I see it lacks a minute-hand. She must have wandered into Duo's chamber and found your old striking clock. It is a wonder Duo has not lost it, for he has little regard for anything that does not bark or swim. I press my lips to the top of her head, breathing in the baby moistness, then I tell her she must take it back to Duo. She slides off the bed, naked except for the clock dangling from her fingers.

Tonight memory washes over me like a benediction, a sudden jasmine on the night air. My fleurs did not come this month and I am fierce with longing. At supper, when I realized that Franny was with child, I was gripped by an envy as sharp as childbirth pain, then by relief. What woman wishes to be made a mother when she is a grand-mother? These past months, I sometimes thought I was carrying William's child inside me, my blood flowing one month then not the next, but now I know that my womb is as infertile as a girl's again.

—

I was older than Franny is now when my fleurs finally began. I became hydroptic with the gathering blood while keeping a vigil at your deathbed.

Week after week, I ministered to your decomposing flesh, wondering how such a body had performed such feats of love. Death was to be your crowning achievement, the news your many friends awaited. You faced towards the east, dreaming no doubt of your grand effigy in Paul's.

What became of your vow to die in the act of love and share a single grave with Ann? I read through your poems once again, counting your unkept promises to her. I had taken her part for so long, I hardly knew which was my mother or myself.

Once you bragged of being canonized by love, but now you hankered for real sainthood. You even had an acolyte who was copying out your sermons for posterity. But Izaak Walton was doing more than that. He was copying down the case for your beatification from your own canny lips. You told him story after story, each destined for the *Life of Donne*, a plan I did not grasp until, years later, I set eyes upon that fiction.

On the evening before your death, I heard you tell Walton, *I were miserable if I might not die*. He made a notation in his little book, splashing ink in his haste to get it down. When he went into your library, I crept up behind him and covered his eyes with my hands. Rooted by the hope it might be Constance, he dared not move, his eyelids sucking heat out of my palms. Pushing my small breasts against his back, I leaned over to read the book still quivering in his hand.

There in his perjuring script were the makings of a saint. He might as well have pimped for Christ at Calvary. There was no mention of your incontinence, or the poultice of flesh-eating maggots, or the loathsome flatulence you blamed on the dog beneath your bed. Every sanctimonious word you had fed him was there in his messy handwriting. The man's fists were made for ironmongery, not penmanship. Why did you let him drudge for you when I would have run your errands blithely? Even then I guessed the answer—although I was a better secretary, he was a far, far better fool.

Walton's eyelids were shut and throbbing for some time before a doubt began to stir inside him. I suppose my boyish figure did not press against him as he imagined Con's should do, for he spun around and stared at my matted hair and the pock-marks on my face.

Let me at least know a man's kiss, I begged, *for I have always loved you.*

At that, he jumped as if I had scalded him. His words sear me in memory even now. He shoved me away and called me—oh, the sting!—*Constance's little sister.*

I locked Bess's door, throwing myself on her narrow bed and wetting it with my tears. Well before dawn, I came to your bedchamber to relieve Bess and send her to a mattress I had barely slept on.

Your death was driving me out of all patience. Why could God not claim you in a timely fashion? On the bed in front of me, you were basking in your future martyrdom. You had been given a surfeit of love and squandered it while I could not scrape up even a taste for myself. As I stood marvelling at your bony frame laid out in its smug cruciform, a hunger claimed me. In my bones and marrow, my sinews and my gathering blood, I was a woman grown. I could not wait for love to seek me out. If I was to taste love, it must be now.

I crept into my old bedchamber and stood next to the sleeping bodies of Mr and Mrs Samuel Harvey. Con was so big with child that Mr Harvey was lying on a pallet on the floor, snoring contentedly in spite of this mistreatment. On the table was what I had come for, one of Bess's remedy jars. It was a salve for Con to use on Mr Harvey—dried honeysuckle steeped in grease to anoint a body benumbed and cold. *To bring him round*, I had heard Bess counsel Con, *when nought else will do it.*

I added some aromatic resin to the salve and began to rub your limbs, skirting bedsores and mapping subterranean knots. You lay like a corpse ready for dissection, your skin so papery it punctured as easily as Saint Sebastian's.

You had so railed against Ann's voluptuous spirit in your sermons that the audience sat rigid with attention, eager for more of the Dean's sins with his dead wife. Well, I was amorous too, but I was flesh and blood, heavy with new womanhood and bruised by the deceit of men. I cursed all faithless lovers and wished them turned to stone. But you were not rock yet, and I might still get some answer from you that no other man would give me. I worked the ointment deep into your skin, watching the inky veins burst through their purple banks, for even the dying cannot ignore a kneading palm. As my fingers sank into your flesh, your pulse quickened and your skin warmed under my hand, its female cunning startling both of us. I scarcely needed to move my thumb to see its fruit. I licenced my roving hands and let them go—before, behind, between, above, below.

All at once, the ligature around your heart broke open in a glorious haemorrhaging flood and you were rampant with remembered love, bartering your immortal spirit for one more minute in a woman's arms. My mother drove me forward, but oh! I was willing. *Drawn by my perfume*, I whispered, *you will slide into my labyrinth like a bee into an orchid.* And in that lyric rush, if I sang out my name as Ann, then thrust my tongue deep in your mouth, who was to blame, my mother or myself? Though you were a brittle ossuary with bones as porous as a bird's, I would break bones to taste forbidden love. But at the last tumultuous moment, just as I held your pleasure in my palm—when you were about to die unconfessed and forfeit your grand sepulchre in Paul's— some pity called me back, and instead of sucking out your soul in one last greedy kiss, I withdrew my tongue and let you hang between the utmost pleasure and the utmost pain.

You lay with one foot in the grave, another in heaven, one eye straining west and the other yearning east. I ran my tongue around my lips, tasting a slight bitterness, then drew a pin from my sleeve and pricked your tongue to jerk you back and fire you off.

Your eyeballs fell back with a *smack* into their sockets, and I said good-morrow to your soul as it sped past. Why not?—I had saved it from eternal death, such nocturnals as priests should never taste. As quickly as the blood had reddened your skin, it now withdrew, bleaching the flesh behind it, until all the blood had ebbed back to your heart.

I left you there for the philosophers to dissect. They would discover whether your lungs were smoky and your heart combust, and whether your soul had been made vehement by God's fire or left behind like a jelly cooked from the finest winter plums.

—

William is right—I must stop sleeping in my father's bed. It will make a good midsummer bonfire, for the oak is full of dry rot. Why has it taken me so many years to move from one bed to another? There is plenty of space in William's bedchamber for both of us. We have lost so much time, William and I. Soon the morning star will rise, the night-flowers will close, and he will stir, his leg gliding across the sheet to discover what lies in its path. I press my fingers to his heart and feel this clock pulse, not in a case of silver, but of skin, the beats quickening whimsically at my touch. Here is a heart within my grasp. I have only to reach out in the moonlight to claim it.

If I move, William will learn I am no disembodied spirit. Perhaps—it would give him such delight—I will let him find me here this time, a great star fallen in the dark from some accident or change of heart. My morning-gown lies crumpled on the floor. This once I do not feel like writing, as is my habit, in the hours before the house awakes.

How hard it is to have a wife who loves the smell of ink and paper! How much William would rather I did needlework like other women. However, I will not subject him to more torment than a gentleman can bear. At the end of each book I have written: *If I die first, do not publish it and do not burn it and between these, do what you will with it.*

I have not been very observant about William lately. His arms may be pale, but they are well muscled from lifting bolts of cloth, and his hands are brown from being in the country. I rub my cheek against his chest, picking up the garlicky scent of pike, a bold, manly fish that pounds upriver lustfully but, once it is there, breeds only with its mate. I hear a lost river thrumming beneath William's skin, with floodgates longing to be opened. How easy to caress his aging thigh with scented palm, to turn his veins into a conduit of blood, to command him to rise and fall and do my bidding, for this man is already waking to my touch.

Come, William, I see Venus rising like a pink nipple on the plump horizon. Shall we make that clock of yours run faster? Let us bed down together in this new dawn and weave a silken tent of arms. Such feats are not reserved for extraordinary lovers, and my love for you has grown over the years to marvellous proportions. Let us die together in the act of love, so death cannot divorce us. When our grave is broken open, our souls shall take flight together, assuming limbs of flesh, and lips, ears, loins, and brows. But first let us speed darkening time and savour this long night of love.

About ten days ago a large pike was caught in the River Ouse, which weighed upwards of twenty-eight pounds, and was sold to a gentleman in the neighbourhood for a guinea. As the cook-maid was gutting the fish, she found to her great astonishment a watch with a black ribbon, and two steel seals annexed, in the body of the pike; the gentleman's butler, upon opening the watch, found the owner's initials, J.D. Upon a strict enquiry, it appears that the said watch had been owned by a descendent of the old Dean of St Paul's, John Donne, and was sold to a gentleman's servant, who was unfortunately drowned about six weeks ago, on his way to Cambridge, between this place and South Ferry. The watch is still in the possession of Mr John Roberts at the Cross Keys, in Littleport, for the inspection of the public.

VALEDICTION

Warmest thanks to my husband, Orest, and to my writing partners June Hutton and Jen Sookfong Lee for their generous critiquing and encouragement over many years. Thanks also to Thomas Wharton, Cynthia Flood, Paul Headrick, Keir Novik, Karen Novik, and Lynne Neufeld for careful readings, to Langara College and Booming Ground for their support, to N.P. Kennedy for his wit, and to Alexander Novik for being a source of wonder and delight.

While writing this novel, I read seventeenth-century writers for inspiration, particularly John Donne, Izaak Walton, Samuel Pepys, Ben Jonson, William Shakespeare, Anne Clifford, Robert Burton, John Evelyn, Margaret Cavendish, and John Aubrey. I have consulted the usual scholars and biographers but, after all is said and done, this is *my* seventeenth century and I have invented joyfully and freely. The characters entered fully into the spirit of it, contributing in surprising ways to their own fictionalization, John Donne most liberally of all. Perhaps this is fitting, for he confided to a friend, long after becoming a priest, "I did best when I had least truth for my subjects."

I would like to thank my agents Dean Cooke and Suzanne Brandreth and the enthusiastic team at Doubleday Canada, especially Maya Mavjee, Kristin Cochrane, Martha Kanya-Forstner, and Scott Richardson. Above all, I would like to acknowledge the guidance and encouragement of my editor, Lara Hinchberger, who has been *Conceit's* champion from the beginning.